A Face like a Flint...

Forging Faith, Fitness & Fortitude

A Kinesiologist's Devotional

Patrick Greak

WALDORF PUBLISHING

Published by Waldorf Publishing
2140 Hall Johnson Road
#102-345
Grapevine, Texas 76051
www.WaldorfPublishing.com

A Face Like Flint… Forging Faith, Fitness, and Fortitude
—A Kinesiologist's Devotional

ISBN: 978-1-64764-904-3

Library of Congress Control Number: 2020930152

Design by Baris Celik

Dedicated to my mom who first inspired me to write

The things of the body are good; the things of the intellect better; the best of all are the things of the soul.

Remembering these things, we set our faces resolutely against evil…

-        Theodore Roosevelt – 1908

Introduction

It is said in the portent prophecy foreshadowing Christ's life and death, through the augur Isaiah that Jesus' daily countenance praxis was to, "Set my face like a stone." (Isaiah 50:7; NLT) This physical consuetude preceding His life reflects the deep determination and perseverance needed to fulfill the Father's ultimate destiny for Him as Savior of mankind. This same type of rugged discipline is needed to participate in/ dedicate oneself to a fitness/ athletics program. God's nature, as well as many who participate in these physically taxing endeavors, is composed, bucolic and stolid. These qualities take hold of our behavioral health because we actualize the fact that God knows everything, and thus peacefully acknowledge that we are ultimately in limited spheres of control. In the ways/ properties of fitness and health, exercise helps us put into perspective the larger more consequential issues in life.

It is also interesting that although Jesus was clairvoyant and knew His ending fate and the horrid suffering he would endure, he "Was always pressing on to Jerusalem." (Luke 13:22) In acquiring these formidable forces for good, (faith, fitness, and fortitude,) we can learn life lessons and positive personal qualities from exercising that would otherwise lie dormant, shrouded in mystery and unmanifested. As in the end, only three qualities will remain, (faith, hope, and love) these three attributes (faith, fitness, and fortitude) will stand the test of time.

Also, these qualities will deliver crushing blows to the enemy in our daily lifestyles, as well as God's zenith defeat of evil. According to a poet that Norman Vincent Peale references, "There is an unseen battlefield in every human breast where two opposing forces meet and where they seldom rest." Exercise mimics the ongoing eternal war because it is both physical and spiritual in nature. We cannot fully fathom or comprehend the spiritual realm God has created and presides over. For Jesus said, "My kingdom is not of this world." (John 18:36) These rulers and authorities exercise their dominion in an unseen world/ kingdom that is eternal and everlasting. At the same time, God created human beings in a physical/ earthly constitution and in his own image. It is a physical world that God gave Adam presiding power over. Exercise abides in this tangible realm, as can be experienced, evidenced and understood by sensations of pain, fatigue, and the exertion/tension required to overcome inertia and create a kinetic neuromuscular force. However, in the alternate aspect of conditioning - the invisible emotional and philosophical spheres - a battle of will/ volition takes place when exercising that pushes to the core of a man or woman's inner being. Vince Lombardi said of the perpetuated heart-based struggle: "It is essential to understand that battles are primarily won and lost in the hearts of men." The theoretical or philosophical nature of man ultimately dictates the actions that take place in the concrete/ physical realm. In relation to the power to triumph over specific life challenges/ divinely-authored tests, God has endowed in men's spirits this ability to cope and overcome. Jesus' pivotal position on the theme of overcoming adversity was clarified when he stated: "The kingdom of God is already within you." (Luke 17:21) A perpetuated amaranthine struggle exists in every woman's and man's heart, as all humans are fallible beings.

The purpose of this book is to establish, substantiate and expound on complex and in-depth connections between the word of God and the practice of physical exercise or the discipline of kinesiology (knowledge base of movement science) as a whole. The aim is to provide an impetus to stimulate reflection upon the entries, and ultimately contemplation on Biblical truths to accomplish one or more of four results: 1) fomenting an autochthonous relationship with Christ (evangelism), 2) inculcating a sagacious preexisting faith in Christ (discipleship), 3) cultivating/ percolating the motivation to stimulate real-life 'deeds/ works' of faith done in practical ways, and 4) linking the spiritual realm to our everyday physical endeavors to promote a holistic health and balanced lifestyle. Results can be achieved in conjunction with God's promise to accord an incorruptible belief that He will grant eternal awards for His servants. Motivationally, relating exercise and Christianity in a metaphorical and literal manner can bring about sincere Christian fellowship emulating the example of the original early church as depicted in Acts 2:42.

Table of Contents

January: Strength Training and God's Divine Strength

<u>January 1st</u>:

A More Powerful Entity than Strength? There is great emphasis in American culture on the connotations of the word 'strength' with accomplishments in physical form. However, there is a term with mightier implications: wisdom. Wisdom begins with the fear of the Lord (Proverbs 9:10), and also brings to fruition a sense of immediacy and urgency to the gift of life and expatiating nature of the calling of the Gospel. When we realize that there is no guarantee of existence tomorrow, we become more fully immersed in and aware of, the precious gift that life is.

Wisdom comes from the heart, not the mind or body, and is therefore knotty. King Solomon says of wisdom's seeming opacity, "Though I have searched repeatedly, I have not found what I was looking for." (Ecclesiastes 7:28). However, the quality of wisdom is existential in the physical realm. For example, God uses the activity of walking to emphasize wisdom's earthly existence: "When you walk, their (the wisdom your mother and father impart), counsel will lead you." (Proverbs 6:22) Solomon also used a person's vitality of countenance as a gauge of wisdom possessed: "Wisdom lights up a person's face, softening its harshness." (Ecclesiastes 8:1) Wisdom is also eternal in nature and imparts these infinite gifts to us.

"Wisdom is better than strength." (Ecclesiastes 9:16)

<u>January 2nd</u>:

With Movement There's Improvement Exercise has been proven to substantiate the specific area of self-esteem qualitatively annunciated as self-efficacy. The definition of the term self-efficacy means the ability to bring about a sought after desire.

A specific area of the brain, the amygdala, which deals with survival, can become inhibited over time so that we can face stressful situations through exercise. Psychoanalyst Linda Graham states of this happening: "Remembering a moment of previous coping when we're facing a daunting task or situation can help us return to our window of tolerance, where we can cope more easily.' (183) GABA, an inhibitory neurotransmitter, allows the prefrontal cortex to assume responsibility in guiding us through the extenuating circumstance imposed by physical fitness activities.

Lifting weights has been shown to help people with the capacity to simply believe in their heart that they can do what they want and physically bring it to actualization. Strength training helps humans develop a chutzpa, in a way no other activity can, through overcoming resistance and staying focused on the task at hand in order to make every repetition toughed out count by adhering to a strict form and proper technique.

"Blessed are those whose strength is in you." (Psalm 84:5; ESV)

January 3rd:

Courage Conflagrated Indubitably Exercise provides the building blocks both of and for courage. Regarding the former, the properties 'of courage,' in exercise you must create entropy from a zero-sum situation of bodily rest. This categorical shift in anatomy & physiology takes a vast effort. Prior to obtaining and nurturing physical courage, however, the genesis of moral courage must come from an external source – Jesus Christ. The sprouts of courage are born from the seeds of faith in Christ as the sole means of salvation.

Regarding the latter property - 'for courage,' a coherent testing and battleground for all types of inconspicuous, yet displayable courage exists in a weight room. The sound of iron weights and dumbbells clanking together in a forceful yet coherently patterned manner, the dry caking of talcum powder on your hands necessitated by the grip of a barbell, and the sting of sweet seasonal sweat in the sebaceous glands and on the brow subcutaneously dripping into the eyes, the smell of 'teen spirit,' bodily odor emitted from governed toil, the numbness from callouses on the hands exuberated in usage from chronic grasping of fractioned surfaces, make us want to beckon the call of masculinity. This includes unleashing impetuosity on the resistance, so that man's inner vehemence is not released in a derelict manner. King David, on his deathbed, implores his son Solomon upon succeeding his kingship to, "Take courage and be a man." (1 Kings 2:2) Because once moral courage is established in rugged faith, serving God becomes almost a natural and reflexive behavior.

Is courage merely present physically? No, because public displays of determination are not the only means of expressing bravery. Although the Bible extols physical courage, it is not the only format. As Dr. Bill Bennett states, "Courage is more than readiness to encounter danger or death, it is not afraid of ridicule when one believes himself right." (180)

January 4ᵗʰ:

A Cognitive Realization of Mortality via Fitness "Teach us to realize the brevity of life, so that we may grow in wisdom." (Psalm 90:12) Exercise has a natural manner of implanting in the soul the fact that our lives are transient in nature. The meanings of the word 'strength' infer intensity of cognizance for one of the five senses, or an extreme expression of vigor. However, the spiritual wisdom gleaned from fitness is morally superior to that of the somatic gifts that are actualized from working out. Wisdom must first be established, to discern right from wrong, before the strength a person has to offer can be fleshed out with physical human effort.

January 5th:

Exercise Entails Dynamic Distortion Benefiting Verve The disruption of homeostasis that exercise initiates in the body causes dynamic physical alterations that bring about pain and a feeling of discomfort. Immediately following when you stop the exercise (especially running), an acute sensation of recovery, as opposed to maintenance of labor, ignites a dynamic distortion of physiological functions. The process causes you to actually feel even worse than while working out as you return to resting state: tasting metallic mucus in your throat, your lungs lowering functionally from laborious levels of deep inhalation previously un-tapped aquifers, and seemingly un-collude from an expanded adhesion to the ribs, and the heart dumps its glut of blood from a full amount to the point of what feels like explosion in it, re-distributing to oxygen-starved muscles. The experience of 'dutiful' activities including running, lifting weights, or other effort based movement is not even close to how bad you feel once the partaking of the activity is over.

However, if you just focus on the moment you are in, not thinking about the exertions that were present in past workouts or even earlier in the present endeavor, you become stronger and better able to deal with the present. You know that the pain of running can only get a little worse as you continue to go on, and just accomplishing the task of placing one foot in front of the other becomes a reachable goal. Instead of focusing on the upcoming five, two, or even one mile ahead you want to finish, the focus becomes the next 100 yards, or 50, or even just the next step as you acknowledge and recognize the pain, but don't let it influence you to quit. This method is effective because the Bible says that serving the Lord is never done in vain no matter what the specific human behavior entails.

One veteran of the Iraq war poignantly states how she used exercise as a coping mechanism during and after a deployment as an effective antidote to anguish. "To stay sane, I also exercised, often running through the desert, trying to let go of the horrors with each drop of sweat. Whenever those awful moments surface, I tap into what has proved to be my most vital medicine: exercise. Running and weightlifting help me shed PTSD (Post Traumatic Stress Disorder) like other people shed pounds." (211)

"I even found great pleasure in hard work, a reward for all my labors." (Ecclesiastes 2:10)

January 6th:

The Struggles Make us Stronger through Exploiting the Writhe of This Life The Psalmist Asaph entreats what he sees as an unfair situation to God by saying in Psalm 73 that the, "proud…prosper despite their wickedness…their bodies are so healthy and strong." (verse 3-4). Asaph is jealous because of his perception that the abundant life is going to those who don't deserve it. A similar scenario could play out at any high school or college when a young man or woman does not have the physical makeup they want and are jealous of those who seem to not even spend much time or effort working out, yet have ripped muscles or toned/ sleek bodies. Not everyone will get the physique of a bodybuilder from working out, but keep in mind that sex appeal is not the exclusive benefit of fitness either.

But to delve deeper into the spiritual meaning of Psalm 73, the middle of the verse says that the dubious sinners, "seem to live such painless lives." (Psalm 73:4). Asaph concludes that although God seems unjust, pain drives the godly to do better things and follow through on their resolutions to God and man. As William Ellery Channing, a Unitarian preacher once said, "I would not change, if I could…our subjection to physical laws…and the necessity of constant conflicts with the material world. I would not, if I could, so temper the elements that they should infuse into us only grateful sensations… and the minerals so ductile as to offer no resistance to our strength and skill." (213). Exercise is one example of a skirmish mutually beneficed by the mind, body, and spirit against gravity, nature, objects, or other humans.

It is an unusual situation in the Bible we have happening here that the unjust are blessed with vitality and precociousness. However, Asaph comfortably concludes that when he goes into the sanctuary, he leaves God's business and role to, well…God! A similar sentiment is seen by an American who had to change careers following the recession of 2008. After a hard and long day's work, Mark Judge states that he found spiritual value in work as an usher at the National Geographic Society by musing on the evening bus ride home, "I felt spent. But I also felt alive." (214).

January 7th:

Meet With Mettle Your Tribulations Head-On My high school track coach Tony Munson once remarked to me and the other 10% of athletes that showed up for practice on a holiday afternoon that "You aren't supposed to feel good during your training or in the middle of a workout. You feel good following the workout." Armed with this knowledge, it is amazing to think that Jesus went through with exactly what he didn't want to at the very time he felt the least like doing it. Prior to His arrest and subsequent torture, Jesus said to the disciples, "My soul is crushed with grief to the point of death." (Mark 14:34).

I once heard a pastor, preaching on the very subject of Christ's obedience in bewildering pain in the crucifixion that Jesus' physiological senses were on extra alert. Sensation-wise, the hurt his captors placed on Him Good Friday, was even more intense as his nerves felt the agony amplified many times over what would have been perceived in a regular circumstance, as Jesus was facing a real medical condition known as hematidrosis.

We could compare the stark physical drudgery of carrying a heavy cross to lifting weights. This mindset fosters a sense of kinship with our brother Christ and friends who are fellow partakers of pumping iron. The main point of including this aspect in the story of the over-all Gospel is that he mustered up the courage to meet his fate head-on. Following the Savior's example, we can develop one aspect of bravery by sharing in his physical distresses in pushing ourselves past resting comfort levels in workout embarkings. We can compare this situation to what happens when we run/lift weights and the internal impetus to stay motivated by reading herbalist and elementary teacher Penny C. Royal words: "Since illness is blocked by circulation, exer-cise is important to increase the circulation. It is usually needed the most when you feel the least like doing it." (215).

"Yet I want your (God the Father's) will to be done, not mine." (Mark 14:36)

January 8<u>th</u>:

Guaranteed Muscle Gains and Failsafe Forgiveness If I could only recommend one aspect of fitness for someone to partake in, it would definitely be resistance training. Being in the form of calisthen-ics, body-weighted exercises, or external weight training (dumbbells, barbells, or bands), increasing strength is paramount. Because resis-tance induced fitness helps in rehab, maintenance of therapy gains, in-creased efficiency of ADL's, a better posture and physique, and simul-taneously elicits a spike in heart rate, these modalities reign over other aspects of kinesiology. But don't just take my word for it; listen to Dr. Ellington Darden, holder of a doctoral degree in exercise science from Baylor: "Building stronger muscles is the single best medicine a man can prescribe for himself. Stronger muscles escalate productivity. Stronger muscles are the key to living longer." (225). Notice what Dr. Covert Bailey, a medical doctor, says is the prerequisite to unlocking this Pandora's Box of strength: "A muscle fiber enlarges in response to one thing – demand. If it's contracted hard enough and often enough, it will get bigger." (226).

Similarly, a guarantee of mercy is slathered on anyone who believes in Christ. The term of slathered is appropriate because Jesus' atoning blood sacrifice literally covers over our sins. Just as muscle growth is the assured repercussion of contraction, three steps are needed to wash away sin: 1) repentance - telling God you are sorry for your sin (Matthew 3:1-2), 2) confession without expiation – confessing to God exactly what you did wrong and getting it out in the open before Him (Psalm 32:3; 5), and 3) beseeching God sincerely for forgiveness (Matthew 9:6). Two theories you can take to the bank as irrefutable: resistance train for health and fitness, and God will forgive any and all who ask of Him.

"But if we confess our sins to him, he is faithful and just to forgive us our sins and to cleanse us from all wickedness." (1 John 1:9)

January 9th:

Strength of Faith is the Basis of Bravery God refers to the specific exercise of deadlifts to make a metaphorical comparison between His beloved people and the nations they will subdue. God says through the prophet Zechariah that he will strengthen Israel to such a degree so that they can conquer whoever they need to by other peoples who were being made weak in comparison. "On that day I will make Jerusalem a heavy stone for all the peoples. All who lift it will surely hurt themselves." (Zechariah 12:3).

The larger context of the verse lies in the fact that this 'stone' is Christ Himself and the message of salvation he brings to everyone on the earth. By making the other nations weak, could it be a blessing in disguise so that they will turn to God and realize their need for Him (and ours today)? The fact that possible injury is mentioned details the fact that a risk is taken by some being eternally and devastatingly lost. Because fortitude was needed for Israel to fulfill its God-given destiny, God makes us strong today and uses that baseline bedrock property to prepare us for his ministry. As Dr. Micheal Yessis says of strength, we need a critical value reached in faith as well to follow the taxing effusion required of the Christian walk. "It is important to understand that strength, especially of the specific muscles involved, is the basis for speed, coordination, agility, and even flexibility." (230)

January 10th:

The Contradiction of True Strength – via Fully Relying on God Paul's God-authored thorn in the flesh is a seeming discontinuity between the battle of strength versus weakness and the meaning we ascribe to the two terms. "Three different times, I begged him to take it away…Now I am glad to boast about my weaknesses so that the power of Christ can work through me." (2 Corinthians 12: 8-9b). While we don't know what the plight was, it could be misunderstood as a curse from God. Typically humans don't think of being weak in any way, for example – in the weight-room, as simultaneously displaying a type of strong disposition. However, this contrast is not dichotomous, because when we let God help shoulder our 'weights', his vast pool of strength instantly infuses our hearts and bodies for boldness. Don't misunderstand my point as being that lifting weights is a messenger from Satan, but rather, a workout accomplishes the same purpose of retaining a humble heart that God will use – as he did with Paul!

"Give your burdens to the Lord, and he will take care of you." (Psalm 55:22)

January 11th:

Proverbial Displacement of the Soul for Godly Growth By the act of moving a weighted implement with a 'force' from the body, we are thrown out of a homeostatic utopian harmony (that the body works very hard to maintain) into a state of chaos. However, the REAL news is that we create and control that distortion into a sense of orderliness with our brains acting out in the instance of sequenced muscular contraction.

There are many instances of 'forces' exerting their proverbial wills onto other people or from nature into a surrounding environment. God is the author of all 'forces' and proves this point in referencing a group of Jews led out of exile back to their home through a Persian official named Zerubbabel. "This is what the LORD says to Zerubbabel: It is not by force nor by strength, but by my Spirit... Nothing will stand in Zerubbabel's way...He is the one who laid the foundation of this Temple, and he shall complete it." (Zechariah 4: 6, 7, 10). The verse alludes to a divine 'force', while another example of this commodity are militaries such as the US army and special operations commandos being called armed 'forces'.

Another reference to divine power occurs in the Psalms when the Bible talks about the end times and the triumph of God's holiness. "The LORD sends forth from Zion, your mighty scepter...on the day you lead your forces." (Psalm 110: 2-3; ESV) When we combine all our efforts in the quest to glorify and please God, we literally become a living testimony and type of living capacity of 'force' in the world that works for the good of our fellow man and Christ's kingdom.

January 12th:

God's Seeming Spurn and Surprising the Muscles Surreptitiously In life, we go through seasons of abundant blessings and vicissitudes of apparent silence from God. "How long, O LORD? Will you forget me forever? How long will you hide your face from me?" (Psalm 13:1; ESV). In fitness, we go through plans of periodization to surprise muscles when things get stagnant, days where motivation is scarce, and times when we seem to be on surpassing our wildest dreams of pre-set desired strength, hypertrophy, or performance goals.

There are also periods where repetition and practice of what can seem like a menial movement exercise get muddled in how much just sticking with the process of a conditioning plan can really benefit. In these situations, we must submit to a higher authority such as a coach and 'buy into' the program he/ she is advocating for our moral and physical growth. Similarly, we must yield to God when life is just plain hard, meaning we must look outside ourselves and this world. Achieving balance in the two realms requires a concomitant view of exercise which, focuses on our own efforts and the physical reality, while placing our soul and eternal future in God's hand. "Enjoy prosperity while you can, but when hard times strike, realize that both come from God. Remember that nothing is certain in this life." (Ecclesiastes 7:14).

We would do well to take heed of the last sentence of that verse and yet, find two apparitions which are opposed to its truth. God is constant, just like a weight we lift. Two hundred pounds will always weigh the same amount, but it may feel easier or lighter based on our current levels of strength/ power. So also, we may perceive God has forsaken us, but is an illusion or mirage clouded by the enemy and our own misgivings. You can always rely on exercise and strength training to brighten a day, just as God will never abandon you! "I can never escape from your Spirit! If I go up to heaven, you are there; if I go down to the grave, you are there…even there your hand will guide me and your strength will support me." (Psalms 139: 7, 8, 10)

January 13th:

Is Exercise Necessary to Please God? Exercise certainly is not mentioned as a requirement in the Bible, but there is a divinely conferred noble purity associated with it. With regard to quenching desire with fitness, Paul remarked, "I pummel my body and make it a slave." (1 Corinthians 9:27; ESV). Did the apostle Paul workout and infer the modality of 'pummeling' to mean exercise? We may never know, but it is in the realm of possibility. Dr. Cooper says of an unseen quality boosted from robust pursuits, "You can bolster your willpower by always exercising at the same time of day." (263). How encouraging that something so seemingly elusive a quality as an indomitable will can be enhanced through natural God-bestowed athletic training.

I have heard it said with regard to physical preparation that the equation, 'Sweat more in training, bleed less in battle,' is applicable. While truth exists in this sentiment, there is triteness to the statement, as it simplifies the subject. What is accurate is that through bodily preparation, you become more obedient to God in the process; tougher and able to handle the trials and tribulations that almost surely yet unexpectedly arise in the middle of ministry practice. Exercise bequeaths self-assuredness in purpose, enabling you to fight fear with faith, so much so that you are willing to place yourself in potentially tumultuous situations to defend and spread the Gospel of truth.

"Even though I walk through the valley of deep darkness, I will fear no evil." (Psalm 23: 4a; ESV).

January 14th:

Don't Deceive Yourself Waiting for Optimally Primed Conditions The best time to start lifting is the right now! Do not delay, but after being educated enough on safe lifting techniques and philosophy, go at it! However, is there an ideal time of day for weight training? Circadian rhythm experts state that "Body strength and pain tolerance peak in the afternoon." (296). Armed with this knowledge, it may be useful to lift between 2-5 pm, when the midday fatigue has worn off, and you are released from the stress of the daily grind, yet releasing the stress simultaneously in the act of moving bars and dumbbells. You can push yourself to new repetition or weight amounts as strength coincides at a high point, and try new lifts or simply increase the volume of the total workout as pain acceptance levels reach their zenith.

Like beginning a strength training program, you shouldn't delay confessing your faith in Christ/ placing trust in him for eternal security, for: "Indeed, the 'right time' is now. Today is the day of salvation." (2 Corinthians 6:2). We are not promised tomorrow, and I don't know about you, but when I go to sleep at night I like to know if I'm not going to see morning again, where I will spend eternity!

There is no perfect time to start strength training or to become a disciple of Christ. If you wait for ideal conditions, you will be rooted in good intentions perpetually. God's love for us should soften our hearts and beckon us to invite him to lead us in our ventures. "Today, if you hear his voice, do not harden your hearts." (Hebrews 3:15; NIV). There's no time like the present, and God speaks to us as he has since the dawn of ages from a position of strength.

<u>January 15th</u>:

The Ectopic Ambiance of an Athletic's Weight Room   The weight room is a unique atmosphere where you encounter people with all types of personalities and in varying states of disposition while executing their lifting routine. In a ferocious yet controlled situation, you see people in all their fluxing states with regard to athletics or other fitness goals: angry about not playing enough, humbled by their state of weakness, trying to get 'swole' to impress the ladies, brute effort and intensity taken out during and on the lift, and intimidated when comparing physical feats among others.

There is a certain unadulterated rawness of tone present in the air in a weight room. Seeing men and women exert forces on equipment can be freeing and socially impactful. We get to see our friends and brothers grow, but we also see them in the most negative conscription they can exude in fights, pride, or verbal exchanges. Christian author Suzanne Hadley Gosselin, herself also in an intense state of raising four young children says of what can be an overwhelming pressure to measure up to, "Allowing others to see us at our worst, is simply a part of life." (297).

The same comparison and desire to be on a pedestal occurred even under Jesus' servant leadership example during his ministry. The mother of James and John, two of Jesus' disciples, respectfully requested, "In your Kingdom, please let my two sons sit in places of honor next to you, one on your right and the other on your left," (Matthew 20:21) and it ruffled some feathers. "When the ten other disciples heard what James and John had asked, they were indignant" (Matthew 20:4). To build up one's self, while encountering a legitimate social strati- present in strength training, is to prepare to build God's Kingdom and face down predicaments.

January 16th:

Adherence to the Old and Tried Sometimes in strength training, we must go back to the old-school, classic and peerless lifts after trying new equipment and techniques. For example, I consider squats to be the most optimum exercise in existence as it recruits a large amount of the body's musculature. Researchers have discovered that at loads of 50% or higher of one repetition maximum, the squat is an effective means of increasing not only leg power, but also trunk and core strength. (212) In addition, the squat engages much more of the leg muscles available to recruit, as opposed to the contemporary leg press machine. (212) There is just no substitute for the way it requires core stabilization and works both the hip and knee flexors and extensors simultaneously.

As you can go wrong in new lifting variations to increase likelihood of injury, referring back to the 'tried' lifts, that technique is impeccable in decreasing this chance. So also, forsaking the eldest of sins in a contemporary facet, living a paramount lifestyle in concert with a truth older than antiquity itself exists according to God who told the prophet, Jeremiah, "Ask for the old, godly way, and walk in it." (Jeremiah 6:16)

January 17th:

The Discovering of Gods Will/ Revelations In our skeletal muscles, there exist two different types of muscle fibers: fast twitch and slow twitch. Fast twitch fibers are less efficient, contain fewer capillaries, and are used in quick, explosive movements such as weight lifting, sprinting and jumping. Slow twitch fibers contain greater amounts of capillaries and are more efficient at utilizing oxygen for slow energy-combusting activities such as jogging and walking.

Some communications from God come like fast twitch fibers, quickly in the form of advice from a pastor, friends and relatives, or directly from God's word. Other revelations come over time, like slow twitch fibers, from the same source that the prophet Elijah discovered in "the sound of a gentle whisper." (1 Kings 19:12)

January 18th:

Godly and Muscular Growth The second most important theory in strength training is the application of progressive resistance. Progressive resistance theory states that an overload must continue to be applied (through a high enough intensity of force production) by either increasing the weight of an exercise, or the number of repetitions performed.

Many times in our lives it is this maintenance of godly character that is so difficult. The Bible maps out how to attain this character, and there are five pre-requisites to getting to this point. The last trait (godliness) will never be fully achieved. Rather, it is the process, and the sincerity of effort God likes and honors.

"Supplement your faith with a generous provision of moral excellence (1), and moral excellence with knowledge (2), and knowledge with self-control (3), and self-control with patient endurance (4), and patient endurance with godliness (5). (2 Peter 1:5-7)

January 19th:

The Innermost Capacities of Spiritual Armor Core strength and stability are of utmost importance to any athletic training regime. Developing core strength ensures durability to perform common activities of daily living. Strength of the midsection refers to the ability to flex, extend, laterally flex, and rotate the torso against external forces. Stability refers to the functional capacities of the trunk to maintain proper posture in walking and other activities.

The first piece of spiritual armor listed in Ephesians chapter 6 is the belt of truth, also located centrally in the anatomy of the body. Veracity to Jesus Christ as Savior and deep knowledge of his truth in the Bible is essential to have before one can meet the challenges of daily life with the proper holistic defense.

"Stand your ground, putting on the belt of truth." (Ephesians 6:14)

January 20<u>th</u>:

Jesus Gave All he had so we Can Reciprocate Jesus came not only to purchase for us eternal life, but also so we could have abundant life on this earth. Exercise helps us claim this copacetic experience to the fullest degree by helping us in one manner to achieve holistic wholeness. Dr. Cooper says of people who exercise that they are: "not only increasing the raw power of their bodies but are also tapping broader physical and psychological resources that spill over into their other pursuits." (16)

"My purpose is to give them a rich and satisfying life." (John 10:10)

January 21st:

Strengthened for a Higher Spiritual Plane Superseding Fear Exercise mimics the ongoing battle that takes place on earth relating to an eternal war. Exercising causes the anticipation that we will have the fortitude/ perseverance to push through the temporary hurt and discomfort associated with it. This allows for a higher quality of life and a deeper, anagogical experience of life in all the daily adventures we encounter.

The ancient French knight Jean De Breuil said of the thrill of physical testing and the morality struggle men and women face daily, "Do you think someone who feels this is afraid of death? Not in the least! He is so strengthened, so delighted that he does not know where he is." (32) The force of love is so powerful that it forms a buffer to the fear of death.

"Such love has no fear because perfect love expels all fear." (1 John 4:18)

January 22ⁿᵈ:

Proper Directing of the Natural Wild Working out allows man a vent or soliloquy of catharsis and a means of outlet for deep-seated fervor which exists from origins of a state of divine instillation. As we pump out repetitions against the resistance of metal paraphernalia, we acquire a release for a man for which his "growth, his energy, owes chiefly to that striving of the will, that conflict with difficulty which… the material world does much more for our minds by the pains it inflicts," according to a preacher who catered to assisting blue-collar laborers (239).

We do not have to like or try to inflict pain on our bodies when lifting weights, but there is an undomesticated, feral domain to our souls for which lifting weights cater to exasperation thereof. President Roosevelt aptly described this nature in a speech where he castigated Americans not to lose this driving desire. "The overcivilized man, who has lost the great fighting, masterful virtues…whose soul is incapable of feeling that mighty lift that thrills 'stern men with empires in their brains' – all these, shrink from seeing the nation undertake its new duties. These are men who fear the strenuous life." (240).

One Biblical character who certainly did not hesitate to enamor feats of strength and effort was Samson. The liberation of the prementioned fervidness came out in Samson in the following Bible story. "Suddenly, a young lion came roaring toward him (Samson). The Spirit of the Lord came upon him mightily, and he tore the lion apart as one tears apart a young goat, and he had nothing at all in his hand." (Judges 14:5-6; Amplified Bible). Remember that it was God who imparted the vigor to his Spirit in the first place. In this example we see a man conquering a foe in the form of battle in man versus beast, while in weight training a man seeks to master his own self-doubts and insecurities of embattled weak areas, thus building godly character.

January 23rd:

The Ultimate Unseen 'Authority' I believe that exercise strengthens the unseen, inner characteristic that encompasses what is referred to as 'the heart'. Physical exertion does this by preparing our souls for what we will do in eternity.

James A. Michener, author of Sports in America, shared this feeling when he wrote: "The exquisite moments I have known in sports have related more to the dance of the human figure than anything else; the spiritual freedom I have often found in games has derived specifically from the dancing body seeking new forms and new releases." (39)

Perhaps Michener chose the metaphor of dance because you must feel the movements deep in the recesses of your spirit that choreography requires to make an artistic expression, which requires an act of the heart. Jesus often referred to the heart, and this is the intersection where exercise meets the spiritual and becomes good for the soul.

"For whatever is in your heart determines what you say. A good person produces good things from the treasury of a good heart." (Matthew 12:34-35)

January 24th:

Courage in the Struggle God has implanted in humans a hunger for eternity and to be godlike in virtue on this earth. We all long to be brave and remain courageous during the battles we face in this life as they occur in spite of the stress they cause. Exercise offers a perceptible way to develop this bravery. Yet, God alone is holy, perfect, and set apart from humans.

The Bible alludes to God being a warrior in the literal and figurative sense. Perhaps it is because there have always been conflicts in both the seen and unseen realms. Therefore, we can relate this actualized example of strengthening our physical bodies, and use the experience to our advantage to compare to mental and spiritual struggles.

"Who is the King of glory? The LORD, strong and mighty; The LORD invincible in battle." (Psalm 24:8)

January 25th:

Genetic Rejuvenation and the Spirit-Filled Life A fascinating aspect of exercise just recently illuminated is its role in 'turning on' more of our beneficial genes. Dr. Dean Ornish conducted a compelling study that should motivate anyone to begin lifestyle changes. "We found that comprehensive lifestyle changes were able to significantly increase the DNA-repairing enzyme telomerase in only three months." (53)

Similarly, when our lives are conducted with the primary goal of pleasing God, we are able to accomplish great things that invoke a connotation consistent with improving the human condition. This is possible because Christ came to give us abundant life.

"Under the new covenant, the Spirit gives life." (2 Corinthians 3:6)

January 26th:

The Prevailing Nature of God's Kingdom and Human Movement Kinesiology is a new and emerging field (the most rapidly growing major at colleges/ universities) in America that has thus far stood the test of time in terms of its theoretical and practical uses to improve quality of life. It is a scientifically researched and proven discipline that can literally change a person's life. Dr. Isadore Rosenfeld, in his book about alternative forms of medicine, says of kinesiology that "it is a proven technique of muscle testing, training, coordination, and rehabilitation that is widely and effectively used by athletes and dancers, and in the treatment of sports injuries." (66)

Similarly, the Bible – the living word of God, has stood the test of time. Jesus says that the word, specifically His good news (the Gospel), although having enemies, existed before the world began and is still the only source of truth to this day. "The Kingdom of Heaven has been forcefully advancing, and violent people are attacking it." (Matthew 11:12) In stark contrast to what our notions of Christ might be, he claims to be a force of division. "I came not to bring peace, but a sword." (Matthew 10:34) This sword is the Bible, the living word of God.

January 27th:

The Physicality of Spirit Growth In a blatant reference to brute physicality, the Bible states that we should "Take a new grip with your tired hands and strengthen your weak knees." (Hebrews 12:12) It is interesting to note how the Bible uses the literal comparison of kinesiology diction - the verbs 'grip' and 'strengthen' - in reference to how a person should respond to God's spiritually based discipline.

In the context of the passage, God's discipline shows and proves that he loves us. "As you endure this divine discipline, remember that God is treating you as his own children." (Hebrews 12:7) As Dr. David Lipschitz states, the trials of hardship, which also encompasses fitness endeavors, yield big results. "There's simply no substitute for hard effort...Research has clearly shown that for weightlifting to have a significant effect on muscles and bones, you have to strain." (82) Strain, or maximum effort, is the only way to grow physically or in godliness, in physique or spirit.

January 28ᵗʰ:

Love Spreads in Dying to Ourselves Exercise provokes a qualitative (compositional) alteration in bodily physiology (such as fat percentage reduction) and lifestyle. It makes sense that a source (human movement) powerful enough to change makeup in muscle size, strength, and stamina, causes the old pattern of sloth to 'die'. Jesus said, in relation to our spiritual lives, "Unless a kernel of wheat is planted in the soil and dies, it remains alone. But its death will produce many new kernels." (John 12:24) When we die to the desires of this world and its god, our love spreads like a wildfire to neighbors, and can save a soul or deepen a brother/ sister's faith.

St. Francis echoed this sentiment 1,000 years after Christ when he wrote, "For it is in pardoning that we are pardoned, and it is in dying that we are born to Eternal Life. (84) Just as physical changes due to exercise are personal in nature, faith also comes from within. John C. Maxwell says about the inherent desire embedded in each person to find fulfillment in God/ faith, "God is sufficient to give them the desire to change, but the choice to act upon that desire is theirs." (85). Just as exercise must originate with a personal decision, faith comes first from within - the heart. After the decision is made via individual freedom to trust/ place faith in Christ, then we come together to form the body of Christ. Fellowshipping in arenas such as love for each other, the act of exercise and the love of exercise build true communal experiences.

January 29ᵗʰ:

Creating Muscular and Spiritual Growth Through Inroads

According to Dr. Ellington Darden, a relatively new means of muscle growth called 'inroads' has been postulated. The concept states that if you start lifting at 100 percent of maximum strength and lower the load following multiple repetitions until it is 20 percent less (meaning at 80 percent of maximum strength) and finish the last two to three repetitions at this level with extreme difficulty, you have made an inroad. In describing this theory, both quantitatively and qualitatively, Dr. Darden says, "This combination inroad followed by intense failure seems to be the primary stimulus for the muscular growth process." (108)

Coming back stronger by pushing through soreness to weight train again should teach us a lesson that we need to grow in faith/ spirit as well. In our relationship with God, an effort also must take place on our part: we should crave spiritual sources of sustenance. "Like newborn babies, you must crave pure spiritual milk so that you will grow." (1 Peter 2:2) Spiritual milk can come from a variety of sources such as the Bible, fervent prayer, fellowship with other believers, and wisdom derived from parents and ministry elders.

Eventually, we must mature as Christians enough to grow past only growing our own spirit, into building others up. A lifestyle of stewardship – giving of time, talents, and treasures (more than just philanthropy) should be adopted for the kingdom of God.

"In the same way, let your good deeds shine out for all to see." (Matthew 5:16)

January 30th:

Obtaining a 'Supernatural' Physical Gift In the arena of physical exertion, youth athletics and adult fitness programs gravitate towards some similarities that American servicemen and servicewomen undergo in basic and advanced occupational training. Some of the undertakings military trainees undergo include running short sprints and long distances, gravity-resisted body weight training/ calisthenics, and improving core stability to ambulate and maintain fighting postures while carrying a constant load of 70 to 80 pounds for prolonged periods. Also, the inner qualities of deep resolve are developed in military and civilian fitness endeavors mutually.

Although athletics is not a literal battle, it is worth noting that my favorite football team, the Philadelphia Eagles, hired Shaun Huls as their chief sports science coordinator. Huls was previously employed as the training director for the Navy SEALs, thus supporting the hypothesis that physical training traverses several different forms and reasons for employing physical abilities in many arenas.

God blessed the Israeli army with military victories. Dr. Rex Russell says of these ventures, "Advice...was given, to the Israeli armies when they were the greatest 'against all odds' winners. They seemed to have supernatural fighting skills, particularly when they were obedient to God." (134) Is there any denying that the American armies have faced down some potent enemies as well? To compare with another generation, it is said of Jesus as he entered teenage years that he "grew both in body (or stature) and in wisdom, gaining favor, with God and people. (Luke 2:52; GNT) Physical endowment can be a sign of God's favor and a blessing doled out for many different reasons.

"The horse is prepared for the day of battle, but the victory belongs to the Lord."   (Proverbs 21:31)

<u>January 31st:</u>

Resiliency is Reinforced via Resistance Training By teaching us to give a full effort in lifting and running, and therefore to all enterprises, exercise helps us acquire temperance. Temperance is listed in the oldest translation of the ancient Bible (King James Version) as a fruit of the Spirit. If you reflect on what the word means relating it to a weather climate not varying much in regards to temperature and remaining a constant mildness of nature, personality corresponds to this quality after imbibing on fitness. Because your mind and body both focus on an external object outside of yourself (weight plate, barbell, running trail, etc.), yet the input of the effort is germinated from inside the mind and heart, and then manifested in perceptible corporeality of movement, people who regularly workout are hard to rattle or make squeamish.

The Bible says that this developed attitude of restraint without sternness is a blessing from God. "For the righteous will never be moved; he is not afraid of bad news; his heart is firm, trusting in the Lord. His heart is steady." (Psalm 112:7-8; ESV). When we can keep our composure even though the enemy tries to submerge us in chaos and make us distraught to leech us of our joy, we know God is at work. By allowing us to embrace struggle, faith is affected with a compositional change in attitude and corporal industry of muscle force. We know that God has worked on us physically and spiritually to stay obedient, measured, and steadfast in our faith despite the process of laboring through difficulties.

Dr. Covert Bailey says of this phenomenon, "People who are involved in sports are harder to ruffle. Everyday trials and tribulations seem petty after you've been knocked down on the basketball court… Little things just don't get to you…These are the psychological benefits of exercise – hard to prove, hard even to discuss, and yet so important." (232). God implants his virtue and character into us using the process of attaining an untenable psyche, uniquely suited only to the palpability of kinesiology.

February: Running the Race – Endurance and Cardiorespiratory Training

February 1st:

The Matthew Effect Ignites Prevention of Apathy Exercise can prevent burnout from everyday activities such as work, relationships, and predictable hobbies or leisure-time endeavors. So also, God desires us to serve Him and advance His kingdom in multiple facets – a spiritual concept known as stewardship. For Jesus said, in the parable of the talents, regarding his servants who make patient, fruitful use of their gifts, "To those who use well what they are given, even more will be given, and they will have an abundance." (Matthew 25:29)

This spiritual concept is also intertwined with the Newtonian/astronomical/ physiological laws that govern physical activity. An authoritative book in fitness research/ application by C.P. Gilmore says, "People rust out before they wear out because they fail to realize that the human body was made to be used for as long as a person lives." (152)

God desires us to transfer this physical epiphany we get from working out, into a productive and active lifestyle of stewardship. Stewardship means a complete 'sellout' to love God, our neighbors (friends and enemies), and those less fortunate. We accomplish these heavenly goals by sacrificing the aforementioned leisure time into godly quests. This concept of 'live-to-give' includes a coalescing of time, talents, and treasure consecrated to God in acts of service towards others.

February 2nd:

Why Give Up When Manual Work Stifles Evil? It is when we work the hardest that we tire the most. And it is because we put an all-out effort into our work or workouts that we feel emotionally and physically at ease afterward. Exercise helps us relax better when we get done working and have leisure time. The Unitarian preacher William Ellery Channing said of this phenomenon in a speech to the Mechanic Apprentices' Library Association: "I believe that difficulties are more important to the human mind than what we call assistances." (159) Dr. William Bennett, also a firm believer in this development of the 'whole-man' who is both intellectually astute and physically capable, said, "Hard manual labor and study are both necessary to build true manly character." (159)

Practically speaking, occupational health and output/ efficiency are products of solid, hard work, and as the Bible says, we cannot know how this effort may benefit us down the road. "Plant your seed in the morning and keep busy all afternoon, for you don't know if profit will come from one activity or another – or maybe both." (Ecclesiastes 11:6) The truth expounds on the theme of manifold blessings from physical toil, as does the American/ Unitary preacher Channing. He elevates the value inherent in work even to the unseen world of blessings in the same speech referenced earlier in this daily entry. "It has a far higher function, which is to give force to the will, efficiency, courage, the capacity of endurance, and of preserving devotion to far-reaching plans." (159)

February 3rd:

Is it the Acquisition of Goals or Pursuit of Fulfillment That We Crave? When I played football and partook in off-season training, the time spent devoted to strength and conditioning was more fulfilling than attainment of a good game performance. This makes sense, because, as Norman Vincent Peale says, "Happiness actually is found in striving for a goal rather than in settling down to enjoy the attained objective." (167) When you achieve a goal of scoring a touchdown or having X number of catches/tackles/ yards gained, it is fulfilling to an extent, but then comes the deep desire for a new challenge and the ever present question: what next?

Good coaches relayed to me the message that character is who you are and what you do (having integrity) when no one is watching. A tool the enemy employs is convincing us that 'no one will know.' This fact occludes together the lessons of the Bible and exercise, because most offseason work and preparation is unseen and unknown by others. Endurance is developed because of this secret undertaking, and the Bible is quite clear of the positive benefits regarding the trait of endurance.

"By your endurance, you will gain your lives." (Luke 21:19; ESV)

February 4th:

On a Different Metric Of Health By Imitating Christ Taking up a consistent aerobics program can yield such great results with oxygen uptake and efficiency of its distribution that a heart may beat up to "13 million fewer times per year." (170) Because the heart can pulse forcefully and eject more blood per contraction, it is required to do less to sustain the oxygen needs of the brain and muscles.

Spiritual training of consistency towards prayer life and allowing self-discipline to stand up to and defeat temptation will eradicate sinful behavior. Dr. Kenneth Cooper postulated that persons with healthier hearts or higher levels of cardiovascular fitness (evidenced with V02 max, defined in the previous paragraph) operated on a different physical level because not as much effort needs to be provided to maintain homeostasis/ bodily equilibrium at rest. Spiritually, this equates to living on a higher plane more in tune with God in our daily lives.

"I discipline my body like an athlete, training it to do what it should." (1 Corinthians 9:27)

February 5th:

During the Toughest Points, we Parley Past Mediocrity Don't let plateaus or slow incremental growth in strength or endurance deter your personal fitness practices. Long-term goals are to be reached for, but should not sour the minor victories and growth in the short-term. The effort you give in each workout contains an inherent lesson, and the laws of physiology will eventually be extended to yield gains in physical attributes and skill enhancement.

In his advice to young men, Scottish writer Thomas Carlyle curtailed the attitude that should be imposed upon the aforementioned situation. "Neither let mistakes or wrong directions discourage you. Let a man try faithfully, manfully to be right; he will grow daily more and more right." (173) The validity of this quotation is evidenced and proven in the fact that even Jesus needed exertional help and received it at the toughest point in his life – carrying His cross to be crucified in the face of unsullied exhaustion.

"As they led Jesus away, a man named Simon happened to be coming in from the countryside. The soldiers seized him and put the cross on him and made him carry it behind Jesus." (Luke 23:26)

February 6th:

A Godly Point of View Gives Us a Unique Perspective In an individual's response to exercise, there is an observable physiologic phenomenon rooted in psychology that I like to term 'perceptual set.' This quality refers to the dissemination of thoughts and, following overflow of emotions evoked prior to, during, and following an exercise bout.

For example, runners who engage in the fruition of stimulating this effect include the following scenario, as described by Dr. Covert Bailey: "Two people might claim the same pace, for example, a nine-minute mile, and therefore the same level of fitness, but one does it at 85 percent of maximum heart rate while the other is only at 70 percent." (180) Due to varying cardio-respiratory efficiency levels, one person would perceive a mightier effort had to be undertaken and given to complete the run.

Similarly, Christian faith is personal in nature and unique to each individual. The man of stalwart ancient faith, Job, also links together this mind-body phenomenon and proclaims it to be truth coinciding with man's creation. "But there is a spirit within people, the breath of the Almighty within them, that makes them intelligent." (Job 8:32) Because we cannot fully know how each person responds to the external stimulus of the Gospel (Romans 10:17), faith must come from within, just like the drive needed to cross the finish line in a competitive or recreational run. Armed with the knowledge that we were created each from God's divine nature(Genesis 1:27), we must look inward (to have heart or courage) and vertically (toward God) for true faith before we can live it out and expand our sphere of influence horizontally to others.

February 7th:

Exercise Assists in Comprehending God's Nature and Attaining Proximity to Him

"The heavens proclaim the glory of God. It rejoices like a great athlete eager to run the race." (Psalm 19:1,5)

Contained in a Psalm written by David, the comparison of the joy of competition to the glory and splendor of creation is substantiated. Understanding that the Scripture is referring to a track event should cause us to reflect on all the training that goes into the sport. You must run longer distances at slower paces to build endurance/ stamina as a partial portion of the program. In addition to running the expanse of the race being trained for, you must traverse shorter distances at 100% or above intensity effort-level to build anaerobic capacity, in proper training for the race.

In this consideration of all the preparation that goes into prerace efforts for which there is no circumvention, physically, the experience of butterflies exists. This form of anxiety aids in preparing the body with increased blood flow to extremities that will be utilized and release of adrenaline /norepinephrine into the bloodstream. Mentally the urge to not disappoint compiles in the mind so that there is no perception that the training was done in vain. As my uncle once said to me, "If you cross that finish line, you can do almost anything."

This metaphor of athletics related to nature is not vague at all. Rather, the beauty of it is that God's glory is proclaimed in creation as much as in athletic endeavors from which we assimilate in pieces the very nature of God and His relationship to us through exercise. The fact that the Bible uses athletics in similes professes the truth that God smiles down on physical training and innumerable self-sacrificial elements present in team sports.

February 8th:

God is Faithful So We Should Trust His Anointed Processes Everyone undergoes silent battles and all are faced with conditions and situations they would rather not confront. Many times exercise falls into this category of 'nonessential' activity that while not meaningless, does not ultimately seem necessary or mandatory in obligation. As with many tough situations, it is often what we perceive that misleads us. Running a continuous 5K after just one week of cardiovascular exercise at a low intensity, such as walking, can seem intolerable, unattainable and discouraging.

Having shed a negative connotation to fitness in the prior paragraph, I have to emphasize that exercise is a self-induced, not God-initiating, personal activity. God makes us free so that we can have all the more joy in working out, feeling as though it was our accomplishment. Participation in these movement-based programs and athletics can actualize in a loss of a game or being unable to finish all we planned in a workout. Facing bitter defeat allows us to become better at forward motion after the sting subsides.

While competition is good, children set an amiable example in how they 'play,' for how adults should conduct themselves as Christians in trying moments. "Children exposed to healthy competition will soon learn that the reason they play sports isn't to win at all cost, but to strive to win by playing as hard as they can within the boundaries of a set of rules." (198) Regardless of what happens in a game, the sun will rise again on a new morning, and defeat is not an absolute finality.

"The righteous person faces many troubles, but the Lord comes to the rescue each time." (Psalm 34:19)

February 9th:

Yielding to God's Plan Causes Body & Soul-State Multiplications Methodically Being an athletic trainer my freshman year of college required me to do what seemed like giving up on my dream of being a professional football player. I had to yield to other student-athletes of the same age, yet endowed with a superior talent, playing the sport who I perceived as being more blessed than me. It was difficult and took effort to watch others participate while I did not, but it was only temporary in nature, and eventually, I accepted that I could learn much from the situation.

In fitness, and specifically in strength training, you have to put forth a little extra bit of effort than you think you can muster going into it and that you actually precipitated in the previous workout. The expenditure of energy in muscle usage to lift a heavier weight or increase the number of repetitions can be discombobulating, as the agony of muscles twinging past their previous point is supervened by blood engorgement and filling of fluids in the interstitial spaces. But this state of stinging is only temporary in nature. In reality, you only have to experience the throbbing ache for maybe five to 15 seconds of time – a short duration in the large scope of life – and you are counted braver by others and in your own inner heart for sustaining just the attempt.

So also, we are like exiles on this earth, aching for something more than mediocrity that our souls are thirsty for. But this life is temporary in nature. Eventually, we will arrive circumspect to eternal life through grace by faith in Jesus Christ, and even to the point of inheriting a reward for the earthly struggles we battle daily.

"There is wonderful joy ahead, even though you have to endure many trials for a little while." (1 Peter 1:6)

<u>February 10th</u>:

The Naturality of Experiencing Visceral Enhancement via God's Creation An amazing aspect of creation exists in human toxin elimination and how it relates, during exercise, to the natural amazingness of plant life. Plants take in carbon and release oxygen into the external environment. In direct opposition, human beings require the uptake of oxygen and guess what is released into the air when running: H20 in the form of water/ sweat excretion and carbon in the form of metabolic by-products emitted through increased respiration which gives off carbon in the breath.

Also, Jesus uses a metaphor of soil and crop growth to indicate how we humans operate spiritually. "The good seed represents the people of the Kingdom." (Matthew 13:38). Just as the earth nourishes us and sustains us with atmospheric molecules necessary for survival (and never more apparent than when we are panting from an intense roundabout), God says the grain produced from precipitation helps yield a harvest of souls through His word. "It is the same with my word. I send it out, and it always produces fruit." (Isaiah 55:11). The physicality we derive from God transposes with the spiritual realms, and this is evident by experiencing a good fatiguing run in God's fresh air and created nature.

February 11th:

Take Exercise One Step at a Time, Spiritual Walk One Day at a Time Have you ever noticed that when you set out to run one mile exactly, the third lap (or the time between 50% and 75% of the trek) is the most difficult to persist through? Perhaps your mind and body rebel because you are hurting from hustling, but are a tad too far out to envision crossing the finish line of the fourth lap and completing the end goal of a mile.

So also, often when things seem the bleakest is the time when a major blessing is right up the track (pun intended). The times that we undergo trials might be disguised blessings from God. We must remember never to blame God, even if it seems like He is unfair to us or we even go so far as to question His pre-emptive goodness toward humans and singular holiness. To take up walking (or running) by faith each day and not by sight (or what we perceive), continuing to give an all-out effort, is the one and only solution.

The Nebraska strength coaches embellish us to take this difficulty as a possibility/ opportunity for salubrious growth. "Though the goal is seemingly impossible, you must continue to persevere, because a burst of progress is just beyond the horizon. There are no shortcuts or secrets to achieving your maximum performance potential." (229).

"For you know that when your faith is tested, your endurance has a chance to grow." (James 1:2)

February 12th:

Consistency is the Key to Conditioning and Receiving Consecrations My friends and fellow weight lifters in college always said that when you start a regime back up after a prolonged period of rest that you should, 'savor the flavor' of getting sore and observing positive alterations in muscle strength and size. In running travails, if you start out walking a mile, then running a half a mile, then walking two miles, running one mile at a slow pace, then progressing up your runs 400 meters at a time, you will notice that the initial single mile pace no longer makes you short of breath. When stamina increases, it is based on an exercise science theory of SAID (Specific Adaptations to Imposed Demands).

After surpassing initial states of lifting and running consistently, you will see all types of conditioning results taper off in gain. The body has adapted to the conditioning program and needs a compositional change in mode. Mode is the type of exercise you do and all the choices you have for fitness variables. For example, to enhance anaerobic conditioning, you can run sprints, jump rope, or climb stairs. If you vary the mode of exercise, you will never get bored in individual workouts or stale in your long-term routine.

Nebraska's strength coaches succinctly surmise the surreptitious nature of exercise. "Every player has reached a plateau in his training in which no further progress seems possible regardless of unrelenting endeavor. Don't become discouraged when you reach a training plateau; they are normal and necessary for your progress. Most of your time is going to be spent on a plateau." (229) Jesus gave wisdom on prayer life and its mediums and modifications, which can compare to fitness efforts. Just as your body will be obliged to eventually hypertrophy, consistency in prayer life is guaranteed to benefit as befitted by the following verse's finality punctuated not by a question mark, but by an exclamatory guarantee.

"If you then…know how to give good gifts to your children, how much more will the heavenly Father give the Holy Spirit to those who ask him!" (Luke 11:13; ESV)

February 13th:

Well-Being Spills Over Into a Godly Discernment of Erudition My uncle once made an interesting remark about running for fitness. He said that he would start jogging distances to get in shape when he saw someone running with a smile on their face. Interestingly, he is right that most runners don't seem happy during the act, but I don't believe it's an indication they are in pain, but rather being focused on the task because it resonates power to other areas of life too. Dr. Charles Stanley writes that "Spiritual growth is imperative from God's point of view not only for our spiritual well-being, but for our general happiness as well." (231) It is fascinating that God cares about all aspects of our lives so much that even the area he is most concerned about (obedience to His law), he uses to infuse power into other various mediums of daily existence such as trotting in displacement motion for a length of time.

In what may seem like common sense, it is alluring and rewarding to experience not getting short of breath as quickly or intensely when running at a moderate pace after you have done it for about six months. The tight, constricted, and concerted effort of lungs to draw breath gives way to a steady inhalation that is not as taxing – which could endow happiness to the point of exuding joy through facial expressions. Training through exercise for an extended time concerts the power of human health processes in such a way that spills over to spiritual growth, just as Dr. Stanley emphasized that spiritual growth gives way to maturity in all areas of needed virtue.

"But solid food is for the mature, for those who have their powers of discernment trained by constant practice to distinguish good from evil." (Hebrews 5:14)

<u>February 14th</u>:

The Direct Opposite of Fear is Not Only Courage but God's Unconditional Love Exercise does not have to be transitory in nature but can integrate with a reality-based resolution to persist in life's challenges. Just as Christ was afraid of what lay ahead, but paced on unfazed, we learn to last for the long-term benefit through chronic consistently applied aerobic exercise. The theme of perseverance is expounded on in the opening scene of 'A Knight's Tale.' While Chaucer ambles by a band of friends he describes what initiative he has left. "To trudge: the slow weary yet determined walk of a man (or woman) who has nothing left in his (or her) life except the impulse to simply soldier on."

In what can be a haunting discourse contained in Revelation, Jesus speaks to the church in Philadelphia of the ancient world that our patrolling onward has manifold spiritual rewards. "I know all the things you do….You have little strength yet you obeyed my word… Because you have obeyed my command to persevere, I will protect you from the testing that will come upon the whole world." (Revelation 3:8-10)

The lessons of exercise contain in themselves the ability to put aside the finite and flashy for a consistent concord of durability, which will furnish an unseen source of stamina. To continue on steadily despite facing downright overwhelming odds provokes the question: what is the meaning of it all? Yet proposing this mystery brings an exhilarating pursuit that one can codify purpose from fitness.

"Men in rags, men who froze,

Still that Army met its foes."

February 15th:

Receiving the Promise of Rest for Recuperation and Restoring Buoyancy Manual labor and concerted exercise differ in function, but either makes rest and relaxation time all the sweeter. Why else would God refer to an aspect of heaven as rest unless by some measure he authored life as a means of work and toil in its entirety? The writer of Ecclesiastes tapped into this aspect of laborious applications yielding benefits money could not purchase. "People who work hard sleep well, whether they eat little or much." (Ecclesiastes 5:12).

Figurative work which prepares us for the destiny God has prescribed that we shall do in eternity, allows us a deeper appreciation for recuperation and helps us find joy in the small details of monotony inherent in work. Many jobs in the 21st century economy no longer rely on broad swathing movements of the body to till and cultivate the land. Instead, our efforts are repetitive in small, specific and specialized motions that can tax a joint over time, giving rise to an industry referred to as 'ergonomics'. How to purposefully direct energy in work is a fascinating topic, in exercise just as much as when we work for God's kingdom. However, whether fitness comes from occupation or intentional physical activity, it is honest and allows us to exemplify what we are capable of with the body God gave us.

"For all who have entered into God's rest have rested from their labors, just as God did after creating the world." (Hebrews 4:10).

February 16ᵗʰ:

Get Busy Trying for God, and then Relying on God Sometimes I think we negate the enthusiasm of a daily dose of exercise because we feel like it is not the ideal time or situation to begin. We want to have diet, daily interactions with others, and stress levels in tow before we try to achieve a good workout session. But in these situations, the exercise can help make up for the lack of a copacetic nature of the day as a whole. God calls us to action 'where we are,' not where we feel it is an ideal environment for us to engage.

In addition, hard work can combat feelings of despair. A Protestant pastor once said, "The best antidote to grief…is action," and Dr. Bill Bennett states the healing and problem-solving aspects of fitness by saying, "Good, hard work is often the best way out of a tight spot" (273). The call to action via movement is one hallmark of a spiritually fervid life, but is only one, not 'THE' only one. Hard work can take many on many forms of demonstrations and should not be exclusively limited to exercise. In fact, it might be good to step back from working out for a time so we can divert our mediums to other modes, like prayer or reading. Exercise is effervescent, but should not solely be relied upon to grow us closer to God. Rather, we should work hard for the kingdom of God in all aspects and arenas being honestly dedicated as an offering to him.

"Gracious words are like a honeycomb, sweetness to the soul and health to the body." (Proverbs 16:24; ESV).

February 17ᵗʰ:

Parental Processes Fatigue So Thriving in Weariness lies in Muscle Usage Exercise causes an introspection of why we partake of it, and how it supplants suppositions suggesting it isn't necessary. It can help you become that man you aspire to be deep down. In fact, Fox News writer Gary Wilkerson suggests we look within ourselves as men if fitness is lacking, to help us become better fathers by bringing it into a daily or consistent routine. "Go deep. Even check the way you eat or lack exercise. These things can cause us to lose the vast amount of energy it takes to father the active nature of children in this (young) age." (278). Being a father takes enormous energy reserves, and while I haven't been one, I have worked with children, learning that interacting with young boys and girls can be physically and emotionally draining.

Working out regularly gives us a chance to focus on something that is concerned with our personal, individual needs, recharging our bodies and spirits with vast resources of vitality reinvigorating us for daily challenges. A recompensing takes place in our souls when we further fitness. As I heard one fellow student at TCU say about her taking and making time for running, "I know it's about me, and I can focus on my needs for a while." It is not selfish to take time for ourselves, but rather, shows a dedication to God himself that we long to serve him and take a temporary respite (is that an oxymoron to compare working out with rest? – I don't believe so) to operate within his divine will in the future. If scripture says God places a premium on bodily health and abilities, we should too!

"Our bodies were made for the Lord, and the Lord cares about our bodies." (1 Corinthians 6:14)

February 18<u>th</u>:

Exalting Vigor Exalts God There is dignity and divinely intentioned purpose in work, and the first task given by God was labor, specifically manual toil in the fields. Catholic intellectual George Weigel says of manual effort that "Work, with all its rigors and hardships, was a participation in God's creativity, because work touched the very essence of the human being as a creature to whom God had given dominion over the earth." (299).

In today's information and service-based economy of the United States, few jobs require constant physical exertion. Rather, many who are active regularly achieve their energy expenditure of work in an indoor gym setting. Therefore, we can elevate as ennobling the task of working out to God-authored status. And there is no feeling quite like the cessation of an exhausting workout. As Mark Judge states of the spiritual worth of work, rejoining the workforce in a part-time job after losing his full-time employment during the 2008 recession, "But I will be changed I think…one night after work I was riding home…I felt spent, but I also felt alive." (299).

"For even when we were with you, we commanded you this: If anyone will not work, neither shall he eat." (2 Thessalonians 3:10; NKJV).

February 19th:

Plodding on in Daily Ventures In exercise and fitness, we must patiently wait for physiological results. Plodding through daily training, takes perseverance and a strong commitment. This physical trudging prepares us to 'Wait on the Lord.' This 'waiting' or having the patience to allow God's framework/ plan for our lives is a godly activity, is a form of prayer in and of itself, and bestows spiritual strength. Dr. Charles Stanley says of this process: "Sometimes God wants to answer our prayer, but the timing is not right. We don't like waiting around, especially when it looks like a unique opportunity might slip away." (183)

It takes trust in the physiological anabolic enhancement process that God ordained to give results from exercise. The faith in the goodness of the future can be related to having patience in finding an understanding spouse, obtaining a fulfilling career, seeing through an educational venture, and just purely finding the grit and wherewithal to rise in the morning in the face of mounting daily challenges.

"Wait on the Lord. Be brave and courageous. Wait on the Lord." - (Psalm 27:14)

"Be still in the presence of the Lord, and wait patiently for him to act." (Psalm 37:7)

February 20th:

The Inner Spirit Potentiates Life-Altering Zeal At lactate threshold, the body's production of the by-product of exercise (lactic acid) exceeds physiological capacity to clear out the acid from the bloodstream and muscles. Lactate threshold is of utmost importance to an endurance athlete as it determines the intensity he/ she can maintain in endurance-based exercise while lactate pools in your extremities, leaving inadequate blood and oxygen supply to the brain. This increment intensity of exercise will inevitably drop, as the body can only accomplish so much.

God's word also sets our hearts and minds ablaze and compels us to fight for the holy and just in this world. "His word burns in my heart like a fire. It's like a fire in my bones!" (Jeremiah 20:9).

Dr. Covert Bailey says of this metabolic phenomenon: "It's lactic acid that causes the sharp, burning pain we have all felt...that burning sensation is the origin of the expressions 'go for the burn' and 'no gain without pain.'" (184) So also, God's word can be shocking in meaning by bluntly correcting our false motives, pretenses, and actions.

"The words of the wise are like cattle prods – painful but helpful. Their collected sayings are like a nail-studded stick with which a shepherd drives the sheep." ("Ecclesiastes 12:11).

February 21ˢᵗ:

Be a Good Man, But Not a too-good Giddy One Exercise is a clean, honest, and good leisure activity. We know it is good for the body and mind through recent scientific research and discovery. But there is also a spiritual goodness inherent in fitness. This can be discovered when Paul exhorts believers to: "Fix your thoughts on what is true, and honorable, and right, and pure, and lovely, and admirable. Think about things that are excellent and worthy of praise." (Philippians 4:8).

Working out is not an activity intended for someone who lives like a square, and yet it still has purity to it. Teddy Roosevelt sums up how to avoid this predicament of not being pretentious in youth so as to become an upright and steadfast grown man: "The boy can best become a good man by being a good boy – not a goody-goody boy, but just a plain good boy." (300). Certainly pushing yourself to new goals in weight loss, strength gains, or athletic prowess is excellent and worthy of praise. For example, the specific training of jogging can impart indefatigability into our bodies and hearts both concurrently.

February 22ⁿᵈ:

Learning God's Composure from Ancestral Diviners Dr. Vaughn Bryant, head of Department of Anthropology at Texas A&M, said regarding the physical activity level of our ancient ancestors, "We estimate that on a hunt, prehistoric man might have covered about 10 miles, routinely." (6)

Similar to what we have promulgated with modern efficient machinery, except that machines are inanimate, our bodies were created by God to have the capacity for endurance physically and spiritually for the lifelong calamities that are bound to occur. We were built to handle the stresses and pressures that are inevitable with being a follower of Christ and prepare us to spend an eternity with Him.

"So I (Paul) run with purpose in every step." (1 Corinthians 9:26)

February 23rd:

Feeding the Craving for Courage through Faith and Fitness Faith is often the father of courage. Exercise cannot give birth to true faith, but it can nourish and deepen it. Exercising and achieving fitness goals help build that invisible quality of courage that God so vehemently admires and admonishes us to kindle in our hearts.

"This is my command – be strong and courageous! Do not be afraid or discouraged. For the Lord your God is with you wherever you go." (Joshua 1:9)

February 24th:

A Serious & Shameless Grit Not Stodgy in Nature Jesus used the parable of the persistent widow with his disciples, "To show that they should always pray and never give up." (Luke 18:1). Jesus never promised us that because someone is a Christian, he or she will never face difficulties, trials, or calamities. On the contrary, if the very Son of God had problems, surely all other humans will too.

A poem entitled 'The Quitter' by Robert W. Service echoes this persistence that Jesus talks about:

"It's easy to cry that you're beaten – and die; but to fight and to fight when hope's out of sight – Why, that's the best game of them all! It's the keeping-on-living that's hard." (9)

Fitness gives humans a way to develop this shameless doggedness of effort through physical exertion, psychological steadiness and mental stability (maintaining motivation for each workout). Persistence in exercise routines will eventually, through practice and consistency, transpose its effect on prayer life too.

February 25th:

A Simultaneous Clandestine & Transparent Scientific Process Martin Luther, who is primarily responsible for ushering in the protestant reformation, once wrote about his own prayer life that God answered in mysterious ways with long-term effects. "Indeed God sometimes deferred, but notwithstanding he came." (17)

Accomplishing fitness goals can take some time, along with an immense amount of sustained effort. Not seeing results as quickly as we hope for can be disheartening. But like God's response to prayer, results are eventually inevitable. Being a matter of science weight loss has been pinpointed in regard to how it is achieved. Prayer, not being a science, must be adhered even that much more consistently and ardently, to yield even greater fruit.

'I tell you, you can pray for anything, and if you believe that you've received it, it will be yours." (Mark 11:24)

February 26th:

Forward Motion Requires Absence of the Past Incongruences

I press on to reach the end of the race and receive the heavenly prize." (Philippians 3:14)

To achieve success in any fitness endeavor, you must conclude being fixated on past failures, where consistency in frequency of sessions was not present. It is imperative to begin with fresh aspirations for a new exercise program. Notice also that Paul refers to life in the metaphor of 'race.' It is curious that in many instances Paul alludes to physical properties and athletic endeavors, using them as allegory and/ or metaphors for our spiritual walks.

God offers us clean slates and forgiveness of sins through the blood of Christ. If we have faith in God's promises, when we believe, we are able to do ALL things! Even more encouraging, is that a prize awaits us at the end of our story, culminating in unequivocal terms that we will be rewarded for every good thing we do!

February 27th:

Neuroscience and the Laws Governing Exercise Delving into the practical side of exercise psychology, when we confront the sorrows that occur in life, we can learn much from them. We should try to understand what God, in an adroit manner, is teaching us through the twinging. The minister Dr. Charles Allen says of combating this cumbersome yet necessary emotion, "Healing means bringing the person into a right relationship with the physical, mental, and spiritual laws of God." (131)

Of science as a whole, Dr. Allen says it is an "Organized effort to learn the laws of God and how they operate." (131) These 'laws' also control the effects and result of exercise, yielding humankind, "To seek the truth and know when truth is found." (131) Jesus said this truth would set us free, (John 8:32) and ultimately we see the nature of God's laws evidenced when proper fitness programming constitutes measurable results.

At the same time, we have this truth, along with the proven resource of exercise to face down negative thoughts and help sadness to recede naturally. Norman Vincent Peale, says of the formidable forces combined, (truth and exercise) "There is indeed a 'prescription' for heartache. One element in the prescription is physical activity. Get busy walking, riding, swimming, playing – get the blood coursing through your system…and emphasize the physical aspect of activity." (132)

"Sorrow is better than laughter, for sadness has a refining influence on us." (Ecclesiastes 7:3)

February 28th:

Let Your Effort and Hustle Exhibit Your Faith Jesus used the illustration of physical activity to demonstrate a faith harbored within the heart. "If a soldier demands that you carry his gear for a mile, carry it two miles." (Matthew 5:41). The context of the passage is such that when a calamity occurs, do not give in to desperation, but just keep soldiering on. Also, the verses following and prefacing Jesus' statement urge us to be eager to help others in palpable ways, even if it means exerting to a maximum bodily effort. Regarding the fact that observable exercise in the service of others (such as walking with a lonely friend, helping a senior carry groceries, or playing football with youth as a coach) should be encouraging, because if we are good stewards of our bodies, there is something everyone can do in a kinesiology manner to serve.

March: Reducing Idle Time Via Athletics, Fitness, and Recreation

March 1st:

The Narrative Aperture Effect of Performing with Persistence Strength training too sporadically, or in my opinion, less than once per week, although beneficial, will not yield optimal results. It takes performing the same grueling exercises multiple times to cause gains in strength or hypertrophy.

When we lead clean, godly lives, every day becomes an adventure with more and more to look forward to. When our hearts are pure, every day becomes exciting with new experiences ready to be had. We no longer have to be considerate to tedium, because there are always fresh relationships to be cultivated and, physically, a diaspora of training regimens to imbibe in.

"The way of the righteous is like the first gleam of dawn, which shines ever brighter until the full light of day." (Proverbs 4:18)

March 2nd:

Drama Follows Rules when Steeped with Godly Fear One reason organized sports are fun to play is that all athletes must play under the same set of rules, and the outcome is not predetermined. Organized sports, whether competitive or recreational, are an excellent way to improve fitness.

"And athletes cannot win unless they follow the rules." (2 Timothy 2:5).

We must also follow the commandments God has given us. God gave us the law in order to show us his goodness and infallibility, and allow us to realize and spurn our sinful nature. Godly fear, allows us a dispensation of thought during exercise from the heart itself. Through fear we simultaneously obey God and permit a constructive means of transposing eustress on the body through sustained physical effort.

March 3rd:

Only the Deity's Opinion Matters Ultimately, the Bible gives us wisdom and tells us how to find favor in the sight of people and God: "Let not mercy and truth forsake thee; write them upon your heart. So thou shalt find favour and good understanding in the sight of God and man." (Proverbs 3:3-4 KJV)

Many people seek fitness for the changes in bodily shape and proportions that they feel will make them popular. Motivation from this source means that seeking popularity is not a bad venture as long as it does not become an obsession. However, true and eternal fulfillment comes from seeking to please God, as this is our primary purpose in life.

"For thou hast created all things, and thy pleasure they are and were created." (Revelation 4:11) Notice that past tense term 'were' and present tense term 'are' have been chosen by a celestial being to express the truth to John. Since God has control, even over the past, we ought to be motivated that previous misgivings or underutilization of exercise can be righted. Chronic health conditions can always be at least partially encumbered by a healthy lifestyle that includes exercise.

March 4th:

Invest Vigor of Emotion, Physicality, and Service in all Endeavors Former President Theodore Roosevelt once said, "In short, in life, as in a football game, the principle to follow is: Hit the line hard: don't foul and don't shirk, but hit the line hard." (12)   Exercise bestows upon us something to give a full effort and pour ourselves into, in order to build ourselves up to the greatest potential. Not shirking requires having the discipline to apply ourselves fully whether to exercise, at our professions/ career, serving in the church, relationships, and personal life, especially when our motivation levels are low. As stated in the University of Nebraska athletic performance manual: "Discipline is doing the right thing at the right time." (72)

"Work willingly at whatever you do, as though you were working for the Lord rather than for people." (Colossians 3:23)

March 5th:

Warming the Body, Mind, and Heart via Prayer & Toil Plato once remarked, "You know that the beginning is the most important part of any work." (13).

My good friend and I used to remark to each other, before we began a lifting workout that "The hardest part is getting started." Once the sweat and adrenaline get flowing, it is easy to continue to push yourself and achieve new heights in a workout. And my friend and I were rewarded with a post-workout sense of positive personal accomplishment for finishing the feat.

The hardest part to attaining a fervent prayer life is just to begin to pray. Not by reading about prayer or listening to a lecture/ sermon about prayer, but by simply doing it.

A good starting point is to thank God for the day beginning in the morning, and the individual blessings you received the previous day.

Jotting down a 'list of gratitude' for gifts makes us more cognizant of just how fortunate we are and lets us uniquely pray for each inheritance in our life. Following the intellectual stimulation of writing, we can creatively look into the future for what we would like God to continue or begin to bequeath to us and supplicate for His favor.

"Never stop praying." (1 Thessalonians 5:17)

"Devote yourselves to prayer with an alert mind and a thankful heart." (Colossians 4:2)

March 6th:

Human Strength Singularly is Insufficient without Godly Study Regarding the acquisition and maintenance of fortitude, the Roman philosopher Seneca once remarked, "This strength of heart, however, will come from constant study, provided you practice, not with the tongue but with the soul." (14)

It is interesting that bravery could be developed from a practice as seemingly dichotomous with physical strength as the activity of studying. However, an indomitable will must be developed in all areas of life if we are to overcome our challenges and subsequent battles in the eternal war. A holistic approach to health and well-being is necessary, not just in the physical and mental realms, but more importantly, morally and spiritually.

'Nor is great strength enough to save a warrior." (Psalm 33:16)

March 7th:

Walking Elicits Unique Worship in Conjunction with the Holy

Spirit Walking is a great mode of exercise for people of all fitness levels. A movement pace of three to 3.5 miles per hour or greater is likely a high enough intensity to elicit fitness benefits. Harry Truman, while President, walked a mile and a half every day and said of the activity: "If you are going to walk for your physical benefit, it is necessary that you walk as if you are going someplace." (15)

Aside from the movement-oriented benefits of walking, it is a great way to collect your thoughts and regain composure after encountering a stressful life event. The rhythmical movement is the perfect medium to allow purposeful prayer, a rote memorization of scripture, and a proper flow of thoughts into and out of the mind.

"Let the Spirit renew your thoughts and attitudes." (Ephesians 4:23)

March 8th:

A Mutually Beneficial Social Contract Americans hold a unique responsibility and obligation to be an example of freedom in both public and private life. Thomas Jefferson said of this responsibility that our actions echo to successive generations in posterity. "We feel that we are acting under obligations not confined to the limits of our own society. It is impossible not to be sensible that we are acting for all mankind." (199)

So also, our fitness goals achieved can serve as a leadership-by-example process. It is possible that our improvement and dedication may foster another person's interest in living a healthy lifestyle. What higher existential freedom is there than a calling to take care of our mortal bodies in preparation for the eternal work we will perform in God's kingdom throughout eternity?

"For you have been called to live in freedom, my brothers and sisters." (Galatians 5:13)

March 9th:

The Internal Dialogue of Prayer and Promenading Thomas Jefferson once remarked that "of all exercises, walking is the best." (27) Perhaps Jefferson went for leisurely walks to stimulate his mind when he had writer's block as he drafted the Declaration of Independence.

Walking is the perfect exercise/medium to collect your thoughts. You can also use this potent physical antidote against chronic disease, to memorize Bible verses or repeat inspirational quotes. The rhythmic cycle stimulates the mind potentiating it to acquire spiritual wisdom just as our moods have ebb and flow. As much as we might hate to admit it, our attitude toward God may fluctuate like the cross-crawl pattern of our gait, allowing us to coincide the two and improve character. Walking speed and labor, much like prayer, can range in intensity and duration in order to elicit the specifically desired effects.

"Humbly accept the word God has planted in your hearts, for it has the power to save your souls." (James 1:21)

"The earnest prayer of a righteous person has great power and produces wonderful results." (James 5:16)

March 10th:

Salt in Exercise Studios of Sociology The Bible makes use of the edible substance salt to connote the inner faith of a Christian. Paul says to "Let your conversation be seasoned with salt so that you will have the right response for everyone." (Colossians 4:6)

I believe this metaphor of salt has direct implications to how we behave in a free-spirited, casual atmosphere such as the gym. Many times talk can become crude and impure. The Bible implores us to have our public life and speech match the fervor for Christ in our private lives of contemplation and mindfulness.

Saint John Chrysostom, early church preacher, had this practical advice to offer on the matter: "If we are doing any type of good work, we should season our actions with the desire and remembrance of God. Through this salt of the love of God, we can all become a sweet dish for the Lord." (33) Certainly, as we literally exude salt in propensity of effort, we can diffuse an embodiment of Christian behavior and convey its very character.

March 11th:

Strengthening the Sinews and Spirit Causes Disregard for Sin
Exercise offers a recreational activity that is far better than the sedentary and catabolic activities of drinking alcohol, smoking, or binge eating. It could be the answer to your being more productive on the job and playing recreational endeavors harder and for a longer duration.

I believe that fitness and athletic involvement has kept many young men and women from choosing an unwholesome path for their lives. Many wise persons have stated regarding the eternal war between right and wrong that you're either part of the problem, or part of the solution. Exercise and Fitness are part of the solution, being on the side of good in this world. The sense of tranquility that you feel after a vigorous game or bout of exercise is unparalleled. Exercise is, "a much purer high with tremendous long-term psychological, medical, and physical payoffs." (34)

"Dear friend, I hope that all is well with you and that you are as healthy in body as you are strong in spirit." (3 John 2)

March 12th:

Exhilaration Early in the Day via Spiritual and Physical Exertion Methodist Minister Edward McKendree Bounds, who some say wrote the greatest book on the subject of prayer in Power Through Prayer, once wrote, "The men who have done the most for God in this world have been early on their knees. He who fritters away the early morning, its opportunity and freshness…will make poor headway seeking Him (God) the rest of the day." (37)

Christ utilized a delicate, yet intentional balance between public and private life. Beginning a day with exercise following prayer can be an invigorating experience. You get a sense of accomplishment and the day seems unlimited with its possibilities and adventures. It is not unmanly to think and meditate and pray in the morning about any area of your life.

"Never be lazy, but work hard and serve the Lord enthusiastically. Be patient in trouble, and keep on praying." (Romans 12:11-12)

March 13th:

Assurance in Attainment of Victory over Adversity What an advantageous opportunity for adversity involvement in athletics offers! Alluding to these tests, Grantland Rice, the American sportswriter and broadcast journalist, wrote the famous words: "For when the One Great Scorer comes, to write against your name, He marks – not that you won or lost, but how you played the game." (42)

Jesus actually gave us a guarantee that we will face problems in life. "Here on earth you will have many trials and sorrows. But take heart, because I have overcome the world." (John 16:33).

I believe that God, who has the whole scope of our life in view, can use present and past adversity to prepare and mold us for what lies ahead. Athletics offer a robust ground for the cultivation of character through the physical, mental, and emotional challenges they entail.

March 14th:

Exercise and Moral Pathways of Life   George W. Bush has written that he used exercise to develop self-control prior to becoming president. He has stated that "I ran harder and longer as a way to discipline myself." (67) It is fascinating that physical activity provided a canvas for pondering what eventually occurred for Bush: an epiphany of what he should do and which direction he would proceed within his life by faith.

Even the most powerful man in the world, for a time, needed what we all need: the fruit of the Spirit. Self-control/ discipline is listed as a gift profiteered by the Holy Spirit, against which there exists no law. (Galatians 5:23) Paul compared the journey of life to running a race and how useful and necessary this quality of discipline is when he wrote, "All athletes are disciplined in their training." (1 Corinthians 9:25)

March 15th:

Embrace Conditioning For the Love of the Task   Just as Christ embraced the role his Father gave him in life because it glorified God, we should embrace the richness and fullness of life that exercise confers upon us. Exercise quantifies and broadens our experiences with physical limitations, therefore enabling us to work at maximum efficiency in other areas of life.

"Don't be dejected and sad; for the joy of the Lord is your strength!" (Nehemiah 8:10) The aforementioned verse offers an interesting comparison: that strength actually is derived from existential innate joy. The genesis of that expansive joy stems from our faith in God.

Reverend William Jewett Tucker implores us to become leaders because of the joy it entails. "The one solution of our present troubles...the presence of men qualified for leadership, whose great qualification is not a sense of duty, but the joy of the task." (95) Much can be compared to exercise in this quotation, or as some might even elevate as an equation: namely that we should involve ourselves in athletics/ exercise because we love it. Also, we should be motivated to reap the benefits and naturally unmitigated virtuous qualities that conditioning instills in us.

<u>March 16th:</u>

The Confluence of Fitness and Work God exhorts us to give a passionate means of hardihood to any enterprise we choose to undertake, including fitness. Provided the circumstances please the Lord and/ or benefits others to improve the overall human condition, there is no reason not to pour our whole selves into any cause undertaken. "Whatever your hand finds to do, do it with all your might, for there is no work or thought or knowledge or wisdom in Sheol." (Ecclesiastes 9:10; ESV)

This full temerity in fitness/ athletics prepares us for the vocation we are called to fulfill in our professional lives. For example, following the loss of a national championship game in 1994, the Nebraska Cornhuskers strength coaches sum up the attitude and 'buy-in' needed to undertake that task of coming back stronger with perseverance for the whole season. "This resolve did not focus on winning the national championship, but focused on what it takes each day to get the job done. This involved sacrificing certain comforts and making a commitment each day to prepare thoroughly and work hard. If everyone concentrated on doing his part each and every day, the national championship would take care of itself." (110)

There exists no more important endeavor than to link the mystique of mind and spirit together with our earthly vessels practically, through the binding forces of faith and arduous work ethic.

"With God we shall do valiantly." (Psalm 108:13; ESV)

March 17th:

Is Yoga Godly and Christian in Nature? Yoga is a form of physical activity that through concentration, bodily positions and focused breathing, can ease your mind and 'center' you. To be centered infers that you reach into your inner core being or the 'subconscious' mind. Psychologists say this autonomic aspect of our brain's function on its own and without personal volitions. This area encompasses not just the mind, but also the heart.

Evidence of this area was given by none other than our Savior. Christ said, "Don't let your hearts be troubled. Trust in God, and trust also in me." (John 14:1) The Bible also has this calming and reassuring aspect to it when we imbibe on it. By giving hope for the future despite the fact that we live in a chaotic world, Jesus comforts us in the fact that he will right the wrongs/ injustices of life in a fallen world. "God blesses those who hunger and thirst for justice, for they will be satisfied." (Matthew 5:6)

Yoga's benefit is that of relaxation and enhanced flexibility through use of synergistic muscles physically speaking. "Yoga can

direct manner, God states that indolence equates with evil. In Jesus' parable of the talents, God personifies His viewpoint toward a lackadaisical attitude and lifestyle: "But the master answered him, 'You wicked and slothful servant!'" (Matthew 25:26)

On the contrary, God elevates physical activity to the level of ennobling status, championing it on nearly the same level of importance as working for living wages /income. Oftentimes, in manual labor environments, they many times are one in the same and reciprocate a burgeoning of godliness in character.

Because there is a striving of will against inertia, and a practical derivation of spiritual qualities, exercise decries sin and promotes chasteness. Exercise burns off literal energy in excesses, and stifles temptations while instilling a concomitant virtue that is difficult to produce in elocution or using literary devices. Dr. Charles Stanley explains this paradox relating to both important qualities of exercise and faith, and their plenitude blessings excoriated and excavated. "An untested faith is weak and ineffective. Just like our muscles, our faith must be exercised against some resistance. When we face trials with wisdom and endure them with godly perseverance, we will find blessings we never thought possible." (179)

"Never be lazy, but work hard and serve the Lord enthusiastically." (Romans 12:11)

March 23rd:

Don't Get Duped Into Inactivity – Lose Yourself in Vibrant Effort The book of Proverbs is quite outspoken in admonishing us to avoid laziness. In many different contexts, Solomon writes of his specific abhorrence for that quality and its sloth, about 20 times (word choice used - depending on the translation). This percentage of alluding amounts to being mentioned in two-thirds of the whole volume of chapters in the book of Proverbs. Clearly then, there must be a reason why physical activity is so important, and is even put on the same echelon as work, which can include manual labor actions. Exercise combats the 'dull' or 'gray' notion of not putting into action the call to Christian servitude. This fact is evidenced by James who wrote, "But be doers of the word, and not hearers only, deceiving yourselves." (James 1:22; ESV) Not only is an inactive lifestyle ungodly, it leads to discontent of the heart, or inner man. President Roosevelt said, "A mere life of ease is not, in the end, a very satisfactory life." (193)

From an athletic's standpoint, you always have to concern yourself with who is investing more time training to become more skilled through pure work effort. Fitness-wise, it only takes several missed workouts to develop a pattern of avoiding that discomfort which at times marks exercise. Pioneers in the strength and conditioning field write regarding this area, "Without discipline, you have a deadened conscience. You are 'doped' by your lesser peers or emotional feelings…that keep you from being the most you can be." (194) I believe Job was giving mankind a warning to employ our bodies with constructive activities when he remarked, "I was at ease, and he (God) broke me apart." (Job 16:12; ESV)

March 24<u>th</u>:

If you have a Backbone from Fitness You're Bound to Offend Somebody Exercise does not seek to palliate the passion present in a man's heart, but rather, to properly and productively channel it. Jesus Himself showed passion at times, one example being in the Gospel of John chapter two when he drives out the money changers selling sacrifices and seeking to make a profit in the temple. When he did this, Jesus' disciples remembered in their minds and hearts from an earlier prophecy (Psalm 69:9) that Jesus would anger the religious authorities in doing so. "Passion for God's house will consume me." (John 2:19)

Jesus even offended the Pharisees in another manner because of their stodgy and haughty perception of themselves as more godly in character than average Jews. "Then they scoffed, 'He's just a carpenter'… and they were deeply offended and refused to believe in him." (Mark 6:3) Similarly, exercise is for anyone and as Jesus worked with His hands, he knew the value of manual labor and the peace of mind amid living a clean, honest life with daily physical toil. In these two examples of passion and work, Jesus evidenced that while spiritual matters are more important, bodily efforts can heighten spiritual experiences and ultimately entrench our faith.

March 25th:

When Good Men do Nothing, The Gospel Implodes Jesus remarked at the end of a parable regarding the dispensation of spiritual gifts and call to action for spreading the Gospel, "But from those who do nothing, even what little they have will be taken away." (Luke 19:26) This is a striking statement and should stir in our hearts a trifling bit of inadequacy and perhaps even a fear that we have not done enough in service to God. While this type of referenced reverence is quintessential, we should be stimulated and prodded on to serve God because we love Him.

In kinesiology terms, a no-can-do attitude and lack of action circumvents into a literal atrophy or– wasting away -of muscle tissue and functional strength capacities. Augmentation then ceases as there is no new formation of capillaries in the muscle and subcutaneous skin tissue. Thus, the growth of existing muscle fibers cannot occur via the successive stages of usage and slight damage, with the body sending a dearth of nutrition and medicinal substances for regrowth, leading to an anabolic state.

Exercise is a specific aspect of health in which we interact with on a singular and concurrent social level to inspire our teammates/ peers. It carries with it senses of accomplishment that methodically merit gains in areas of physical and psychologically rooted benefit difficult to expound on. In the same parable mentioned above, God conveys that with great ability comes a conferring of responsibility: "I'm a hard man who takes what isn't mine and harvest crops I didn't plant." The fleshing out of energy expenditure yields manifold blessings, as Dr. Kenneth Cooper says: "Just as strong belief can produce significant benefits in other areas of health, your deepest personal convictions, including your religious faith- can become the key you've been seeking to unlock the door to better fitness." (203)

March 26th:

Sacrifices of Others Improved the Human Condition; You Have the Same Obligation "Live as people who are free, not using your freedom as a cover-up for evil, but living as servants of God." (1 Peter 2:16)

You are free to feel good about the person God made you to be. You are free to work out for the enjoyment of it in itself and the manifold blessings of mental/social/ emotional remunerations the activity entails. Not only do the physical aggregates accentuate over time from exercise, but you are also free to not fear via not worrying what others think about you if you stand out as different.

The Nebraska strength and conditioning coaches sum up this behavior marked by resolve to live for Christ and the goals we set in life by saying, "We had been that close to winning the championship; now each player was responsible for reaching deep down within, giving it all he had." (209) Notice the inner drive developed by kinesiology and its coexistence with both spiritual and physical components. Freedom implies a sacrifice of comfort so that experience -hardening and reconvening for a grueling off-season training program can yield results down the line of time in the next season.

The concluding quote for this entry that follows from Norman Vincent Peale, shows that prefacing physical training there must be a spiritual commitment to something one believes in overriding even exercise results, before true muscular prowess improvement can occur. "Jack Smith, operator of a health club, says that while he probes his patrons for physical flabbiness, he also probes for spiritual flabbiness because, he declares, 'You can't get a man physically healthy until you get him spiritually healthy.'" (210)

March 27th:

Is Seeing Believing or is there a Deeper Craving? Certainly, visibly affirming with your own eyes the consummation of colleague's fitness journey results is better than merely hearing him/ her talk about them. To see a physique altered, a heavier weight lifted, three minutes shaved off a three-mile run, or 70-plus push-ups pelted out in a two-minute time period (as the US Army tests for muscular strength and endurance) rouses a desire in the viewer to attain that effect his- or herself.

This may be the reason for the differences dispensed in two neighboring chapters from the Gospel of Matthew relating Jesus' stances on good deeds. In the first allusion to visibility of works, Jesus says, "Let all your good deeds shine out for all to see, so that everyone will praise your heavenly Father." (Matthew 5:14). Secondly, in a seeming contradiction, Jesus then tells the same crowd (in the Sermon on the Mount), "Watch out! Don't do your good deeds publicly, to be admired by others, for you will lose your reward in heaven." (Matthew 6:1)

Maybe the discrepancy exists in not trying to be noticed, but being humble and not expecting recognition for each individual weight training repetition completed. Likely, it is the attitude we approach fitness and sports with, and not trying to 'tell' people you've worked hard, but 'showing' it off in the game performance. Nebraska strength coaches summate the need for 'buying into' a training program and how the finite computation of motivating athletes for continued participation is so vital. "Many programs fail because the athletes do not believe in them. They question what the coach is trying to accomplish or feel something else will work better. The same is true with a conditioning program; if an athlete does not believe in the program, he will not be motivated to put full intensity into his workout." (228)

<u>March 28<u>th</u>:</u>

A Brotherhood of Shared Service & Conquest in Overcoming Immorality A practical means of encouraging teammates and fostering friendship exists in the atmospheric context of a weight room. There is a certain service in spotting lifters, monitoring technique, and loading/unloading /racking weights that bonds young men. Through the shared difficulty of all in the interest of moving resistance implements - to be better athletes and develop discipline that is easily transferrable - a unique brotherhood is born.

The effects of these experiences are cumulative in nature by deepening faith and/ or character. Nebraska strength coaches expound on this theme of teamwork fleshed out in a game situation. "A team that has strong unity unleashes the greatest effort possible from each player and coordinates it, so the team works together as a unit. A team without unity may get great effort from each player, but the efforts are not in harmony with the rest of the team." (248).

An example of not being a team player occurred in my life during my junior year of high school. I had injured my back and hamstring to the extent that I knew I would not be able to play that fall. When I went into the head coach/ athletic director's office to relay the news, a man who I looked up to immensely and respected, he told me that there were multiple ways he could still use me for the varsity team if I wanted to remain in athletics the last period of the school day. I have always regretted that I did not take him up on the offer, and therefore, was not fully there for my friends. It was an opportunity to show true service to my brothers on the field, rejoice in their successes, and likely learn new avenues of growth to help me later. None of my friends dogged me about it, but since then I have always looked at the following Scripture in a new light and with a sense of regret for that decision.

"And whoever wants to be first among you must be the slave of everyone else." (Mark 10:44)

March 29th:

America in Prophecy? As men desire an adventurous quest to go on or an overarching theme to disperse in the course of their lifetime, working out gives us a taste of the divine. Many believe that we will have celestial tasks in heaven, and certainly bodily striving in this life brings pleasure therein or afterward. How could the unseen effect of fitness be transmogrified into an inexplicable circumstance of winning the invisible/ eternal war? Matters of God such as these remain a mystery and are difficult to annunciate in a literary manner.

The fact that men will divert their intentions to either good or evil, as in the case that young boys will choose either sports/ academic clubs to be part of or gangs that appeal to the desire for innate toughness, is irrefutable. The youth must be directed to focus their desires for benefit of others in a grandiose way. Exercise offers a gallant avenue of toil. For example, Isaiah described an absolute momentous acting on God's part (in what seems to be a mostly earthly manner) against evil: "Behold, the name of the LORD comes from afar…He will cause the descending blow of his arm to be seen...Battling with a brandished arm, he will fight with them." (Isaiah 30:27; 30; 32) Who is 'them' at the end, and what young man would not want to be a part of that scenario, especially to be on the predetermined winning side?

Isaiah spoke of a chosen people that are special to the God of Israel, and kinesiology acts as an adjunct to discovering one's prodigious purpose. "Throughout the earth, the story is the same—only a remnant is left, as when an olive tree is beaten, as at the gleaning when the grape harvest is done." (Isaiah 24:13) Judging from this perspective, excoriating evil has to do with a chastening from fitness. Is it possible that the hard work of many predating the USA was part of the prophecy of Isaiah as indicated in the verse at the end of this entry? Manifest destiny is a debatable proposition, but the following verse makes the possibility worth pondering for our purpose as a nation: "They lift up their voices, they sing for joy; over the majesty of the LORD they shout from the **west**." (Isaiah 24:14)

March 30th:

Becoming Steady & Even-Keeled but not Anesthetized to Christ's Call The Bible says that "Wisdom gives strength." (Ecclesiastes 7:19.) And exercise imparts wisdom which makes you level-headed because of the inherent intensity and breadth of its experience. If you encounter the bounds of your body's physiology, you become acutely aware of the vast pool from which to draw this inner fortitude, giving stoutness to the heart, vigor to the will, and acuity to the mind. These properties amalgamate into courage exemplified in fitness/sports that can't help but spill over into noble actions on a daily basis.

It is my personal belief that intense exercise increases the physiological capacities of both pain threshold and pain tolerance. To feel the muscles tighten, tweak and fatigue while contracting fervidly and desiring immediate furlough, helps us be even-keeled in stressful situations. Dr. Covert Bailey identifies and summates how the social makeup of fitness-based competition strengthens our spirits: "In competitive sports, players love to trade insults. Then, when they're off the court, they can laugh about the other little insults in life." (232).

If you feel yourself becoming calloused by the monotonous aspects of daily life, exercise will jolt the soul into a greater ambiance. The senses will no longer be sequestrated by seeming injustices that don't get fixed here on earth, because "We rejoice in the hope of the glory of God. Not only that, but we rejoice in our sufferings, knowing that suffering produces endurance." (Romans 5:2-3; ESV)

March 31st:

An Idle Mind and Body is the Devil's Workshop Exercise helps us combat the sin of foolishness so easily wrought in even a little idleness, and therefore promotes a abstemious mindset and lifestyle. Literally, you have to live clean to adhere to a properly patterned exercise regimen. You cannot be drunk, high, or stoned and still workout safely and/ or effectively. Avoiding these temptations because they detract from your sports and fitness goals is a positive end result of athletic involvement. You cannot mix holy living with evil and expect God to bless you, just as you cannot drink in excess, smoke, and/or use illegal drugs and still hope to enhance your physical physique or functionality.

Nebraska strength coaches aptly describe the dilemma of following God (and becoming a better person and athlete), or following the enemy and the temptations of the world (and descending into chaos and a sinful life/ ungodliness). "As drinking, using drugs, and smoking accelerate the process of catabolism, your body must work overtime to recover. It cannot keep pace trying to recover from both intense workouts and bad habits." (256). If you follow friends who are bad influences, you will profligate your exercise gains and all the hard work you have put in will have been in vain. The New Testament links this quality of sobriety and seriousness to being ready to go to work intensely for the kingdom of God, in whatever form and fashion that may take.

"Therefore, preparing your minds for action, and being sober-minded, set your hope fully on grace." (1 Peter 1:13; ESV)

April: Health – Physical and Spiritual

April 1st:

Emptying Yourself in the Service of Being a Soldier for Christ
Exercise gives birth to the desires of a person's thought and inner heart life leading the man or woman to desire exuding and possessing gallantry. What drives a man that's making him want to be brave is fleshed out in a practical way when physically exerting himself? "The work of a man's hand comes back to him." (Proverbs 12:14; ESV)

The undertaking of kinesiology is one we can pour ourselves into with exuberance because there is no wrongdoing involved in it. The equation of offering effort whose starting point is the desire to be brave and encounter the epic expresses heroism in the consequential movement. The yearning to rise above mediocrity gives us a chance to show what we are capable of in fighting through fatigue to show human courage in fitting (pun intended) fashion. The West Point student prayer exhibits this fact by saying, "Encourage us in our endeavor to live above the common level of life," (271) as all cadets enrolled must achieve an extreme level of being fit for future missions. And yet as exercise is one method of showing bravery, it is not the only one and is a means or way and not the end in itself, as Dr. Bill Bennett says, "Sometimes the size and strength of a body mean less than the kind of heart it carries inside." (272)

April 2nd:

Athletes and Soldiers Obey Just like Stanch Christians Is it possible that some of Paul's New Testament letters were influenced by his attendance at the Olympics? In several instances and locations, Paul refers to life as a race or compares the Christian walk to how athletes contend. "An athlete is not crowned unless he competes according to the rules." (2 Timothy 2:5; ESV).

The previous verse was written after Paul made his second missionary journey which took him through many Greek city-states. And in preceding verses, Paul mentions his friend Onesiphorus who, "When he arrived in Rome he searched for me earnestly and found me." (2 Timothy 1:17; ESV). Since we know chronologically that Paul was in Rome following his second mission trip that included Greece, historically he could have attended Greek Olympic Games and made the statement in verse five based upon his impression of them. For example, we know from written passages that the Olympics existed long before Christ: "According to historical records the first Olympic Games began in 776 BC as a series of athletic competitions between the various city-states of Greece." (289). This veritable relating of instances shows that Paul favored physical activity as an overall good and godly experience beneficial for the building of Christian character.

April 3ʳᵈ:

Innumerable Benefits of Outdoor Exertion The orphic benefit that spending time outside has on the human body and psyche cannot be denied. In a physical sense, trees uptake the carbon dioxide that humans give off as heat/ energy and release back into the environment oxygen that we so desperately require.

To delve deeper, exercising outside increases the effectiveness of a workout session's health impact exponentially. For example, the founder of the scientific method so readily used in a widespread effort by medical researchers, Francis Bacon physicalized this transcendent nature of exercise added to the outdoors. "Almighty God first planted a garden. And indeed it is the purest of human pleasures. It is the greatest refreshment to the spirits of man." (153)

The fantastical effect creation and natural settings have are also emphasized by Jesus in the Gospel. After healing a man with leprosy, Jesus commanded the man to take a sacrifice to the Jewish priests. "Take along the offering required in the law of Moses….This will be a public testimony that you have been cleansed." (Luke 5:14) The fact that Jesus respected the law from the Old Testament's practice of animal sacrifice, when he was the very fulfillment of that law, speaks volumes about the cleansing/ renewing effects of God's creation and partaking of natural environments. When we combine this experience with fitness, there are numerous possibilities for physical, mental, and spiritual growth.

April 4<u>th</u>:

Nourishing the Spirit Via Examination and Exercise Proper postexercise refueling is essential to build larger and stronger muscles. After a weight training session, the body's cells are literally hungry for a certain type of nutrition needed to effectively rebuild traumatized tissues. The specific necessities include simple carbohydrates – needed to spike insulin levels which the hormone, in turn, helps drive in nutrients inside the cells – as well as complex carbohydrates depleted in the session plus 15-40 grams of protein.

So also, man needs to be fed spiritually. Jesus made this surprising admission in a strikingly humanistic topic employed by Satan to bait Jesus into rescinding his divine purpose by taking the easy way out when he craved earthly food and irreverently requesting his Father to turn stones to bread (he had been fasting for 40 days). Jesus said to the Adversary, "No! People do not live by bread alone." (Luke 4:4) We need our souls' thirsts quenched through the truth of the Bible.

An interesting comment I heard spoken by George W. Bush after a 10-mile bike ride with military veterans was, that he had concluded that exercise is addictive. If substances such as nicotine chemically alter the brain, exercise can become a desired and also essential aspect of a healthy lifestyle craved by the body much like food itself.

"So whatever you eat or drink, or whatever you do, do it all for the glory of God." (1 Corinthians 10:31)

April 5th:

A Proper Self-Esteem and Body Image Being satisfied with your bodily figure and constitution brings about a unique and healthy type of pride. Godliness combined with good fitness levels make for a powerful combination and provide a cumulative and exponential effect on the quality of faith. If your faith in God is in abundance, the small details of life seem to fall in line and exercise helps us tangibly put our faith into action. This detail is not overlooked in the Bible, and part of Joseph's rise to success in Egypt was that he ate healthily and took care of his body, presumably through working out, and because of the deep faith expressed and held in his heart, God blessed his efforts. "Joseph was a very well-built man." (Genesis 39:6)

Debra Norville says of the way we and others view our bodies, "I do think all of us, men and women, have a higher sense of self-confidence if we believe we present well to the outside world." (129). God even lists the particular attributes of strength and health as a reward for fearing Him and imbibing upon behavior that is careful to adhere to His commandments.

"Respect the Lord and refuse to do wrong. Then your body will be healthy, and your bones will be strong." (Proverbs 3:7-8)

April 6th:

Definition of God's Property According to the Underappreciated Founding Father James Madison, fourth President of the United States, gave an interesting definition of the term 'property': "In its larger and juster meaning, it embraces every thing to which a man may attach a value and have a right. Conscience is the most sacred of all property." (5)

Perhaps conscience is so sacred because our bodies are temples of the Holy Spirit. Therefore, we should attend to the well-being and physical health of the temple with unction, as we are God's property. God places a prime potentiation on the body if he deemed it exquisite enough to house his own Holy Spirit! Working out can be said to be equivalent with 'temple-building.' This perspective leads us to a stronger inner spiritual devotion dedicated to serving God with our earthly vessels. Once we have given our human composition into his hands, our souls will follow suit.

"Don't you realize that your body is the temple of the Holy Spirit, who lives in you and was given to you by God? You do not belong to yourself." (1 Corinthians 6:19)

Jesus himself compared his body, the – 'word made flesh,' with the very temple that took nearly 50 years to build and that Jews believed housed the presence of God. "Destroy this temple, and in three days I will raise it up. But he was speaking about the temple of his body. When he was raised from the dead, his disciples remembered he had said this, and they believed." (John 2: 19; 21-22). If Jesus placed this premium on a structure that was held sacred in creation, it should motivate us to workout taking care of the corpus, and this property of 'conscience' within it spoken of earlier, will resultantly be impeccably clean.

April 7th:

Theories Abound and the Mysteries of the Kingdom Strength and Conditioning is a very practical field. Knowing which muscle groups an exercise activates is a matter of fact. However, there is also a deeper, more philosophical area of this field which must be undergirding the program as a whole. Machines or free weights? One set of an exercise or multiple sets? 30 or 90 seconds of rest between exercises?

In much the same way, a Christian's moral center begins with Jesus' method of teaching. Jesus used parables of earthly, practical activities of daily life such as farming and fishing, both of which required physical attenuation, to convey a deeper meaning about the kingdom of God. We should take to heart what God is teaching us during our earthly experiences as we seek His will and guidance.

"The Kingdom of Heaven is like a fishing net that was thrown into the water and caught fish of every kind." (Matthew 13:47).

April 8th:

Mimicking God through Recovery and Reflection Proper rest for athletes and fitness enthusiasts is important for two reasons: To prevent overtraining, and to optimize the strength and hypertrophy one does achieve through training. There are two aspects of rest that must be adhered to in order to maximize results and stave off overtraining: getting enough sleep every night and the proper space of time between workouts.

In life, we need quiet time with God to repent, beseech/ supplicate, and to listen to Him so that we can be obedient to His will. If God rested on the seventh day, certainly humans need rest as well. God promises rest for his people in both the physical and spiritual aspects of repose.

"Therefore…the promise of entering his rest still stands…we who have believed enter that rest…For he has somewhere spoken of the seventh day in this way: And God rested on the seventh day from all his works." (Hebrews 4:1-4)

April 9th:

The Therapeutic Value of Exercising Solitarily with Nature There are healing properties in purposeful solitude and silence. Thomas Carlyle proclaimed: "Silence is the element in which great things fashion themselves together." (76) A long run or walk in God's creation has innately immense physiological and psychological benefits. These benefits include observing the sounds of nature that bring an inner peace. Exercise connects man to nature.

"For ever since the world was created, people have seen the earth and sky. Through everything God made, they can clearly see his invisible qualities." (Romans 1:20)

April 10th:

The Harvest is Plentiful, But Needs More Workers Essential to finding a successful vocation is discerning a legitimate human need that requires assuaging to be met and filling it. The kinesiology major is the fastest-growing degree in the United States because of the need for therapeutic exercise professionals. Weight loss, rehabilitation, sport-specific conditioning and injury prevention are all areas of the sought-after movement-based field. As these exercise authorities improve living capacities in their clientele, we do also in our spiritual lives, as we have needs that can only be met by friends, family, and other mentors/ counselors. Jesus refers to the Holy Spirit as a helper as well.

"And I will ask the Father, and he will give you another Advocate…He is the Holy Spirit." (John 14:16-17)

April 11ᵗʰ:

Feeding on God's Word for Respite and Rejuvenation Proper nutrition is an essential complement to any well-designed fitness program. A post-workout protein and carbohydrate supplement is needed after a strength training workout to help replenish exhausted resources of energy, and build new muscle tissue from the microlevel damage done to the area known as the 'Z line' in a muscle fiber.

In the same way, our souls need constant nourishment. This source of sustenance is the Bible, the living word of God. When tempted by the devil to turn stones into bread (as Jesus had been fasting for 40 days), Jesus referred to the truth in Scripture from the Gospel (originating from earlier scripture in Deuteronomy specifically).

"People do not live by bread alone, but by every word that comes from the mouth of God" (Matthew 4:4)

It is also interesting to note that Jesus was 'led by the Spirit' into the wilderness, for the specific purpose of facing temptation from the devil (Matthew 4:1). Armed with this knowledge, we should embrace the challenges of life as opportunities for growth in godliness. Exercise offers this palpable quality by providing a difficulty you must meet and defeat: starting and completing training sessions. "Finishing is better than starting." (Ecclesiastes 7:8)

April 12ᵗʰ:

Humility Coexisting with Success is Commendable Fitness

is not about being better than others; it's about continually better-ing one's self. Competition is good, but is best utilized with a dose of moderation. Stay humble despite the physical prowess you may have developed through hard work. Do not constantly compare your achievements with others' and what God may have blessed them with.

Norman Vincent Peale has elaborated on self-sufficiency in an interesting manner. The goals you set are achievable in regards to de-veloping this humility, a deep faith, and a conviction that our efforts in exercise and diet yield concrete/ real results. Peale iterates that when we live to please God alone, our lives are lived at a fixed maximal ca-pacity. "Your subconscious…may say to you, 'you don't believe any such thing.' But remember that your subconscious mind in a sense is one of the greatest liars in existence." (114)

To be truly content with peace of mind is a great blessing in and of itself. Exercise defeats the lies of Satan, who says, 'you are too far gone' to lose weight or attain a healthy lifestyle in practical, daily behavior.

"I observed that most people are motivated to success because they envy their neighbors. But this too is meaningless – like chasing the wind." (Ecclesiastes 4: 4)

April 13th:

Blessed Are the Poor in Spirit Asking for help from a personal trainer or fitness expert is the first step, after seeing a physician, which many people take in their quest for general health and weight loss. It is not easy to admit that you need help and takes quite a bit of fortitude to place trust in someone you don't know that they will help you reach your fitness goals. This is an admirable quality for one to possess, to reach out and admit imperfection/ insufficiency on our own abilities alone.

For along with the apostle Paul, every human says, as God has ordained it, that when we are weak, in actuality, we are strong. This paradoxical statement can seem a questionable confutation in relation to strength training principles. However, God told Paul in his times of suffering: "My grace is all you need. My power works best in weakness." (2 Corinthians 12:9)

April 14ᵗʰ:

Physical and Spiritual Rewards We Can't Even Perceive In Matthew chapter 6 verse 6, Jesus states that there is a reward for private prayer. The rewards of exercise can be anatomically discernable and practical matters at times. Being more flexible so as not to injure your back, or improving functional capacity in tasks such as being able to carry and move objects easier are prime examples. In addition, there are chemical composition changes at the cellular level unlocking keys to vitality. Physiologists are only beginning to understand these factors, which in the end, yield good health promotion. Similarly, there are rewards for following the Bible and God's laws.

"But if you look carefully into the perfect law that sets you free, and if you do what it says, then God will bless you for doing it." (James 1:25)

April 15ᵗʰ:

Persistence Can Be Important to the Level of Omnipotence Sometimes you can dread starting a workout before it begins. It can seem like such a large, looming task in the future that we overthink it. Overcoming this discouragement by dogged perseverance through the day's plan develops character. So also, this persistence helps us to overcome fear that may have deep roots in our subconscious related to an inferiority complex.

"The Lord is for me, so I will have no fear." (Psalm 118:6)

"Why should I fear when trouble comes?" (Psalm 49:5)

April 16th:

A Genealogical History of Faith and Fitness The young men of ancient Athens recited the Athenian Oath when they turned 17. It says in part: "Thus in all these ways we will transmit the City, not only not less, but greater and more beautiful than it was transmitted to us." (8)

Today, we are called to transmit the Body of Christ, which is found in and through the church, in better condition - by prayer, by our faith and deeds, by our private and public/ corporate worship - than we found it. This transmission begins with the honoring of our own bodies and keeping them healthy and pure, as God made us good, with marvelous workmanship, along with all of His creation.

The church is a body of believers, not an institution. So also, a fitness or sport organization can be an institute, but the spirit that is found within that body in a cohesive community state of brotherhood/ sisterhood ultimately is responsible for changing peoples' lives. When we love God and others, we share our blessings, and these processes of both healthy physicality and true evangelization occur naturally.

"God has put all things under the authority of Christ, and has made him head of all things for the benefit of the church. And the church is his body." (Ephesians 1:22-23)

April 17<u>th</u>:

Divine Matters are Imputable but Demystified from Exercise
"Murmur not at the ways of providence," said Thomas Jefferson in
a letter to a young man sharing his namesake (11). Although nearly
everyone struggles with some form of doubt, it is unbecoming for
human beings to question the way God carries out His will and plan.

"Accept the way God does things, for who can straighten what he
has made crooked?" (Ecclesiastes 7:13).

Exercise can help us take our mind off perplexing problems for
a moment's reprieve. While exercising, many times, we are able to
collect our thoughts in an organized manner as our mind drifts in and
out of certain situations. In this time, we are able to frame the best
possible solutions for our problems.

April 18<u>th</u>:

Bating Bacteria to Death and Prompting a Godly Image Dr.
Cooper, alluding to a research report from the University of Michigan,
writes that: "Joggers and other enthusiasts may get sick less often because of an increase in body heat caused by exercise. The increase in
body temperature, which lingers after the exercise may make it harder
for invading bacteria to grow in the body." (20)

While this statement is fascinating, it really shouldn't be surprising. For God creates humans in His own image and endowed our bodies with a plethora of resources, internal and external, that afford us
the opportunity to achieve a healthy and productive life span. "So
God created human beings in his own image. In the image of God he
created them; male and female he created them." (Genesis 1:27) It is
interesting to note that many of these expedient factors of prevention
and healing are actually 'activated' through the acting out that is con-

spicuously visible in exercise.

April 19ᵗʰ:

Habituation Forms a Habitat for God to Indwell & Foster Health In my adolescent years, exercise morphed from a one- or two-hour daily habit into a way of life. Eventually, my love for the field of kinesiology would become a lifelong career and venture-seeking calling. So also, our Christian walk should be formed by a daily relationship with Christ. In our daily lives, we must be able to make our actions good in minor details, along with large life-changing decisions. In Romans Chapter 12, Paul lays out the two prerequisites for discerning God's will for our lives: making our bodies a pleasing sacrifice to the Lord, and refusing to think like the world.

"Give your bodies to God…Let them be a living and holy sacrifice…let God transform you into a new person by changing the way you think. Then you will learn to know God's will for you." (Romans 12:1-2) Giving our bodies to God would definitely entail taking care of them through fitness achievements.

April 20ᵗʰ:

Physical Work Emboldens Our Walk of Faith Jesus' trade as a carpenter allowed him to place a high value on hard work and physical exertion. He likely faced personal and professional dilemmas with his family and patrons before He began His public ministry.

Thomas Paine quite possibly may have had Christ's example in mind in his exhortation for courage in his writing entitled the American Crisis: "I love the man who can smile in trouble, that can gather strength from distress, and grow brave by refection." (160) Christ's work prepared Him for the insults, ridicule and false accusations He would face later on. On several occasions Jesus paralleled the earthly physical lessons, such as the manual labor that accompanies farming, with spiritual anecdotes such as the kingdom of God.

"My nourishment comes from doing the will of God who sent me, and from finishing his work." (John 4:34)

April 21st:

To Enjoy Pure Health is to Relish Obedience The best-kept secret of exercise as a whole is, that if done within safety constraints, it is enjoyable. Speaking both acutely and chronically, you feel euphoric after every bout. H. Robert Superko, MD cardiologist and founder of Berkeley Heartlab in California says, "Once I've gotten someone to begin, I don't have to worry about them backsliding, as exercise sells itself." (31)

A person's relationship with fitness can parallel their relationship with God. The more we love God and love others, the better off we are physically and spiritually.

"Blessed are those who obey the words of prophecy written in this book." (Revelation 22:7)

April 22nd:

Life Abundant George Washington once wrote in a letter to his adopted grandson regarding moral conduct, "I do not mean that you are to become a stoic, or to deprive yourself in the intervals of study of any recreation or manly exercise which reason approves." (40)

In this admonition, Washington refers to both recreations and exercise in a figurative, literal, and altruistic manner. In broad-based/ figurative meaning, exercise encompasses a variety of activities that are good, healthy habits that can fill idle time. In the literal sense, exercise conveys a sense of effort in something that exists in reality and can possibly perpetuate an effect that begins with the body and extends distally to other areas of life. In the altruistic view, it is likely that many young men and women have avoided delinquency and/ or lustful indulgences from this formula. Washington's suggestion still rings true for youth today.

"Good planning and hard work lead to prosperity." (Proverbs 21:5)

April 23rd:

Keeping a Lighthearted Outlook Problems do not seem so big when viewed by the personality of a phlegmatically inclined human being. The sensations of peace and tranquility that follow a workout make difficult issues seem less looming. Exercise helps us to put failures and mistakes in a larger overall context.

Shakespeare, the ancient sage, said that "A light heart lives long." (48)The entire book of Ecclesiastes could only be described as a lament in the most melancholy of tones. However, the author seems to imply that we should have an overriding theme in our hearts, and actions that examine life with a hopeful, lighthearted attitude for the future and in the face of despair, is godly in nature.

"Yet true godliness with contentment is itself great wealth." (1 Timothy 6:6)

April 24th:

The Limits of Human Wisdom God's word and commandments are no doubt for our good, but they don't always make sense in the earthly meanings of literature. In the end, we don't always have the proper amount of wisdom to discern God's will. This ontological opposition plays out in the tangible, physical world as well. Dr. Kenneth Pelletier says, "It is a paradox that oxygen, which is absolutely essential for all animal life, is toxic under conditions that allow its reaction with sensitive biological compounds." (54) What Dr. Pelletier means is that the same life-giving oxygen that enriches our life-blood actually increases the activity of free radicals which are responsible for the propagation of chronic illnesses and aging.

To humans, God's word can at times give the false appearance of dichotomy. The apparent fraction exists because the god of this world exists and flourishes on the practice of deception. Exercise can hurt. Foods that are not healthy can taste good. What is pleasurable is not always Biblical. But in the end, God alone knows what is best for us.

"My ways are far beyond anything you could imagine." (Isaiah 55:8)

April 25th:

Warmth of the Body and Soul An interesting phenomenon of exercise was described by Dr. Ellington Darden, who posited that exercising shortly after a meal boosted metabolism. He coined the phrase "exercise induced post-prandial thermogenesis." (55) The meaning of this phrase is that the body burns more calories using this method because of an increase in core temperature. Blood is diverted to the digestive organs, so exercising at this point exacerbates combustion of calories.

The effect this theory initiates can be compared to the mercy, empathy and compassion we develop for our fellow humans when our walk in life mimics our Savior Christ's example. Just as exercise creates lasting warmth physiologically, we develop an inner empathy for our brothers and sisters emanating from the heart and the genesis of brotherly love.

"Your love for one another will prove to the world that you are my disciples." (John 13:35)

April 26th:

An Unnamed Feeling Comes to Life Emrika Padus, an editor of Prevention Magazine, has an interesting definition of the physical and psychological phenomenon that occurs after a particularly lengthy and strenuous bout of exercise. "Your exhaustion was a strange kind of sensuous pleasure. It seemed to fill your whole body with a sleepy warmth, a sensation of having lived." (64)

Physiologically speaking, this mysterious/ recondite experience can be explained by one physical law: postexercise oxygen consumption. The heart rate remains elevated after physical activity which provides literal warmth due to increased levels of blood circulating.

Mentally and emotionally, this peace of mind comes from being a man truly seeking to walk in God's ways. The effect that exercise has upon the body coincides with the spiritual effect of having a fervent prayer and fellowship-filled life ultimately guided by the truth of scripture.

"The Lord has sought out a man after his own heart." (1 Samuel 13:14; NIV)

April 27th:

A Pagan Practice in Christianity? God cares so much about our physical well-being that he ordained sleep for restoration, food for sustenance and nutrition, and exercise as an impasse key to holistic health. "Happy is the land...whose leaders feast at the proper time to gain strength for work." (Ecclesiastes 10:17) Just as food gives strength, exercise can contribute to godliness. Norman Vincent Peale said of this relationship between vigorous activity and godliness: "God must surely be interested in our having good, strong, sound bodies." (70)

An interesting occurrence for kinesiology transpired in 393 A.D. At that time, the Emperor of Rome, (Theodosius - a Christian) banned the Olympics because he "disapproved the 'pagan' emphasis on bodily rather than spiritual health." (71) What a tremendous mistake and miscalculation that God, who created earth and humans in physical form, objects to it in some way being enhanced or focused upon with and through fitness. The fact that the Bible alludes to the specific phrase 'strength for work' is evidence for strenuous activity's validity and confirms the value God places on physical activity.

April 28th:

Exercise is Never a Futile Endeavor In a course entitled 'measurement and evaluation of kinesiology' at TCU, we as students were exposed to the concept of hypokinetic diseases. Hypokinetic literally translates to: deficient or lacking in movement. Regression in the ability to perform activities of daily living, which unfortunately occur at times in geriatric populations in the form of falls and broken hips, belongs under this umbrella of symptoms for hypokinetic problems. Exercise has been proven to prevent and in some cases, treat chronic diseases, such as those caused by low levels of fitness.

Dr. Sheri Colberg, an expert in the field of diabetes treatment and prevention says: "People who engage in moderate exercise regularly are at lower risk for many chronic health problems including heart disease, obesity, hypertension, type two diabetes, and certain cancers." (74) In reality, our own placated natures, which emanate from a mindset that we cannot influence our very health, makes an indelible imprint at times. As a result, these hypokinetic diseases are manifested. "Much of what we attribute to the aging process – muscle atrophy or loss of flexibility in joints – really results from disuse." (74)

However, it is never too late to reap the benefits of exercise, because God ordained the results: "So refuse to worry, and keep your body healthy." (Ecclesiastes 11:10)

April 29th:

Exercise Has Metamorphic Properties Exercise is not only transformative in regard to bodily shape and appearance; it also possesses healing and preventative aspects for the treatment of chronic illness. In reference to healing properties, Dr. Lipschitz says that exercise, "Also stimulates the release of hormones and cytokines, natural chemicals that promote feelings of energy and well-being. (86)

In allusion to the preventative qualities, Dr. Lipschitz says, "Evidence also suggests that exercise reduces the risk of breast and prostate cancers by modulating hormone levels." (86) That God instilled natural 'comeback' properties in us to help us face earthly challenges, there should be no doubt. Exercise acts as a catalyst to unleash these naturally occurring phenomena.

Jesus evidenced that he possesses this healing power (emphasis on present term 'possesses') in his lifelong ministry by curing the sick. "A Roman officer came and pleaded with him, 'Lord, my young child lies in bed, paralyzed and in terrible pain.' Jesus said, 'I will come and heal him.'"(Matthew 8:5-7) Exercise is a key cognate in unlocking this healing mystery built within our existential DNA.

April 30ᵗʰ:

Childlike Faith Iterates Health & Longevity John Wesley, the itinerant Anglican preacher who ushered Methodism into existence gave six trite, practical, and effective means to achieving the overall life of health and wellness. These practices included: 1) "To my constant exercise," 2) "To my never having lost a night's sleep," 3)"To my having slept at command," 4)"To my having constantly risen at four in the morning," 5)"To my constant preaching at five in the morning," and 6)"To my having had so little pain, sorrow, or anxious care." (117)

It is also likely that his belief in the power of fitness and a healthy lifestyle was an important psychological mechanism, and coincided with what Wesley says was the number one factor (constant exercise). Belief in the power of God to produce forces not prevaricated and that we cannot materialize alone is amazing in considering Wesley's longevity and quality of life.

Also interesting is the last reason listed as a means of incurring health. I must disagree in one respect that no pain or sorrow leads to encompassing well-being. Indeed, God put Jesus through trials, and we learn lessons from sorrow, displeasure and failures. Also, a trial such as completing an exercise session, involves some aspect of the upcoming sensation of physical discomfort. Perhaps the simple yet effective faith was all it took for Wesley to achieve fullness, fulfillment and longevity.

May: Injury Prevention & Overcoming Sin Temptations

<u>May 1st</u>:

A Path to Peace and Tranquility through Physical Activity
The serenity prayer could take on several meanings. In one sense, it means being vested with the inner strength, born of an ability to let go of situations we cannot change. On another level, it means having the wisdom to discern when circumstances are within our power to alter. The Bible is quite emphatic that this type of wisdom begins with fearing God, and that no relational trust will be canonized vertically (with God) or horizontally (with our brothers and sisters in Christ) without it.

One aspect of life we do have control over is the power to live a good lifestyle and to not be apathetic about our physical health. Norman Vincent Peale gives a good explanation on how exercise is something we have prevalent power over. "A sensible program which substitutes physical activity for fruitless brooding reduces the strain on the area of the mind where we reflect, philosophize, and suffer mental pain. Muscular activity utilizes another part of the brain and therefore shifts the strain and gives relief." (136).

When we balance appropriately the characteristics of reverential fear leading to wisdom and love leading to trust, we raise our faith and subsequent blessing to a new level.

"The fear of the Lord is the beginning of wisdom." (Proverbs 9:10; ESV)

<u>May 2nd</u>:

The Synergism of Body and Spirit When Falling Even as Christ Did To replace engrained habits that are sinful, we must satiate our time with activities that build up both body and spirit. The two entities are not mutually exclusive; they are companions in nature and influence each other. Prayer is the most effective medium to subsist on when temptation strikes. As Benjamin Franklin stated in his autobiography, detailing a plan for moral certitude, "Contrary habits must be broken, and good ones acquired and established, before we can have any dependence on a steady, uniform rectitude of conduct." (171)

Exercise is also a proven method of avoiding sin against God, by instilling a uniform fear/reverence/ awe for His might. Jesus also procured the aspect of attaining physical and spiritual strength through simultaneous devotion and obedience in the book of Revelation's message to the church in Philadelphia. Exercise is morally valuable because it develops and hones the trait of persistence. Though we may fail, we gain strength in the process and are additionally rewarded for trying.

"You have little strength, yet you obeyed my word and did not deny me. Because you have obeyed my command to persevere, I will protect you." (Revelation 3:8, 10)

May 3$\underline{^{rd}}$:

Can Both Health and Godliness be earned? "It is for discipline that you have to endure. God is treating you as sons." (Hebrews 12:7 – ESV)

A colleague of mine who was a personal trainer at TCU (Texas Christian University) once said to me that he pursued our particular avenue of work because people, "only get one body, why not help them make the most of it." A noble prospect for him, this optimistic outlook details the very reason why the field of kinesiology is in existence.

Yet beyond the mere physical capacities exercise brings about, the theorem of discipline is fostered and cultivated, as these two postulates (exercise and discipline) are congruently wired. A registered dietician writes in a book about preventing and reversing type II diabetes that "Exercise is often easier said than done. You simply have to make it a priority. You're worth it." (185) The last statement of this quoted author's is the most relevant and profound – and God says our bodily health is worth it too.

Discipline through physical perseverance is garnered for future use as extemporaneous servanthood to God. Plasticity of personality is brought about, quenching the need to know how to handle ourselves as followers of Christ in every instance. Character-based discipline is obtained by obeying God, and he gives it to us in trying situations, so why would we not aim in our lives to develop our own form of the precious attribute? Notice the specific diction employed in the following verse by use of the term 'trained,' as it takes sustained effort to build our bodies, mind, and spirits.

"For the moment, all discipline seems painful rather than pleasant, but later it yields the peaceful fruit of righteousness to those who have been trained by it." (Hebrews 11:11)

May 4<u>th</u>:

Jesus' Ministry Included Physical Health and Balance in all Undertakings Balance is important in both the physical and spiritual spheres. To be healthy in body and spirit is an organic by-product of seeking God and propagating a robust relationship with Him. Balance is defined broadly as a state of equipoise in emotional health and concurrent biological homeostasis within the processes of organ systems.

Instinctively, we know that balance is necessary in the arena of sports and in the process of rehabilitating an injury to restore functional capacity. Amazingly, we can attune a conditioning program to achieve more balance by utilizing free weights to a certain degree over machines. Dr. Covert Bailey elaborates more on this fact of the importance of synergy in a training program. "Balance is a more important factor in exercise than had been realized. When we balance a weight, we use more of a given muscle, different fibers and levels of the muscles are brought into play at the same time." (190) Similarly, when we attain a holistic state of fettle, we can tap into levels of blessing and an endowment of godliness and well-being that exceeds all previous expectations.

This harmonious state is achievable and evidenced as so by the fact of Jesus' healing of any and all disease in His time on earth, as well as his ability to bring soul-healing through His sinless shedded blood. "To each is given the manifestation of the Spirit for the common good…to another gifts of healing." (1 Corinthians 12:9 ESV) Caring for others by trying to bring balance to their lives to the degree it is desired personally, we naturally become receptive to God's bountiful blessings.

May 5th:

Is Exercise Defendable Even though it can be Dangerous? Certainly, there exists some element of risk in lifting weights or undertaking strenuous aerobic activity. This level of danger may not cause exercise to be slathered with the designation of 'perilous,' but strains, sprains, cardiac complications, or even death can and have occurred when partaking of the activity. Tim O' Brien, a Vietnam War veteran, expounds on this same theme of facing hazardous situations that can be compared to the gleaning character through fitness: "You're never more fully alive than when you're almost dead." (200). A workout should have an aspect of teaching that guides us to thankfulness for a healthy body that can send transmitting signal from the brain to all body parts like modem technology, and the unseen values that our involvement with it dins. In the same breath, kinesiology is not an activity for thrill-seeking adrenaline junkies, as it takes a concerted, steadily applied devotion to derive results.

"The prudent sees danger and hides himself, but the simple go on and suffer for it." (Proverbs 27:12; ESV).

<u>May 6th</u>:

Sin Begets Soul Ailment and New Unclean Desire; Fitness Affords Magnanimity The unquenched feeling of chasing a new type of sin and the enduring fulfillment of chasteness from living 'clean' (including incorporating fitness) are diametrically opposed. David went so far as to remark that deteriorating health was a symptom of unbridled behavior. "There is no health in my bones, because of my sin." (Psalm 38:3b; ESV). Adam's one-time wrongful act saddled mankind with a foe he could not fight much less defeat, while Paul elaborates that one man, Christ, also bought atonement from this exponential evil with his bravery.

I have had one of my best female friends tell me that she feels 'icky' when she has gone a few weeks without invoking physical activity. While, on the other hand, a female coworker said she felt so energized and ready to take on the day's ensuing challenges from exercising for over an hour in the morning before work. The acute quelling in an act of sin never does mollify desire or result in complementing of self-realization, but rather, only awakens a fresh craving to plod on further in disobedient behavior from a sense of fleeting and guilty gratification that must continually be sought as we develop a tolerance for the previous sin's euphoria.

When we are ardently following God, our undertakings will forsake sin in favor of pure actions. "How much more will the blood of Christ...purify our conscience from dead works to serve the living God." (Hebrews 9:14b; ESV). Notice that God is alive and implied as busy in both the supernatural realm as well as in Christ's divine, yet fleshly execution of the Father's plan on earth. Inactivity does not bring satisfaction, yet only leads to conscripting of greater ills, while exercise brings a lasting and godly sense of spurring-on and spiritual satisfaction.

May 7<u>th</u>:

Give Retribution to Unfairness of Life-Maintaining Dignity that Equipoise Exercise Bestows Take out the disillusionment at the wrongs perpetrated against you on the weights or by running at a faster intensity/pace or for a longer distance. Righteous anger is just in certain circumstances, and can be followed with appropriate action. Resisting desire for retribution against someone who has shown wrongdoing against you doesn't allow Satan a foothold, and simultaneously re-patterns thoughts of vengeance with mercy. Examples of godly behavior stemming from righteous anger include voting as an expression of freedom, singing in concert with a congregation of believers in mutual befuddlement at the test/ trial you are going through, or praying to God in earnest repentance (even if you have righteously judged against an enemy) out of reverential fear and awe. The Bible explicitly explains this phenomenon of peaceful reprisal by admonishing us to: "Be angry, and do not sin." (Psalm 4:4; ESV).

The previous reactions and courses of behavior are all noble and appropriate, but a means of intentionally acting out based on feelings contained inside, in a positive manner against an enemy that is absent, is owned in an exclusive manner as an aspect of working out. The retribution committed can be internal (increasing one's own running stride pace), or external (trying to move a heavy weight in the direction of intended displacement) in an application of force emanating out of an apparently indignant spirit. An unsettled matter becomes disclosed in the open for the waywardness to be subverted in the form of intentional exercise movement. The feeling of injustice is properly directed with mentor guidance in the controlled environment of a gym, court, track or field, and therefore, crystallizes the case as concluded.

May 8th:

Civilization Was Built Based on Manual Labor Exerted During the Building of the Temple Scripture actually demarcates the time period when man's notion of a 'society' was birthed. A prophecy from a minor prophet says, "Let your hands be strong, you who in these days…were present on the day that the house of the LORD of hosts was laid. For before those days there was no wage for man, neither was there any safety from the foe for him who went out and came in, for I set every man against his neighbor." (Zechariah 8:9-10). God also summates the ultimate lack of law and order in society bequeathed by a negation of godliness where there is no ultimate source of moral authority except individual prerogative: "Everyone did what was right in his own eyes." (Judges 21:25).

It is interesting that this formation of a symbiotic, spiritual and service-oriented economy of man is annotated by the admonition of fidelity to a physical reference - strength in a grip. Perhaps the imagery of the hands writhing in work or joined together with fellow man bestowing a sense of brotherhood would have been captivating to the Israelites in a time when physical labor was profitable and not stodgily looked down on as inferior. It is also interesting that this society was built around the centralized location and idea of the temple, or - being in the very presence of God.

Henry James, an American writer, comments that society benefits humanity because it, "Fits man for the recognition of inward and infinite good, by enabling him to resist the domination of the outward or sensible sphere. The way it enables him to resist this domination, is by gradually supplying his natural wants." (259). With necessities provided, man can turn inward to reflect on the heart, or the courageous meaning of our actions. With the heart governing, 'strong hands' can be given to us by God to help us repudiate immoral actions, setting us up to serve God and our brothers through societal stratifications.

May 9<u>th</u>:

Don't Get Distracted by Fitness 'Cliques,' Simply Grind in Effort to Be 'Salt' In the fitness 'bubble' it can be easy to get caught up in too much competition with our contemporaries. Being weaker, smaller in musculature size, or slower in movement speed can be humbling. True knowledge, which God puts a premium on obtaining throughout the course of the Bible, can also cause us to get dejected. Understanding the evil that occurs on earth, and not underestimating it, can lead to an existential sorrow solicited in daily carriage.

Do we feel powerless and too small to make a difference when we get sad at the epiphany that many bad things happen on earth? Or do we strive with our hardest efforts (in which exercise enthusiasm is contagious) to make a difference knowing that if we - the salt of the earth - did not exist, how evil would the world be then? But James, denoting an earlier insight from Christ that this is, as Shakespeare said, where the 'rub' comes in, says, "Believers who are poor have something to boast about, for God has honored them." (James 1:9). This 'poor in spirit' attitude should kindle forth humility and spur us forth into a cold dark world with the motive to bring light forth in the shadow.

Basic knowledge of kinesiology is a prerequisite to avoiding injury and bringing success to your athletic endeavors or leading by example to others in being fit and practicing safe workout methods. Dr. Cooper says of this revelation, "After you take that first leap of faith, it's necessary to embark on a disciplined program, which can gradually turn your beliefs into a long-term reality." (264).

"My people are destroyed for lack of knowledge." (Hosea 4:6; ESV)

May 10th:

Manliness Stereotypes May Have Some Truth but Salvation Gives Way to Only Good Lifestyle I once read of a miraculous recovery by a man severely injured in a car accident. The article, in the east Texas newspaper Longview News Journal, had the doctor who treated the man make an almost startling admission: that the man's level of fitness and healthy physique helped him to survive despite the drastic injuries he sustained to the head, torso, and lower body. Isn't it amazing that exercise literally has the power to save your life!? So also, the impetus of being saved can initiate a devotion to a life-changing level of fitness.

It is true that the temperament and practical habits associated with masculinity are often physical in nature without regard to the psyche or moral habits. Dr. Bill Bennet describes this mindset: "It is natural to think of men first as physical beings and to describe manhood as muscle, strength, power and actions." (266.) Just as the inner man is developed through corporeal prowess, Jesus links holiness in practice to physical health. "The eye is the lamp of the body. So, if your eye is healthy, your whole body will be full of light." (Matthew 6:22; ESV).

May 11th:

Taking the Harder Way on the Course of Pursuing Christ
Earning gains in cardiorespiratory fitness and muscle strength/ size
is a process and, while a definite formula exists for its achievement,
it takes time and consistent resolve. Overcoming sin in our life can
happen on repeat, but like kinesiology, takes a concerted fight in order
to consistently defeat the barrage. As we resistance train, we use muscles in an 'overcoming' sense to move our body or an object, while
dropping the sin burden in a spiritual walk helps us enhance and literally speed up our service to God as we are able to take on sequen-
tial and more consequential tasks. "Let us strip off every weight that
slows us down, especially the sin that so easily trips us up." (Hebrews
12:2). We prevail over a weighted element in strength training, and we
avoid an obstacle to become stronger and swifter in the running of the
proverbial 'Christian race.'

The same desire that propels us to work out drives us to imbibe
on sensual pleasures! Or does it? Surely God would not situate these
two entities on the same sideline. Just as we enact physical changes
to our body over time, requiring minute or large changes in exercise
programming, sin gets easier to beat after we exhibit discipline for the
first initial time. On the flip side, Peter Marshall says, "But after the
first giving in to temptation, our defenses are weaker the next time."
(273). After a sin is committed, tolerance takes form, and the altered
gratification of the senses is no longer sufficient to satisfy the longing
that the enemy carrots us with. "Then, after desire has conceived, it
gives birth to sin." (James 1:15; NIV).

The yearning for gratification is fleeting, and does not coincide
with the pure motif to merit exercise results. For example, we know
that a weightlifting session will suffice to satisfy a muscles' need for
use, thereby increasing their work capacity in a lasting fashion. However, lust, wantonness, and general malaise offer no continuing benefits. The former chaplain of the US Senate (Peter Marshall) elaborates
further on this theme and the quote referenced earlier: "These are sins
of desire…and we desire, not with our body, but with our spirits. The
body supplies us the vehicle of consummation…the means of gratifi-

cation of a base urge." (275).

Not Wearying of Sustained Effort and Temptation Resistance
No strength training exercise, cardiovascular response posed by as-
sortments of movement, or flexibility drill is truly new. "Nothing under the sun is truly new." (Ecclesiastes 1:9). All exercises have been
done before by athletes training and competing long ago. Therefore,
we should not become weary of repetition of the same programs in our
exercise prescriptions. The ultra-toned, yet pliable muscle, is the least
compromised in both new and repetitious usage, and therefore, in the
least amount of danger for injury.

We should also not give up resisting and defeating the same temptations that may plague us over and over again in our lives. Defeating
the enemy time and time again, with similarly themed extenuating
circumstances that arise from lies, is the mark of a mature faith.

"Resist the devil, and he will flee from you." (James 4:7)

May 13<u>th</u>:

Being a Pupil of Moral Courage Exercise and self-perception
of body appearance, like anything, can become both an obsession and
unhealthy addiction. Under the right temperament and in the appropriate amount/ frequency however, exercise helps produce gallantry.
Regarding the personification of exercise, Socrates remarked, "If you
treat it properly it should make them (men) brave, but if you over-
strain it, it turns them tough and uncouth." (1) It makes sense then,
that godliness requires a type of training, through many means such as
resisting temptation, as well as a sustained effort over time to live out

the deepest levels of faith in our daily walks.

"Train yourself to be godly." (1 Timothy 4:8)

May 14ᵗʰ:

Physical Education Improves Character & Capacitation of Mental Faculties The founding fathers of America knew the importance of physical exertion and listed it as one area of parenting, public education and a good youth domestic health policy not to be neglected. John Adams said to his wife Abigail, with regard to fitness of America's youth in a letter written in 1775, that "Their bodies must be hardened. Without strength and activity and vigor of body, the brightest mental excellencies will be eclipsed and obscured." (2) The ancient physical and moral courage extolled by the Bible is developed through vigorous physical fitness and conditioning activities.

"Remain in fellowship with Christ so that when he returns, you will be full of courage." (1 John 2:28)

May 15ᵗʰ:

Exercise Aggrandizes Confidence James gives the practical advice that we should not hastily get angry at our circumstances or at others: "Understand this, you must all be…slow to get angry. Human anger does not produce the righteousness God desires." (James 1: 19)

I believe that exercise helps reduce our irritations at small things that would normally get under our skin. Working out produces self-sufficiency abasing the irritation that our own subconscious hurls at us when we make mistakes or fail to live up to our own expectations. When our confidence grows from succession of a vigorous workout, we no longer need to get angry (at ourselves especially) when we fail in certain aspects of our lives or in small matters, as we all will at times.

May 16th:

Holding an Adherence to the Truth In the field of kinesiology, there can be a good deal of misinformation. These misnomers could possibly discourage someone from starting an exercise program. As it relates to a geriatric population, there are two examples: it is impossible for muscle to hypertrophy after age 60, and it is dangerous to work out after a heart attack. In the same manner, people we know can often emanate words that hurt or discourage us. This should serve as a lesson that gossip can hurt people and we should try our hardest to avoid it.

"Do not take to heart all the things that people say, lest you hear your servant cursing you. Your heart knows that many times you yourself have cursed others." (Ecclesiastes 7:21-22 ESV)

May 17th:

Obtaining and Exhibiting Humility During a Plateau is Perplexing There exists in every person a genetic ceiling to our athletic/ fitness training results. We must accept the body God has allotted us and to not strive beyond the hereditary boundaries he has put in place, even as we work as hard as humanly possible for results. So also, we must repent of our sins. This was John the Baptist's main theme: repentance.

"Repent of your sins and turn to God." (Matthew 3:2)

We must look to God for forgiveness and realize we do not have the power to make it to heaven on our own; we need grace and part of that equation includes being humble enough to admit that fact.   We must accept the limitations God has given us in our physical and spiritual beings.

"To the humble he gives favor and grace." (Proverbs 3:34)

<u>May 18th</u>:

A Natural Sense of Euphoria An 'exercise high' from endorphins is usually all the mood perception transmutation that people who consistently work out need. Drug abuse is far less common in physically active teenagers. (7) Alcoholism is also less prevalent in physically fit adults (7). The Bible says that we should exhibit self-control and be sober-minded.

To feel a sense of accomplishment at the conclusion of a workout transcends petty/ feigned reality alteration, found in the 'buzz' that alcohol and drugs impose, which is ultimately a lie. Eventually, a tolerance builds, and more of the substance is needed. Exercise, however, composes a sense of reassurance and inner comfort. The body needs a dynamic experience, an expanding and simultaneous tautening of our physical capacities to new heights. These experiences are crucial for the body and spirit to be assuaged mentally and spiritually.

"For those who get drunk, are drunk at night. But since we belong to the day, let us be sober." (1 Thessalonians 5:7-8)

<u>May 19th</u>:

An Anabolic Derivation in Physical and Spiritual Health

Exercise results in an elevated resting metabolic rate. Specifically, the addition of new muscle tissue expedites elevated caloric expenditure at rest. As we allow ourselves to be infused with God's divine strength, particularly when we feel weakest emotionally, he gives us an exalted fervor and enthusiasm for everyday life. We operate on a higher plane of physical and spiritual power.

"But he that is of a merry heart hath a continual feast." (Proverbs 15:15 KJV)

May 20<u>th</u>:

The Call of Conscience and Disregarding of Malady Thomas Jefferson gave a profound definition of conscience to his daughter Patsy: "You will feel something within you which will tell you it is wrong and ought not to be said or done: this is your conscience, and be sure to obey it. Our maker has given us all this faithful internal monitor." (10)

There is a difference between feeling tired or sore during/ after a workout and feeling pain. We must learn to differentiate between the two if we are to avoid injury. Poor technique and/ or overexertion can cause anatomical strain to soft tissues resulting in injury. We must know our limits and operate within the physical boundaries that our bodies are capable of surmounting.

Similarly, there is a difference between right and wrong, which is always discernible as black and white. We should not push the envelope with the freedoms God has given us, which ultimately lead to sin. Exulting in lustful or haughty activities is as harmful to our spirits as overextending the limitations of our physicality are to our God-given health.

"If you do anything you believe is not right, you are sinning." (Romans 14:23)

<u>May 21<u>st</u>:</u>

A Dynamic Biological System Gives Astuteness to the Soul "A wise person thinks a lot about death." (Ecclesiastes 7:4)

It is possible that exercise can increase our earthly longevity, but ultimately it is God who decides when we die. The older we get, the wiser we get. Exercise induces us to think much about death, because we know that life, like each individual workout session, eventually ends. Recognizing this incontrovertible fact occurs as we experience our physiological dynamic nature being altered from a workout. Exercise also makes us aware of our physical and spiritual limitations.

"How short is life…We blossom like a flower and then wither. Like a passing shadow, we quickly disappear." (Job 14:2)

<u>May 22<u>nd</u>:</u>

A Threefold Fulfillment of the Law by Engaging in Exercise A great way to show love to your brothers and sisters in Christ and exemplify the servant leadership he calls us to have, is to participate in group workout sessions. Invite people who may not know as much about exercise to become more fit with you. This takes the knowledge you have in the field and wields it in a much more powerful way than if you workout only for vanity and personal achievement.

You will be using your expertise in a threefold manner as God calls us to do: to make new friends (Luke 16:9), to show love to others and therefore let the Spirit of God be present in your workouts (Matthew 18:20), and to bear fruit (Matthew 7:17).

"A person standing alone can be attacked and defeated, but two can stand back-to-back and conquer. Three are even better, for a triple-braided cord is not easily broken." (Ecclesiastes 4:12)

"If you love your neighbor, you will fulfill the requirements of God's law." (Romans 13:8)

May 23rd:

Primordial Roots of Fighting for Survival Exercising induces the 'fight or flight' syndrome which is manifested by the survival instinct. This phenomenon occurs due to the challenge that a workout presents. You must 'fight' for 30 minutes to an hour to overcome the physical obstacle working out presents and the desire for immediate cessation of a set or session as a whole. Nebraska conditioning coaches describe the internally gushing environment of the tussle: "Adrenaline, cortisol, and growth hormone are released in the bloodstream in response to…excitement….The adrenaline shifts blood from the digestive organs to the muscles." (26)

So also, our spiritual lives are a constant battle and struggle against our adversary Satan, who tempts us in various ways. We must 'fight' to resist the devil's schemes.

"And I have remained faithful. And now the prize awaits me." (2 Timothy 4:7b)

May 24th:

The Futility of Self-Pity Exercise improves the human condition by allowing us to lead fuller, richer lives in many ways. In one aspect, it makes life a grand adventure by taking our physical prowess to a new level. One thing exercise cannot do, however, is make life fair.

A great example of the unfairness of life occurs to the Israelite army after they suffer a defeat to the men of Ai because of one man's sin (Aachen). Joshua did not know what to do at this point, so he laid prostrate/ face-down on the ground in despair. It is fascinating that instead of comforting him, God said to Joshua: "Get up! Why are you lying on your face like this?" (Joshua 7:10)

Learning from this passage, it is apparent that God does not approve of groveling. Calvin Coolidge echoed this sentiment when, in his autobiography, he wrote about the death of his 16-year-old son upon becoming the United States President: "The ways of Providence are often beyond our understanding." (60)

May 25th:

Exercise 'Winnows' Ungodly Motives The battle against leading a sedentary lifestyle can take on a life and context of its own. This 'fight' winnows out all that is contradictory to the healthy life God intended for humans to live and enjoy. God knows our true motives, and also implants the notion within our minds and hearts that it is possible for us to live this active lifestyle with copious amounts of vim and vigor.

Dr. Lipschitz says of this outward manifestation of an inner struggle that it takes time. "Push yourself. I know, exercise doesn't feel very good at first. You're going to tire quickly, and you might be a little sore. But if you push yourself just a little harder, your strength and endurance will increase faster than you can imagine." (83) God will help us through the journey, in ways we cannot fully comprehend. Just as He knows our motives, we also know that he wants us to have fit and healthy bodies.

"The LORD's light penetrates the human spirit, exposing every hidden motive." (Proverbs 20:27)

May 26th:

The Divine Blessings and Value of Freedom It is my belief that the individual freedoms we enjoy as Americans are God-given. This belief was substantiated by Thomas Jefferson in the Declaration of Independence. And this is also true of every human being, including those that live in other countries and do not have the literal or theoretical freedom we enjoy in America.

Norman Vincent Peale says, "God has confidence in us. he gives us the power of private judgment. He makes us free moral agents… He leaves us free."(87) A call to live according to the dictation Christ preached is just that: to live in perpetual freedom (from sin). Philosopher Thornton Wilder remarks about this patriotic perspective, "The American sense of personal identity is not those of Europeans. The literature written in that language (American) is one of the greatest glories of the entire human adventure." (88)

Exercise is an example of exhibiting personal freedoms. A workout session can lift a sagging spirit. And because of dual freedom from 1) Christ, and 2) the Bill of Rights, we personify this right through fitness: "A merry heart doeth good like a medicine." (Proverbs 17:22) Exercise invokes a metamorphosis of sorts. Fitness imparts upon us a soothing balm, a 'linctus', to our disposition. Only a free man can truly obtain and appreciate these blessings.

May 27th:

A Greater Alacrity of Faith and Service Exercise preempts the utilization of glucose, turned into ATP (adenosine triphosphate) for energy. The 'spark' let off by the fracture of one phosphate group (from a total of three present) from the adenosine molecule lets off a release of sudden, extemporaneously available source of fuel.

In relation to this catechism which yields energy, God also wants us to be 'on fire' for the Gospel, constantly striving to please Him and to love our neighbors. "I know all the things you do, that you are neither hot nor cold. I wish that you were one or the other! But since you are like lukewarm water, I will spit you out of my mouth!" (Revelation 3:15-16). This statement should actually frighten us, because God would rather us to be 'cold' than 'lukewarm." There must be an inherent danger or detriment to not pleasing God.

Dr. Lipschitz says of resistance training that it "lowers the risk of diabetes because muscle tissue takes up glucose or blood sugar, much more readily than fat tissue." (92) Only when we train hard, at this higher level of intensity/ utilization, even described as a burnout (inducing maximal muscle fatigue) can we reap the total benefit. So also, God wants our 'life-song' to be zealous and speak to his glory/ the renown of a holy name.

<u>May 28<u>th</u>:</u>

Eccentric Exercise – Resisting the Resistance Many times, our efforts in resisting evil involve abstaining from the values of the god of this world, and resultantly are defensive in nature. "Pure and genuine religion in the sight of God...means...refusing to let the world corrupt you." (James 1:27) The pieces of armor, listed in Ephesians, are all defensive in nature with the exception of the single offensive weapon: the Bible itself. "And take the sword of the Spirit, which is the word of God." (Ephesians 6:17)

A study done by an Austrian doctor showed that walking downhill improved glucose tolerance by 25 percent, as opposed to a nine percent improvement in patients who walked uphill. The reasons for this are complex, but suffice to say, eccentric exercise (resistive and lengthening in nature) is as or more important in contributing to muscle stimulation compared to concentric (tightening and force-making in nature) training. "Walking uphill shortens muscle fibers….In contrast, when muscle cells resist a force, they stretch out. It is possible that longer muscle cells use more glucose compared to shorter muscle cells." (109)

Be sober "well balanced and self-disciplined", be alert and cautious at all times. That enemy of yours, the devil, prowls around like a roaring lion "fiercely hungry", seeking someone to devour. But resist him, be firm in your faith "against his attack—rooted, established, immovable." (1 Peter 5:8-9, Amplified Bible). So also, we must fight eccentrically in the daily battle, to maintain our moral values and remain vigilant forces against evil and for good. The end result will be, "Christ, will Himself complete, confirm, strengthen, and establish you." (1 Peter 5:10)

May 29th:

The Power of Human Movement 'Kinesiophobia' is a real medical condition, mainly afflicting persons who have received little amelioration/ reprieve from their pain or lack of functionality. The definition of this term is found in the book A Nation in Pain: "People with chronic low back pain often avoid exercise out of fear that exercise, indeed any movement at all will make their pain worse." (112) However, a study was done, documented in this same book, that "The people who completed the exercise program did a reality test," (112) in which they could see that pain did not worsen with activity when movement occurred.

Indeed, in cases where ambulation is lacking, the fear of unknown factors takes over, and a loss of flexibility, lessened core stabilization, and overall deconditioning sets in causing activities of daily living to become difficult to perform. Similarly, as William Bennett pointed out in his commentary/analyzation of a prayer from G.K. Chesterson, "Men, like Chesterson, who have a sense of their own deep imperfections sometimes turn away from God and prayer. They should not." (113) When these types of attitudes/ moods occur extemporaneously, it is good to remember that "The Lord is a friend to those who fear Him." (Psalm 25:14) A healthy reverence for God is good, but you must also believe in His unconditional love, grace, and blessings for those who do follow the Lord.

"But the love of the Lord remains forever with those who fear him." (Psalm 103:17)

May 30th:

The Antiquity of Defeating Sin The physicality of effort works to spiritually harmonize your whole being with the ultimate source of power. By expanding your sphere of influence over the domain you can affect, you simultaneously relinquish to God what is not in your ability to domineer. The blithe attitude gives you a rugged stolid quality, both in life's journey for yourself, as well as in pleasing God. Exemplifying this type of trust allows us to stop fighting the battles we are not strong enough to win.

Norman Vincent Peale delves into this subject using the allegory of football. "The late Knute Rockne, one of the greatest football coaches the century has ever produced, said that a football player cannot have sufficient energy unless his emotions are under spiritual control." (114)

The antiquity text of Genesis (through the relationship of Cain and Able) was the first to state that God ultimately had to be in control of your life for you to be happy. God gave us free will, not only in the sense of freedom, but also to defeat the forces of evil that we are capable of in what can be perceived as minor battles faced each day.

"Why are you so angry? Why do you look so dejected? You will be accepted if you do what is right. Sin is crouching at the door, eager to control you. But you must subdue it and be its master." (Genesis 4:6-7)

May 31<u>st</u>:

The Assimilation of Thought and Action Would you believe that assuming the posture of a singular stretch is synonymous with the very act of worshipping God? How to worship is a critical question to the Christian faith and is not left to the imagination in the Bible. If we are to show how we acknowledge God's sovereignty over us, we need to know the proper manner of gamesmanship. Lying prostrate was one of the few postures chronicled in the Bible regarding how Jesus prayed. The term worship in Hebrew is associated with assuming the 'Child's Pose' Stretch. This stretch is used particularly in rehabilitative and injury prevention circumstances.

If you doubt that God likes us to assume a physical alignment to demonstrate our mindset of humility, awe, and reverence, look no further than Scripture: "Oh come, let us worship and bow down, let us kneel before the LORD, our Maker." (Psalm 95:6; ESV). Max Lucado elaborates on how the physical is an efferent showing of what is occurring on the inside – the heart and soul: "Worship adjusts us, lowering the chin of the haughty, straightening the back of the burdened. Worship properly positions the worshiper." (302).

"When all the people saw...the glory of the LORD...they bowed down with their faces to the ground on the pavement and worshiped." (2 Chronicles 7:3; ESV).

June: Mercy and Salvation

<u>June 1<u>st</u>:</u>

The Power of God Evidenced In what could seem like a stark incongruity, exercise to stave off and/ or treat certain chronic illnesses could serve a purpose for God to bring glory to Himself.   In describing this apparent discrepancy, Dr. Rex Russell states that "Some illnesses glorify God." (130) The pathway that this phenomenon follows is hard to understand because, "Like many people today, the disciples automatically associated all sickness with sin." (130)

To back up this theory, we can turn to the words of Christ Himself. When asked whether a man was born blind because of his sins or his parents' sins, Jesus replied, "It was not because of his sins or his parents' sins. This happened so the power of God could be seen in him." (John 9:3) This power, or otherwise translated 'works' to which Jesus refers, also have the application practically evidenced in medical fitness professionals and the exercise 'prescriptions' that they give patients as a source of treatment.

These avenues of referentially pointing to God ultimately glorify Him, because he ordained the power of human movement to accomplish miracles, through sound, honest, hard work. It also proves modern science correct: God designed us to move and remain active the majority of the time.

"Thank you for making me so wonderfully complex! Your workmanship is marvelous – how well I know it." (Psalm 139:14)

June 2nd:

A Servant of God but Not a Slave to Sin The relevance of athletics and competition at any age is proved by the apostle Paul in the New Testament. He uses this connection of physically based training in preparation for spiritual warfare by saying, "We urge you, brothers to admonish the idle (or – undisciplined.)" (1 Thessalonians 5:14; ESV)

The reasoning behind this employed simile is interesting and has practical implications for how Christians should live. Paul refers to the fact that he could possibly be labeled as a hypocrite. This staunch opposition would be subsidized by telling people to follow God's law, and yet not obeying it himself. He makes clear his heart's antithesis to hypocritical behavior later in the same way as earlier mentioned by saying, "I fear that after preaching to others, I myself might be disqualified." (1 Corinthians 9:27)

Notice the use of the term 'disqualified,' exhibiting a connotation of banishment from participation in/ involvement with an athletic context. The diction translates to no longer having the same impact to spread the Gospel in the spiritual sense. It is my belief that Paul uses this comparison because of the meaning of sports in general - many people participate in fitness-oriented games and activities. Paul wanted believers to know that we should stay humble in attitude towards God and our neighbors because as a prophet said, "Lord...we have all sinned against you." (Jeremiah 14:20) Being pushed to our physical exhaustion capacity can and does accomplish the feat of planting the seed of servitude in our hearts.

June 3rd:

Abundances of Faith, Intensity of Exercises, and Excesses of Merriment God actually commanded the Israelites to be joyful.

(Nehemiah 8:10)   A jubilant disposition is acquired through a workout program, and gives a permanent/ lasting effect when finishing a workout session, that no one else or a set of circumstances can take away.   It is quite possible that God created exercise for the precise reason of it making us merry.

Jethro Kloss, an herbalist and practitioner of holistic medicine, had this to say about what takes place at the denouement/finality/ closure of each training bout, progressing through consistently practiced fitness programs: "Oxygen, the elixir of life, is one of the best blood purifiers, and one of the most effective nerve tonics. Useful work in the open air will bring new strength and vitality, and give a happy and cheerful attitude of mind." Especially interesting in this pithy position statement is that exercise can actually alter the rhythm/ vibration patterns of the nervous system.

Perhaps the greatest source and reason for joy in working out is that it solidifies the irrational truth for our being forgiven of our sins, which is in essence, undefinable. "What joy for those whose record the Lord has cleared of guilt." (Psalm 32:2) The disciples also felt joy, in its complete and fullest meaning, when they saw Jesus ascend and knew they had tasted firsthand the one truth. (Matthew 2:10) A similar intensity of exuberance occurs when feeling cleansed and renewed from exercise. Although this sense of euphoria disappears over time, the joy of the Gospel never abates. Max Lucado bloviates on this principle by stating, "Someone who tastes God's grace is the hardest worker, the most morally pure individual." (139) Embrace the circle of advantageous challenge and reward that fitness offers!

June 4<u>th</u>:

Guaranteed Results and Assurance of Mercy Exercise results are fair and in proportion to the amount of time and effort given. Exercise does not bestow better results on specific persons or groups more than others. I once heard a former colleague of mine state to his physical education class that, "This is the only class that can guarantee positive noticeable results. No other subject can guarantee results for sure even if you study hard. But if you work hard in physical training, you will reap the benefits."

Even people in the most denigrating positions of disability or illness can benefit from increased fitness levels. The Merck Manual elaborates on this phenomenon by stating, "People who have substantial disability, may think exercise is beyond them. However, continuing to exercise after rehabilitation is over can help them maintain the gains made and may help them function even better." (150)

So also, it is never too late to sincerely repent and become a recipient of God's mercy. The truth of this statement was evidenced at humanity's low point, which God has turned into the highest trajectory of our hope: at the cross. The criminal next to Jesus assiduously asked for mercy and received it abundantly. "Then he (the criminal) said, 'Jesus, remember me when you come into your Kingdom.' And Jesus replied, 'I assure you today you will be with me in paradise.'" (Luke 23:42) What other example could be more affirming and comforting to humanity as a whole?

"Repent of your sins and turn to God, for the Kingdom of Heaven is near." (Matthew 3:2)

June 5th:

Testing Bodily Boundaries Breeds Humility   There exists a genetic ceiling to every individual's athletic/ fitness potential. In acknowledging a predetermined latency that God has endowed us with, we come to peace with our body image. In this way, we strive to improve, but accept the body God has given us.

So also, we must repent, realizing we cannot make it to heaven on our own – we need grace. John the Baptist starkly presented this truth to people prior to Christ's baptism. "Repent of your sins and turn to God, for the Kingdom of Heaven is near." (Matthew 3:2) We must be humble enough to repent, just as we must humbly accept our genetic limitations in athletics and fitness.

For example, I begrudgingly accepted the fact, at age 15, that I would never play professional football. But this discomfit was beneficial to me, as I pursued other paths and became more appreciative of the many other manifold blessings I was receiving. King Hezekiah, also felt this notion after having 15 years added to his lifespan in the midst of illness, saying, "But what could I say? (Isaiah 38:15) For he himself sent this sickness. Now I will walk humbly throughout my years because of this anguish I have felt." In this respect, athletics prepared me, and is a vehicle for many young men, to test their physical limitations, preparing them for the expansive properties of adulthood.

"The Lord opposes the proud, but favors the humble." (Proverbs 3:34)

June 6th:

Repentance is Yielding and Returning to a Spirit Stronger Than Humans Our bodies all plateau eventually in the context of attaining fitness results or eliciting athletic potential. We must accept the body God has given to us and be thankful for the health that a holistic wellness program can give.

We cannot attain salvation through strength of arms or desire; it is a gift through grace. We must be humble enough to repent in the same manner that we must be humble in attitude toward our physical constitution. The 'good news' of the Gospel is just that – that we can alter our spiritual health through Christ and hope in His salvific nature. The amazing aspect of fitness is that we contain the power to alter our physical health. Fitness, in this manner, melds the qualities of fortitude and faith into our psyche.

Repentance - acknowledging we are sinners, and humility - admitting that we need lifestyle alterations, are the first two steps in making these physical/ spiritual, and quantitative/ qualitative amendments.

"There is forgiveness of sins for all who repent." (Luke 24:47)

June 7th:

Every Drop of Sweat has a Price and is Counted in Consecration to Christ A friend once told me that while guilt brings feelings of suffocation, grace is freeing. It is important to note that God says we cannot earn his forgiveness undeserved, which is what grace ultimately is.

Resulting rewards of exercise will always be equated with a 'price': complete devotion of resources to a program and stonewalling of distractions and hindrances to achieve fitness goals. While life is not fair, exercise in a sense is because the weight room, track, or training fields are always there to be utilized with honest corporal industry. Teddy Roosevelt referred to this phenomenon, and I will use the metaphor he propagated of 'effort' being similar to achieved physical assets: "In this life, we get nothing save by effort. Freedom from effort in the present merely means that there has been stored up effort in the past." (192)

Similarly, grace is not free, as it came at a very steep and high price, but it is free for us today. We cannot acquire grace similarly to bodily health gains, Christ paid the price previously and we reap the benefits of his suffering.

"So it is God who decides to show mercy. We can neither choose it nor work for it." (Romans 9:16)

June 8th:

God Relentlessly Pursues us to Propagate for His Kingdom Heart rate recovery is a measuring tool that can be used to inspect cardiovascular fitness. The term refers to how quickly the heart beat returns to preworkout levels after being pushed to its limits, or even just slightly raised to deliver more oxygen to muscles. This process of coming back to resting homeostasis following giving the heart a proverbial 'gut-punch,' can be euphoric. As blood pressure, circulation, and the amount of heartbeats per minute all slow down at the conclusion of training, a good sensation sets in from satisfaction of a job well-done.

So also, a return to God and the true source of life can be invigorating. We can feel peace and sense God's presence when we repent and ask for forgiveness, lifting a weight off our shoulders that is similar in nature to finishing off an exercise session. We can feel at ease that our repentance will yield mercy because Christ paid the price we couldn't. Proving this point, Jesus used the metaphor of a man finding a lost sheep he owned, by actively seeking it out. Thus Jesus evidenced that God pursues sinners allowing grace to flourish in first-time conversion, or a return back to - Christ. "And if he finds it (the lost sheep), I tell you the truth, he will rejoice over it more than the other ninety-nine that didn't wander away." (Matthew 18:13)

June 9th:

Not just Spurning Miscalculation but Having Confidence of Accomplishment Proverbs 16:26 states: "It is good for workers to have an appetite; an empty stomach drives them on." Besides avoiding retribution from a supervisor, a quest to be competent can propel an individual's work ethic. Wanting to do a good job, and not just experiencing the fear of being overtly less grisly than our counterparts, will motivate us to apply potency on each and every repetition in the weight room.

Jesus actually states that an arduous dedication to labor and/ or exercise and belief in its capacity for instilling moral value is part of the way to heaven. "Work hard to enter the narrow door to God's Kingdom, for many will try to enter but will fail." (Luke 13:24) Such an important proposition likely spurred someone to proffer Jesus the presupposition, (wanting to avoid damnation) "Lord, will only a few be saved?"(Luke 13:23). The fact that Jesus affirms some will try and fail means the clarity of focus on Christ must take preeminence in our hearts. Christ must have dominion over our motives and subsequent actions, and the 'narrowness' mentioned regarding the path means it won't be easy.

Jesus was articulate in his diction, and purposefully did not parse words to the question mentioned above, knowing exactly of how to state what he meant. A great analogy to how the above processes transpire is given by Dr. Kenneth Cooper. "The physical experience of stretching can serve as a kind of metaphor when an opportunity for growth arises. Just as stretching the spirit through effort and discipline is required to achieve spiritual progress, physical improvement depends on increasing the flexibility of various parts of the body." (222)

June 10<u>th</u>:

David found recompense and direction from God through his Intensity in Battle King David, in his God-commanded war efforts, pursued his enemies - the Amalekites, in a flight so vigorous that one-third of his men could not handle the wearying nature of the mission. "So David and his 600 men set out... but 200 of his men were too exhausted to cross the brook." (1 Samuel 30:9-10). After all, this decision was instructed by God himself and gives an insight as to how fierce an effort he covets. "Slothfulness casts into a deep sleep, and an idle person will suffer hunger." (Proverbs 19:15 ESV) Indeed, being doped into a steady cycle of slumber dulls the senses and cuts us off from divine guidance.

The high expectation God entreats from us exists in a literal and metaphorical aspect and can flow from passion in exercise that is converted into strength of soul. The abetting pair of exercise and evangelism was never meant to be perfunctory.

Peter even questioned whether his and the disciples' vocations were worth giving up in order to follow Christ, and what they would receive in turn. Peter wondered whether the encompassing journey was worth it all. "Peter began to say to him (Jesus), 'See, we have left everything and followed you.' Jesus said, 'Truly I say to you, there is no one who has left house or mother or children or lands for my sake who will not receive a hundredfold now in this time...with persecution, and in the age to come eternal life.'" (Mark 10:28-30; ESV). Notice that Jesus prefaced salvation with persecution, enameling the fact that Christians are under a heavy burden in this life to push through, similar to a grueling workout - but it is worth the fight!

June 11ᵗʰ:

The Fairer Sex Brings out the Proper Strength and Better Angels of a Man A close female friend once asked me, while we were watching World's Strongest Man together: "How is that (moving and lifting heavy objects) fun?" I rubbishly replied that what's fun to men and women are two different qualities, but her proposition made me reflect. Just as male and female perceptions differ in a dual nature;

everyone has a dark or sinful side. Paul attests to this and says: "We all once lived in the passions of our flesh, carrying out the desires of the body and the mind, and were by nature children of wrath." (Ephesians 2:3: ESV). It is precisely this worldly wanton configuration the enemy influences in our souls that gets emancipated through weight training in a healthy manner, instead of in other ungodly and aberrant ways.

The liberation of the Spirit involved in strength training, when combined with repentance, allows us to view God as we should, in reverence that leads to a new awareness of his real presence. Dr. Charles Stanley elaborates on this phenomenon by saying, "He (Satan) knows that when we go to God in this way (with prayerful repentance), we'll see sin, wickedness, and carnality in our hearts as we have never seen before." (238). When we allow the inner man to exist and conquest untamed in the weight room, it makes us, in turn, more civilized and godly in the specific details of everyday life and thus become more godly in our nature, purer in our thoughts, and more divine in our behavior.

"These are the promises that enable you to share his divine nature and escape the world's corruption caused by human desires." (2 Peter 1:4)

<u>June 12th</u>:

Indicative of Life-Strength through Christ's Cross Concretes Salvation & Cohabitation of his Spirit Exercise, and specifically the 'mode' of running, is no matter of rote recitation movement accomplished by simply shuffling feet. An aerobic base is required for long lengths of endurance training, but a base level of quadriceps strength, eccentric contraction ability of the hamstring, and general flexibility of the hip/groin/ lower abdominal area is needed for concerted distances. Even the 'father of aerobics,' Dr. Kenneth Cooper, teaches that the qualities of strength and cardiorespiratory capacity do not have to be mutually exclusive. "Both are good, but each serves a different purpose. Calisthenics builds agility, coordination and muscular strength...Aerobics builds basic fitness and endurance. A highly conditioned person needs both." (258).

Job, in his complaint to and about God's seemingly lacking semblance of justice, even goes so far as to suggest the possession of strength present can serve as a clinical vital sign of life. "But when people die, their strength is gone." (Job 14:10). Indeed, I have learned academically that just by doing knee extension exercises consistently to train the quadriceps, gait/ walking patterns can be improved in elderly persons who struggle to walk efficiently.

So how do we reconcile being weak in spirit as pointing more to God's strength and omnipotence? We have to come to grips with the fact that mercy and justice can coexist in God's characteristics through, and only through, the crucifixion of Christ. With the scorns and sufferings undergone, he purchased for us a source of strength beyond confounding circumstances of life, knowing that our eternal salvation is secure.

June 13^{th:}

Conquering Previous Sinful Habits by Creating New Ones Cultivates Wholeness The receiving of Christ as Savior should cause a conversion, a change in the manner of how life is lived. There is some element of resolve necessary to cast aside sin that has long plagued the previously unconverted in the past that only the Gospel has the power to alter. Scholar David Field elaborates on how this revelation should appear to God and our neighbors: "The qualification of entering (the kingdom of God) is a radically changed lifestyle, characterized by repentance and faith. All who submit to him...find that his royal power is immediately available to help them conquer bad habits and live lives which really please him." (286). Notice that the requisite for the new lifestyle is characterized by spiritual sorrow for sin girded by a deep belief in Christ. Living healthily can be part of a coherent pattern of evidencing how we have placed our trust in Jesus.

David, in a repentant psalm, proposes a connection between slavery to sin and a lack of whole health. "For when I kept silent, my bones wasted away through my groaning all day long." (Psalm 32:3; ESV). But, God can forgive and clear the slate clean to restore health through a right relationship with him. As proper nutrition bestows a healthy translucent flush of sufficient circulation in the skin, faith in Jesus serves to nourish us spiritually, as well as physically. "I am the bread of life; whoever comes to me shall not hunger." (John 6:35; ESV). It is no coincidence that leading a godly life gives holistic wellness effects, as God wants us to lead a full life equating to the potential he placed in us. Health is a natural biproduct of living 'clean' or in accordance to Christ's teachings.

June 14th:

The Sin Situation Solved via Atonement The ultimate function of the body as a whole and its integrated organ systems is to maintain homeostasis. But our souls crave something deeper than complacency. Man is at his optimum when solving problems and inventing solutions. "Improving compliance to exercise…known to decrease disability is an important and complex subject. The term compliance can have subjective, even paternalistic connotations." (291).

The return to balance after the extreme degree of exertion has been reached, detailed in physiologic stress after a workout, can be euphoric when post workout elevated oxygen consumption takes place. This phenomenon makes us thankful for the health we DO have plus reiterates that tomorrow, indeed not another moment, is guaranteed but the one we are currently in.

The chief problem of sin and joining with its solution - the cross, places us in good standing in the eternal war on the side of Jesus, as he is willing and able to absolve sins. "So I will prove to you that the Son of Man has the authority on earth to forgive sins." (Mark 2:10). And holding faith in Jesus' mercy is the centrifuge for effective comportment change, especially in off-the-field conduct and fitness-supplemented endeavors. Exercise physiologists have recognized this factor and denote that lifestyle modifications are initiated.

June 15th:

Exercise Gives a Collected Emotional State Similar to Sin Absolving "Oh, what joy for those whose disobedience is forgiven, whose sin is put out of sight!" (Psalm 32:1). I can tell a difference in sleep quality, duration, and patterns on days I work out. Confessing sin and placing it in the hands of God gives an inner soul/ heart peace. We sleep better and don't have to walk around with the proverbial guilt's and the monkey on our back.' Exercising relieves us that we have done what we can to make a significant contribution to our short- and long-term vitality, just as forgiveness puts us at ease that we won't be condemned.

June 16th:

The Real 'Avengers' and True 'Immortals' Amass God's army runs very literally! "Like war horses they run." (Joel 2:4). The humanistic inflection of how heaven's armies traverse is described in a vivid (and either utterly horrifying or stirringly inspirational) depiction. "Like blackness there is spread upon the mountains a great and powerful people; their like has never been before...Fire devours before them, and behind a flame burns." (Joel 2:2-3: ESV). Can you imagine witnessing this? We should tremble at the very thought of having a front row seat to view the spectacle (if indeed it comes in the reader's lifetime).

But notice that in one verse this prophecy of future history is described as terrible – "For the day of the LORD is near, and as destruction from the Almighty it comes (Joel 1:15; ESV)", while simultaneously in another verse it's identified as glorious – "For the day of the LORD is great and very awesome." (Joel 2:11; ESV). Could it be that the forgiven in Christ will shout in adulation for their regeneration into a heavenly body, while the wicked will tremble in panic and revulsion as they witness a righteous God execute vengeance with invincible beings? "Like warriors…like soldiers…They do not jostle one another…they burst through the weapons and are not halted." (Joel 2:8; ESV).

Notice also that kinesiological diction giving way to natural phenomenon is used in describing their movement patterns: "They leap on the tops of the mountains, like the crackling of a flame of fire." (Joel 2:5; ESV) This description indicates that physical work will happen on judgment day. To prepare for it via exercise helps us to understand better its implications and gives stoutness to our hearts for the effort we have and will put forth as forces for good in the eternal war. And through all of this, God proclaims in a stunningly summative verse that he still offers divine mercy to any: "Yet even now, declares the LORD, return to me with all your heart…who knows whether he will not turn and relent." (Joel 2:12,14; ESV)

June 17th:

A Manumission of Inner Feelings Exercise and sports provide the means of a venting mechanism for deep-seated emotion. Exercise is nature's greatest mood tranquilizer and stress reliever. The alleviation process is accomplished by the uptake and utilization of excess blood glucose, cortisol, epinephrine, and norepinephrine, saturating and flowing freely in the bloodstream, to stimulate combustion in physical activity.

While the Bible is not explicit in the faculty of the emotional or physical relenting of stress, it does compare this 'release' to the phenomenon of death for easing of practical, real-life anxieties. "Can the dead live again? If so, this would give me hope through all my years of struggle, and I would eagerly await the release of death." (Job 14:14) Even Jesus sought out this freeing of calamity on the cross by crying out to God regarding a reprieve from abandonment before 'releasing' His Spirit.

"Then Jesus shouted out again, and he released his spirit." (Matthew 27:50)

June 18th:

Salvation Requires Facing the Uncomfortable When following a diversified fitness plan, one must explore new possibilities to 'shock' muscles into stress that ultimately leads to new growth. Body weight exercises, calisthenics, core stabilization drills, yoga and Pilates are all examples of unorthodox strength training methods. Analogous to this variation and progress, salvation is an ongoing process that continues throughout life's seasons.

"Work out your own salvation with fear and trembling." (Philippians 2:12 ESV)

June 19<u>th</u>:

Life May Not be Fair, But God is Good Fitness teaches convalescence through having to exercise despite the pain of muscle fatigue. Sometimes we might fail to reach our goals or even injure ourselves because of overtraining in overzealousness. However, the Bible teaches us to keep trying when we get knocked down. Moral fortitude is developed by focusing on what is truly important: working to please God.

Robert W. Service, a well-regarded poet and writer, had this to say about the quality of wielding moral persistence: "'You've had a raw deal!' I know – but don't squeal, buck up, do your damnedest, and fight." (73) '

"Fight the good fight for the true faith." (1 Timothy 6:12)

June 20<u>th</u>:

What is Grace and why is it Amazing? We may be able to 'earn' a better, more muscular and supple body. We might, in addition, be able to 'earn' an improvement in overall health and also 'earn' prevention of chronic disease before they begin. These three qualities that we imbue come through repetitive trekking of hard work in exercise. However, we cannot 'earn' eternal life. This gift, this ultimate gift, is given to us by God through grace.

"God saved you by his grace when you believed. And you can't take credit for this; it is a gift from God. Salvation is not a reward for the good things we have done" (Ephesians 2:8-9)

June 21<u>st</u>:

Christ Invades and Puts to Rest the False Dark Identity Working out helps us develop our true identity. This occurs because exercise, whether aerobic or anaerobic in nature, boosts self-confidence. We feel a certain sense of control over our lives, and in one sense, we do make our own destiny of physical health manifest as we would like it to be. However, our true identity is found in Christ alone, and when we give him control, others see Him and not us.

"It is no longer I who live, but Christ lives in me." (Galatians 2:20)

June 22nd:

Peace with God Manifested Exercise can be healing in many ways, just as the process of repentance, confession, and forgiveness is spiritually healing. With the modality of exercise, we restore our connection with nature and our own spirit. Dr. Dean Ornish elaborates on this topic by saying, "In other words, when you go all the way to the healthy end of the spectrum, your body often has a remarkable capacity to begin healing itself." (47)

The calming, rewarding sensations we obtain from exercise have emanated from God's mercy and convolute with the peace that only Christ can offer.

"Therefore, we have peace with God because of what Christ our Lord has done for us." (Romans 5:1)

June 23rd:

The Past is Over Anyone who has ever been involved with athletics has made a mistake. Even the person living the most 'strenuous life' (as Teddy Roosevelt described) has skipped a workout. Similarly, everyone has past sins they are ashamed of.

Letting these previous actions dictate your present or future status is the work of the enemy. Max Lucado sums up the heart of this situation: "You…have to make a choice. Do you rise above the past and make a difference? Or do you remain controlled by the past and make excuses?" (49)

"And the blood of Jesus...cleanses us from all sin." (1 John 1:7)

<u>June 24<u>th</u></u>:

The Search for Perpetual Life There is not an existential 'fountain of youth.' Not even for an extreme fitness enthusiast who never misses a workout and always eats healthy. Dr. Kenneth Cooper substantiates this fact by commenting on even those that exacerbate aerobic fitness gains to the recommended level. "It will enable you to live a healthier and more productive life, but it is not the fountain of youth. It will decrease the severity and frequency of many medical problems…In that sense, maintaining your exercise routine is buying you a lot of health insurance." (162) Exercise can increase longevity, while simultaneously improving quality of life and reducing morbidity, but the mortality rate of all humans is still 100%.

Therefore, exercise increases our humility and lets us take charge of the things we do have control over. We have control over our eternal destiny – when we place our trust in Christ. When you are facing fears or cannot see the whole scope of God's plan for your life on earth and the hereafter, Max Lucado says to remember this: "Earthly fears are no fears at all. Answer the big question of eternity, and the little questions of life fall into perspective." (51)

"And anyone who believes in God's Son has eternal life." (John

3:36)

June 25th

Rapid Health Enhancement & Instantaneous Forgiveness Every day is a new day filled with endless possibilities of improving fitness stratums, regardless of what level you are currently at. It is never too late to make lifestyle changes that are conducive to prompting superior health.

If you are starting on a new resistance/ strength training program, you are very likely to see rapid improvements in strength and coordination for activities of daily living. These gains occur because of the improved working efficiency of the neuromuscular system. So with God also, it is never too late to repent.

"The faithful love of the Lord never ends! His mercies begin afresh each morning." (Lamentations 3:22-23)

June 26th:

The Healing Power of Exercise Regarding the medicinal aspects of exercise, Dr. Dean Ornish says, "A single exercise session can lower your blood pressure by 5 to 7 mm/Hg, which may persist for as long as twenty-two hours." (52) Today, after much research, there is little disputing the fact that exercise has inherent healing properties.

Similarly, prayer has power that even exercise cannot tap into. Prayer centers our minds and hearts and provides an inner peace. The Agnus Dei is an ancient Catholic prayer that was first used in reference to Christ as the perfect sacrificial offering for the atonement for all of humanity's sins. It ends with: "Lamb of God, you take away the sins of the world. Grant us peace."

"Then you will experience God's peace, which exceeds anything we can understand." (Philippians 4:7)

June 27th:

Defining Salvation and Holistic Health Fitness is defined by the US President's Council on Physical Fitness and Sports as: "the ability to carry out daily tasks efficiently with enough energy left over to enjoy leisure-time pursuits and to meet unforeseen emergencies." (59)

Without a comprehensive sense of direction in what you are trying to attain, you will not be able to reach that aspiration. Without a reference point of beginning, there can be no comparison from baseline testing to the current to show progress. In these cases, it will be difficult to maintain fitness to the optimum level or possibly improve at all.

Similarly, God gives us a clear-cut method/ definition of how to attain forgiveness for our sins and eternal salvation: "If you confess with your mouth that Jesus is Lord and believe in your heart that God raised him from the dead, you will be saved." (Romans 10:9)

June 28th:

The Ancient & Continuing Search for Truth Marcus Aurelius, the emperor who led Rome through a time of prosperity known as 'Pax Romana', waxed eloquently about the virtues of hale and hardy masculinity: "Let the deity which is in thee be the guardian of a living being...who has taken his post like a man." (77) Could it be that unknowingly, Aurelius was referring to the Holy Spirit?

It is likely that in referring to this 'deity,' Marcus Aurelius taps into a source of freedom beyond that of which even the empire and 'civilization' of Rome could offer. "Wherever the Spirit of the Lord is, there is freedom." (2 Corinthians 3:17)

It is in this duality/ intersection of tangible and ephemeral work that we find the true meaning of freedom we are endowed with. We strive to make enthalpy out of a chaotic world which is dark and meaningless without the hope of Christ.

We reach the conclusion that as humans, we desire our existence to project into the external environment as a formidable force for good, of which fitness is one means to do so. Today, we still echo the sentiment of President Eisenhower: "That all who yearn for freedom may experience its spiritual blessings."(79) Exercise is a literal and figurative exhibition of liberties and a discipline of work which yields manifold results.

June 29th:

A Spirit of Power Putting life situations in God's hands to be totally at His disposal can be a freeing experience. Instead of attempting to control external situations which are outside our capacity/ jurisdiction, we give power to God to work through us. "May you be strengthened with all power according to his glorious might." (Colossians 1:11; ESV) Power is given to us in order that we might make it through the sorrows we will face: "He gives power to the faint." (Isaiah 40:29; ESV)

Also, God's power exists so that he can do what we cannot do on our own ability: salvation. "The Gospel…it is the power of God for salvation to everyone who believes." (Romans 1:16; ESV). In the same manner, aerobic training benefits many organ systems, including but not limited to the musculoskeletal, cardiovascular, and pulmonary.

However, besides amounting to these capacious effects, the benefit of a cardiorespiratory endurance program, "Fine tunes the nervous and hormonal systems." (103) The bodily power begotten from aerobics on us will have an effect similar to the result of Samuel Johnson's prayer, in which he said he desired to be, "More pure in my thoughts and more regular in my desires." (104)

June 30th:

Is Posture Important When Praying? An interesting intersection between physical and spiritual realms takes place when praying and deciding which posture is best to take while in the practice. Is it required during prayer to be kneeling or prostrate to present oneself before God? These positions affirm an attitude of humility in the presence of majesty when approaching God.

It is said in the Gospel of Matthew that when Jesus asked to be delivered from his death and suffering fate, he, "Bowed with his face to the ground, praying." (Matthew 26:39) King David also alludes to this interaction, and said that when praying for his enemies nonetheless that "I prayed with head bowed on my chest." (Psalm 35:13 – ESV) It would likely do us well when we supplicate/ beseech God that we yield in posture and desire. Indeed, kinesiology could play a role in answered prayers if we humble ourselves in both body and spirit.

"God blesses those who are poor in spirit and realize their need for him." (Matthew 5:3)

July: Servant Leadership – Following Christ's Example

<u>July 1ˢᵗ</u>:

Faith and Fitness Require an Aspect of Self-Denial Certainly involvement in athletics or adherence to any exercise program requires a certain amount/ level of self-denial. Attaining this quality means putting aside one's temporary pleasures in order to accomplish a long-term goal. It also involves contributing to a goal that is larger than one's own individual aspirations. We have a great example to follow in Christ, who shared in our humanity so that we might one day share in His divinity.

"If anyone would come after me, let him deny himself and take up his cross daily." (Luke 9:23).

<u>July 2ⁿᵈ</u>:

Breaking Out of the Box of Complacency To garner fitness gains from a cardiorespiratory (aerobic) style workout, certain intensity must be realized. Heart rate must be elevated to 65% of its maximum capacity. Ideally, after surpassing the beginner's phase, a cadence of 120 steps per minute (two steps per second) must be attained.

Similarly, to grow in our relationship with Christ and our obedience to Him, we must, at times, step out of our daily monotony/ routine to love God and love others. The Golden Rule is the authority of the Christian's daily life walk with the Lord and provides us with the 'spirit' rather than the 'letter' of law which should guide our daily reactions to any situation.

"Do to others whatever you would like them to do to you. This is the essence of all that is taught in the law and the prophets." (Matthew 7:12)

July 3ʳᵈ:

Moral Courage Conceived From Athletics Speaking from personal experiences, football in Texas reigns supreme in the realm of athletics and goes hand-in-hand with faith. I can say with almost absolute assuredness that whatever I accomplish in life will be due in large part to the moral lessons I learned from playing football and off-season conditioning.

Coach Ken Purcell, former Athletic Director of Denton ISD, Texas echoes this sentiment. "If we're not teaching values, then we're wasting too much money on a game." (301).

Adolescent boys long for ways to prove themselves to others, and football coaches can be great role models to whom they look to impress and learn from. The coaches' work-ethic rubs off on the players, as many times they work much more than a 14-hour long day. To work hard towards a goal of performing underneath those 'Friday night lights' instills a sense of accomplishment and underscores the substantial value of thorough and dedicated preparation. The value of honest hard work stems from these experiences and spreads to committing a full effort in work, faith-life, relationships, family and friend concord, and many other undertakings.

Coach Purcell lays out the mentality of Texas toughness and arduous work ethic, which is foundational and expected out of all young men and women in Texas. "I grew up in ranching and agriculture. Coaching in Texas is very similar in work ethics. You work until the work is done. It's a bit like cattle or the wheat harvest. When the wheat harvest comes in, you just have to get it in. The wheat is ripe; you've got to get it cut. A wheat harvester will cut it all night to get it done, and as a coach, you have to prepare for the opponent over the weekend." (301).

"And we know that God causes everything to work together for the good of those who love God." (Romans 8:28)

July 4<u>th</u>:

Freedom and its Inspiration Exercise can provide the sustenance for an almost surreal experience of pure and unscathed freedom. The tone of the atmosphere in this medium of human expression is a bit dichotomous; serious and tedious, yet consequentially casual and informal.

Joy fills our hearts as we imbibe on a social quality known as shared humanity. Each soul faces struggles during a workout, and as they do, we see our brothers and sisters push through exhaustion. Conquering previously unreached limitations, we are inspired to inculcate this determination into our individually unique personalities.

Although war is a horrific reality, the ancient French knight Jean De Brueil had this to say about the comradery and brotherhood that extolled from it: "If we see that our cause is just and our kinsmen fight boldly, tears come to our eyes." (32).

"A glad heart makes a happy face." (Proverbs 15:13)

July 5<u>th</u>:

The Vanity of Perception It is a tragedy to live only for a striving of fame and posthumously acquired glory. George H.W. Bush summed up succinctly the Lord's purpose for earthly power. "For we are given power not to advance our own purposes, nor to make a great show in the world, nor a name. There is but one just use of power, and it is to serve people." (46)

The reference to negative qualities the former president gives applies to the vanity that sports superstardom can impose. In a nonathletic fitness endeavor, this vanity can manifest itself as an obsession over bodily physique. The paradox of worldly treasures that fame offers allows us to understand that we should pursue storing rewards in heaven for eternity.

"Let someone else praise you, not your own mouth – a stranger, not your own lips." (Proverbs 27:2)

July 6th:

Others Before Self & Servant Leadership True renown and proper fame are not to be attained on this earth. Instead, a legacy is what we should aim for. Jesus spoke of this temporal, worldly praise and its fleeting nature when he said, "When you pray, don't be like the hypocrites who love to pray publicly on street corners and in the synagogues where everyone can see them. I tell you the truth, that is all the reward they will ever get." (Matthew 6:5)

The real results of fitness must be personal first (not to say that you cannot ask for help/ assistance) and corporate second. To lead by example is the true practicality required to become a servant leader. To attain this level of nobility, we should specifically pay attention to the example Jesus gave by washing the feet of his disciples on the very eve he knew he would be apprehended.

Sir Walter Scott, a Scottish poet and novelist, alluded to the theme of a created legacy through the context of a poem about a lack of patriotism, inducing pride and arrogance: "High though his titles, proud his name…

the wretch concentrated all in self, living, shall forfeit fair renown." (61)

July 7th:

Exercise Makes 'Shared Humanity' Visible The camaraderie developed by those who partake in the shared experience of fitness/ athletic endeavor is a powerful phenomenon. A copacetic community perspective of attaining better, healthier lives is forged in the crucible of hard work/ struggle. The quest for health enrichment, through the quality of vigorous manual effort, can also be described as the trait/ theme of 'shared humanity'. We see our brothers and sisters working hard for personal health, and while this quality is a personal demonstration of individual freedoms, it inspires us all to be devoted to the optimum common good that we ascertain in each other.

Exercise creates coalescence of the community as a whole, uniting people of all backgrounds regardless of race, gender, and socioeconomic status, to work together for a common good goal. The theme of 'shared humanity' is echoed in ages past by an ancient unknown Norse poet who said, "Rich did I feel when a comrade I found, for man is man's delight." (80)

"Behold, how good and pleasant it is when brothers dwell in unity." (Psalm 133:1)

July 8th:

Bearing Fruit With Fitness The reason for, and gain of good deeds is to bear fruit. Fruit is the result of a constant walk of faith with our friend, brother, and redeemer: Jesus Christ. Fruit can take on the meaning of earthly/ physical results or heavenly/ eternal rewards. A prime example of physical fruit transcribes when a therapist successfully rehabilitates an injury, or a personal trainer helps a client lose weight and adopt healthier lifestyle habits.

In fitness, there is a bluntly stated law of yielded results: "Exercising more intensely, will elevate what doctors call your exercise tolerance. The better your maximum exercise tolerance, the longer you're going to live." (81) 'Tolerance' means that you have enhanced endurance and increased fitness levels through previous high levels of exercise intensity, leading to a need for higher doses of arduousness in succeeding workouts.

The Bible reiterates this fact by saying, "Each of us did the work the Lord gave us." (1 Corinthians 3:5) 'Work' refers to bearing fruit. Ultimately, it is God who "Makes the seed grow. The one who plants and the one who waters work together with the same purpose." (1 Corinthians 3:7-8) To have true meaning in life, we must 'work' hard to bear spiritual fruit. We do this because of the heavenly reward that awaits us, but more so because we love God, and we love our fellow brothers and sisters in Christ and want to point them toward salvation.

July 9th:

Personal Belief Begets a Stronger Community Many people interested in fitness and/ or Christianity, question 1) whether a wellness plan that includes a fitness regimen/ exercise prescription, written down on paper, really has the power to give practical effects of weight loss and buttressing overall health. Another valid question people wonder is 2) can God truly reveal Himself to us through the written word (the Bible)? These issues of 'trust' are the intersection of faith and science, in terms of believing in the goodness of our bodies as God created us. The answer to these questions as matters of reason and faith is: yes to both!

In relation to the latter, the key is found in the word of God itself:

"All scripture is inspired by God and is useful to teach us what is true." (2 Timothy 3:16) The power of the written word encompasses a certain anagoge carried with it. Dr. Ben Carson quotes a theologian, who said, "In the best books, great men (and women) give us their most precious thoughts, and pour their souls into ours. They give to all who will faithfully use them, the spiritual presence, of the best and greatest of our race." (89) The last four words are a reference to the perfection and holiness of Christ.

Relating to the former question, exercise literally affects our lifestyle in an impactful manner. These alterations are continuous, lifelong and eternal - influencing our minds, bodies, and souls. It is proper here to mention that the YMCA's mission statement is: "To put Christian principles into practice through programs that build mind, body, and spirit for all." (90) Notice both the practical nature (body), intellectual (mind) and sublime (spirit) aspects of Christian principles. William Bennett astutely asserted that "The founders of the YMCA perceived that the way to make an impact on culture is to be firmly established in one's spiritual life." (91)

July 10th:

Temporal Discomfort Repulses a Lukewarm Psyche God places our apathy/ inaction to living out the Christian faith via our good deeds, and keeping ourselves undefiled from this world, in the same ranks as the sin of pride. "Sodom's sins were pride, gluttony, and laziness, while the poor and needy suffered outside her door." (Ezekiel 16:49) Notice the trifold nature of these sins: to our own bodies, to our spirits, as well as the community as a whole.

Exercise can provide an avenue out of this lifestyle of self-centeredness by compelling us to examine our own health motives, and therefore care about the wellness of our friends, family, and neighbors/ communities. Sigmund Freud was mistaken in his assertion that "mental life was originally directed by the 'pleasure principle'; that is, by the need to avoid pain and to obtain pleasure." (94)

If we forsake the transient instant artificial gratification, we automatically activate the quality of self-control God has embedded in the depths of our spirits. Because Christ himself suffered in the flesh and underwent the discomforts inevitable in all human life, we should expect to undergo these sensations as well. The key then, is to listen for and be on guard for the "Sound of a gentle whisper" (1 Kings 19:12) that God can use to direct and speak to us.

July 11ᵗʰ:

Mutual Courage Builds Intimacy Through Shared Experiences The product of shared trials, such as those experienced in exercise, results in a closer, more intimate friendship. When two or more persons complete a workout session together, the mutual toughening of their bodies results in a fostered sense of belonging with regard to social networks. A refined outlook on our own inner character, as well as that of friends, is the subsequent result.

Although fitness and sports are not war, the common commodity of pushing through a human experience, such as the onset and subsequent conquering of fatigue, bonds us together in a special way. In the book, All Quiet on the Western Front, the author elaborates on how two German soldiers grow closer through experiencing the hazards of war together. "We are two men, two minute sparks of life; outside is the night and the circle of death. We sit on the edge of it crouching in danger, now we are so intimate that we do not even speak."

Humans are attracted to instances that foster a degree of mutual courage. The contrivance developed through mastering apprehension and mustering bravery before and during exercise, develops a kinship like no other.

"A friend is always loyal, and a brother is born to help in time of need." (Proverbs 17:17)

<u>July 12<u>th</u>:</u>

Gaining Prudence From Exercise Many athletes in the malleable age of teenage years look up to their coaches, but are not 'friends' with them during this time period. During later years, the effort demanded by the coaches bears its fruit in the lives of young men and women. It is at this juncture that, as stated by Dr. Leon Kass, "Concentrating on material wants and bodily ills, while ignoring moral and spiritual deficiencies...undermines the worthier goal of...philanthropy governed by help really means." (99)

Biblically, this principle of prudence in the training of athletes, and the amount of feedback they receive is definitively supported. "The prudent are crowned with knowledge." (Proverbs 14:18). By knowing and employing the craft of giving feedback adroitly and subtly, coaches shape young men and women through the crucible of exercise. Dr. Bill Bennett alludes to this principle – saying, "Ancient Greek philosophers considered prudence to be one of the most important virtues because it allows us to make good decisions in putting other virtues like courage and perseverance into practice." (100) Courage, in concert with the moral and spiritual sense, is a natural by-product of involvement with athletics/ exercise.

<u>July 13<u>th</u>:</u>

Courage from Christ's Example It is interesting to note that the Gospel of John begins with the mystical and proceeds to the physical. "In the beginning the Word already existed. The Word was with God, and the Word was God." (John 1:1) However, the emphasis then shifts later into the 'human realm' and how Jesus embodied God. "So the Word became flesh." (John 1:14)

Jesus has been in our human position before, so we know he experienced the same bodily limitations and Newtonian laws that govern physical science and human activity. To accentuate the spiritual aspect of John's first verse, family practice physician Dr. Scott Morris says that "Jesus' disciples knew body and spirit had something to do with each other." (135) Spiritual law controls the natural laws, but God created them in accord with one another.

Imagine the amount of walking that took place to meander from town to town with a very intentional nature of evangelism as the goal. To elaborate on the earthly aspect of Christ's life and God's creation, Dr. Scott Morris says, "The enfleshing of Jesus, God's own Son, says something of what God thinks of being human. God created the physical world and called it 'good.' God created human beings and said, 'very good'." This physical proximity can be thought of in a very practical manner that Jesus is right by our side always as our side, including while we exercise. This theological reality instills courage in our hearts.

"And be sure of this: I am with you always, even to the end of the age." (Matthew 28:20)

<u>July 14th</u>:

Acquiescing to Christ Despite Self-Reliance Exercise teaches the quality of self-reliance. The process of accomplishing this feat originates with improving the ability to perform physical 'activities of daily living (ADLs).' Improving the capacity to perform ADLs is especially beneficial to the elderly who may have an impingement for reaching down and picking up objects, carrying weighted items, or rotating/ twisting the torso to simultaneously reach with arms. Absolute strength is of exceptional value to improving our abilities to achieve ADLs. However, at a certain 'critical value' exertion of higher forces will not yield greater skill (ADL) levels.

In our faith walks, we are not strong enough to save ourselves or absolve our own sin. Like the thief on the cross next to Christ, we all reach moral disrepute and stagnation. Homer wrote, "You cannot fight beyond your own strength." (155) This fact is comforting in one respect – that Christ alone is sufficient to offer salvation. In another respect, it can be discouraging because we have to incur meekness to obtain true moral and physical strength. "Blessed are the meek, for they shall inherit the earth." (Matthew 5:5; ESV) The proper viewpoint of demureness is extolled by King Solomon: "He who rules his spirit (is better than) he who takes a city." (Proverbs 16:32; ESV) In the proper perspective of the eternal, meekness seems a small price to pay for residency in permanent paradise.

"If only there were a mediator between us...I would no longer live in terror of punishment, but I cannot do that in my own strength." (Job 9: 33-35)

July 15th:

True Fellowship is a Beautiful Commodity Comity - the shared mutual experience of facing and overcoming difficulty in regard to fitness goals and social interaction definitely exists. This facet of community and individual development is elaborated on in The Daniel Plan. "Being engaged in community will improve your health – and not just physically. Friends can improve your emotional and spiritual health." (165) In this manner, each devotee of fitness becomes a natural leader by example. "You are not just receiving influence; you are an influencer as well. If you develop and keep healthy habits, your friends and family are more likely to develop them." (166)

I can't help but draw parallels between these theories and writings regarding fitness communities and the early church. The disciples and other apostles had forged a bond beyond which no one on earth had ever seen in the history of mankind. This mutual endeavor united Christians based on Christ's divinity. I have felt this bond in the gym with those I partake in workouts with, and it is unbreakable. Communities are defined by common interests, and combining fitness and faith indeed fosters a formidable force and formulates fortitude.

"And all who believed were together and had all things in common." (Acts 2:44; ESV)

July 16th:

To Die To Self Through Boldness in Both Faith and Fitness
Certainly, Paul showed physical courage during imprisonment/ bondage and in chains for preaching the Gospel. He did this while also showing spiritual courage that his eternal destination of heaven was guaranteed and that "My life will bring honor to Christ, whether I live or die." (Philippians 1:20) Paul was bold in this sense that his purpose in life, fulfilling the Great Commission and presenting grace to the Gentiles, spurred him on. "I fully hope and expect…that I will continue to be bold for Christ." (Philippians 1:20)

Boldness is defined as: showing or requiring a fearless, daring spirit, or standing out prominently. Certainly, as Christians, we should stand out prominently in this world that Satan is the god of. Exercise also requires and purveys this type of intrepidness. In a workout or sporting event, competition proclivity sets in, and we feel empowered to push past our normal everyday capabilities. Our teammates, friends and faith compel us in this arena. Dr. Peale says of this occurrence, "Boldness creates a state of emergency to which the organism will respond. Your pride, your competitive instinct, and your sense of obligation will see to it that you do." (168) In what some might consider as rhetoric too asperous, Dr. Martin Luther King echoed Paul's sentiment in positing the aphorism, "That if a man hasn't discovered something he will die for, he isn't fit to live." (169)

"For to me, living means living for Christ, and dying is even better." (Philippians 1:21)

July 17th:

We all Have Individual Gifts and Roles in Defending the True Faith A 'fight' can take on many forms. Cortisol and adrenaline are released into the freely circulating bloodstream during preparation for the execution of physical activity. This process entails mechanical work via usage of relaying neuromuscular messages that spur contraction processes. The psychological and sensory challenges that exercise embellishes implicate these reactions. We must 'fight' through muscle fatigue, getting 'winded,' and acidic muscle burn from excess hydrogen ions to the point of conclusion in an aerobic or anaerobic training session.

This trudging was elaborated on by General Douglas MacArthur when talking about the daily unambiguous bodily challenge which inversely, led to demonstrable opportunities for the unique exhibition of skill and talent that the soldiers he commanded in World War II faced. "Of even greater importance is the human element – the troops who fight the battles...the human equation was strikingly expressed by a unique flavor that is the essence of that elusive and deathless thing called soldiering." (178)

While this courage is easy to recognize practically in action, especially in a conscription military setting, it is not easily formulated into oral or drafted language. The quality matches the daily battle we face, in fitness/ athletics, and on our spiritual journeys as we resist temptation, stand our ground and defend Christianity's truth.

"I have been appointed to defend the Good News." (Philippians 1:16)

"But now I must write, urging you to defend the faith that God has entrusted once for all time." (Jude 3)

July 18ᵗʰ:

Simply Handling A Matter Efficiently With No Exaltation
When viewing the movie Gladiator for the first and following successive times, one aspect of the opening battle scene depicting Roman conquest of Germania stood out to me: the laconic businesslike method and implacable highly focused demeanors that the Roman infantry soldiers displayed just moments before literal life-and-death encounters. Grimly and almost stoically, the Roman ground-troops steadily advanced while their enemy combatants nonobsequiously yelled, jeered, gestured, and mocked them. In this extremely physical, and yet regrettable arena of war, balance and stability to hold one's ground based position and strength with skillful endurance to properly utilize weapons with forceful precision and yet stunning lethality, are definitely prerequisites. However, do not misunderstand me in thinking that I recommend never exuding emotion, for zeal is a desirable quality.

So also, God does not flash from the sky daily to prove his might but implants an awe of Him and His power in our hearts. We are humbled by his divinely mighty nature, and so exercise relates to God in that it is not impetuous. Christ followed the Father's predetermined fate in the physical sphere and did so obediently and with a reverent attitude, "He was afflicted, yet he opened not his mouth." (Isaiah 53:7; ESV)

Dr. Peale posits that a situationally aware, yet poised attitude, which condones the performing of exercise, is essential. "The controlled person is a powerful person. He who always keeps his head will always get ahead. The cyclone derives its powers from a calm center. So does a person." (189) It takes forsaking vain pleasure and fleeting temptation to lambast in the temporary anguish of exercise, and please God by following Christ's example of handling physical affliction with magnanimity. "Yet it was the will of the LORD to crush him; Out of the anguish of his (Christ's) soul, he (the Father) shall see and be satisfied." (Isaiah 53:10-11)

July 19th:

How Does One Become a True & Respected Leader? Exercise can be a conduit to developing leadership in many ways. One completely physical and observational manner is to demonstrate the movements of weight training to your peers, clients, or younger participants in the discipline, and so become their visual mode of how the lift is properly performed.

That is to say, we can use our chances as athletes and fitness enthusiasts to be an example to others. While sanguinely heaving of large weight masses is impressive to adolescents, ultimately the real impact on them will be made in the moral department. We should not workout only to make ourselves more appealing to the opposite sex, achieve personal satisfaction, or sport performance enhancement, but to be a character-based (rooted in being a 'little Christ' or Christian) influence on others. When we strive to benefit others, we subconsciously become natural leaders.

"My life has become an example to many, because you have been my strength." (Psalm 71:7)

"Work hard and become a leader." (Proverbs 12:24)

July 20th:

Many Generations Have Believed in the Eternal Unseen Theory is important in kinesiology just as much as practical applications. The science of movement is very complex and is a culmination of three fields: psychology, physiology, and physics. Laws exist that govern any and all bodily movements. So also, God reigns supreme over the seeable world, but there is something else going on that compels us to discern the notion that purely seeing is not believing. Qualitative and/ or conceptual qualities are developed during and after a workout.

If there is not a viable plan set in place for strength and conditioning, no matter what the goals, it is like traversing a road with no eventual destination. So also, Christ came and was quantitative proof of God's love for humanity. "Christ is the visible image of the invisible God." (Colossians 1:15) The theory for this mysterious plan is laid out for all Christians in the first five verses of the Gospel of John. The realization/ fulfillment came in Christ's sinless life, death and resurrection. But the practical application of Christ's truth ultimately trickles down to us in the words he spoke to 'Doubting Thomas.' "You believe because you have seen me. Blessed are those who believe without seeing me!" (John 20:29)

July 21st:

Extending Christian Virtues via Lifestyle Example Paul exhorted the Romans, in the theoretical sense, to, "Put on the Lord Jesus Christ." (Romans 13:14; ESV) While it may make sense that we should reflect our values to the outside world, how exactly do we proceed to nondeceptively radiate the light of the Gospel and Christ's example to our neighbors? Colossians 3:12 (ESV) gives us practical advice of what seven qualities to exhibit to a world in need of God's love. "Put on then…compassionate hearts, kindness, humility, meekness, and patience. And above all these put on love." When love is guiding us, we will naturally do the right thing and don't need to give heed to apprehension or hesitation because our lives will not be ruled by fear.

From a health and medical standpoint, Dr. Scott Morris also delves into the practicality of being an iridescent light in the darkness: "We call these pieces of clothing God gives us 'the virtues.'" (191) Exercise imbeds, develops, and gives us a chance to show these six qualities as an example to others. Dr. Morris says of his free medical clinic, "Whether we're running exercise programs, nutrition classes, or personal counseling, we want to see the virtues play out in as many ways as possible." (191)

Therefore, fitness speaks to this concept of mutual beneficence to us and others, and not just in an earthly manner.   Rather, what we give off in the physical sense points to a greater evanescence of spiritual truths. Dr. Morris goes on to describe the process further by saying that in his business designed to help the working poor, "The goal was that these virtues be not just an intellectual concept, but, a reality for people as they're exercising, swimming, eating, and so on." Our whole lifestyles, including fitness formations, when consecrated to Christ speak volumes in ways we may never know.

<u>July 22<u>nd</u></u>:

The Sooner You Realize Nothing Can Make Life Fair the Better In athletics as in life, we must learn to handle perceived failures with a phlegmatic attitude, shrugging them off while simultaneously skimming important lessons from them. Children who participate in youth sports and/ or physical education of any form expose themselves to potentially self-induced disappointments stemming from competitive game losses, comparison of body features, or not being as athletically inclined as their fellow students in testing or achievements. However, encountering these injustices in a compassionate environment supervised by responsible adults, teaches valuable lessons of life, with one in particular: life is not fair!

Knowing the ache of losing a race, being slower than others in a game of tag, and undergoing a heart-wrenching experience such as missing a basketball shot in front of friends, helps children to learn from difficulties. An enlightening research study that was conducted with youth soccer programs in Los Angeles, pointed out by the president of the American College of Sports Medicine relayed the point that "coaches had more impact on kids' sense of self-worth than either the parents or teammates!" (198)

A godly coach, following the template of the Bible passage at the end of this entry will be cognizant of these factors, and will recognize the tough times kids can go through when competing (and also that adults encounter too in early stage fitness capacities), and will modulate his or her coaching traits. Knowing how to offer constructive criticism as a fitness instructor or mentor involves showing a combination of gentleness along with firmness.   Enthusiasm to praise successes while also not pandering can be a fine line of behavior to mesh. But a good coach always acts with the child's/ clients' self-perception in mind and makes use of every lesson imparting opportunity wisely.

"The Lord is close to the brokenhearted, he rescues those whose spirits are crushed." (Psalm 34:18)

July 23<u>rd</u>:

Don't Have Indifference, Be on the Side of Freedom Functioning for Christ Dr. Kenneth Cooper, in his second of many published books, delves into the matter of fitness as if it were a kind of morality mission birthed from his Christian faith. "When I introduced aerobics as a new concept of exercise, my chief aim was to counteract the problem of lethargy…so widely prevalent in our American population." (208) In a sense, the doctor is saying that engaging in a workout, either privately or publicly, is a way to battle apathy towards life when it gets you down. No doubt, we have the freedom to get lost in our feelings, and forget about working for God's Kingdom. But freedom in that sense is combated simultaneously by the crucial freedom to fight, go against the grain, and put others before yourself.

Jesus referred to this freedom when he replied to an inquisitor how he should handle the drafting of a will between himself and his brother for his father's property rights. "Friend, who made me a judge over you to decide such things as that?" (Luke 12:14) Shocking, that God in the flesh would relinquish his ability to preside over and pontificate a provision of the matter. Instead, Jesus indicates through his action and seeming inaction, that he believes deeply in the human freedom. In the same Gospel chapter, Jesus remarks to a crowd: "Why can't you decide for yourselves what is right?" (Luke 12: 57) Exacerbating the trying nature of, yet ultimately positive outcome of fitness is one means to an end of championing true freedom.

"So if the Son sets you free, you are truly free." (John 8:36).

July 24th:

Being a Light in the Darkness through Christ for Others A fitness success story can inspire many others to reach for their goals in a multitude of ways. Especially for those who have a proverbial 'high mountain' to climb in losing weight or excess body fat, we honor such people for having the self-discipline to show restraint in diet and persistent consistency in working out. As Jesus said, "Let your light shine before others, so that they may see your good works and give glory to your Father who is in heaven." (Matthew 5:16; ESV).

Siphiwe Saleka, a Harvard university graduate who also had Olympic aspirations in swimming, had gained many pounds and saw his health decline after becoming a truck driver. In the unique course of his personal life and exercise journeys, Saleka designed a 13-week program and began implementing it to improve fitness and well-being for professional truck drivers commenting that "I'll have people confess they're embarrassed to exercise in front of others. 'I'm 270 pounds. What if folks see me doing burpees and make fun of me?'" (217) Albeit tragically, even professional athletes or Olympians face the facet of consternation and mocking over their performance. However, Saleka posits the ultimate motivation for helping one's own, or others in their desires to improve health, "What if they see you and think, 'Hey, if he can do it, maybe I can too?' I say to them, 'Why not set a healthy example and be a light like Scripture asks of all of us?'" (217). This stance echoes Jesus' instructions to, "Use your worldly resources to benefit others and make friends." (Luke 16:9)

July 25<u>th</u>:

Perception of Threat and Its Ensuing Motivation to Start Moving Forward The instinct of survival plays a role in exercise program adherence and consistency. In fact, a lack of some type of 'fear' preceding a pending experience implies that we are not properly aroused to meet the challenge that a workout or game experience should infer.

Jesus' death transcended physicality, as brutally damaging as it was to His flesh. So also, danger arouses the acute heightening of the senses when lifting weights or running. The boy who performed a dangerous rescue in a true article written by C.H. Claudy, beautifully annotates how a spiritual identity overrode the hurting his body underwent. "As the fright in a measure subsided, my body ached in protest against the strained position of the muscles; and then I suddenly forgot pain." (107). Tapping into these elite and vast aquifers of fortitude bubbles up from our faith in God, and illustrates that if we are following His will, we can tamp down the forces of fear in any daily enterprise.

Although not exclusive to fitness or war situations, FDR referenced these aspects of valor in his D-Day address to America. "Our sons, pride of our nation, have set upon a mighty endeavor, a struggle to preserve our civilization…Their road will be long and hard, but we shall return again and again, and we know that by Thy grace, and by the righteousness of our cause, our sons will triumph." (105).

"Remain in fellowship with Christ so that when he returns, you will be full of courage and not shirk back from him in shame." (1 John 2:28)

<u>July 26<u>th</u>:</u>

The Question on Everyone's Mind: Is there a Formula for Extreme Growth? In an interesting twist of events, after John the Baptist is imprisoned by Herod, his disciples report to him about the Messiah's activities. Although John knew Jesus to be the Christ and had himself baptized the Savior, he sent these same disciples back to Jesus to ask him, "Are you the Messiah we've been looking for and been expecting, or should we keep looking?" (Luke 7:19). Jesus' response is also fascinating in that he doesn't give a flat-out yes-or-no answer. "Then he told John's disciples, 'Go back to John and tell what you have seen and heard.'" (Luke 7:22)

Perhaps Jesus did not give a one-worded response because he knew how personal and individualistic faith is. Also, Jesus knew his words would reverberate throughout the following generations and did not want to alienate any possible future believers. Finally, Jesus was aware that talk is cheap and so he mentioned phenomena that were observable for proof. So also, a fitness guru or even a professor cannot surmise and dispense information in an algebraic equation such as: three sets of ten reps for squats done three times a week will cause you to gain three pounds of muscle in the lower body. Jesus was certainly not overconfident and felt no compulsion to assert his factual superiority to mankind, although when he did at times it was for our good. Comparable to how spiritual faith in Christ grows mysteriously, Dr. Covert Bailey sums up the strength training apparatus built into humans by saying, "Only a few maximal or near maximal contractions a day are necessary for muscle growth." (218)

July 27<u>th</u>:

Lead-Up Skills to Ambulation and the Greatest Trial Ever Conceived Standing up sturdily as a baby is a momentously difficult task and developmental milestone. Many lead-up skills such as sitting, creeping and crawling must be divined before a young child garners the strength and balance necessary to walk. The toddler eventually has to take a leap of faith and just go for it.

So also, Jesus was in great distress on Holy Thursday evening while residing at the Garden of Gethsemane. "He (Jesus) was in such agony of spirit that his sweat fell to the ground like great drops of blood," BUT – "At last he stood up again." (Luke 22:44-45). I believe the main point of including this aspect in the story of the Gospel is that he mustered up the courage to meet His fate head-on. The fact that we gain the audacity to ambulate and continue to take risks in movement toward God's will when his arrest was inevitable, helps us draw upon the supreme example of courage that Christ exhibited when standing up to meet fate at that particular pre-ordained point in time.

July 28th:

It is Not Awkward to Allocate Time and Emotion in Fitness and Faith To make exercise convivial and consistent, you must become comfortable with being uncomfortable. Jesus and the cross offend people and stir up dissension, just as he predicted he would. "Don't imagine that I came to bring peace to the earth!" (Matthew 10:34). Exercise disrupts both the figurative and literal peace that healthy humans experience at rest.

Perhaps because exercise is serious and we wish to be unflappable for its duration so that we can flesh out our resolve and justify our 'power'- it causes discomposure. Yet our attitude can remain lighthearted in our minds and hearts because we are thankful for the ability to move unhindered that many handicapped persons would give almost anything to excise their predicament which prevents them from doing so.

Similarly, following God and purveying repentance publicly causes conviction of self over sin and can result in a social display of embarrassing emotion, fear and cringing. Jesus' words seem harsh to a man he provoked to follow him who had just lost a father. "Let the spiritually dead bury their own dead! Your duty is to go and preach about the Kingdom of God." (Luke 9:60). Yet this type of raw and sincere faith is what God desires, even demands, and is undoubtedly developed from facing hardship of exercise.

July 29th:

Letting Go of Self to Enjoin Aid to Others and Thereby Your Own Best Interests In every workout you do, you essentially are prefacing a growth in strength (and arguably additionally in authentic arduous faith too by essentially mimicking Christ) with an example of weakness. You are always weaker in the present tense (meaning –

current workout), than you will be following its conclusion or during successive sessions to come. The detailed process is laid out revealingly by Dr. Ellington Darden: "Before muscular growth is complete, overcompensation must occur...strength not only recovers to your previous level of 100 pounds, but it must increase...Your fatigued muscle compensates back to 100 pounds, and then overcompensates to 101, 102, or even 103 pounds of strength. (245).

Christ also had to become weak prior to receiving the endowment of his contemporary full authoritative power. "Christ is not weak when he deals with you; he is powerful among you. Although he was crucified in weakness, he now lives by the power of God." (2 Corinthians 13:3-4). We follow his life authorship plan when we partake of this exercise cycle without succumbing to temptation of believing the superficial lie that strength means we are reigning sovereign over our lives. In this manner, we do not succumb to what can materialize as a "vicious cycle." Rather, we can indent the arcing and circularly re-traceable pattern of Satan (in that he tempts all in the eldest of sins using the newest of methods) by persevering simply to continue facing each day in the struggle of life that can become exasperating at times.

<u>July 30th</u>:

He did it all for You, he did it all for Everyone Jesus was no Pollyanna. The most detailed depiction of his crucifixion in art, media, or literature doesn't come close to doing justice to the horrific nature of the event. Also, scholars estimate that the crossbeam that Jesus carried on the way to Golgotha weighed approximately 125 pounds. (254). Can you imagine carrying uphill a standard 45-pound barbell with 40-pound plates on each side that you typically use to bench press or squat, mounted for an extended period of time on your neck, back and shoulders?

It was indeed Christ's passion originating from love in his heart that kept him from becoming cumbersome to death or not fulfilling all of the Father's pain-based obligations so that we could be cleansed by his blood. In an indirect way, you can say that Jesus rejoiced in his suffering because he knew that through that event, we would be freed from the penalty of sin. In a similar manner, as Jesus displayed courage, we can find meaning and enjoyment from our work, and also/ especially from toil that may seem like drudgery, but entails micro-sieving our musculoskeletal system for its own betterment. "There is nothing better for a person than that he should...find enjoyment in his toil. This also, I saw, is from the hand of God." (Ecclesiastes 2:24; ESV).

Jesus' fate was non annullable, but we have the power to influence our soul's health through fitness. Jesus is our brother in the 'church of iron' because he experienced the raw despotism of lifting a heavy object, but for us and not his own personal improvement. In this way, we can become closer to him by following his lead in adhering to God's law and lifting. Although not a commandment from God, I believe we please him when we workout and never give up to discouragement, in much the same way as the ancient Latin prayer 'Anima Christi' alludes to, "Passion of Christ, strengthen us." (253).

"For to this you have been called, because Christ also suffered for you, leaving you an example, so that you might follow in his footstep." (1 Peter 2:21).

The Thought Blueprints Become Reality in Body Building In the context of chronic fitness, we are better off in health and are better people at the conclusion of a workout session than we were preceding it. Just as context in reading is important – as the previous sentence can ascribe a different meaning to its successor – increased strength means you can amplify the load, type of exercise, amount of repetitions, or time of rest between sets, because of previous hard work in the weight room extoling you get to this point.

So also, God's word is literally alive and a dynamic document in the power it holds and how it can affect a life. "For the word of God is living and active." (Hebrews 4:12a; ESV). The second adjective listed (active) means that the Bible is still as relevant and powerful as ever. In being 'active,' the Greek word implies a gush of energy emitted. Each time we read and do what the Bible says, we are better off than we were prior to that obedient act being carried out. But more than just the physical outpouring of energetic substances, the Bible is, "Piercing to the division of soul and of spirit." (Hebrews 4:12b; ESV). I don't know about you, but I had always thought the soul and spirit were the same beings. To delineate between the two compositions gives personification to thought life and heart attitude which ultimately drives us to follow Christ's example (as he was the word that became flesh), in keeping our bodies lively or 'active' in all means of Christian service, spiritual growths and fitness conduits.

August: The Refining Fire – Overcoming Adversity

<u>August 1<u>st</u></u>:

Contending With and Yielding to Our Creator A fascinating nugget of truth is found in the Book of Ecclesiastes: "To increase knowledge only increases sorrow." (Ecclesiastes 1:18) Why would the act of increasing knowledge, which God states the attainment of in other Biblical passages to be good (Proverbs 2:10), result in a negative effect? The link between striving to attain goals and grief can be seen in exercise. The better the body that we attain through hard work, the more we pursue greater achievements. Knowledge of how to properly workout only induces a craving for that which we have not yet conquered or accomplished in the fitness sphere.

I believe that God instilled this type of passion in every human being in some form or fashion. Everyone strives to be the best he or she can be in a work field, educational capacity, athletic endeavors, or other specific goals. God confirms this earlier stated truth regarding knowledge and sorrow by saying that we even try to compete with Him. God states: "My Spirit will not strive with man forever, for he is indeed flesh." (Genesis 6:3; NKJV)

It is healthy to keep an accurate account of our relationship with God, through physical labor and our extrinsic actions that are born from faith. Dr. Herbert Benson, who is a professor at Harvard Medical School, says of these public and/ or private displays of outward action, "Adding strong belief to meditative prayer may trigger even more potent natural healing through the additional release of certain chemicals in the brain and nerve cells." (137) Dr. Benson elaborates further that he, "Does not rule out the possibility that healings may also occur through outside, divine intervention." (137). What an encouraging fact: that godly knowledge and true, pure hard work can yield natural and supernatural results.

<u>August 2<u>nd</u></u>:

The Authenticity God Desires and People Respect Exercise begets a certain humility not bestowed upon the participator in any other facet of life, leading to a sincerity of personality. Only prayer or defeating a personal illness is likely to impart this humble attitude in the same manner or above the level that physical activity bestows. Deep repentance gives this authenticity and forms/molds in us into acquiring the attitude God desires. An example of this occurs in the life of David, pleading for God's mercy to intervene in his life and save himself and fellow countrymen. "'I'm in a desperate situation!' David replied to the Lord. But let me fall into the hands of the Lord. So…the Lord relented." (1 Chronicles 20:13, 15)

Jethro Kloss postulates that outdoor bodily exertion gives: "buoyancy and strength, and maintains a healthful mental balance, free from the extremes resulting from artificial life." (140) God also suggests that the acquisition of fitness levels yields subconscious benefits of persona in the New Testament: "In the Lord your labor is not in vain." (1 Corinthians 15:58) Obviously, the word labor alludes to many activities/ facets of life, but includes the practice of working out regularly, and being genuine in our personal interactions with others.

The physiological responses to exercise are robust and plentiful, but only partially understood in their mechanisms. For example, there are aspects of exercise we do not have conscious control over no matter how hard we work, such as nerve signals sent via saltatory conduction. The value of heart and inner drive is inestimable, and former President Calvin Coolidge elaborates on the development of this trait, which exercise can help give (self-esteem/ confidence) in saying, "Nothing in the world can take the place of persistence. Persistence and determination alone are omnipotent." (141)

<u>August 3<u>rd</u>:</u>

The Contentious Blessings of Labor Exercise carries with it the contention of multiple rewards. Job refers to both the humanly and divine capacity built-in a person when he remarks to his friends: "My strength is continually renewed." (Job 29:20). What is fascinating about this literary nugget is that Job is philosophizing on his blessings of a previous day, while simultaneously experiencing as great a struggle as any person in history has (only outflanked by Christ). We know that Job had tremendous financial, familial, and bodily health blessings. If Job could count his blessings in a calamity, it makes sense that working out could instill a deeper appreciation for the good gifts that God imparts.

God has ordained the laws governing the resulting exercise capaciousness. By convalescing through fatigue, conditioning develops in the participant's true grit. Norman Vincent Peale refers to this quality and disposition by saying, "The secret of life isn't what happens to you but what you do with what happens to you." (142) We should take a healthy amount of pride in our fitness accomplishments because, "People should enjoy the fruits of their labor." (Ecclesiastes 3:13)

<u>August 4<u>th</u>:</u>

Does Being a Man Entail or Require Fighting? In the movie Troy, Achilles tells his cousin and warrior-protégé Patroclus, "I taught you how to fight but I never taught you why." Achilles is a fascinating character in literature, combining history with what is most likely myth. The ramifications of his statements are perplexing and dichotomous as well. The aforementioned discussion ultimately leads to Patroclus' death at the hand of the Trojan prince Hector.

The author of The Iliad, the ancient oral tradition extraordinaire

Homer, knew even in a pre-Christian era that there was a constant struggle between good and evil. This discernment from Homer led him to expound on many themes in his literature of how divinity interweaves through the physical world and human life on earth. This tangible world implies the same 'physical' meaning as is protracted in exercise and bodily work.

It requires heart and true grit to stay in the eternal war on the side of godly/biblical morals. Paul references this fact in his second letter to Timothy. "I have fought the good fight, I have finished the race." (2 Timothy 4:7) William J. Bennett waxes eloquently on the theme of continued eternal war and how we should conduct ourselves in service to God. "You have to be able to recognize when the time is right to fight, and then you have to know how to get through the tough times. Courage in adversity is half the battle, but it does not always win the battle. We are always in the forge, or on the anvil; by trials God is shaping us for higher things." (151)

Exercise can act as a brace by aiding us in acquiring and maintaining a taut backbone when we confront evil head-on and stay true to our deep-seated convictions stemming from faith.

August 5<u>th</u>:

Exercise Strips to Bare Authenticity Ben Franklin posited the axiom, "What you would seem to be, be really." (154) Authenticity of personality is a contagion to pride because you do not feel the need to charm anyone when in possession of a clear conscience and secure identity. One of the most physically and mentally rigorous preparatory situations, that of West Point, echoes this sentiment in its cadet prayer so that students there may winnow out the superfluous elements, "Suffer not our hatred of hypocrisy and pretense ever to diminish." (97) Sincerity of actions is an antidote to that hypocrisy that Jesus faced, opposed, and taught others to guard against in their lives too. "And why worry about a speck in your friend's eye, when you have a log in your own? Hypocrite! First get rid of the log in your own eye." (Matthew 7: 3, 5)

During a workout, there is no faking a true identity when the fatigue of workout alarm sets in. Will you respond to the demands? Without the proper effort, barbells, dumbbells, and weight stacks will not overcome their static position of zero inertia on their own. You cannot make weight lifting and strength training a dramaturgical display or vaudeville showing. It takes sufficient energy and application of continuous disciplined forces to move the weight, for which the origination of volition springs in our internal core belief system. When the veritable personality is rooted in Christ's example, others spot this radiance easily.

"Jesus led them up a high mountain by themselves. And he was transfigured before them, and became radiant." (Mark 9:2; ESV)

<u>August 6<u>th</u>:</u>

Do Tests and Temporary Damage to Muscles Fortify the Soul? In order for strength and hypertrophy gains to become maximal, the overload placed on engaged muscle fibers must be of a high enough percentage of maximal force/ intensity to elicit microtrauma. The damage to the muscle must be sufficient so that repairs can be made to enlarge preexisting muscle fiber. The referenced area of conflict in the body due to structural derangement is known as the Z lines that, "Lend stability to the entire structure. They may also play a major part in the relaying of nerve impulses." (158)

God can cause distortions of pleasantness in our lives in order to 'test' us. Actually, this disturbance is proof of God's love. In order to prune us to produce more fruit from a vessel that already yields a bountiful return, God does what is analogous to the cellular process of becoming bigger and stronger. "He prunes the branches that do bear fruit so they will produce even more. You have already been pruned and purified by the message I (Jesus) have given you." (John 15:2-3)

King David even precipitously calls out for God to initiate this refining process. "Test me and know my anxious thoughts." (Psalm 139:23)

<u>August 7<u>th</u></u>:

Does Stress in Moderation Have Healing Ability? We grow stronger through some aspects of stress; specifically exercise eustress, which yields fitness and health results. Because it takes a concerted effort and consistent dedication to obtain these benefits, they are that much more appreciated. Thomas Paine elucidates the positive nature of these rewards, while also figuratively alluding to God-given spiritual aspects of faith growth. "What we obtain too cheap, we esteem to lightly: it is dearness only that gives everything its value." (160)

It is not selfish or narcissistic to desire a fit body and achievement of optimum health. It is also humanly natural to want to reap rewards that we will not acquire until the next life. The physical trials we endure from exercise prepare us to withstand hard times and to never give up the quest of attaining eternal value.

"So when your faith remains strong through many trials, it will bring you much praise and glory and honor on the day when Jesus Christ is revealed to the whole world." (1 Peter 1:7)

<u>August 8<u>th</u></u>:

God Causing Your Spirit a Kinesthesia Means he Has an

Eye on you for Good Purposes Many fitness and rehabilitation experts recommend performing exercises on an unstable surface that the feet come in contact with to enhance balance. Balance is a performance-oriented aspect of fitness that is vital in sports and not always easy to restore via post-injury rehab protocols. Armed with this knowledge, it is important to remember, according to motor control expert Dr. Mark Latash that "Humans become aware of balance only when it is seriously endangered." (177) For example, hiking on uneven terrain (with undulations) increases the lower body's capacity for correcting a variation in one's center of gravity, making it more efficient in handling unforeseen perturbations when walking or performing other synchronized multi-joint movements. "Any displacement of a joint creates elastic forces that resist the displacement." (177)

In our spiritual walks, God tests us with modulations in our plans, both minute and complex/ long-reaching. It is tough when going through adversity as it can be confounding, but in reality, we should revel in the fact that God counts us worthy of enduring trials.

"God tested Abraham's faith… 'Take your son, your only son – yes Isaac…Go and sacrifice him as a burnt offering'." (Genesis 22:1-2)

"For everyone will be tested with fire." (Mark 9:49)

August 9th:

Temporary Pain Gives Way to Lasting Rewards "We are children of God…provided we suffer with him in order that we may also be glorified with him." (Romans 8:17 – ESV)

Exercise can be a means to an end. The act encompasses suffering in that the body is tested with mental and sensory anguish. The fact that the Bible compels us to 'suffer' denotes the importance that

God places on humans facing earthly tribulations.

I recall seeing an advertisement in a football magazine for Marine Corps recruiting that stated, "Pain is weakness leaving the body." The recruiting tool is itself a wise motivational aphorism and rhetorical paradigm for potential military servicemen/ women that winnows to the core of inner strength and perseverance through trying circumstances.

Methodologically, this broad sense of unambiguous rousing is only one way in which exercise brings us closer to Christ. In addition, it points to a promise of eternal/ heavenly glory accrued in this earthly shell.

<u>August 10th:</u>

Gaining Courage Because the Incomparable Reward Exists in the Next Life Solomon employs a useful metaphor to juxtapose the injustices of this life along with seeming incongruence of spiritual matters. To make this point, the author of Ecclesiastes shows that continued effort displayed in the example of physical prowess, despite not knowing what the final end result will be, will ultimately develop into answers in a faith-walk and be rewarded in the end by God, if not also in this world. Using a lament in order to illustrate that this life is not fair because we live in a fallen world which brings on many frustrations, the wise king of Israel said: "The fastest runner does not always win the race, and the strongest warrior doesn't always win the battle." (Ecclesiastes 9:11)

On the canvas of physicality in football and its demonstrative emphasis on building practical bodily perseverance, the directors of the strength and conditioning program at Nebraska say that heart or courage is many times a paragon of virtue exceeding raw athletic ability. Coaches often give starting positions to, "The one who is the most persistent and most determined in his pursuit of a spot on the team. We consistently see players who come in as freshmen with less ability than other players, but eventually earn more playing time than their more talented teammates." (201)

While we don't have to aim to purposely face persecution, it may happen, because the author of our faith has faced it. Seeing physical results from exercise helps us to quell the anger that can ignite in our hearts at the unfairness in our lives because God's ultimate nature encompasses fairness. While results in this world can be palpable, failure should not depress us into quitting, but spur us on to sanguinity and pressing ahead to exceed others' expectations and our own.

August 11th:

Every Repetition Counts, Every Action is Preceded by a Decision While each workout counts as a major accomplishment, consistency is the key in returning to the seeming tedium of all repetitions and undertakings of successive days to achieve fulfilling results. Fitness affords us with a forward-leaning vision for how we will improve and reach our literal life-altering goals. It is worth noting that God impels us not to rest on our laurels, in a great example of speaking to the disciples after witnessing the very ascension of Christ. "Men of Galilee, why are you standing here staring into heaven? Jesus has been taken from you, but someday will return in the same way you saw him go!" (Acts 1:11)

The disciples could have been left discouraged believing they didn't do enough for God, or even indignant that the angels failed to recognize the gravity of their faith and how much they had sacrificed previously to follow Jesus. Instead of birthing a bad attitude, Christ's followers were motivated just like we feel today in completing a bout of exercise or the realization of the Gospel's power hitting us head-on: looking forward to the future gains and the resulting forces our dreams demand.

In a similar proposition, a dialogue takes place between the leaders in The Fellowship of the Ring. After Gandalf's fall, Aragorn focuses on pressing on to the dismay of his comrades:

Aragorn: Legolas, get them up!

Boromir: Give them a moment for pity's sake!

Aragorn: By nightfall these hills will be swarming with orcs!... We must reach the woods of Lothlórien. (234)

Kinesiology ignites a fire in the heart that pushes us forward in our ideals of spreading the Gospel and fostering a sonorous faith.

August 12<u>th</u>:

Exercise can Brace us Against the Tumultuous Vicissitudes of Triumph and Tragedy You don't have to show a plethora of emotion while working out to get results. Regardless of your body language (aside from keeping mechanically good posture throughout the lift), gains in fitness are not dependent upon paroxysms being extradited in a gregarious outward showing. In one sense, weight training can help us overcome lust and sexual immorality by teaching us how to corral our urges and direct them into proper godly channels. "But if there is no urgency and he can control his passion, he does well not to marry." (1 Corinthians 7:37).

I once heard a pastor say that the 'shoes' referred to regarding the armor of God were really spiked stabilizers that allowed infantry soldiers in old style of hoplite (large shield) warfare to face the onslaught of the coming army in a defensive manner. Therefore, many of the struggles we face need to be conquered by quelling feverish urges of the moment, regardless of the form of sin. "Stand your ground...For shoes, put on the peace that comes from the Good News so that you will be fully prepared." (Ephesians 6:14-15).

In an interesting case study of this seeming stoicism, Joseph put his ultimate trust in God despite his desperate situation. It is likely that Joseph's healthy diet and a rigorous daily regimen which developed his body and thus allowed him to deal with his problems with powerful rulers of Egypt. The Jewish historian of antiquity – Josephus – detailed this attitude of Joseph in the following manner: "He demonstrated that wisdom was able to govern the uneasy passions of life." (241). In the same way, we can grow our poise and piety through the self-control that exercise imparts.

<u>August 13<u>th</u>:</u>

Rise Like A Warrior in the Fight Against Satan the Feign In many lower body exercises such as the squat and deadlift, the objective of the lift is literally to stand up straight and tall. God also uses this phrase and metaphor to equipoise elevating ourselves from earthly dispositions into a state of accord with the Father. Jesus exemplifies this facet of unshakeable fortitude, but only after petitioning for a free pass from the cross. "Abba, Father, all things are possible for you. Remove this cup from me." (Mark 14:36; ESV). Notice that Jesus' statement is not a request, for there is no question mark at the end of the sentence. Therefore, Jesus made a demand that the crucifixion not take place, making his next statement: "Rise, let us be going see, my betrayer is at hand," (Mark 14:42; ESV) even more staggeringly brave in that he knew the end was at hand, yet with no hesitation continued in fighting on.

Obedience and submission that God wants from us are not synonymous with resignation of all volitional faculties. The act of rising up against the frowns and flatteries of this life takes fleshly and messy gumption. Jesus rose up to confront the forces of darkness, and when we fall, we can follow his example of standing up straight and tall in the arena of exercise, as well as gloating over our unseen enemies. When this takes place, you can feel the intrathecal pressure increase in the abdominal cavity as a physical sign that spiritual strength is swelling and surging to new levels of power. Jesus' courage becomes yours not as an example, but in present tense transubstantiation, "For though I fall, I will rise again. Though I sit in darkness." (Micah 7:8)

August 14th:

A Price Was Paid – Freedom is Never Free When we face the 'slings and arrows of outrageous fortune' in exercise goals by not obtaining a model's physique, not increasing our bench press one repetition maximum by 50 pounds quickly, or not dropping a minute from our fastest mile time expediently, reality smacks us as the heartache protrudes into the soul with potent poignancy. However, when we look back on seasons of life with fondness, it is often the difficult times that give us the most intense feelings of nostalgia.

Keep in mind the seeming latent yet prophetic verse that exalts Christ before he ever became human: "I will make him my firstborn son, the mightiest king on earth. I will love him and be kind to him forever." (Psalm 89:27-28). How striking it is that prior to this realization of a position of power, the Father's love also encapsulated sending Jesus to endure the physicality of literal torture. Jesus was made a prisoner of war – the eternal war – and in descending to hell so won the fight against Satan that we don't have the strength to muster an expression of self-defense against.

Jesus even questioned – privately to Peter, James, and John – why he had to face the ultimate moral dilemma: being burdened by every sin committed on his strikingly divine-less form of sinewy soma. "And how is it written of the Son of Man that he should suffer many things and be treated with contempt?" (Mark 9:12; ESV). Jesus recognized injustice and pointed it out; even as we still face the bewildering beckoning of the eldest of sins presented in the newest of ways. When we look back at how far we've come in fitness pursuits, it is the overcoming of our calumny the enemy tries to exploit, that exfoliates the superficial unveiling the fondest of memory perceptions. The ultimate victory is Christ's defeat of these evil elements, but bear in mind; even Jesus had to be humbled first.

<u>August 15th</u>:

An Ellipsis That Christ Endured so he Could Identify with us
When talking with a friend who had just finished boot camp for the Army as well as OCS (officer candidate school), I asked him how he toughed out the grueling physical exercise (known in military circles as simply 'PT') aspects that take place in the ten weeks of its duration. He replied that you just had to learn to 'embrace the suck.'

So it is in exercise that you have to give a literal and figurative 'piece' of yourself to improve. The terminology used in this context encompasses reference to the combustion of fat cells burned off in the physical sense. In intellectual properties this diction refers to becoming property of the US government/ military and succumbing (or a better word to describe the courage and self-sacrifice given by our veterans would be welcoming), to the fact that you will lose your rights temporarily in addition to putting your very life on the line so that others can live in peace and plentitude. Many servicemen/ women cite the verse of John 15:13 as to reasons for motivation to take on such a monumental, influential and important task.

God is not unable to identify with our calamities, for he created the very world that would later collaborate trying hardships with blunt force into the fleshed human world. In fact, Philip Yancey goes so far as to say that this grappling with the spiritual holiness of God and reconciling it to a fallen world we face every day with its problems is a sign of strong faith and evidence that God is at work even today in each person's singular subjective experiences. "We may not get the answer to the problem of pain we want from Jesus. We get instead the mysterious confirmation that God suffers with us." (247). Imagine, the discomfort we feel in exercise and the mentality it takes to subdue it was experienced by God. In the same breath, we encounter exercise training as a means of embracing a struggle that helps us put off the old man and our former ways to rid ourselves of avarice and cowardice.

"For you have been given not only the privilege of trusting in Christ but also the privilege of suffering for him." (Philippians 1:29)

August 16ᵗʰ:

Fostering A Gift in Flesh that is not Feathered James 1:17 tells us that when we feel compelled to act or, 'know what to do' and not follow through - it is a sin. Could it be argued that not taking stewarded care of our earthly form and subsequent behavior falls into that category? The founding fathers propounded that freedom did not just exist in the theoretical sense of being left alone by the government, but in having the ability to the 'free exercise thereof.' These modes imply freedom of worship, assembling in fellowship with our brothers in a peaceful way, voting for our leaders, and speaking unhindered without threatening the safety of others.

In the same way, fitness is an 'exercise' (pun intended) of knowing what to do and following through by acting. In one sense, Paul refers to an otherworldly aspect that working corporally imparts by being an example to others and earning an honest living so that we can provide for our own means. "And I have been a constant example of how you can help those in need by working hard. You should remember the words of the Lord Jesus: 'It is more blessed to give than to receive.'" (Acts 20:35). In another sense, Paul seems to sense a synergistic synthesis of self-worth from working, and hearkens to a spiritual element in being able to aid another. Also elaborating on the former benefit of labor, true strength is surprisingly fleshly in simply weathering a storm, such as in allowing you to move forward with resiliency, just as we pick weights up, then put them down in a matter of fact manner but yet find meaning in the activity.

G.K. Chesterton alludes to how the physical can lead to the spiritual by implying that Jesus suffered as much or more in the bodily manner along with metaphysical degrees in order to recompense for our wrongs. The following poem focuses on how time did not stop or nature did not negate the physical pain for even the son of God, but the crickets kept chirping, and Jesus not only acquiesced, but was happy for future generations who would receive mercy.

"Men say the sun was darkened; yet I had

Thought it beat brightly, even on – Calvary:

And he that hung upon the Torturing Tree

Heard all the crickets singing, and was glad." (249).

August 17th:

Exercise is gritty, not glamorous. Angela Duckworth, in her research, concluded that grit (a hard to measure/ quantify attribute) was the most important commodity in predicting K-12 academic success and graduation rates for cadets at West Point. At the same time, human participles of participation can only be exaggerated to a certain extent. At some point, we must relinquish hegemony to God to get the best out of this life and an assurance of salvation. "The Spirit alone gives eternal life. Human effort accomplishes nothing." (John 6:63).

If we are not gaining a translucent vantage point of our soul-health and strengthening the spiritual existence in our workouts, we are missing the point.

You cannot hustle your way into a deeper faith, earn salvation based upon exuberant exercise, or gain a meaningful marriage from fomenting muscle contraction. There is nothing sexy about leg pressing 500 pounds, and a female is not going to be attracted to marriage based on watching you bench press a heavy weight. The lack of congruency between espousing effort and results in matters such as these or answers to prayer can be frustrating.

But the advantages of trying with toil and results in these aspects of life experiences are complementing and not contradictory in a deeper analysis. Combining the two qualities leads to confidence and merit in all aspects of comportment and inner heart/ feelings life – a much more prized proposition than if these two factors were mutually exclusive. Dr. Cooper sums up the situation well by stating, "Intrinsic belief has the capacity to spark major personal enrichment in every area of life – including dramatic improvements in physical health, emotional well-being, and levels of fitness." (255). What comes from within, manifests in a fleshly form of behavior during a game or training session.

<u>August 18th</u>:

Is it Beneficial to Run or Lift with a Chip on Your Shoulder? It was said of Michael Johnson by commentators at the Olympics of 1996, that he ran with a chip on his shoulder. He said he tried to 'run angry.' You could see the tangible evidence through manifestation in his visage of furrowed eyebrows and narrowed glance immediately prior to, and during his sprinting (200-meter dash) and glycolysis activation (400-meter run). Exercise can help us control anger. Envisioning others as a threat can work in athletics, but off the field/ court/

track, was the competitor just your brother all along? This beast-like perspective can help us advance in life, and need not be suppressed, but diverted into positive application of energy to educate and train youth for following Christ's example. He bore the very anger of God at sin in his body, so that we might face God not as judge, but as loving Father. An anger management solution appears with blowing off the steam on the track or on the weighted implements. 'Control your temper, for anger labels you a fool." (Ecclesiastes 7:9).

August 19<u>th</u>:

Don't Let the Flame of Wonder and Ambition Be Extinguished
Exercise broadens our perspectives by reenergizing our youthful ambitions. When we are children, we all have big dreams. Along the way, we can get subdued by becoming pessimistic to the world's harsh ways. In young adulthood (defined as ages 18-35) it can become easy to fall into the privations of this world, but exercise gives us a feeling of accomplishment that we are capable of almost anything. When you manifest your thoughts of preceding exercise planning/ routines into a reality fleshed out during an exercise session, an indelible imprint is footed in our psyche that – maybe our childhood dreams weren't overly outlandish – and instills an innate sense of optimism. Don't lose the fire that God put into your heart, but rather, stoke the flames with the igniter of fitness as the crucible that refines us and makes us tempered in steadfastness of soul.

"Don't let anyone think less of you because you are young. Be an example to all believers in what you say, in the way you live, in your love, your faith, and your purity." (1 Timothy 4:12).

<u>August 20th</u>:

Overload Principle Encompasses Broad Spectrums The primary theoretical underpinning of any resistance training program is the overload principle. The overload principle states that the strength, endurance, and size of a muscle will increase only when the muscle performs/ contracts for a given period of time at a certain amount of its maximal strength and endurance capacity. The American College of Sports Medicine defines the phenomenon, stating that "For a tissue (in this case muscle fibers) to improve its function, it must be exposed to a load to which it is not normally accustomed." (195)

It is my belief that God gives to humans from His own hand a form of overload principle in our earthly endeavors: testing. Why we are being tested or the eventual fortuitous nature may be made clear later, or perhaps never (only to God or to us in eternity). Eventually, testing makes us better Christians as we can empathize with human sufferings. Also, in arcane ways, tests are different from temptations. When we stare down trials resolutely and conquer them, we are made stronger in God's sight as well as in our own notions of self-confidence.

"For you test us every moment." (Job 7:18)

"These trials will show that your faith is genuine. It is being tested as fire tests and purifies gold." (1 Peter 1:7).

<u>August 21st</u>:

Exercise Offers Contention to Egress Virtue Exercise is difficult and can be tedious at times. Exercise causes a certain amount of discomfort by temporarily disrupting the biological homeostasis that the body attempts to maintain. Horace, the Roman philosopher, once wrote, "Difficulties elicit talents that in more fortunate circumstances would be dormant." (4) Physical exertion can bring out the best in us by allowing us to surmount this form of difficulty.

"Physical training is good." (1 Timothy 4:8)

August 22ⁿᵈ:

Exercise's Effects are Inestimable until Acquiesced John Jay, a founding father of America once wrote in a letter: "The remark that we seldom estimate blessings justly till we are about to lose them for a time, or altogether, is, I believe, frequently true." (12) Usually, fitness gains and spiritual fire are lost slowly, almost in a conceding freefall, until the passion has left and a gray state is all that is left.

We never fully know or appreciate the impact fitness has on our bodies until we see corporal results. Even then, physiological changes occur at the cellular level that we don't know about. We do not fully comprehend the blessing that good health is until we have faced illness or incapacity. That we will face physical ailments as part of God's larger plan, which comes in the form of trials and testing is a certainty.

"Is not all human life a struggle? For you examine us every morning and test us every moment." (Job 7: 1; 18)

August 23ʳᵈ:

The Proof is in the Personification of Physicality St. Augustine of Hippo, a Latin Church priest, said this of God's response to man's supplications, "He gets it, however, only when he ought to receive it, for certain things are not refused us, but their granting is delayed to a fitting time." (24)

Augustine is obviously advocating a certain type of inner perseverance/ endurance in prayer life. Persistence in exercise that comes from an indomitable will and achieves physiologically noticeable results requires consistency. Paul compares the physical concept of a competitive race (or marathons would be more accurate analogous and concurrent with human experiences) to the exponentially summative experiences that we accumulate over a lifetime in our walks of faith.

"And let us run with endurance the race God has set before us." (Hebrews 12:1)

Exercise Affliction Will Fire up Fear of God Faith is not rational. When you ponder its meaning, exercise is logical in that we reap results, but not reasonable or rational. It is not rational to subject your body to the unforgiving laws of nature. Exercise tests these limits that nature puts on our bodies.

Exercise can prevent/ treat/ heal some chronic disease conditions, but people always think: 'It won't happen to me.' Fear is simply not a motivating emotion. Fear of God, however, results in a different reaction. For evidence of this, you only need to look as far as the dispersion of the Ten Commandments. In the presence of God, the people of Israel saw a cloud of smoke and lightning and were frightened.

Moses told them: "Don't be afraid, for God has come in this way to test you, and so that your fear of him will keep you from sinning." (Exodus 20:20)

August 25th:

It is no Shame to Suffer for Shunning Sin Injuries, setbacks, and plateaus are inevitable in strength, speed, and endurance training. It is natural to be confounded initially regarding the proper actions to take in order to process multiple theories of training, then to rectify the situation of staleness after original improvements. As the poet Robert Burns says in a poem that cries out to God in supplication:

"But, if I must afflicted be,

To suit some wise design,

Then man my soul with firm resolves,

To bear and not repine! (36)

We should not hold on to our sorrows for too long, lest we give in to the weapons of the enemy: self-pity and despair. Jesus never gave in to these tactics; instead, he always maintained hope in the promise that His Father would never abandon Him.

"Dear friends, don't be surprised at the fiery trials you are going through, as if something strange were happening to you. Instead – be very glad – for these trials make you partners with Christ in his suffering." (1 Peter 4:12)

August 26th:

The Benefit of Temporary Failure Exercise and athletic competition speaks to us in manners that no other occupational faculty can reach us through. This complex path exists in the fact that we experience a definite, black-and-white resolving of conflict upon cessation of a workout. Win or lose, we feel relief in knowing that the struggle has ended and we are better for having navigated it.

An example of this indomitable will being developed through another avenue of God's choosing is found in Job. Even though he was, as God said to Satan, "A man of complete integrity," he found himself looking for a clear-cut explanation as to why life can be tumultuous: "Is not all human life a struggle? Our lives are like that of a hired hand, like a worker who longs for the shade, like a servant waiting to be paid." (Job 7:1-2)

It is proper and fitting that the "struggle" that this life conjugates is compared to work. The truth of this simile exists since all exercise is also literally work, and a seeking of resolution to end the conflict physiologically inherently presented in and of itself.

August 27th:

The Inherent Value of Calamities The Psalmist wrote a sentence that should catch our attention: "Those who plant in tears will harvest with shouts of joy." (Psalm 126:5) Perhaps God embedded this lesson in Psalms to teach us that if there is no struggle or difficulty, there is no enhancement for an individual's singular expansion or of the human condition as a whole.

Happiness and peace of mind can be a result of exercise. When working out, we must mentally be able to block out all negative thoughts to focus on what we would like to achieve in the weight room, on the treadmill, or the specific mode of exercise we choose. If we are gloomy or weary, we still must feel the rush of adrenaline or butterflies in our stomach to get the proper benefit of a workout.

Frederick Douglas, the staunch American abolitionist, echoed the words of the Psalmist almost prophetically when he said in 1857 that "The whole history of the progress of human liberty shows that all concessions yet made to her august claims have been born of earnest struggle." (62)

The Logic Behind Exercise & Discomfort We have all heard the cliché phrases regarding the physiological status of brain and muscle tissue such as 'use it or lose it,' and 'rest = rust.' While there is an element of truth in these idioms, the relationship between exercise and faith goes much deeper.

Pain is a God-given sensation that occurs as an 'alert' signifying to us something has gone awry in our homeostatic physiology. You don't have to exercise to the point of pain to see results. However, pain with movement is sometimes unavoidable in the rehabilitation field. Recent useful research has concluded that "To date, there is no scientific evidence that activity and exercises are harmful, or that pain-inducing activity must be avoided." (111) On the contrary, the Bible states that we will experience pain in our lifetime, and even goes a step further in saying we should help shoulder the burden of our neighbors' pain: "Remember also those being mistreated, as if you felt their pain in your own bodies." (Hebrews 13:3)

Pain exists in many states, including mental and emotional. The physical nature of soreness from Z line muscle fiber disruption lets us know we have 'alarmed' our neuromuscular system and the motor units recruited to move the body. Pain lets us know and reminds us that we have an unspoiled/ unalterable eternal security with God in heaven, giving hope for the future. It is my belief that exercise affords us patience and a sense of hope in this truth of heaven: "There will be no more death or sorrow or crying or pain." (Revelation 21:4)

<u>August 29th:</u>

The Phenomenon of God-given Tests and Trials The term strength is not only a physical quality to be expressed. It also has a connotation of an indomitable will and perseverance. It is interesting that General Douglas MacArthur desired his son to exhibit, "the meekness of true strength." (124) Participation in fundamentally sound strength training actualizes resiliency and convalescence.

It is observable in the Bible that God ultimately uses trials to strengthen us. "For the Almighty has struck me down with his arrows. God's terrors are lined up against me." (Job 6:4) True character strength compels us to carry on even when the odds seem insurmountable. An example is when an athlete gets injured many times but carries on with rehabilitation and doesn't become bitter or resentful toward God. Dr. Kenneth Cooper elaborates on this strengthening process of the mind, body, and spirit. "Certainly, if we remain close to God through obedience, prayer, and other spiritual disciplines, his strength will flow into us. At the same time, it's incumbent that we take care of our bodies, including our muscles." (125)

The Bible says of Job that when the depths of his physical health was tested, despite being at the point of death, that he "Did not sin by blaming God." (Job 1:22) Obedience to an exercise program yields manifold blessings, but ultimately we should also observe spiritual exercises such as yielding to the will of God. "Listen! Obedience is better than sacrifice." (1 Samuel 15:22)

<u>August 30th:</u>

Being Transparent Forges a Bond in Shared Difficulties I had a lesson in humility taught to me by an Army Ranger during the setting of a weight lifting session. As coworkers at our job, we had downtime each day that we made use of by utilizing the rehab room equipment to workout on for approximately 60 minutes each day. We had previously maxed out (lifting the highest amount of weight for one repetition) on a bicep curl a week earlier and we both were at the same level on the weight stack for that amount.

I had always thought of myself as 'tough' from enduring the hot Texas high school football two-a-days. But during this context of lifting, I learned that there are people with more 'heart' or 'courage' than me. We set the weight stack at 70% of our max, and commenced to perform a set to failure. I thought I had done good lifting for 11 reps, but my friend followed me and gruelingly pushed out 20 reps. I was floored that his pain tolerance and willpower were way out of my league. Since we both had the same baseline strength amount on the exercise, the only available explanation was that my coworker was able to display more fortitude.

When humility presents itself, we can easily throw our hands up in dejection thinking that what we do does not matter or won't make a difference. Or, we can let the humbling nature of the experience spur us on to acquiring new and previously unattained virtues. During a lift, there are many ways we can broaden our horizons, and forge a bond of brotherhood.

"But a real friend sticks closer than a brother." (Proverbs 18:24)

August 31st.

The First Instance of Anti-Semitism and Its Kinesiological Resultant The ancient Hebrews faced many trials and adversities in their 40 years post-Egypt before inhabiting the promised land. The least of which was not their first battle experience, (with no military training mind you) against the Amalekites, who were described by Josephus as, "The most warlike of the nations that lived thereabout." (310). What happened as the conflict ensued is described more than adequately as kinesiology and the power of prayer taking hold of each other.

Josephus describes the vehement event as such: "So the armies joined battle; and it came to a close fight, hand-to-hand, both sides showing great alacrity. And indeed while Moses stretched out his hands towards heaven, the Hebrews were too hard for the Amalekites. But with Moses not being able to sustain his hands, thus stretched out (for as often as he let down his hands, so often were his own people worsted)…he bade his brother Aaron to assist him in the extension of his hands. When this was done, the Hebrews conquered the Amalekites by main force." (310).

A fascinating depiction of how God literally strengthened his own possession Israel in hand-to-hand combat. The use of kinesiology is employed in the earliest intimation of bodily movement or position in solemn prayer – with results! Still today, many people raise their hands when praising or reading from the text of the Bible. But perhaps even more noteworthy is the fact that the Hebrews gained courage knowing that war could only take their lives at worst, but not harm their souls! "And how valuable God's assistance is, they had experienced in abundance of trials; and those such as were more terrible than war, for that is only against men…yet had all these difficulties been conquered by God's gracious kindness to them." (310).

September: Persistence and the Power of Prayer

September 1ˢᵗ:

Physical Work Emboldens Our Walk of Faith Jesus' trade as a carpenter allowed him to place a high value on hard work and physical exertion. He likely faced personal and professional dilemmas with his family and patrons before He began His public ministry.

Thomas Paine quite possibly may have had Christ's example in mind in his exhortation for courage in his writing entitled the American Crisis: "I love the man who can smile in trouble, that can gather strength from distress, and grow brave by reflection." (160) Christ's work prepared Him for the insults, ridicule and false accusations He would face later on. On several occasions, Jesus paralleled the earthly physical lessons, such as the manual labor that accompanies farming, with spiritual anecdotes such as the kingdom of God.

"My nourishment comes from doing the will of God who sent me, and from finishing his work." (John 4:34)

September 2ⁿᵈ:

The Continuation of Faith in the Face of Wariness Muscular endurance and aerobic endurance are two separate entities, but equally important components of fitness. This dual nature of stamina is also of paramount value in an athletic setting of sports performance.

"But those who trust in the Lord will find new strength. They will run and not grow weary. They will walk and not faint." (Isaiah 40:31)

Notice that this scripture invokes the long-term activities of walking and running. The continuation of volition in the face of fatigue is vital and requires and indomitable will in sports and also in life. Certainly, every person feels weary at times, but like physical endeavors, if we rely on God, we can persevere through anything.

September 3ʳᵈ:

Discipline Embodied to Frame Christian Behavior Fitness teaches and develops forbearance through having to renewably motivate yourself by maintaining adherence to a preplanned program. Self-control is listed as a fruit of the Holy Spirit, and is one of the marks of a mature Christian. The patience created by and exhibited in chronic exercise compels us to choose a harder right over an easier wrong. Adherence to a designed exercise sequence teaches a certain abstaining quality from the temptations of this world.

"But the Holy Spirit produces this kind of fruit in our lives... self-control." (Galatians 5:23)

September 4ᵗʰ:

A Fire Set Ablaze in the Very Bones of Anatomy The Methodist minister E.M. Bounds once wrote: "True prayer is a working force, a divine energy that must come out, that is too strong to be still." (18)

Exercise affords a dissipation of energy into the external environment that otherwise would stay bottled up inside, flowing in the bloodstream. Lack of physical activity likely causes an angst that could be repealed by the utilization of substrate and the dissipation of activity hormones. The human body is approximately 20% efficient in converting ATP into energy. 20% of the fuel from foodstuffs is utilized as energy, while the remaining 80% is released as heat energy.

In the same way, prayer is an expression of and source of energy for our souls.

"Does not my word burn like fire?" says the Lord." (Jeremiah 23:29)

The Moment of Truth Many early Christians had the authenticity of their faith tested to the point of death. Marcus Aurelius – the Roman emperor, said of the martyrs in his only written reference to Christianity: "O for the soul that is ready at any moment to be separated from the body. This readiness must come from a man's own judgment, not from mere obstinacy, as with the Christians." (19)

Marcus Aurelius was mistaken that Christians derived their strength from obstinacy. Rather, it flowed from the wellspring of genuine faith.

Exercise cannot create this dogged/ persistent faith on its own, but if trust in Christ is preemptive, exercise can strengthen this faith and make it increasingly dynamic.

"For when we died with Christ we were set free from the power of sin. And since we died with Christ we were set free from the power of sin." (Romans 6:7-8)

The Proof is in the Personification of Physicality St. Augustine of Hippo, a Latin Church priest, said this of God's response to man's supplications, "He gets it, however, only when he ought to receive it, for certain things are not refused us, but their granting is delayed to a fitting time." (24)

Augustine is obviously advocating a certain type of inner perseverance/ endurance in prayer life. Persistence in exercise that comes from an indomitable will and achieves physiologically noticeable results requires consistency. Paul compares the physical concept of a competitive race (or marathons would be more accurate analogous and concurrent with human experiences) to the exponentially summative experiences that we accumulate over a lifetime in our walks of faith.

"And let us run with endurance the race God has set before us." (Hebrews 12:1)

September 7th:

Beyond the Patronizing Crowd and Into A Private Cavalier Faith A father once counseled his son on a certain aspect of maturing that: "We find a blessing upon charity when it is secret and unostentatious: that charity is best which exercises a spirit of discernment." (35)

This surreptitious attitude also proves true for the training you put in for a sport or fitness purposes. There will not always be a crowd/ audience to applaud you in the daily grind of working out. Many times the best results will come from hard work when no one is watching.

Similarly, Jesus taught His disciples that secret prayer yields the best results. "But when you pray, go away by yourself, shut the door behind you, and pray to your Father in private. Then your Father, who sees everything, will reward you." (Matthew 6:6)

<u>September 8th</u>:

The Undocumented Power of the Inner Life In an exercise program, as in all facets of life, we must remind ourselves constantly that as Henry Wadsworth Longfellow said, "Things are not what they seem." (56) There are many dramatic, life-altering effects of exercise that we are not even aware of. Atherosclerosis being reversed from a healthier vacillation of blood flow through a system of capillaries, vessels and main arteries is one example.

So also, being God's child causes us to take some turns we may not have anticipated or do not fully understand. In these cases, we should remember that God is ultimately in control. If we try to comprehend everything or make sense of it all, we might miss out on the subtle, lesser-recognized blessings that God bestows on us every day.

Jesus said: "Look below the surface so you can judge correctly." (John 7:24)

<u>September 9th</u>:

The Limits of Self-Reliance and Personal Strength Contretemps provide the impetus for change, the fuel needed to inspire thirst in a quest for God. Abraham Lincoln once remarked, "I have been driven many times to my knees by the overwhelming conviction that I had nowhere else to go. My own wisdom, and that of all about me seemed insufficient." (96) Experiencing a bout of misfortune can and should stand to reinforce an attitude of dependence on the Lord. In this manner, exercise mimics the effects of calamity in a positive manner.

Just as prayer rouses the spirit, exercise invokes an emotional stirring that is needed to complete a training bout or to finish a physically demanding game. Exercise can be a catalyst that makes us desire to know God on a deeper level.

Certainly, King David was a muscularly robust man, a consequence of training for battle. The women from Israel praised him upon his return from battle by saying, "Saul has killed his thousands, and David his ten thousands." (1 Samuel 18:7) And yet, David was wise enough to never rely on his strength alone. Regarding David's enterprises and eventual rise to king, God said to Samuel, the prophet in the selection process: "Don't judge by his appearance or height… So Jesse sent for him (David), and the Lord said, 'This is the one; anoint him.'" (1 Samuel 16:7; 2)

<u>September 10<u>th</u></u>:

Being On Fire for Christ The end result of prayer is that the soul is nourished. Much like the body is made stronger through the discipline of fitness literally and figuratively along with proper recovery/ nourishment, a spiritual act of feeding the soul takes place and in the invisible realm through prayer. Saint John Chrysostom described this happening in a homily by relating the earthly/ physical setting as proceeding up and into the eternal: "What it (the soul/ eternal) receives is better than anything to be seen in the world (earthly/ physical)." (101)

It is interesting to note that just as exercise literally emits energy as heat, God's Son allows us to reveal and project our true identity to the external environment. In the same sermon, Chrysostom states that: "Prayer is the light of the soul." (101) The fact that we can be lights in the darkness exists because Jesus lives in us. "The Spirit of God, who raised Jesus from the dead, lives in you." (Romans 8:11)

"No one lights a lamp and then covers it…A lamp is placed on a stand, where its light can be seen by all." (Luke 8:16)

September 11th:

The Inner Will in the Face of Danger The organic instinct of self-preservation plays a role in adherence level to an exercise program and attaining the level of 'maintenance' in the stages of change theory. The existence of danger elicits a heightened sense of awareness. President Franklin Delano Roosevelt put it candidly to the American people in a radio broadcasted speech on D-Day in 1944. Tapping into the prowess of Americans both domestically and abroad, knowing the vastness of difficulty for the enterprises that lay ahead, Roosevelt said dauntlessly: "Let not the keenness of our spirit ever be dulled." (105)

The same pugnacity is developed from exercise in an emotional and spiritual form. "As Dr. William Bennett says, "The virtues of battle – loyalty, bravery, and duty – make men immune to cowardice." (106) While this concept holds true physically, Scripture states that a step deeper and richer as meaning is conferred in terms of perseverance in a spiritually testing manner: "Can anything ever separate us from Christ's love? Does it mean he no longer loves us if we have trouble or calamity...or in danger, or threatened with death? No, despite all these things, overwhelming victory is ours..." (Romans 8:35-37)

An example of courage in adversity was given in a Boston Magazine named The Youths Companion: "Scientists will tell you that in moments of great and sudden danger, the instinct of self-preservation overcomes mere fear." (107) In summation, it is a fact and true notion that the force of faith is more powerful than the force of fear.

September 12th:

Fighting Smarter, Not Harder Knowing when and how to workout is an art as much as a science. We must concentrate our muscular/bodily efforts wisely to achieve results. This is true of fitness as well as facing calamities in life. Dr. Bill Bennet expounds on the relation-ship between godly wisdom and facing conflicts by drawing upon a higher/ proper/ intended power: "You have to be able to recognize when the time is right to fight, and then you have to know how to get through those tough times." (119)

Far too often, we focus on battles that are inconsequential in the long run. "They (Israel) have worn themselves out, but it has done them no good." (Jeremiah 12:13) Applying the proper force in a workout leads to an ability to practice and personify this practical wis-dom in everyday life.

But this type of fight is only half the battle. We must also battle the unseen qualities in the waging of warfare of the spiritual realm. "But if you don't believe me when I tell you about earthly things, how can you possibly believe if I tell you about heavenly things?" (John 3:12) In a blatant physicality allegory in the book of Jeremiah compar-ing the human to the spiritual dilemma facing Israel, God gives words to assimilate and ponder: "If racing against mere men make you tired, how will you race against horses?" (Jeremiah 12:5)

September 13th:

The Circular Pattern of Godly Vigilance Over time, exponen-tial fitness gains increase cardiac output both during exercise and at rest. Cardiac output refers to the amount of blood ejected from the heart into the circulatory system with each pump. Increased usage during exercise yields greater production and efficiency of the heart and circulatory system at all times. It is estimated that for persons who engage in physical activity (three times per week for 20 minutes at a moderate intensity), the heart will beat as much as 13 million times less per year than that of a sedentary person.

In our spiritual lives, our hearts need to be kept 'in-tune' to the moral wisdom antiquated in Biblical truth to work functionally and effectively. If we give our hearts over to an idol such as seeking vain-glory, temporal rewards, or lustful desires, we do not keep our heart in proper spiritual health. We must 'exercise' our hearts in the dual nature of the physical and spiritual contexts. Spiritually, this can only be accomplished by staying in the proper undefiled nature from the god of this world. Commitment requires holding true to convictions when temptations arise. Inclusion in this godly cyclical pattern occludes to us by spending time listening for God's voice in our daily lives.

The Book of Proverbs states that we should "keep your heart with all vigilance, for from it flow the springs of life." (Proverbs 4:23; ESV) Keeping in harmony with God means public displays of faith and an internal belief that provides a moral compass for daily guidance. Guarding our hearts makes us 'rulers' over our lesser and darker personality traits.

"And he who rules his spirit (is better) than he who takes a city." (Proverbs 16:32; ESV)

September 14th:

Workers in the Field Will Not Go Unnoticed or Unrewarded Persons working in the field of kinesiology and its specific disciplines have a great opportunity and obligation to be builders of what is characterized as the temple of the Holy Spirit. It is a transparent and highly visible responsibility for professionals in coaching, training, designing, demonstrating and lecturing in terms of instilling godly virtue into those they serve via what can be in nature at times - extreme physical discomfort or challenge.

In the subsequent cascade effect of one's actions, the result is giving God's love to others, creating a domino-falling aspect that spreads to our neighbor. The provider of 'temple-health' is blessed by seeing the fruit of their efforts empower others, which creates a chain of a bigger domino to each person influenced. Especially in children, the powerful experience of unadulterated fatigue when exercising reaches across age thresholds and teaches that if you can just hold onto that effort a bit longer until the conclusion of a game/ practice/ conditioning session, no goal you set is too difficult to accomplish and actualize through hard work. The power of pure unalloyed love cemented in observable effects is a causation that Christ said would be rewarded.

"And if you give even a cup of cold water to one of the least of my followers, you will surely be rewarded." (Matthew 10:42)

September 15th:

A Placid Solitude of Recuperation Relaxation time takes on a new meaning after a bout or a string of daily successive bouts of exercise. Jesus also needed time to himself, spent alone with His Father. Separate from the crowds and even His closest companions, the disciples, Jesus found restoration in the quiet solitude of nature. "But Jesus often withdrew to the wilderness for prayer." (Luke 5:16)

If God Himself incarnated as man needed recuperation, certainly athletes and fitness enthusiasts need to take breaks as well. A new and improved approach/ vigor can then be applied in full effort to working out after proper recovery. This recovery will take on a meaning that much fuller, because of the intense effort given to exercise. As Unitarian preacher William Ellery Channing says, "Ease, rest, owes its deliciousness to toil." (159) A lesson we all need indelibly stamped into our psyche: work hard, rest contently.

"On the seventh day God had finished his work of creation, so he rested from all his work. And God blessed the seventh day and declared it holy, because it was the day when he rested from all his work." (Genesis 2:2-3)

Can Prayer Be Properly Perpetrated With Kinesiology? Faith and fitness may be separate entities but can combine to make each other vitalized with birr. For example, it is proper to pray before a workout that it may go well and be beneficial. Prayer that is preparatory in nature prior to a fitness venture is just as proper in essence as it is to pray in trying times or before facing a stressful life event that prompts anxiety.

It is not sacrilegious to combine prayer with exercise. For example, you can focus on deep breathing while stretching and attempting to memorize a Biblical passage. To ascribe a deeper meaning to fitness, that enhances prayer life, or the strength of faith is totally plausible. R. Scott Kretchmar, Ph.D. elaborates on this theme by commenting that "When movement is experienced as joy, it adorns our lives, makes our days go better, and gives us something to look forward to. It may even inspire us to do things we never thought possible." (174)

"Pray about everything. Tell God what you need." (Philippians 4:6)

September 17<u>th</u>:

Do We Know the Means by Which Exercise Activates Spiritual Laws? Although the discipline of exercise science has pinned down in experimental inquiries the measures that govern muscle growth in size, strength, and endurance; prayer and our relationship with God are still mysteries. God rules with spiritual laws, in an unseen world, that we do not know and will likely never discover or prove with any theorem. "What is seen is temporary, but what is unseen is eternal." (2 Corinthians 4:18 – NIV)

Equipped with this knowledge, failures in life and in fitness fruition are easier to handle. Cliff Sheats in his book Lean Bodies impugns, "As long as you are aware that you will have setbacks, you will be easier on yourself. Remember, progress is built on perseverance." (175) While consistency is of utmost importance in establishing an effective healthy lifestyle plan, there will be times of frustration. So too, prayer can be confounding in nature. As Bill Bennett says, "Sometimes God doesn't answer the prayers of men the way men want him to." (127) When we endow our psyche with expectant patience, each ensuing result takes on a meaning celebratory in nature, for both kinesiology and godliness. Notice in the following scripture that both God and man are required to endue patience, and 'wait.'

"So the Lord must wait for you to come to him so he can show you his love and compassion. Blessed are those who wait for his help." (Isaiah 30:18)

September 18th:

God Cannot Be Hurt and He Does Not Hurt Anyone The constancy of God is reassuring. To know that there is an all-powerful, omnipotent deity on our side gives stoutness to the heart. And to know that he can erase our past, with respect to our follies and sins, presently love us as we are, and prepare an anomalous place for us in heaven gives us the ultimate source of endurance for the marathon race that is life. The Bible gives us that very fact: "Jesus Christ is the same yesterday, today, and forever." (Hebrews 13:8)

So also, there is a comforting esculent quality of being able to work out our kinks and stressors through exercise. I find that I discover so much peace at the platform before the precipitous lifting of a barbell. Also, the increased respiration and heart-throbbing, which pulses living crimson blood tissue to the aid of spent muscles during a running expedition will always occur at the attenuation of intensity. There are two constancies that will always be factual and resolute: 1) we can return to exercise to decrease our anxieties and 2) we can turn to God in any situation.

<u>September 19<u>th</u>:</u>

A Balancing Act to Yield to God in Hard Times Exercise helps to level out negative inner thoughts that might make us troubled, angry, confused, or in a firmly set mood. By finishing a natural, real-world challenge of a workout, we feel more confident in other areas because we have earned our own sense of self-respect. Attaining this prize, we inevitably come at other struggles with a sense of collected calm, and even lightheartedness.

An anonymous author relates this truth in a deeper tangent, which suggests our true personality and our heart shines seemingly when situations appear the darkest. How we react during and after occurrences help us grow or deflate the spirit and we remain stagnant in character growth.

"Do you take your rebuffs with a knowing grin?

Do you laugh tho' you pull up lame?

Does your faith hold true with the whole world's blue?" (182)

Notice the use of the term faith in the poem. Jesus might have been scared during his torture and crucifixion, but it is that very reason and experience that seated him at the right hand of God and bestowed upon him all earthly and heavenly authority.

"I will call to you whenever I'm in trouble, and you will answer me." (Psalm 86:7)

September 20th:

Not in Vain Does Man Live, Act or Perish Discipline applied to life in any and all situations rouses a divinely implanted sense of self-awareness. Self-awareness makes us less apprehensive about loving God and approaching him in prayer and/ or worship despite the healthy fear that we have of Him. Exercise is one method of creating the self-discipline needed to live the 'abundant life,' because we force ourselves to expand our physical boundaries in a literally methodical way.

Dr. Peter Gomes elaborates on this relationship of resolving internal conflicts through self-restraint. "Self-awareness makes aware of the…conflict, or chaos, of the self-divided between 'yearning for something more' and the sense of being less than good, which creates the desire for order…Thus, discipline is the process by which we restore order, imposing considered restraints upon our unruly affections." (204)

The Psalmist cries out to God that despite his best efforts to be good, he is in his own eyes disciplined still harshly by the very same deity he is trying to serve. "In vain have I kept my heart clean? For all the day long I have been stricken." (Psalm 73: 13-14; ESV) The definition of stricken is literally: 'to be made unfit.' Because tangible health or the physical nature of the body and brain is implied with the term, we can easily relate to the type of discipline that we bring on ourselves when working out, and compare it to God's discipline. Perhaps exercise then helps us to understand God's teaching us in differing arenas of human experience and integrate it into our daily lives.

<u>September 21st</u>:

Try not to be a Piker Old Pard, For Opportunity may be More Proximate than you know I find it fascinating that Jesus was speaking of the seemingly mere capacity to stay awake as He went into deep prayer minutes before he was betrayed and arrested. While we might consider Jesus' admonition to, "Keep watch and pray, so that you will not give in to temptation," (Matthew 26:41) as a spiritual decree, really he was just speaking simply of the physical ability to fight off sleep.

Although knowing the disciples would slumber way before the culmination of Good Friday events unfolded, Jesus still was disappointed that the disciples didn't believe in prayer enough to influence the forthcoming history. Jesus said to his friends, "Couldn't you keep watch with me even one hour?" (Matthew 26:40). The Messiah had to take the entire situation on his back, which he did without complaining or grumbling. We could learn a lesson from his attitude not to groan about coaches commanding us in conditioning or entertaining a revulsion to the start of our next workout. For in one simple sense, working out makes us sleep better, while also helping us stay more alert to our moral compass despite the energy-draining aspects of everyday existence.

It is when we feel the least like working out, praying, or loving our neighbor in a Christlike manner that our actions appear to God as most important. Echoing this sentiment of stirring our spiritual flames into a conception of action such as physical capacities of fitness, George Washington wrote in his prayer journal, "Make me always watchful over my heart…that neither the loathing of holy duties…may cast me into a spiritual slumber." (219)

"Remember, it is sin to know what you ought to do and then not do it." (James 4:17)

<u>September 22nd</u>:

Preparation is Key in Training and Imploring I can recall vividly the memory of a harrowing experience from several years ago: helping my dad kill a snake. With undaunted perception, my dad observed the snake as it stopped moving, and as we moved forward it was my job to stand five feet to the left side of the snake to corral it if the shovel missed the mark. I acutely realized that I was unprepared to hem it in because I had no equipment of my own and hadn't prepared or been advised what action to take (thankfully my dad severed the snake in two on the first attempted strike).

I can relate this incident to being prepared for a workout session or engaging in a powerful prayer life. Preparing for prayer before you approach God makes the prayer more refined and focused on exactly what are meaning and need to say. In exercise terms, the Nebraska strength coaches sum up effectiveness of preparing for their players' participation in off-season tumultuousness. "Many programs fail because the athletes do not believe in them. They question what the coach is trying to accomplish or feel something else will work better. The same is true with conditioning programs; if an athlete does not believe in the program he will not be motivated to put full intensity into his workout." (223).

I would advise anyone who wants to draw closer to God to practically enhance their power by writing down prayers. I would never approach a workout without writing down the selected exercises to all body parts, as well as the progression/ order of movements to take place. Memorizing verses not only to call to mind in trying circumstances but to pray the Scripture itself back to God, honors Him and is beneficial beyond physical description. Once again Nebraska's conditioning coaches drive home the point of industry in all phases of life that must be properly directed by love for God and neighbor: "It (football training program) is not based on how many games are won, but the success of each player in becoming the best he is capable of becoming." (223).

<u>September 23rd</u>:

The Meticulous Medium of Candor in Importuning God
Who says you can't pray while running or pumping iron? A curious perspective exists when Paul recommends a style/ conduct of prayer in a manner of certain bodily position (arms fully raised in flexion and hands lifted high). "In every place of worship, I want men to pray with holy hands lifted up to God." (1 Timothy 2:8). Although not listed in exclusivity, Paul does give this posture as a prescription for godly worship. Prayer circumstance is not limited to one bodily carriage or rote saying, but must have its roots in sincerity. Faith and submission to God's will ultimately bring about the behaviors exhibited in prayer or quiet time.

Prayer can actually serve as a backdrop for allowing our anxieties and life/ faith problems to emerge in our mind. It is hard to control the thought process and their emergence which drifts away from the topic we are supplicating to God, and our deepest subconscious seethes to the surface. When we allow ourselves to be honest with our Creator, I believe he is pleased. Pouring out your heart to your Savior is a substantial evidence that we believe he is faithful, willing and able to remedy our problems.

For example, the rosary is a repetition of Catholic prayers given with the suggestion to meditate on various aspects of the crucifixion. We practice the imaging of Christ carrying the cross, burying a deep weighted compression wound into his shoulder, the blood flowing down His forehead from the thorns entrenched into his skull, and skin lacerated and horrifically peeled off from the steel and leather-tipped flogging. If Jesus was able to extemporaneously forgive his executioners, and have faith that God was with him permanently, it seems like a smidgeon drop of substantiality in comparison to believe God will hear our silent prayers when we work out. The sagely author Victor Hugo summed up this paradox of heart-wrenching prayer, "Certain thoughts are prayers. There are moments when, whatever be the attitude of the body, the soul is on its knees." (224)

"I tell you, you can pray for anything, and if you believe that you've received it, it will be yours." (Mark 11:24)

September 24th:

Was Paul Lambasted for Being Frail? Paul makes a serious diversion from some modern Christian circles and those outside the belief system who boast that only those with the most impressive physique or physical accomplishments are fit to be leaders in the church or bestowals of what it means to be a Christian man. The Corinthians criticized Paul for being sharper with the pen than he was with his oration, implying lack of a silver tongue. "For they (the Corinthians) say 'his letters are weighty and strong, but his bodily presence is weak and his speech of no account.'" (2 Corinthians 10:10).

Could it have been that Paul had to relinquish his insecurities about physical makeup to God? It is possible that he was self-conscious about his masculine composition, but that never led to him being timid or intimidated when preaching the Gospel. Certainly, he mentions in other areas of the Bible that he worked laboriously with his own two hands while on missions and exhibited a large amount of pain tolerance while being flogged and stranded (treading water) at sea for prolonged periods.

The particular passage mentioned is an encouragement that you can be a Christian man even if you can't bench press 200 pounds. There is nothing wrong with 'muscular Christianity' and I believe many have had their faith enhanced by combining godliness with exercise. However, the call to follow Christ has no physical prerequisites, and in the end, God's extolment of the virtues we display is the most dangerous type of strength we can have toward the enemy. Dr. Kenneth Cooper sums up the paradox succinctly. "Are there any lessons we can learn from King David's experience? Certainly, if we remain close to God through obedience, prayer, and other spiritual disciplines, his strength will flow into us." (227).

Why Afflict Yourself With Literal and Figurative Pain in Flesh & Unanswered Prayers? It is difficult to propound the theory that rhetorical reason explains our 'reasons' to exercise. Although there is a natural inclination to encumber ourselves to a devout prayer life and exercise schedule, there are many times when the good intention remains just that. It follows suit, as if something seems to come too easy in prayer or fitness, then it probably isn't what it initially appeared as. Some investment has to be made of time, effort and resources in any goal attainment.

The principle I am referring to is an accounting profession concept of return on investment (ROI). Perhaps we start to buy into the critics' claim regarding an obtuse nature of prayer that can't seem to follow suit with quantifiable results, while on the other hand, we believe that exercise enhances both physicality and the cherubic. A mindset of distrust only leads to a haughty spirituality in which prayer becomes a sad show-off stunt lacking sincerity. "Beware of the Pharisees…who devour widows' houses and for a pretense make long prayers." (Mark 12:38, 40; ESV)

The most notable aspect of ROI in prayer is that we become godly and focused on pleasing him in addition to consummating a reception of pertinent richness in bodily health. Winston Churchill delves into the aspect of needed faith prerequisite that God works in both flesh and spirit for good when we supplicate. "I did not hesitate to ask for special protection…I even asked for lesser things than not to be killed, and almost always…I got what I wanted. This practice of prayer seemed perfectly natural, and just as strong as the reasoning process which contradicted it so sharply." (233)

<u>September 26th</u>:

Not to the Point of Ultimate Fatigue, But Proceeding yet with Unction In training for total body fitness, anaerobic glycolysis is one aspect of energy system exploitation that should be included in a training program. This type of work effort occurs in sets of strength exercises, runs, or drills lasting from 30 seconds to three minutes. For example, if you properly perform a set of weightlifting for 15 repetitions, a good rule to employ is to let it last approximately 70 seconds. In this time, each concentric contraction would theoretically take 1.5 seconds, while each phase of an eccentric repetition would last three seconds.

Similarly, it would be beneficial and practical to employ a 60-90-second prayer at regular intervals throughout the day. Just as exercising at a high level of intensity for one to 1.5 minutes yields manifold benefits, when relying on prayer ten times a day at 60-second lengths, you are better able to cope with trials, gaining power from prayer of varying forms and at differing times. Dr. Covert Bailey says of these types of training alterations that "The muscles learn to handle greater and greater loads of lactic acid with less fatigue." (236). Lactate is painful to the body mentally plus physically, and a moderate dose of it toughens us, just as praying with consistent discipline allows us to more courageously face calamities.

Paul exhorts his Roman brothers and sisters to literally join the struggle of the Christian walk through prayer itself, just as exercise molds, then hardens the caricature of our inner heart and proceeding outward projection of Christ into the world.

"I (Paul) urge you in the name of our Lord Jesus Christ to join in my struggle by praying to God." (Romans 15:30).

<u>September 27th</u>:

Prayer, Masculinity, and Ritual Rite of Manhood Jesus was not for making public displays of religious expression ostentatiously. Exercise helps in developing self-control, and therefore advances a genuine and sincere faith that is expressed outwardly in a proper manner. Dr. Bennett states – 'it is manly to pray,' (262) and exercise can offer a type of initiation ritual for proper progress from adolescence to adulthood, in a time where an ambiguous teenage angst still exists pervasively among young adults. You don't have to make a big deal of finishing each individual workout, but rather keep it to yourself and bask in the personal inner good feelings and health benefits.

In a sense, self-control is expiated by just learning how to matter-of-factly accomplish a goal, and while you revel in it, do not think yourself superior to other people, a formula that could be applied to heartfelt prayer. Just as Jesus never directly answered whether he was the Messiah, even with the foreknowledge that he had, we can follow in his footsteps by abhorring haughtiness in behavior. Speaking of journalist David Aikman, who faced death numerous times in dangerous war zones and built up a severely impressive resume of in his accomplishments, Dr. Bill Bennett says, "He has faced death, but he knows that a gentleman is called to do his duty despite danger, and at the end 'comes away not thinking he's any better for it.'" (260).

In 1999, Gatorade appealed to having a sense of courageous heart by asking the marketing question: "Is it in you?" Twenty years later the US Army currently echoes this sentiment with the slogan: "Warriors wanted: Do you have what it takes?" Answering both these questions includes putting aside self-recognition for the betterment of a team or other fellow comrades. A disciplined approach that properly applies exertion in manner, mode (form or type of physical action), and intensity both reveals and requires the self-control mentioned earlier.

"When I was a child…I reasoned like a child. When I became a man, I gave up my childish ways." (1 Corinthians 13:11; ESV).

<u>September 28th</u>:

Awe Preempts a Preparation for Prayer & Prompts a Plan for Exercise Entertaining a proper pre-workout warm-up is endorsed by just about every kinesiology expert currently in the profession. What's the best way to go about it and what should this preparing of the muscles consist of? Dr. Covert Bailey explains: "To warm up a specific muscle, do the same movements – but less intensely – that you do during the actual event. It's a walk-through rehearsal of what's to come." (270).

Similarly, prayer can and should occur in any situation and can manifest certain outcomes if prayed about prior to their happening. For example, if you are about to have a big meeting with a boss, praying for wisdom in a 20-30 second timespan while waiting in the lobby for the meeting to begin. If you are making an important telephone call – pray for a good result while the phone rings. Laying out your anxieties to God shows that you trust him and want him involved in every detail of your life. Think about the scenario this way: you would not approach the President of the USA without first mapping out what you would like to say to him/ her. So also we should plan for prayer by recounting our daily sins and confessing them, or by writing down a prayer of praise and worship before bringing it formally to God.

Also, since warm-up includes slower and less forceful/ intense activity but almost similar in movement pattern, we should pray with the prayer embedded in Biblical concepts. "Praying at all times in the Spirit, with all prayer and supplication. To that end keep alert with all perseverance." (Ephesians 6:18; ESV). The verse mentioned makes it clear that God likes to have his word recited back to him (as that's what praying in the Spirit means). The premium you place on communicating with God drives how close to him you are, and the alertness spoken of by this Scripture is a by-product of spending time with him by looking at every life event as God-authored and directed.

<u>September 29<u>th</u>:</u>

Christ is a King Who Fights His Own Battles – and Ours Too!
Is it audacious to expect working out to result in benefits to both social
and cognitive factors? No, the desire to show heart in a workout makes
you brave from a supposed 'impudence.' Jesus stated in a parable, after his disciples requested he teach them to pray properly, that a man
begging his friend for bread in the night, that even though the bonds of
fellowship would not compel the benefactor, "Yet because of his impudence, he will rise and give him whatever he needs." (Luke 11:8; ESV).

Imagine God answering prayer just because you are so stub-
born in your desires that you don't stop with the request and are bold
enough to seek food after midnight! But this is exactly the persua-
sion of how God confers benefits on us in the intangibles if we just
relentlessly keep training day after day, rep after rep. Two experts in
exercise medicine state of these seemingly concealed qualities: "And
the social benefits are often similarly attractive. It helps us look better,
feel better, live more confidently." (288). God honors the stern determination and perhaps, we learn to relentlessly procure patient benefits
in an instant gratification generation.

It is interesting to note that attitude displayed in the movie Troy,
Achilles is told by Agamemnon that "I should have you whipped for
your impudence!" The very noun that describes Achilles' lack of respect for his king relays a purported demeanor that God honors! To
which Achilles responds: "Imagine a king who fights his own battles.
Wouldn't that be a sight!?" Achilles longs to serve a worthy deity
like Jesus in a B.C. era. Even with his refined physical prowess and
nimbleness, Achilles' bravery does not satisfy his soul with satiety
that comes from working out with the motive to honor our God-given
bodies. What is troublesome to man and the world, reeks of opportunity to God.

"Therefore the LORD waits to be gracious to you." (Isaiah 30:18;
ESV).

September 30th:

A Proper Proposition in Prayer Outpouring via Meekness
Warming up is necessary and beneficial in fitness. Covert Bailey even goes so far as to say that muscle contraction patterns can be more synchronous with a warm-up. "A warmed up nervous system helps you to coordinate intricate movements." (293) However, a prerequisite of achievement is not needed before prayer. Instead, what is desired by God is that we approach him with reverence. With this correct mindset, we can ask in expectation girded by faith that yields results. Indeed, as we approach God with the attitude of humility, we can achieve, (yet not earn) but still experience redemption from our sins. Jesus shared with his disciples an example of a tax collector who did not raise his eyes to heaven but beat his breast in sorrow standing at a distance from the congregation saying, "O God, be merciful to me, for I am a sinner. I tell you this sinner…returned home justified before God." (Luke 18: 13-14).

Exercise also humbles us by making us realize that our body is sensitive in certain aspects of needing increased temperature and blood flow to deliver oxygen and nutrients via speeded circulation prior to lifting or running. And yet, all the while we don't relent on placing the burden on it from imposed physical demands. We become wise through this mediating situation of linking exercise precipitously to health, compelling us to pray first in recognizing God's singular sovereignty and our need to petition for mercy, before we make requests.

October: Psychology of Faith, Fitness & Sports

October 1st:

Sometimes You Must 'Zone Out' to get in 'The Zone' To ponder on the ways and means of God following a workout can be a divine experience. We can feel contented and fulfilled following a training session as both the mind and the body are disposed to receive wisdom and physiological recuperation. "Meditate within your heart on your bed, and be still." (Psalm 4:4; NKJV). Here God talks about reflection, upon our lives and how they conform to his will. I believe God wants us to do ALL of the following four practices: work hard, play intensely, rest peacefully, and reflect internally.

It is worth noting that God doesn't say strictly 'pray' in the formal sense of the term, but if we think on scripture, recount our blessings, and focus on sin and shortcomings that we would like to shore up, we please him in these pursuits. Could these four qualities be a form of prayer that God answers? Dr. Bill Bennett sums up these spiritual experiences comparing them to fitness: "A man sharpens and strengthens his body through exercise; he sharpens and strengthens his mind through thought and reflection – like spiritual calisthenics and study. Much like a body goes to waste without exercise, so, too, will a thoughtless mind." (296).

October 2nd:

A Morally Based Sociology There is always something to learn during and following a training session. We may learn about our ability to push through obstacles. We may shave time off our sprint or long-distance running performances. In addition, our friends can teach us much from a workout. More important than technicalities of biomechanical form, congregational fitness yields moral lessons. When our friends give a maximum effort, we are too inspired. "Two people are better off than one, for they can help each other succeed." (Ecclesiastes 4:9)

It is worth noting that this type of comradery is unique to the kinesiology atmosphere. Most certainly, the bonds of fitness and competitive fellowship unite persons across race, ethnicity, and socio-economic stratospheres in these experiences. Exercise groups can be analogous to the early church and the new believers in Christ in one respect: people were so sold out to giving their all to the Gospel and each other.

It is likely that wholesome social networks are as critical to achieving fitness goals and health habits as the inner drive and deter-mination that sprout from within individuals. It is said by Dr. Dean Ornish, regarding a unique community of fitness friends in The Daniel Plan that "This Harvard-trained physician discovered that it is rela-tionships that ultimately impact our motivation to exercise and eat healthily. It is love that transforms our health, fitness, and lives more than anything else." (147)

"For where two or three gather together as my followers, I am there among them." (Matthew 18:20)

"We are in this struggle together." (Philippians 1:30)

October 3<u>rd</u>:

Humility Offers a Contrast to Masquerading An individual's true character is revealed during the struggle that exercise and athletic competition offer. During what can be perilous moments with regard to stinging grief from fatigue, competitive outcomes, and potential in-jury, the true heart and courage are exposed. These qualities can even be developed through exercise if they are not already present in a participant's mindset. Roman philosopher Lucretius says of this physical and character-refining process, "Look at a man in the midst of doubt and danger...and you will learn what he really is. It is then that true utterances are wrung from the recesses of his breast. The mask is torn off; the reality remains." (148)

Alluding to this theme of pure fortitude, the West Point Cadet Prayer includes a snippet which illuminates the hardship and extreme endeavors that army soldiers will no doubt encounter in military service. This prayer implores self-sacrifice: "Oh God our Father...suffer not our hatred of pretense ever to diminish." (97) Because soldiers face life-or-death situations on the battlefield that involve intense aspects of physicality, if they are not sentient of their true character and personality that God endowed them with, it will be next to impossible to direct subsidiaries with truly open leadership.

"Be humble, thinking of others as better than yourselves. Don't look out only for your own interests, but take an interest in others too. "(Philippians 2:3-4)

October 4<u>th</u>:

It's Never Too Late to Rise Above Inundated Circumstances There is a certain quality embedded within exercise that can yield defeat over the dark corners in our life. By seeing the free will that God bestowed upon us "in action", we can rise to the occasion with the intuition that it's never too late to improve health and/ or revamp your outlook. A psychological healing mechanism is definitely in play when devoting our bodies to a consistency of anything good, especially fitness. Instead of fixating on the negatives and daily bombardment of bad news, we gain peace of mind during and after a workout.

A perfect example of this phenomenon is of an avid runner/ competitive marathon enthusiast Michael Agyin. Diagnosed at age 5 with deafness, and then at age 33 with type II diabetes, he searched for something to ignite a sense of purpose and meaning in his life. "I felt ashamed, scared. Already being deaf, I didn't know if I could deal with another health issue." After finding consolation in a progressive program of walking, jogging, and running further and further, he regained his will to live. "It made me feel free. I ran so far that diabetes can't catch me." Passing on this superlative effect to others is now one of his missions, founding an organization that donates shoes to disabled persons. "Running saved me, and I just want to pass that blessing on to others." (172)

"You will keep in perfect peace all who trust in you, all whose thoughts are fixed on you." (Isaiah 26:3)

October 5<u>th</u>:

Hit the Weight Room in Obedience to God to Debride Depression Exercise has a candid effect for good on balancing out our mental health and emotional faculties. Exercise purges vice in general, by eliminating and repudiating self-pity, and replacing it with effort that surmounts an obstacle in concordance with positively connoted thoughts. Brain power is used, quite literally in the uptake of copious amounts of blood glucose, which inspires us to push past previously actualized victories in fitness gains.

The clinical term for a prolonged state of unhappiness and pessimistic outlook - depression - can conceive a sense of helplessness that we do not own in our gut the gumption to overcome negativity. This false notion of inability or insufficiency in our deepest moment is proved false during a workout. Medicinal aspects of exercise have been proven. Although aerobic exercise has long been posited as an elixir for combating depression, weight training is also emerging as another form of therapeutic modality. Research done at Auburn

University concluded that "Male students who weight trained for 16 weeks showed significantly more improvement in self-esteem than a control group." (176)

Strong core belief in Christ coinciding with moderate to intense vigor in fitness makes for a powerful foe to Satan. Both the combination and conjugation work as a weapon in its own right as a role of an adjunct to the word of God in our mental/ neurological health.

"We take captive every thought to make it obedient to Christ." (2 Corinthians 10:5; NIV)

October 6th:

Motives for Working Out are Pure, Honest & Unfiltered One fascinating element to exercise is that its expansive properties and the application of these principles encompass no ulterior motives. Exercise is not a passive-aggressive means of revenge or retribution. Even if our main desire is to build a supple, appealing physique, there is no wrongdoing in this motivation and subsequent action taken on its part.

Although weight loss is the goal for many beginning a new fitness program, a plentitude of coagulating positive results come about in addition to this outcome. Being attractive to the opposite sex through a lean, muscular appearance is not a sin in and of itself, I believe. This motive is elaborated on by a college kinesiology text to support continued participation: "Although no weight loss may be seen, inches are usually lost around the waist, hips, and other parts of the body, thus resulting in perhaps a trimmer and nicer appearance." (187) In this sense, exercise itself and the philosophical reasons for its use alluded to in the introduction to partake in it, are chaste.

"But I, the Lord, search all hearts and examine all secret motives." (Jeremiah 17:10)

October 7th:

A Legal & Clean Drug to Give Good Temperament According to Dr. Travis Stork, a well-respected and medical authority on television, exercise connects a man to his inner self. Would you believe that God Himself also refers to his own thoughts? Does God indeed, like man, possess a mind? In the physical notion of this reflection/ rhetorical question, we will not know until the next life. However, the most heavily tested man outside of Christ, Job, comes to this very conclusion upon philosophizing on why such evil befalls him. "What are people that you should think about them?" (Job 8:4) The book of Jeremiah confirms the belief that God does control his own intellectual decision maker when God says to the prophet, "They built up high places of Baal…to offer up their sons and daughters to Molech, though I did not command them, nor did it enter into my mind." (Jeremiah 32:35 ESV)

The aforementioned doctor says of the unique capacity exercise holds, leading to his participation in it, because it affords benefits in impalpable ways. "Personally, the number one reason I am active is that it helps boost my mood." (188) Think of the power ascribed to exercise in this quote, that it can influence something as fickle and abstruse as mood. Additionally, Paul relates prayer to the intellectual side of life as well, despite its mystique. "I will pray with my mind also." (1 Corinthians 14:15) Is it possible that exercise sets our mind ablaze on the things above, and in so doing matches it to the will of God and His purpose for our lives? Peter links discipline hand-in-hand with the nature of the brain when he says, "So think clearly, and exercise self-control." (1 Peter 1:13)

October 8th:

The Liberty of Free Thought in Physical Endeavors and Service Isn't it amazing to know that the Creator God has thoughts Himself? "LORD…your thoughts are very deep!" (Psalm 92:5; ESV) We also have internal dictums that offer vicissitudes at all times, even when – especially when, we pray or engage in fitness activities. How should we regulate and direct our thoughts when praying or exercising our bodies? Apparently, God wants our thought genesis to proceed forth from humility and not from any other emotion. "The Lord knows the thoughts of the wise, that they are futile." (1 Corinthians 3:20; ESV).

Because working out is humbling in itself; it helps us to have discernment over how we should control our thought life and in turn, our temperament. When working out or praying, we should focus on how the elements of the activity make us increasingly emulate God's qualities. Any workout or prayer is done freely of our own will, and God is pleased when we give of our bounties joyfully and happily. "Then the people rejoiced because they had given willingly, for with a whole heart they had offered freely to the Lord. David the king also rejoiced greatly." (1 Chronicles 29:9; ESV)

An enthusiastic workout is more effective in every aspect, and it entails the very spiritual aspects of God: "Yours, O Lord, is the greatness and the power and the glory and the victory and the majesty." (1 Chronicles 29:11; ESV) When we focus on these attributes, they mysteriously inhabit themselves in our very souls too. Dr. Rex Russel elaborates on letting God be the director of our lives so that we are not deceived, and what happens when we don't. "By uncritically following the lead of our culture whether in the areas of truth, morals or health, we allow ourselves to be led into a needless death." (191) The statement is drastic but true; however, the good news is that prayer and exercise combat this incorrigibleness, and even more so when done with joy and gratefulness that we have the very opportunity to perform them.

October 9th:

Benefits Abound in Being Humble and Teachable in Beliefs and Behavior "Work with enthusiasm, as though you were working for the Lord rather than for people." (Ephesians 6:7)

Fitness beckons out to us in a uniquely physical manner that we all need: the bodily rejuvenation resources that exercise imparts over the long-term, as well as acute medicinal profits derived. However, God ultimately ordained the beneficial effects to occur in a more adroit personage, as he does with many of his gifts and blessings. When we exercise with enthusiasm, we enact the self-fulfilling prophecy that health enhancement will take place in an observable quality. The ACSM (American College of Sports Medicine states that the genesis of motivation leading to avidity begins with core notions that encompass exercise results: "Beliefs are seen as the fundamental driving force behind behavior." (196) Since working out is in itself a literal act of human behavior, the Bible says we should engage in it willingly but not unwittingly. God blessed the efforts of Jews to rebuild the city walls because of their work ethic: "At last the wall was completed to half its height around the entire city, for the people had worked with enthusiasm." (Nehemiah 4:6)

The invisible nature presiding over exercise that entails motivation to begin, perseverance to continue, and examining areas that cannot be quantified, are also alluded to by the ACSM exercise prescription manual. "A successful approach is to assess an individual's education level, resources to facilitate change, readiness to learn, and personal beliefs. Such individually tailored education and counseling are more likely to result in long-term change." (197) Exercise rouses passion in other areas of our lives, and Paul refers to these qualities' benefit to character endowment and effects on humans in the spiritual realm. "Since you excel in so many ways—in your faith, your gifted speakers, your knowledge, your enthusiasm…." (2 Corinthians 8:7)

October 10th:

Effort can be Forced but the Following Artifact won't be Efficient The Bible is not what I would call a very psychologically driven book. The compilation of separate authors and chapters is woven together prophetically more through the use of raw facts, narrative, and laws. God expects that His injunction imparted on us to love Him and live in fear of His wrath would be sufficient to make us obey. Rarely is the thought process of the patriarchs or Jesus Himself revealed to enlighten our modernity.

There are many reasons to exercise, but the best motivation comes from within, deep in the recesses of the heart in its existence as our earthly soul. God expects that our love for creation, which includes the complexity of our human bodies, furrowed yet revamped from exercise, is sufficient to motivate us and thereby, evidence to us the truth in his word. No one can really 'make' you do anything you don't want to, but God desires that we should desire Him (Hosea 6:6), and we should want to be good stewards of his physical and spiritual gifts. Dr. Kenneth Cooper sums up the connectivity of these traits well by saying, "The belief required for a 'fitness conversion' involves a conviction about your body and health that should be an outgrowth of your basic spiritual worldview." (221)

"I will put my laws in their hearts, and I will write them on their minds." (Hebrews 10:16).

October 11th:

A Scrupulous Escape from Harsh Reality to Rewarded Fable Unlike a drug that gives a mood or mind-altering chemical cascade effect, exercise is not just an evanescent escape with no chronic observable effects. As we need a force preceding antiquity with which to align ourselves, once we realize that seeking our own prideful ambition is futile, we can then align ourselves with physicality that is in accordance with God's will. Exercise offers a stark and defined undertaking that allows us to almost make it a moral story of its own and is not temporary in nature. When life doesn't always cut black and white, there are patterns of adaptation and resoluteness of ending to a workout session that all humans crave.

Do our very souls need defense? Just as the body must undergo straining to underpin its foundation of musculature for maintenance of quality and efficient movement, a soul needs protecting. Dr. William Bennett says of man that "Studying is how he defends his soul." (250). Just as we must have a plan or an elementary understanding of how exercise affects our natural health in the breadth of an active lifestyle, devising a quick fix that shuns long-term commitment is adverse to spiritual health. Dr. Bennett also notes that "Courage does not follow rutted pathways," (251) so we know that a one-size-fits-all workout regimen or faith journey is a false notion.

"I have heard Israel saying, 'You disciplined me severely, like a calf that needs training for the yoke.'" (Jeremiah 31:18). In the behavioral habits listed in the verse above, we come to realize that we are always serving someone – either elements of evil or godly endeavors. The word 'yoke' can mean to put to work, and that definition further carries the connotation that effort is done either willingly and gladly as a servant, or begrudgingly in a required slavish manner. The good news is that although the Scripture refers to 'training' for an animal, it is a metaphor that entails the similar rewards for humans if we use our free will for passions that are eternal in form.

October 12th:

A Psychology of Willingness, not Requirement Certainly there exists in incremental exercise an element of the psychological phenomenon known as delayed gratification. If we continue to press forward with applicable asceticism from listlessness replaced by muscle usage and contraction, we achieve the very object of our desired ends. While goals are important, too rigid a set of requirements causes trepidation. Is it possible that approaching fitness with a happy-go-lucky perspective helps us to overcome this intimidation and fear we have of the quality of evil?

Author Randy Alcorn, relating this flabbergasted attitude of how overcoming evil and exercise coincide, while speaking about the overflow of work he does in preparing a book, says: "At times it's very difficult. I do it anyway because I anticipate the reward that could never come without paying the price. In exercise and eating habits, study and work and spiritual disciplines, we often make short-term sacrifices in the interest of long-term gain." (262).

When we overcome by continuing on and eventually do more than we thought we could in lifting weights or time spent running, we conquer a preconceived notion that evil cannot be competently combated. Further elaborating on this theme, Alcorn says of this proposition, "Doesn't it seem at least possible, that a good God could have legitimate reasons for allowing evil and suffering to continue for the present? If so, then the problem of evil, while difficult, is not insurmountable." (262). Isn't it extremely encouraging and energizing to know that indirectly, and possibly even directly, exercise can contest evil?

October 13th:

Displaying Courage in Competition Routed from Reverential Fear Exercise can have a drastic emotional effect on our hearts, similar to what we feel in fear and/ or reverence of God. When we try to fathom his power and being separated from him or experiencing his wrath, we are immediately brought to a position of humility. Similarly, when we workout intensely or put forth a valiant effort in athletics, we feel a sense of awe for the power our bodies can exhibit in physicality and a sense of gratitude for a healthy corpus.

Sports give men what can be termed a socially acceptable means of feeling and showing sentiments that can later be used in compassion towards women, children, and persons undergoing extraneously difficult trials. As journalist Britt McHenry says: "Men embrace emotion in sports, women should be allowed to do the same," (283). Men can learn from females that do show their inner workings on a more consistent basis, that it is not shameful for them to do so as well. It can be difficult to discern whether these tests from God purpose us to improve our character, make us more thankful, or are simply a part of the vacillating aspects of life. God hearkens out to us in mysterious ways and may be beckoning us to invite him into our lives for the first time or in a deeper manner. "Therefore, as the Holy Spirit says: today, if you will hear His voice, do not harden your hearts" (Hebrews 3:7-8; NKJV).

Exercise can help us make meaning out of difficulties because we volunteer to subject our bodies to the extreme elements and far-reaching physiological effects. Experiencing these far corners of exertion, when we return to equilibrium, we realize that all difficult aspects of life shall too pass in time. As Dr. Covert Bailey says, "The emotional impact of a good walk on a beautiful evening goes far beyond the physiological impact of walking. The psychological benefits of any exercise go way beyond the measurable physiological effects." (284).

October 14ᵗʰ:

Does the Real Church Exist Outside the Sanctuary Walls? Is the Christian faith/ the church in decline? Many people seek real-life experiences for religious expression outside the format of the church and it's worship services. I believe this is why sports are so prevalently important in our culture and that many kids (and adults too!) are so fascinated by and interested in superhero movies.

We must find ways to infuse the culture of the church and faith in Christ into meshing with daily activities – an avenue that is primed for fitness and athletics. The self-sacrifice involved in team efforts emulates Christ's attitude who, "Though he was God, he did not think of equality with God as something to cling," (Philippians 2:6) making it more 'real.' Teenagers in these years following puberty are laying the foundation for the philosophical morals and in the crucible of strength training and conditioning via running and drills, learns how to function in austere situations creating a rugged and mature faith.

I have heard many people in small bible study/ life partnership groups speak about putting on a 'church face,' that all in life is peachy and portray that all is exceptionally good. They may feel as though they can't express their true doubts, fears, and life problems. However, there is no faking it in fitness or presenting a false front, but instead, the authentic personality is expressed, giving comfort that all situations in the walk of faith are on the table to discuss. In a stunning and some would say sacrilegious (but not me!) indictment on the church in modern American culture, Dr. Larry Crabb lays down a thesis of why it's so ineffective. "We are learning not to worship God in self-denial and costly service…The Gospel calls us to higher values of going the extra mile, esteeming others as greater than ourselves, living not for the pleasures of this life…We have become committed to relieving the pain behind our problems rather than using our pain to wrestle more passionately with the character and purpose of God." (294).

October 15<u>th</u>:

Don't Become Comfortably Numb Exercise combats 'numbness,' a feeling that what you do doesn't matter or isn't significant enough to make a difference in your life or the lives of others. We can become cynical as we grow older from adolescence into adulthood and middle-age. The discomfort we feel during exercise as it is taking place sensitizes us to the problems that our world is facing. We want to have a positive impact, instead of idly sitting on the sidelines, and exercise proves to us that our efforts matter. Exercise invokes in us a desire to look both inward and outward for meaning, compelling us to act in multiple manners of service to God and others. Indeed, working out nurtures the flame of the Holy Spirit that gives life to and lies within all believers.

"This is why I remind you to fan into flames the spiritual gift God gave you." (2 Timothy 1:6).

October 16th:

Exercise Unleashes the Vitality of the Discerning Mind The effect that the power of exercise exerts on the mind has long been hypothesized. The philosopher John Dewey once remarked, "There is an impossibility of insuring general intelligence through a system which does not use the body to reach the mind." (3) The relationship between working out and good mental health is now being examined in a scientific manner through research. The Bible links the power of the mind to the strength of our relationship with God.

"Be transformed by the renewal of your mind, that...you may discern the will of God, what is good." (Romans 12:2 ESV

October 17th:

It's Not Fear That Grips Christians; Rather, a Heightened Consciousness Exercise makes us feel alive by heightening our sense of physical awareness. So also, the Bible is actually a living document and personification of God (as His word). Just as we imbibe on elevated oxygen consumption during aerobics, God's word allows us to see his attributes and transfers into us the power of life abundant.

Jesus said , "I come that they might have life, and that they might have it more abundantly." (John 10:10; KJV) Jesus introduced this quality into our world and it stimulates a heightened sense of awareness to the good existing in our world. All around us are positive opportunities, which we will recognize when receptive to the 'still/ small voice,' affording us the opportunity to express our freedoms. Also, it makes us cognizant to the evil elements of our world so that we may resist them.

"It (the Bible) is sharper than the sharpest two-edged sword, cutting between soul and spirit, between joint and marrow. It exposes our innermost thoughts and desires." (Hebrews 4:12)

October 18<u>th</u>:

Strengthening Exercises Delete Victimization From Original Biology American author William George Jordan once elaborated eloquently on the virtue of self-control and the impact it has on a man's life direction. "He should master the weak element within him at each slight manifestation from moment to moment. Each moment then must be a victory for it (the weak element) or for him. Will he be King, or will he be slave? – the answer rests with him." (21)

Notice George's allusion to the 'weak element'. Every human being has weaknesses. Resistance training strengthens the weak muscles of our bodies. Self-control, when practiced gradually, elevates us above the plateau of moral weakness. It is a spiritual tonic that makes our lives more pleasing to God. The Bible gives two nuggets of truth regarding this attribute for anyone who desires a position of authority in the church: first, clarifying that this desire to be an elder is to seek an 'honorable position' (1 Timothy 3:1) and second, that the elder must, "Be a man whose life is above reproach. He must exercise self-control." (1 Timothy 3:2).

October 19<u>th</u>:

The Darkness Fades from Falsification in Yielding to Reality Depression is a human phenomenon that can affect anyone, regardless of gender, race, age, faith, or socioeconomic status. One in four Americans will suffer from depression in their lifespan. (23) What is fascinating about depression is that it can occur in response to life events (extrinsically) or arise out of a chemical imbalance in the brain involving the neurotransmitter serotonin (intrinsically).

The Bible is not silent on the topic of depression. David played the harp for King Saul when he was young to help Saul alleviate and feel relief from his depression. Job, a righteous man whom God tested in astounding ways, was affected by depression.

"Depression haunts my days." (Job 30:16)

"My heart is troubled and restless. Days of suffering torment me." (Job 30:27)

The good news is that exercise has been clinically proven to ameliorate the ill effects of depression. Involvement in exercise steeps our existence in reality of limitations and strength. One such study showed that 75% of depressed patients who exercised for 30-40 minutes consisting of walking/ running three times per week benefited were "essentially well" after three weeks and maintained the results for a year post-study. (23)

<u>October 20th:</u>

Temporary Tensity Unlocks the Real Persona "Know thyself" was an axiom posited by the ancient Greeks who knew that sincerity of heart translated into noble actions and a good reputation among men and their mythological gods. Thousands of years later Shakespeare elaborated: "This above all. To thine own self be true." (143) Befitting this sentiment in posterity, the English poet and Philosopher Samuel Taylor Coleridge echoed this opinion: "But you are likewise born in a Christian land: and Revelation has provided for you new subjects for reflection, and new treasures of knowledge...Self-knowledge is the key to this casket." (25)

The referenced statement above talks of a superior self-knowledge that we discover when we let our true identity be wrapped up in Christ. When Christ controls every aspect of your life, others see Him, not you. Similarly, knowing your own physical capacities and areas you would like to improve on allows you to develop a more tailored approach to a comprehensive fitness program.

"It is no longer I who live, but Christ lives in me." (Galatians 2:20)

<u>October 21st:</u>

Equipping Courageous Action with Precision Athletes and fitness enthusiasts alike know that there is a delicate balance between the mind/ body/ emotions that results in a performance increase referred to as "the zone". Serving as a primary source for the field of strength and conditioning in its infancy, the Nebraska University coaches say when describing this phenomenon: "In a relaxed state the muscles sit back and conserve energy for the exact moment when explosive action is required...the mind is confident and focused on the present task, ready to excite the muscles into action in fractions of a second." (26)

Being in this enhanced state of arousal stimulates increased physical performance while at the same time giving the mind a concertedness and the emotions a stable constitution. Stillness after a workout is necessary while it affords greater recovery and prevents psychological burnout and overtraining. Similarly, we are told to be still by God so that we can yield to and reflect on the will of God, and also allow him to solve our problems for us in accordance with His will.

"Be still and know that I am God!" (Psalm 46:10)

October 22ⁿᵈ:

Distinguishing Holiness from Perfectionism When designing or implementing a conditioning program, do not expect to attain perfection. Workouts will be missed intermittently for extenuating circumstances. Especially when following a vigorous program or a high volume of exercise, it can actually benefit the mind and body to take some time off. Dr. Cooper says, "It's essential to do a personal evaluation of yourself every so often to be sure that you're keeping your exercise routine in perspective with the rest of your life." (30)

God does not expect perfection in everything we do. He knows we are sinners. In actuality, perfectionism can be a negative desire at times. We are not here to gain recognition from others, but rather to store up heavenly treasures in eternity.

"So don't be too good or too wise! Why destroy yourself?" (Ecclesiastes 7:16)

October 23rd:

Pride Caused Satan's fall – Remain Humble Don't work out or participate in competitive sports for the fame or glory it can facilitate. Exercise because you have an intrinsic passion for it. Public displays of affection for fitness, such as showing off a beach body figure or earning the applause of a crowd, often are defined as reasons that Dr. Cooper says, "Remains in the head and never makes it to the heart." (78)

Dr. Cooper goes on to say that beyond the erudition of exercise's effect on the public display of the body, there should exist an inner hunger that family, friends and acquaintances should be able to descry that "has the capacity to spark major personal enrichment…on physical health, emotional well-being, and levels of fitness." (78) Perform exercise with a healthy dose of moderation and with the right motives.

"It is not good to eat too much honey, nor is it glorious to seek one's own glory." (Proverbs 25:27, ESV)

October 24th:

The Similitude of Eternity Practical exercise results create a craving for an ever increasing level of fitness. We are never content with the results, and this is a healthy characteristic, for it keeps us pushing for more. Max Lucado says of this striving in a spiritual context that "We long to see God. The leaves of life are rustling with the rumor that we will – and we won't be satisfied until we do." (43)

We desire more than this world can offer. Exercise parallels this spiritual journey, and in fact, strengthens it by giving us an inner hunger we can't possibly satiate.

"What has a man from all the toil and striving of heart with which he toils beneath the sun? For all his days are full of sorrow, and his work is a vexation. Even in the night his heart does not rest. This also is vanity." (Ecclesiastes 2:22-23, ESV)

October 25th:

The Power of Imaging There is no escaping the fact that we will face problems in life. Seneca, the Roman philosopher put it best: "Where you hide yourself, human ills will make an uproar all around." (44) However, exercise can give us a mental attitude, even if only temporarily, of clarity and acuity.

Even though the clearheadedness is a temporal reprieve, the practice of positive mental imaging has power that flows over into other areas of life. A good workout can clear your mind as your thoughts drift back and forth, and eventually, the image you create in your mind becomes a reality.

"That is why I tell you not to worry about everyday life" (Luke 12:22)

October 26th:

A Healthy Fear God said to Moses after giving the Israelite people the Ten Commandments: "Oh, that they would always have hearts like this, that they might fear me and obey all my commands! If they did, they and their descendants would prosper forever." (Deuteronomy 5:29)

Fear is closely related to the emotion of anxiety. Sometimes you get the butterflies before athletic competition or prior to working out. 'Will I be able to push through and finish to the end?' Your mind races with the question. But fear is a paradox and can be motivating too.

The sensation means you are alive. The adrenaline surges and blood circulation is diverted to your muscles, preparing them for action. Ben Sherwood describes this bifurcation process in an observation that: "Fear drives some people to incredible action while it makes others freeze or freak out." (50)

October 27th:

The False Sense of Task Enormity Beginning a new workout program, or even a single session, can seem like an enormously troubling task in its infancy. Even seasoned veterans of fitness get overwhelmed. At times there can exist an inner timidity about how to get motivated to begin a specific session. We must remember: beginning is half the battle.

Noted psychologist William James commented about this phenomenon that: "Belief at the beginning of a doubtful undertaking is the one thing that will guarantee the success of any venture." (58) I believe it is worth noting that the one vital trait to reaching goals is belief. Belief in what you may ask. Belief in God and the person He created you to be.

Psychologically, we must counteract the lie we construct in the mind that we won't be able to meet up with our own superlative expectations for the desired effort. A certain mental toughness is exuberated in starting to exercise, extrapolated from a sound mind.

"For God did not give us a spirit of fear. He gave us a spirit of power and of love and of a good mind." (2 Timothy 1:7; NLV)

October 28th:

The Mystery of Soul Health and the Metaphysical Aspect of Exercise God responds to our prayers in three different manners: yes, no, and wait. "As for me, I wait confidently for God to save me, and my God will certainly hear me." (Micah 7:7) Many times prayers are answered in what seems to be an inconsistent manner, and the results are unfathomable with respect to how they alter your life. As a prayer found in the pocket of a civil war soldier says, "I got nothing I asked for but everything I hoped for. Almost despite myself, my unspoken prayers were answered." (63)

While God is sovereign and holy, we cannot understand his ways. Exercise, however, offers a black-and-white results pattern. The work you put in will dictate the observable physical differences you will incur.

The fact that God works in our lives in mysterious ways, not equivalent to our efforts as with exercise, should not be cause for despair. Instead, we should find joy in this paradox, for the amazing aspect of grace is that while life is not fair, our eternal destination is providentially secure.

October 29th:

Releasing Toxic Emotions during a Workout Anger is a natural and possibly even reflexive response to life's seemingly unscrupulous dichotomies of unfairness. Even God, the source of all human emotions, expresses this quality: "The fierce anger of the Lord will not diminish until it has finished all he has planned. In the days to come, you will understand all this." (Jeremiah 30:24)

Norman Vincent Peale says of anger: "As an emotion, anger is always hot. To reduce an emotion, cool it." (65) Undoubtedly, the best way to deal with anger is to identify what's causing it and come to grips with it. But even after the root of the problem is exposed, the physiological effects of irritation - increased heartrate and circulation, the tense muscles, and a discharge of cortisol, need to be addressed. Exercise can provide reprieve through a venting mechanism of the inner issues that initiate the anger in the first place. Working out helps a person give up control of what aggravates us, giving us a focus on another mental topic of attention.   Simultaneously, the exercise response is analogous to an anger response. The body releases carbon molecules through increased respiration, and hydrogen and oxygen molecules through sweating. The 'hot' response of exercise energy creation serves to 'cool' this potentially harmful emotion prevents it from being just that: detrimental to yourself or others.

October 30<u>th</u>:

Banishing Unmanly Fear Through Imaging Psychological makeup in relation to mental health and motivation for working out is very present in athletic competition. In a varying manner, in any fitness or exercise program, a sound view of psychology needs to be present. This process is known as positive imaging, and a healthy amount/ dose of it expels fear. In the movie Gladiator, Maximus tells his fellow Roman cavalrymen before battle ensues, "Imagine where you will be, and it will be so."

God created the imaging process and approves of clean thinking. "But you should keep a clear mind in every situation. Don't be afraid of suffering for the Lord." (2 Timothy 4:5) Notice the specific diction choice in the verse with the words: leads (future), letting (present), and control (past, present, and future). Proper visualization of past, present, and future events elicits peace and life or perhaps consequentially peace in life. These qualities are the results of proper imaging through the inspiration of the Holy Spirit. When we do our best and leave the rest in God's hands, we allow an exhilarating experience to unfold in the physical realm, and defeat the fear from the enemy simultaneously.

October 31ˢᵗ:

Achieving Personal Peace through Effort Exercise promulgates a certain calmness, and causes a 'stillness' to occur post workout. This prompted serenity takes place in order for the body to properly utilize its adequate resources for recovery. When trouble strikes, this quality is what God desires from us so that he can intervene on our behalf. "Be still and know that I am God!" (Psalms 46:10)

Specifically, strenuous daily activity aids with the quality of our sleep. Sleep experts say that "Increasing your activity levels is good for your health, your mood, and your sleep. Being physically active builds more sleep drive and can increase deep sleep. If you're awake but inactive or resting for most of the day, you are less likely to have a sound sleep." (93)

It is my belief, that the sense of peace brought on by intensive/comprehensive physical activity can deepen our uttermost sense of trust in God. Jesus himself commented on this theme by saying, "I am leaving you with a gift – peace of mind and heart. And the peace I give is a gift the world cannot give." (John 14:27)

November: Rehabilitation/Movement Science/Motor Control & Christ's Truth

November 1st:

Work Ethic Transforms the Spirit Away From Despair Inevitably, life hurtles many challenges and troubles our way. Exercise is one method that helps us overcome the defeating notion of despair. Despair is a conjugate of depression. Samuel Johnson elaborates on this tepid quality of despair and how it can drain the enjoyment out of life. "The continuity of being is lacerated; and life stands suspended and motionless, till it is driven by external causes into a new channel." (121)

The mention of the term 'external causes' is what we should find encouraging and exhilarating. We can use these factors to get out of a deep rut. The good forces of faith, fitness and fortitude all combat the sense of despair. The Mayo Clinic says of this phenomenon: "During physical activity, your body releases chemicals called endorphins and enkephalins that block pain signals from reaching your brain. These chemicals also help alleviate anxiety and depression." (122)

Thomas Carlyle gives good advice for the power of exercise at 'work' and how this activity or 'external cause' can help us in our travails. "Work, and despair not…let that be my last word." (123)

"To all who mourn he (God) will give…a joyous blessing instead of mourning, festive praise instead of despair." (Isaiah 61:3)

November 2nd:

God's Characteristics Endow us with the Ability to Sow via

Physical Taxing Perhaps because it is one of the five core elements of God's very existence; (along with holiness, love, mercy, and wisdom) Christians are endowed with a thirst for justice in both private and public life. Justice exists in movement science because results will always be equated to the amount of effort and time preponderated by an individual or group. It is likely that this sense of fairness appeals to many involved in maintaining long-term adherence to an exercise regime, as well as to the truth of Christ's Gospel.

But justice goes deeper than mere outer appearances. God's law is just, yet cannot save us because its original existence actually condemns us. We needed a new covenant, which came about in Jesus, to purchase salvation for believers. So too, exercise can increase our health capacity beyond what can be measured. Because of this mutually conducive nature of exercise to godliness, evidenced in the theme of justice, the two entities exaggerate the effects of one another.

Americans hold a unique capacity to safeguard the value and execution of justice – holding it as a beacon to the free world. Dr. Bill Bennett's derivation of American-based justice gives an allegory of how justice in work ethics and faith relates to our unique system of government. "In addition to religious freedom…in America, justice might well give rise to a natural aristocracy, as Jefferson put it, based on talent and virtue…but no aristocracy of birth or rank." (190)

"Don't be misled – you cannot mock the justice of God. You will always harvest what you plant." (Galatians 6:7)

November 3ʳᵈ:

Changing Life Outcomes by Superimposing the Ultimate Mediator's Pattern It may sound strange, and it may be an experience no one else has observed, but following a particularly intense workout, I always get the feeling that time has slowed down. An apparition of hearing musical rhythm sounds slower, and feeling my heart pound less in the number of beats yet stronger in its duty of effect gives me a sense that I have just accomplished something profound. In motor behavior courses, my mentor/ professor said that while motor skill patterns remain stable, the metrics of a movement can alter in their rate of execution. Could it be that exercise attunes us more acutely to God's presence of the Holy Spirit living in us?

Perhaps this experience occurs because both the kingdom of God and exercise are ubiquitous. In respect to the former, God's kingdom is omnipresent in the world, and many early Christians suffered physical pain and death for their beliefs. In reference to the latter, the presence of God cannot be detected through observable signs, (Luke 17:20) just as we are always engaging in physical activity because we have to overcome the force of gravity to simply stand or make any volitional movement.

Jesus gave us instructional advice as to how to handle ourselves if we become persecuted for our faith. St. Ignatius blends this physical endurance of pain tolerance with strong belief that his death of martyrdom will not be in vain. "Come fire, cross, battling with wild beasts, wrenching of my bones, mangling of limbs, crushing of my whole body – only let me get to Jesus Christ!" (202) While working out does increase the ability to cope with physical discomposure, it takes a different and extremely admirable fortitude to suffer for being a disciple of Christ. How fitting, that the foreboding of physical torture afforded those previous Christians a chance to spread the Gospel.

"But beware! You will be flogged with whips...You will stand trial before kings because you are my followers. But this will be your opportunity to tell unbelievers about me. For it is not you who will be speaking – it will be the Spirit of your Father speaking through you." (Matthew 10:17-20)

November 4ᵗʰ:

Jesus Was Practical Plus Theoretical - as is Kinesiology Jesus' power extended to possessing physical healing abilities of chronic diseases. When faced with an assassination threat from Herod Antipas, Jesus did not cower in fear but stayed focused on the Father's purpose for his life. "Go tell that fox that I will keep on healing people today and tomorrow." (Luke 13:32) When presented with what could have been an orthopedic anomaly, Jesus felt compassion and used his healing ability through the avenue of touch to heal a woman. "He saw a woman who had been crippled…She had been bent double for eighteen years and was unable to stand up straight. Then he touched her, and instantly she could stand up straight." (Luke 13:11-12)

To say that Jesus' teaching was all basic in nature or abstract with no fleshly earth component is fallacy. Preparing us for what we will encounter and 'do' in eternity is an aspect of exercise that I believe is of utmost and vital importance. Also, we can show we are Jesus' followers by helping people with chronic illnesses or sedentary lifestyles through the specific area of physical activity encompassed by the term 'exercise.' The American College of Sports Medicine states, "The public health benefits of increasing physical activity within the general population are potentially enormous." (207) Further elaborating on this theme, their (ACSM) exercise guidelines manual further states, "When knowledge of the additional health fitness benefits associated with physical activity is combined with the fact that the list of chronic diseases favorably affected by exercise continues to grow, there remains a clear need for medically – and scientifically – sound exercise programs." (207)

November 5ᵗʰ:

A Compositional Calculus of Freedom in Movement The options of how to execute a movement are fascinating in that we can operate so complex an organism like the human body in an artful and graceful way. Listen to the unique point-of-view that a neuroscientist described in an astounding experience of suffering a stroke. In her perception, which was amenably conveyed during the aspect in which her left brain hemisphere was flooded in blood and the creative recesses of the right hemisphere took over. She described the process of motor learning in the following way: "I was momentarily privy to a precise and experiential understanding of how hard the fifty trillion cells in my brain and body were working in perfect unison to maintain the flexibility and integrity of my physical form. I witnessed with awe the autonomic functioning of my nervous system as it calculated and recalculated every joint angle." (216)

In motor control jargon, what Dr. Jill Taylor just elaborated on is the aspect of neuromuscular 'degrees of freedom'. This term refers to any of the nearly infinite ways and means a joint can rotate, flex, abduct, adduct or extend based upon the input given from the central nervous system or gathered sensory data to produce appropriate muscle contractions. So also, Christ came to give us the freedom to run, dance, and live for Him! The endowment of this gift most importantly refers to its relation with salvation and the assurance of eternal life with God purchased by Jesus. In the earthly sense, freedom implies that we are not controlled or micromanaged, but destined to live a life with access to individual choices at our fingertips (including the many freedoms inherent in and bequeathed by the noun, exercise). The freedom referred to in the Bible is life-encompassing for all aspects of cognitive processes and resultant human behavior.

"He (God) purchased our freedom with the blood of Son and forgave our sins." (Ephesians 1:7)

"So if the Son sets you free, you are truly free." (John 8:36)

November 6<u>th</u>:

Focus on Muscle Shortening in Each Repetition and Feed the Feeling of God's Presence To concentrate fully on a muscle contraction while it is occurring can, I believe, add an innovative and effectual aspect to strength training. For example, to picture in your mind what another observes while you are actively performing the movement makes the effort more fruitful. If you visualize yourself pressing your hands and arms above your shoulders and head as in a military press exercise while it occurs, you actualize in both theory and practice what your intentions are such as gaining strength or hypertrophy.

Neuroscientist Dr. Jill Taylor offers a unique perspective on how an intention is almost just as important as the execution of an activity in describing her initial rehabilitation stages recovering from a stroke. "The process of physical recovery was just like the stages of normal development. I had to go through each stage, master that level of ability, and then the next step unfolded naturally. Methodically, I had to learn to rock and then roll over before I could sit up. Most importantly, I had to be willing to try. The try is everything. The try is me saying in my brain, hey, I value this connection and I want it to happen." (220).

So also, God honors what we intend to do and can cause our efforts to be successful with His aid. God loves a cheerful servant who is eagerly and earnestly willing to take on any task large or small for the good of God's kingdom and fellow neighbor. When we pray or move to satisfy God, we must believe that he honors our efforts themselves.

"Draw near to God, and He will draw near to you." (James 4:8; ESV)

November 7th:

The Spiritual Aspect of Movement If you doubt that God is fond of kinesiology and has not proclaimed exercise as a vital discipline of life, you need look no further than the name he gave to the human race. According to Dr. Larry Crabb, the noun 'Man' in ancient Hebrew language takes on the meaning 'to move'. If you also doubt that God is active in the literal meaning of the verb, pay attention to how God reacts to King Hezekiah's imminent need as Israel is in danger. "This is what the LORD says: do not be disturbed by this blasphemous speech against me from the Assyrian king's messengers. Listen! I myself will move against him." (2 Kings 19:6-7)

It is interesting that God tells Hezekiah to be still, while announcing that He will perform with power acts against their concatenate adversaries. The concept of proper work and its profundity, when adjudicated against needed rest is expanded on by this very commandment. In the English Standard Version of the verse, God states that he will accomplish this feat against Sennacherib by putting 'a spirit in him.' If God moves with the unseen world in mind, could this suggest that movement is an animation of the Holy Spirit within us or an actual outer vibrancy exposited out of our very souls!?

November 8th:

Making Use of Movement to Prove the Power An example of God's interest in physical hale hardihood took place when Peter healed a man from a congenital condition that made him unable to walk not long after Jesus' ascension. "Peter took the lame man by the hand...as he did, the man's feet and ankles were instantly healed and strengthened. He jumped up, stood on his feet, and began to walk!" (Acts 3:7-8). Imagine that God used the canvas of bodily healing into ambulation to get across his point of the saving power of Christ in a very observable way. The kinesiology diction employed in the verse (i.e.

strengthened, jumped, stood, and walk) proves the point that moving activities are indeed important to God's human creation, both in what he sees us do and what we believe about his nature. The power Peter had in Jesus' name was earth/ fleshly bound in its substance of daily normality, yet also miraculous and divine in nature at the same time.

Dr. Covert Bailey reinforces the notion that physicality is an important aspect of life, with consistent exercise concurrently being a type of assiduousness that has mystical properties. "My prejudice is that exercise…can cure almost anything. We're born with a fabulous machine that is able to repair itself almost like magic." (235)

November 9th:

The Cause and Result of Musculoskeletal Collaboration Our muscles are capable of many variable deeds such as acting to lift a barbell, propounding a position then holding it and the whole body in a stable posture, creating forces to overcome gravity in an appendage, or moving any other type of external object. In all of these instances, there is a meticulous metronome of muscle contraction occurring and in turn, the kinetics (energy) give rise to kinematics (results of inner workings producing visible and observable aspects of muscle work).

So also, there are varying types of lifestyles in this life which exist in an unseen realm too – that of the god of this world and those that follow heavenly dictates. Paul cautions us to expunge the former and adopt the latter. "Follow the pattern of the sound (or healthy) words that you have heard from me in the faith and love that are in Christ Jesus." (2 Timothy 1:13; ESV).

In motor control jargon, there are two aspects of muscular bursts and two anatomical areas of the body that are involved in muscle usage: agonist/ antagonist and dorsal (away from body)/ ventral (toward center of body). A pioneer of contemporary motor control theories,

Dr. Mark Latash elaborates on both qualities. "Muscles are unidirectional force generators, they can only pull but not push. That is why one has to have at least two muscles to control movement of a joint; these two muscles are commonly called agonist (a muscle that produces joint a moment of force in a desired direction) and antagonist (a muscle that produces a moment of force against the desired direction.)" (237). Just as the agonist employs the desired use of a muscle and the antagonist must actively go into a stretch not to be used, the Bible exhorts us in both what to do, and what to avoid in patterns of the heart, mind, and behaviors.

<u>November 10th</u>:

Does the Spirit Need Exercise? Do the earthly forms of our souls – our spirits – need avenues of exercising for health and growth just like our bodies? What constitutes spiritual training? If we need to pump the muscles at intervals to maintain their viscosity, certainly our spirits need revitalization and regeneration, just as it is said in scripture that the Holy Spirit accomplishes.

It makes sense that improving the health of our spirits takes time and concerted effort. If our bodies can be damaged from overtraining, our psyches can get burned out and need rest and/ or rejuvenation. Some practical ways I have found to engage in fitness for the fathomable figure of the spirit includes praying in a tense/ nervous situation to place trust in God (for me this means praying in the middle of a tornadic storm instead of watching it or monitoring a radar), controlling the tongue when emotions run hot by focusing on the long-term picture and the blessings we DO have, and extending grace by blessing a neighbor who has injured our pride by praying for that person or offering a good deed as a work of faith. Just as in exercise, there is no one-size-fits-all methodology to spiritual training. If we earnestly commune with God, he will reveal these confidences to true wellness.

"Be a good servant of Christ Jesus, being trained in the words of the faith and of the good doctrine." (1 Timothy 4:6; ESV)

November 11<u>th</u>:

A Contradiction in Teaching Refutes Haughtiness One of my friends that took part in a chair aerobics group exercise class I taught mentioned to me a question about knee replacement surgery rehab that seemed contradictory. A physical therapist had her do a 'quad set' in which the leg affected is straightened out on a flat table, and the quadriceps contracted, which in a circumvented manner slightly hyperextends the knee. This strategy was a contrast and seeming opposition to personal training tips she had received suggesting you should never fully straightened/ lock your knee when doing a leg press, standing squat, or seated knee extension.

It took my mother to educate me as a kinesiology major on the topic, clearing up for me the fact that in the rehab version of a quad set, it is not a weight-bearing situation (as is a squat, leg press, or knee extension where fixed resistances are applied to the sole of the feet and top of the ankle respectively). In a slightly bent or 'flexed' position, the knee can be more tuned in via proprioception with the rest of the body, making it springy in changing directions or utilizing the muscles around it, resulting in a decreased chance of injury.

So also, Scripture can seem daunting or even to contradict itself at times: "Don't answer the foolish arguments of fools, or you will become as foolish as they are. Be sure to answer the foolish arguments of fools, or they will become wise in their own estimation." (Proverbs 26:4-5).

I think the answer to this apparent dilemma is that we don't have the wisdom to be 'all-knowing' as God does. Exercise evokes an emotionally rich experience that makes men more appreciate the perspective of women. We all can learn that true masculinity embodies the fact of caring for, and about the weak without looking upon them with an air of superiority. The sentiment one feels in a workout cannot be fudged, recreated or synthesized with anything else besides a relationship with God. The partnership to the divine is encumbered to deepen during and after-the-fact of a workout session.

November 12<u>th</u>:

God is Mobile Inherently in his Nature You can say God has a stake in kinesiology because he himself is active and not 'in absentia' when speaking of how he intervenes in our lives. God is not confined to a 'space,' even as Jews of the time believed he was present exclusively in the Jewish temple he commanded to be built. This point of emphasis is part of what contributed to the martyrdom of Stephen - the first Christian to be persecuted to the point of losing his life. Stephen's contention was that God had moved with the Israelites in the form of a transported tent carrying the Ark of the Covenant during their 40-year desert wandering period. The claim of exclusivity to a singular place of presence (the temple) made sacrifice unneeded since Christ became the atonement.

Indeed, the sect of disciples in the early days of Christianity's history was referred to as a 'movement,' occurring within ancient Near East culture, a term still used today to describe political or social trends. For example, Jesus said he was the only 'Way.' (John 14:6). To follow God means some type of volitional exertion beyond what we can perform or accomplish at rest. A lively facet of faith is proven to benefit humanity, for example, when analyzing the book of Proverbs. What we perceive as an inanimate object of wisdom itself is personified and speaks to us: "The LORD possessed me at the beginning of his work, the first of his acts of old." (Proverbs 8:22). The Hebrew word synonymous with 'work' in the previous verse is 'way.' Implied in the interchange of semantics is that a path of truth (or 'way') takes honest "'work'"ethic. In one sense, the operational objective of transferring the Gospel to others is accomplished by a free will moving into a predetermined destiny.

"Prophets were moved by the Holy Spirit, and they spoke from God." (2 Peter 1:21)

November 13th:

Don't Let Atrophy and Apathy Coalesce, Put Forth the Strain for Spiritual Stamina Young men are strong in physically related abilities, as a doctor told me at age 25 that I was blessed with youth. "I write to you, young men, because you are strong, and the word of God abides in you, and you have overcome the evil one." (1 John 2:14b; ESV). Few give thought to the temporary lifespan of this gift in motor development, as we all will lose it to some degree. As Dr. Ellington Darden says, "Research done as the University of Rochester School of Medicine shows that the average young man loses a half-pound of muscle per year between the ages of 20 and 50." (265). Even though this foe is biologically inevitable, steps can be taken to remedy muscle and soul atrophy.

The strength of body we have in young age can be converted into godly/ moral strength, and vice versa, a stamina that shines without stipulation. We can let the bodily strength permeate into later life by lifting weights, just as when faith girds every action we take, a spiritual strength sticks. The word of God abiding in young men equals strength, and allows us to overcome evil in our lives. Teenagers and young adults are bombarded with temptations on a daily basis, and the antidote is the addition of morality to resist the Devil from Biblical teaching. The strength we derive from the Bible percolates into our souls, guiding us with the truth, just as strength in movement/ fitness converts to a certain confidence. As the Bible is a living document, it gets somatically and spiritually transferred into our heart when we read, hear, or pray it.

Strength is a foundational ally to fortitude, and fortitude must exist where there is virtue. Dr. Peter Gomes states that the search for wisdom is the foundation of functional virtue. And we all know that true wisdom begins with the fear of God.

"The glory of young men is their strength." (Proverbs 20:29; ESV).

November 14th:

Motor Learning Accords Man with God's Faithfulness Although it might be an auspicious truth, overcoming sin does not have to be a vicious cycle. Coaches drill constantly how an athlete should perform in certain situations, and the term 'muscle memory,' is frequently cited. I would argue from a motor behavior standpoint that muscles do not have an apparatus within them to store information. Also, a motor program cannot be simply selected and then run off, because the environment, anatomical constraints and task goals are unique for each and every movement.

However, practice is not in vain because as social scientist Malcolm Gladwell stated that "Mastery of a skill or art often comes after ten thousand hours of practice." (303). Practicing a skill in the manner most similar to a game situation gives us an unpretentious attitude to simply take care of business without showmanship. Legends are made via purposeful practice, just as faith takes real work post-salvation granting by accepting Christ. Pepperdine women's basketball says that "But then the best lessons are the ones we end up learning again and again. Even when you're a coach. (304). Life is repetitive and if we don't give up, we gain a new nugget of precious wisdom each time we put forth the effort to try.

"History merely repeats itself." (Ecclesiastes 1:9).

November 15<u>th</u>:

Practice Makes Perfect When it's Enjoyed as a Freedom of Expression in Play An expert in aviation crosses over into the subject matter of human factors engineering and motor behavior in describing how novice pilots need to be trained to fly large 737 jets. Chesley Burnett "Sully" Sullenberger III, who famously landed a US Airways flight in New York City's Hudson River after both engines failed, said pilots need to 'develop muscle memory of their experience so that it will be immediately accessible in the future.'" (281). While old theories in motor control tried to explain different movements in terms of 'motor programs' which are stored in the mind (as Captain Sullenberger refers to), and the proper file is pulled for use in the moment, a contemporary view of movement science known as 'dynamic systems,' describes an alternative process.

Proponents of dynamic systems state that real-time alterations occur in each decision made prior to and during an executed task-related goal of each repetition in motion. While biological systems have the storage capacity in the brain to store information about past processes, the motor cortex is nuanced and much more extemporaneous in altering motor patterns constrained by anatomical, environmental, and goal-oriented factors.

Similarly, while many opponents of Jesus claimed he was canceling out the law given by God to Moses, Christ said that his very nature of love would fulfill the law and foster a new covenant of grace. A Biblical scholar elaborates and elucidates this phenomenon: "His radically new teaching cannot be squeezed into the mold of old legalism. It must find new forms of expression, or the old will be destroyed and the new spoilt." (282). While it sounds simplistic, the best way – kinesiologically speaking – to become a better football player is to play the game and the best way to improve speed is to run fast sprints. So also, to put Jesus' new doctrine into practice we should speak, serve, pray, and perform acts with his Gospel as the moral radix.

"And no one puts new wine into old wineskins. For the old skins would burst from the pressure, spilling the new wine and ruining the skins. New wine is stored in new wineskins so that both are preserved." (Matthew 9:17).

November 16<u>th</u>:

Building Character through Kinesiology & Committing to Christ Altering motor patterns is a tricky subject, especially when we are used to employing certain ways of moving habitually. A transition into new means of motor learning from old motor engrams is no more apparent anywhere else than in ballet and dance. Not only is dance an outward expression of a theme or point that a composer develops and the dancer executes, but it projects the 'heart' and intentions of all parties performing onto the audience. Susan Douglas Roberts, a professor of dance at TCU, says of this protuberance that evolved over the course of her career, "I just wanted to go onstage with the patterns so ingrained that they were instinctual. But it was more about the movement patterns and not moving the patterns." (285).

The alteration of changing the main outlook from proximal to distal, or to what happens in 'inward-parts,' (Psalm 52:6) has the effect of changing the perspective to one that is God-authored. When we are God-centered, our movement and behavior is a natural outflow of trying to please God and letting our focus on him direct our heart's desires. Elaborating on this subjugation of control transference from self to God, Roberts takes the concept a step further and equates a focus of what in dance is called the 'third eye,' (the eyes of the heart – as Paul said in Ephesians 1:18; NIV) into Godly character development: "For me, virtuosity is being able to move in my body, not move my body."(285). God originated this notion of morality rooted in him as setting us apart from the cares and god of this life: "Do not conform to the pattern of this world." (Romans 12:2; NIV).

November 17th:

God is on the Move in Many Matters Even though exercise is only one component of life and our faith walk, it pervades all aspects of life. Health of mind, body, and spirit is influenced in the design, implementation, and after the workout recovery experience of strength and conditioning. Jesus put this fact forth in a parable stating, "It (the Kingdom of God) is like the yeast a woman used in making bread. Even though she put only a little yeast in three measures of flour, it permeated every part of the dough." (Luke 13:21).

Working out makes us virtuous at the time, and when we ponder on the reasons why we imbibe upon connivings of training and start to realize the magnificent design of the human body. Reflection reveals how faith can drive a person to want to exercise intensely, exposing an oppositional larceny to personal pride. God's kingdom is everywhere, and God himself is mobile, so why wouldn't experiences of fitness permeate the psyche and in and of itself draw us closer to God?

November 18th:

When Hard Times Strike – Fix your Gaze Above on Christ I can remember a humiliating experience from playing football during my freshman year of high school. I played safety in a cover-two defensive scheme (meaning my main responsibility was not to allow a long pass completion), and the first play of the game in our first game of the year, the team threw a deep fade route on my side of the field against my coverage. I allowed the receiver to outrun me and get deeper down the field than me, and the pass was right on target to him. Not only did he out-sprint me, when made a tackle attempt, he out-muscled me and shrugged me off. I fell helplessly to the ground as he scuttled to the end-zone for a touchdown.

The next morning we had to watch the film, and of course, the opening play was the first clip shown. My friends and teammates laughed at me while the coaches analyzed and offered critique on my flawed technique. However, this experience got me used to having to face a tough situation and realize that failure is not the end of the world. My friends soon forgot about the mistake and I had an excellent season at safety, and the following year as a sophomore I started at both cornerback and receiver having multiple interceptions and scoring several touchdowns. Ken Purcell states of the maturational aspect of athletics, "The old school mentality is that winning is everything, and that doesn't float anymore, because what happens when you lose? You've got to have something to fall back on." (38) What we ultimately have to fall back on during the disappointing seasons of life is the ultimate safety net: Jesus Christ.

"So if you are suffering in a manner that pleases God, keep on doing what is right and trust your lives to the God who created you, for he will never fail you." (1 Peter 4:19).

<u>November 19th</u>:

The Nonlinear Synapses of Neurons, God's Will, and Prayer
One unique function of skeletal muscle is that it acts in a nonlinear manner. That is, there is never only a single muscle acting alone to produce a movement. The level of neurological innervation, and the length of the muscle involved helps determine which muscle groups are recruited. The nervous system allows for fluidity of movement in humans.

A motor neuron follows certain physiological laws in conscripting a muscle to use. "Since neurons obey the all-or-none law, when a neuron delivers an action potential, the response is a synchronized contraction of all the muscle fibers innervated by that single motor neuron." (126) However, sometimes the muscles do not contract properly or the signal from the brain does not ultimately relay the ideal threshold voltage to allow for proper recruitment.

So also, God's answers do not always follow our logic. "My ways are higher than your ways, and my thoughts higher than your thoughts." (Isaiah 55:9) Prayer ultimately follows a nonlinear relationship in terms of what we pray for and what we receive. William J. Bennet wisely elaborates on the subject of prayer: "What we ask for from God might be given to us in a way we never imagined." (127)

"Truly, O God of Israel, our Savior, you work in mysterious ways." (Isaiah 45:15)

November 20th:

The Dynamic Nature of Elocution Proceeding from the Heart
The dynamic systems motor control theory states that we form a neural synergy (force manifold) to help muscles act together when accomplishing a movement goal. The human body acts in a six-dimensional state space that is actually altered by the force manifold when we move. A state space means that there are three directions we can move in simultaneously: frontal (front to back), sagittal (laterally/ side to side) and transverse (rotational), and the same three directions of force that are externally acting upon us.

Just as muscle following laws of usage generates reactions that occur in the unseen world, Christ said that we can actually create situations from the words we speak.

"But the words you speak come from the heart – that's what de-files you." (Matthew 15:18).

November 21ˢᵗ:

The Ripple Effect of Movement and Sin

Inverse kinematics hypothesis states that when you move one joint, it can affect other joints and limb segments not directly connected to the joint being moved. A common practical example of this phenomenon is that when you move your finger, it affects the shoulder joint in multiple facets. This is caused by the viscous properties of the muscle and the connection of limb segments linking together a cascade of effects on one another.

Jesus taught that sin has a domino effect that causes us to commit even greater sins.

"And if the light you think you have is actually darkness, how deep that darkness is." (Matthew 6:23)

November 22ⁿᵈ:

The Fading Futility of Self-Glorification Many athletes play sports to accrue glory in this life and in their reputations after death. But God is clear: glory does indeed fade, and ultimately belongs to Him and no one else.

"I am the LORD. I will not give my glory to anyone else." (Isaiah 42:8)

Don't get side-tracked by striving too much or attempting to be better than others. As Norman Vincent Peale says: "Don't knock yourself out trying to compete with others. Build yourself up by competing with yourself. Always keep on surpassing yourself." (75) The lesson, from Jesus' perspective, is to seek heavenly treasures that await the resurrection of the just and let exercise be a precursor to those rewards.

"Store your treasures in heaven, where moths and rust cannot destroy, and thieves do not break in and steal." (Matthew 6:20)

November 23ʳᵈ:

Spiritual Work in Visible and Invisible Realms Work is defined in physical science as the amount of force exerted, measured in standard international units known as 'joules,' multiplied by the distance an object travels. Work is equal to force multiplied by distance, and can be either internal or external in nature. A basic and elementary example of the work equation exists in analyzing the bench press - an upper body strength training movement. The bar moves a set distance (from the chest to a position of arms fully straightened) but does not actually travel any measurable distance because ultimately, the bar returns from the chest back to its starting point. All the work accomplished by the body is internal and wielded by the chest, shoulder and triceps muscles. The amount of force exerted depends on how much weight is loaded onto the bar. Our lives are a combination of faith (internal) and good works (external).

"So you see, faith by itself isn't enough. Unless it produces good deeds, it is dead and useless." (James 2:17)

November 24th:

Coordinative Structures Envelope Lifelong Legacy and Movement Economy of movements relate motor control directly to our faith. When we relinquish control, we correspondingly (yet not superficially) have more personal liberty in our lives. In motor control, a coordinative structure forms in our movements over time to allow muscles to be entrained as we practice. A neural synergy allows contraction of selected muscle groups hastening together in a specific sequence, allowing coordination of the most efficient movement to take place.

One pattern the neuromuscular system seems to follow is an example of 'coordinative rule'. An example of the rule occurs during prolonged contractions in which, "(turning off) of some motor units is accomplished by recruitment of new motor units." (118) When difficulties strike or failure seems inevitable, it is good to remember that God always opens a new window of possibility when an old door is shut.

The Lord will work out his plans for my life." (Psalm 138:8)

November 25th:

Can We Elicit God to Trust in Us? The Henneman Principle, a theory in motor control, states that the utilization of specific motor patterns through selectivity of motor unit recruitment occurs in order of small motor units (those which do not generate large amounts of force), such as muscles of the eyes, to larger motor units (such as muscles of the back and legs) yielding efficient coordination. The theory comes into play practically to ensure precision in fine motor skills of the hand.

Dr. Mark Latash elaborates on the body's physiological reasoning of this coordinative rule by way of the English/ Language Arts doctrine metaphor: "The Henneman principle can be compared to rules of grammar…which limit the freedom of choosing such combinations (words/ syntax) to grammatically acceptable ones." (156)

Eliminating sinful thoughts and actions produces an abundance of freedom in physical and spiritual senses. The fact that we utilize this freedom relates to the gift of free will and the ability to harness the heart or a profound effort in exercise and a daily faith walk. So also, God says we must be trustworthy in small matters, before he will entrust us with larger responsibilities in His kingdom.

"To those who use well what they are given, even more will be given, and they will have abundance." (Matthew 25:29)

November 26th:

An Unexplainable Torrent Effect of Godliness When we move, our nervous system uses a three-dimensional force manifold that controls forces: the three dimensions we can move in (up/ down, to the side, and rotationally), and the kinematics of the movement (displacement, velocity, and acceleration). Also considered is the effect that the external environment imposes for us. These factors primarily include gravity and many other ostensible qualities of active resistance. A six-dimensional 'state-space' is created that we actually manipulate.

The actions we take in life also have a ripple effect. Our past can be forgiven, but what we do now influences the trajectory our lives will take in the future. Just as factors effect/ influence us, our external environment that includes geographic location/ atmosphere/ surroundings and the people we associate with can have a positive or negative effect.

"Look at those who are honest and good, for a wonderful future awaits those who love peace. (Psalm 37:37)

November 27th:

Glean All Possible Wisdom from Godly Sources From a motor behavior perspective, learning only takes place (for a new or existing skill) when there is knowledge of performance and error correction. Without the feedback from the body's own internal monitors or an instructor, there is no skill enhancement. Dr. Bob Arnot says of the permanent learning process: "Learning takes place quickly and will really stick if you get good error correction. Good students of motor learning don't just like feedback, they love it. They'll be motivated to try harder." (29)

Many times learning in our spiritual life can be challenging. It is a natural phenomenon to get frustrated with someone pointing out flaws. However, God prunes and refines us because he loves us and wants to motivate us to live fruitful lives.

"To one who listens, valid criticism is like a gold earring or other gold jewelry." (Proverbs 25:12)

November 28th:

Perpetual Freedom & the Matthew Principle In motor control, the term 'degrees of freedom' refers to any choice a mover must make to optimally execute a given task. Choosing not to activate a muscle or group of muscles is in itself also a choice. For example, when performing a bicep curl exercise with a dumbbell, it takes a conscious choice to not also contract the triceps as the weight is angularly lifted (in an arcing motion) in elbow flexion toward the body.

This can be compared to the freedom that God gives us and allows us to live our earthly lives in. Theologically speaking, God gives us free will. The endowment must mean that God loves humanity so much that we are given the ability to influence what will happen in life, and more importantly, in eternity.

"To those who listen to my teaching, more understanding will be given, and they will have an abundance in knowledge." (Matthew 13:12)

November 29th:

Exercise Invokes an Epiphany George W. Bush describes a pivotal moment, possibly 'the' pivotal moment in his life against the backdrop of running: "About halfway through the run, my head started to clear. The crosscurrents in my life came into focus."(68) Sports psychologists refer to this mental acuity and focus as being in 'the zone.' Being in 'the zone' allows you to become 'multi-stable,' a motor control term that means easily adaptable and strong enough to face extemporaneous and unpredictable difficulties.

The source of our strength, stability, and succor in life is God. When we relinquish control, we allow ourselves to be in the focused state and become stronger individuals for it. "Don't be afraid, for I am with you. I will strengthen you and help you." (Isaiah 41:10)

In movement science/ kinesiology terms, this phenomenon can be depicted as, "Manipulating visual feedback (that)…can also lead to changes in stability of motion patterns such that previously less stable patterns become more stable." (69) In the larger philosophical view, outside of movement, this means God is in control!

<u>November 30<u>th</u>:</u>

The Paradox of Eustress and Faith Fitness training presents a paradox in the manner in which the body responds and adapts to it. On the one hand, aerobic workouts cause a release of epinephrine. Researchers at the University of Copenhagen have just discovered that exercise can help reduce tumor growth via the release of epinephrine, which mobilizes the immune system's killer cells. (115)

At the same time, adrenaline that is circulating freely in the blood is utilized, or 'burned off' via eustress, especially during aerobic activities. This phenomenon exists so emphatically that Dr. Kenneth Cooper has stated, "The best natural tranquilizer I knew for bad stress at the end of a hard day of work – a physical workout featuring aerobic exercise." (116)

When contemplating the seeming conflict, we can return to the fact that spiritual life does not always follow a linear logic pattern either. Inevitably, we tend to commit the same sins over and over, repeating them – a process in motor control termed 'hysteresis' - many times no matter how much pushback we give to temptation. Oftentimes the dark sides are exposed in words/ deeds that display anger, lust, covetousness, and malice. Even the apostle Paul spoke freely of this daily struggle. "I have discovered this principal of life – that when I want to do what is right, I inevitably do what is wrong." (Romans 7:21) These are powerful words that can make the human predicament seem hopeless. And yet, when all hope seemingly fades, we can still say: "Thank God! The answer is in Jesus Christ our Lord." (Romans 7:25)

December: Longevity, Quality of Life and Eternity

<u>December 1ˢᵗ</u>:

The Implications of God's Physical Creation Sports and/ or exercise done in the outdoors breed a distinctive type of mindset and physical constitution. Perhaps this unconventional mind-body connection to nature exists because God literally created man from earth and placed him in a specific environment. "Then the Lord God planted a garden in Eden, and there he placed the man he had made." (Genesis 2:8) The curse mankind brought upon himself invoked God's laws of labor that "By the sweat of your brow will you have food to eat," (Genesis 4:19) does not annul the blessing of the outdoors conniving inner peace.

Also, physical effort in this natural setting is not profitless. Jethro Kloss elaborates on this topic: "Proper exercise in the open air and sunshine are among God's greatest gifts to man. It gives good form and strength to the physical organism, and all other habits being equal, is the surest safeguard against disease and premature death." (140)

Working outside, whether in manual labor or recreational fitness pursuits connects man with creation and, subsequently, with his Creator. Hamlin Garland goes a step further and postulates that this type of participation develops true godly masculinity. "Do you fear the force of the wind, the slash of the rain? Go face them and fight them, be savage again. You'll be rugged and swarthy and weary, but – you'll walk like a man." (144) Ultimately, the physicality of Christ as a human being is comforting and encouraging. "God made peace with everything on earth by means of Christ's blood on the cross. Now he (God) has reconciled you to himself through the death of Christ in his physical body." (Colossians 1:20; 22)

December 2nd:

Being the Benefactor of a Price We Cannot Pay or Fathom
Exercise is a direct, straightforward process. There is nothing hidden
in the process of acquiring fitness gains. This fact is refreshing to humans because salvation also, although interminable, is non-transient
and evanescent, and cut-and-dried phenomenon. However, it is deep
in the sense of how we try to comprehend it and make sense of the
simultaneous reality pared with the incomprehensible nature of grace.
We cannot quantify redemption in an earthly sense, such as needing
to increase resistance 5 to 10 pounds in weight training exercises due
to hypertrophied muscles needing a further intensive stimuli. Unlike
exercise results, salvation requires a mediator no matter how much we
may try to 'earn' it.

"I need someone to mediate between God and me, as a person
mediates between friends." (Job 16:21)

December 3rd:

**God Forbid we Make Grace Abound or Allow Ambivalence
to Creep in** Health of body becomes a fleeting commodity in the
context of time and biological age. Our true maturity levels, however, come from spiritual advancement. "My health may fail, and my
spirit may grow weak, but God remains the strength of my heart."
(Psalm 73:26) When we have moral courage stemming from the Bible, this gives birth to physical enhancement. Thomas Paine presents
the dilemma in a true manly motive/ light by saying, "He whose heart
is firm, and whose conscience approves his conduct, will pursue his
principles unto death." (160)

Lack of moral clarity in our actions can lead to a bodily language
and viewpoint of irresoluteness, resulting from the fear that God might
be angry or against our lifestyle. When we trust God, we get true

strength to carry on because everything that happens here shrinks in comparison to eternal life with Christ. A Puritan prayer passed down in American history aggrandizes this outlook: "In prayer I launch far out into the eternal world, and…my soul triumphs over all evils on the shores of mortality." (161) Authentic courage comes from faith, not only the transient capabilities that augment with weight training. When we don't cower in fear of God's judgment, we stand bravely in this life because of Christ.

"Because God's children are human beings—made of flesh and blood—the Son also became flesh and blood. For only as a human being could he die, and only by dying could he break the power of the devil, who had the power of death." (Hebrews 2:14)

December 4<u>th</u>:

A Little Bit Each Day, A Little Bit More Each Day is only Necessary Sign Contrary to popular belief, exercise need not be grueling to elicit results. You don't have to push yourself to the point of vomiting during every workout to achieve a valuable/ constructive session. Fitness can and should be enjoyable. We don't need to fret and fume over not working out at the hardest level ever in our life, each time we lace up the cross-training shoes.

Following this line of thinking can disrupt and stifle the creative process that takes place in all aspects of our body during training. Dr. Covert Bailey states this apothegm truth well: "The problem with intense exercise is that it can produce more accidents. In cross-training, we ask muscles that are usually used in one way to move in a different way. By switching from one moderate activity to another moderate activity, you can fool the muscles into thinking they're exercising more intensely." (181)

To relate the aforementioned axiom to faith, I think it is common to yearn for an 'unmistakable' divine sign of salvation. In this respect, we might even be said to be imitating the Pharisees. "Teacher, we wish to see a sign from you." (Matthew 12:38) Jesus concisely and succinctly replies: "No sign will be given...except the sign of the prophet Jonah." However, we should also not despair or lose heart regarding our eternal destinies, for Jesus uttered comforting words in the Gospel of John: "Let not your hearts be troubled. In my Father's house there are many rooms." (John 14:2)

<u>December 5th</u>:

Followers of the Way and Inciting Exercise-Originated Godliness? The self-referential early Christians called themselves 'followers of the Way.' Paul said in trial at the hands of Caesarean governor Felix; with his very life on the line that "I admit that I follow the Way, which they call a cult." (Acts 24:14) Notice that the word 'Way" is capitalized, giving it proper noun distinction and exclusivity by definition. So also, exercise is a way of obtaining a godly based character. Exercise itself is not cursory proof/ existence of character, but rather, the product and fruition of an inner heart-based faith.

In expounding on this interesting theme and apparent opposition, Cicero said the following in 44 B.C.: "The great affairs of life are not performed by physical strength or activity, or nimbleness of body, but by deliberation, character, and expression of opinion."(186) If Cicero was able to wax eloquently on this topic before Christ's existence, then in A.D. times we have a much richer and comprehensive capacity to develop these inestimably valuable traits. One way, yet certainly not exclusively, is to oppress the body by making it a slave to discomfort. Through distress of exercise, we may better appreciate the goodness of the body, sanctity of creation, an inherent value God places on all of human life.

"And endurance develops strength of character, and character strengthens our confident hope of salvation." (Romans 5:4)

December 6th:

The Privilege of Momentary Travails in Christ's Brotherhood
God ordained the shedding of blood for remission of sins. "Without
the shedding of blood there is no forgiveness of sins." (Hebrews 9:22;
ESV) In athletics, blood will sometimes be abdicated in necessity as
part of the sum of our love for the game. In fitness, even while in-
doors, sweat will inevitably seep from our pores at some point. In our
private lives, outside of exercise, it is highly probable that we will encounter trials that merit the jettison of tears. All of these experiences,
however, make us heirs with Christ. "In fact, together with Christ we
are heirs of God's glory. But if we are to share his glory, we must also
share his suffering." (Romans 8:17)

December 7th:

The Emptiness and Eternal Void of Worldly Glory Preceded
by the fear of God and warfare, few things test man's heart more than
athletic competition against other human beings. While Homer wrote
the Iliad to illustrate how men become heroic, the epic played out on
the big screen in the movie Troy showed an interesting juxtaposition
of Achilles' war hungry spirit matched with a lack of contentment.
After he had stormed the beach of Troy and forced a Trojan retreat,
Achilles' body language/ facial consternations almost seem to lament
the acts of war and give off a sense of 'what now' or 'what comes
next?'. Achilles is faced with the prospect that masculine glory falls
short of eternal bliss. Solomon effuses the same stipulations: "When
there is a man who has labored with wisdom, knowledge and skill,
then he gives his legacy to one who has not labored with them. This,
too, is vanity and a great evil." (Ecclesiastes 2:21 NASB)

So what does satisfy the hearts of men if this elusive quality of manly toughness is not even enough to slake our consciousness? To know that we are tough, something that fitness can at least partially satiate, is important to a man's psyche. The object of Achilles' romantic affections poses to him the question regarding the meaning of life. Briseis says, "Why are you here? What do you want?" Achilles replies, "I want what all men want, I just want it more." Achilles, common to many men, seeks to create a lasting legacy through physical prowess. It is interesting that Isaiah prophesies that God will make His Son redeem Israel through unmatched power, even though Jesus demeaned himself with charity, humility and love. Therefore, the ultimate masculinity appears when a man is fortified with inner strength, yet shows outward compassion and love to his neighbors.

"Doom to the pretentious drunks of Ephraim, shabby and washed out and parodies of a proud and handsome past. Watch closely: God has someone picked out, someone tough and strong to flatten them. Like a hailstorm, like a hurricane, like a flash flood, one-handed he'll throw them to the ground." (Isaiah 28:1-4; the Message)

December 8th:

The Meaning of Life Becomes Consequential and Elucidated Exercise is alchemistic in nature in the sense that no one has all the answers to kinesiology's deepest aspects and perplexities. Some people may seem to lose weight with less effort than counterparts, and some professional athletes may be able to pack on layer after new layer of muscle while weekend warriors struggle to 'beef up' proverbial 'chicken legs.' This should come as no surprise, as many training tangential benefits trump up in the unseen or unmeasurable facets, just as God himself is invisible. "Truly, you are a God who hides himself, O God of Israel." (Isaiah 45:15 ESV)

Just as both short-term and long-term results of fitness are inscrutable at times and exercise's results manifesting in bodily function mystify us, we all have religious questions. These include probes into life's ultimate meaning, what happens after death, and how to get to heaven and not go to hell. No one is exempt from these bafflements. God speaks to us in the Gospel about how he expects us to have bewilderments. "He (a farmer who scattered seed) sleeps and rises night and day, and the seed sprouts and grows; he knows not how." (Mark 4:27 ESV) Even orthopedic surgeons do not fully understand the healing process of muscles and bones and yet still fully expect those course's natural qualities to take hold post operation. However, these puzzlements in both the physical and spiritual realms initiate a deep desire to learn, and when we wrestle with inquiries, we ultimately grow a more fortified faith and deeper sense of trust in knowing that we are not omniscient.

December 9ᵗʰ:

Seeking God Yields Health Treasures and Grasping his Unqualified Love There is always new information to become acquainted with regarding the inundation of research in exercise as a science and mode of medication. New nuggets of advice in acquiring of optimal health capacities will always come about. Similarly, Biblical study and godly living mysteriously pass on to us a deeper understanding of God's kingdom. Jesus taught this principle when he said, "Every teacher who becomes a disciple in the Kingdom of Heaven is like a homeowner who brings from his storeroom new gems of truth." (Matthew 13:52)

However, just as there is no amount of finite learning that can totally inoculate us with an exemption from chronic disease, knowledge of God is infinite. In this life, we will never fully illuminate the expanse of God's unconditional love for us. This fact should be invigorating and lead us to honor the bodies we have been given (in one way by engaging in exercise), while instantaneously creating a staunch desire to know God on a deeper level so that we can better serve him. The more we become aware of God's love, the more we want to share it with others, the more he opulently endows us with it!

"May you experience the love of Christ, though it is too great to understand fully." (Ephesians 3:19)

December 10th:

Character is Who You are in Christ's Identity with Impress-ing him Only Paul says in the analogy existing between obtaining athletics fame such as setting world records, and storing heavenly riches/ rewards that "They (athletes) do it to win a prize that will fade away, but we do it for an eternal prize." (1 Corinthians 9:25) What is this 'it' that Paul refers to? Effort! Action! Enduring life's strains light-heartedly for a purpose that gives us an overarching meaning to push on and face each day! I know a Protestant preacher who remarked the following prodding aphorism: "Your life is a mission or a ministry-or your life is wasted."

In the movie Troy, as Achilles seeks advice and direction from his mother Thesis she tells him, "If you go to Troy, glory will be yours. They will write stories about your victories for thousands of years. The world will remember your name." Should we seek this driving factor of lasting personal earthly glory as the impetus behind in all we do and are ambitious for in life?

Every person has to make that individual assertion on his/ her own, as faith is a personal (though at times a simultaneous public) and deep-rooted matter. Regarding the social aspect of faith, we want to be known by others and be connected to a reputation. As Howard Thurman says, "The very spirit of a man tends to panic from the desolation from going nameless up and down the streets of other minds where no friendly recognition makes secure." (205) Should we want to be remembered by people now, in future generations, or strictly by God? The question is both rhetorical and at the same time resoundingly practical for what force ultimately guides our daily actions.

"To everyone who is victorious…I will give a white stone, and on the stone will be a new name that no one understands except the one who receives it." (Revelation 2:17)

December 11ᵗʰ:

Fighting against Fate it seems, but not in Vain A seeming grievous levity burdening humanity is posited by King Solomon during his lament for the entire book of Ecclesiastes. "So what do people get for all their hard work and anxiety? Their days of labor are filled with pain and grief…It is all so meaningless." (Ecclesiastes 2:22-23) The verse seems to be crying out for the meaning of life and why God is so adroit at revealing it. What does fitness have to do with reducing those elusive and hard-to-define characteristics of worry and discovering a sense of poignant purpose?

Exercise gives a coping mechanism by allowing us to become heroic in a uniquely personal way. We rise up above the daily monotony plus seeming mediocrity and achieve a goal-oriented outcome. The pleasure is pure regarding the altruism we obtain from overcoming physical barriers, and gives way to not only letting out frustrations, but building character through striving of spirit. We vent our feelings, similar to confessing problems in writing or voicing concerns sung in song lyrics. There will always be aspects of life we do not exert control over, but grace is freeing and allows physical manifestation of release through concerted effort and giving us comfort that we are powerful yet simultaneously more dependent on God. A poem by an anonymous author sums up the aforementioned mindset while focusing on the ultimate goal and source of motivation.

"I like the man who faces what he must,

Sees his hopes fail, yet keeps unfaltering trust

That God is God; that somehow, true and just

His plans work out for mortals.

He alone is great

Who by a life heroic conquers fate" (243

December 12ᵗʰ:

Is Courage Embedded or Emboldened? Desiring his post-death name to be synonymous with being a valiant hero – Achilles, after being told by a young boy that he was about to fight a giant Messinian man who slew multiple 'heroes' that the boy would not want to face, remarks to the child, "That is why no one will remember your name." Most men desire to show heart or courage and physical accomplishment such as lifting heavy, running fast or plowing through an opponent in a sport is one of many ways to do so. Many women desire gallantry both of themselves and the men they keep company with, as evidenced by the heroine Abigail Adams. "Don't you think me a courageous being? Courage is laudable, a glorious virtue in your sex, why not in mine?" (244)

After defeating the previously mentioned combatant of the Messenians, their king being astounded, inquires of Achilles, "Who are you soldier?" After Achilles answers, he gets his goal – the king answers astonished, "I'll remember the name." But what is interesting is Achilles' answer to the previous question – "Achilles…son of Peleus." The intrepidness Achilles displays stems from an assumption that he is carrying on a hereditary instilled nature of bravery. But the true bravery only comes when we relinquish our pride to lay down our brevity-laced crowns at Jesus' feet. "A warrior is not delivered by his great strength." (Psalm 33:16; ESV). If we are trying to define our masculinity solely by competition with brethren, we are operating with only pieces of the puzzle and missing the mark of Christ's sacrifice.

We all have downfalls in our family tree history or things we were endowed with that force us to face unpleasant realities, but this is where true heart comes into play. When we follow the two greatest commandments, our strength gets multiplied in an algorithmic manner and the Gospel shines above all. While exercise is a key cog in developing fortitude, we shouldn't strive to trample others or deprive God of what he put into the deepest recesses of our beings. Rather true manly (and feminine) courage exists in the unseen world and is hard to define. It comes about not merely when we pump up muscles, but also when we tally up the glory to God and step into the role he has planned for our lives by living with love and zeal at our most vulnerable or doubtful time, and when we think it matters least.

"Let not the mighty man boast in his might…but let him who boasts boast in this, that he understands and knows me, that I am the LORD who practices steadfast love, justice, and righteousness in the earth." (Jeremiah 9:23-24; ESV).

December 13th:

For Some Reason We Remember the Hard Times with Clarity It is the hardship and difficulty existing in the present, and the subsequent surmounting of it, which bestows upon us a memory of nostalgia. Facing down conflict or trouble, doing your best to overcome it with honest hard work, is what allows us to emerge stronger and better equipped after facing it. Because we see things from a limited perspective, we might question, during shortness of breath, what authority our coaches have to make us undergo such seeming torture as running 10-100-yard dashes, increasing the volume of a workout by adding an additional set of 10 reps when we're already fatigued, or pushing us to run a mile as fast as we are capable. The reality is, most of them underwent it too, which gives them a wiser perspective that they can see from to know that their being hard on us is ultimately to mold us into our best overall form and fashion. "He has planted eternity in the human heart, but even so, people cannot see the whole scope of God's work from beginning to end." (Ecclesiastes 3:11)

Fitting fitness to align with maturity breeds a discontent forming a desire to forge forward. As we press on, we push aside the fear and doubt, which ultimately gives way to constructing a true and deeper sense of strength. The philosophical functions freshen over time, with the hardship yielding to a more buttressed perspective due to facing a diversity of difficulties, including those virtuous qualities which exercising exposes and then elates. Jay Demarcus from the band Rascal Flatts sums it up well: "I can count a multitude of blessings, but I have to say that even my obstacles, even the dark times, are blessings. Strange thing to say, I know. But those were the times when I had to dig the deepest, when I've had to tap into that hope, even if it was elusive."(257).

December 14th:

Exercise for Cancer Patients' Well-Being Cancer is just one of the specific fields that exercise science and faith coexist in to bring about healing and soul restoration. Exercise is also a useful tool and can germinate the seeds of thinking positive and having a confident, self-sufficient attitude. Kenneth H. Cooper, MD colludes the two concepts together by saying, "Intrinsic belief has the capacity to spark major personal enrichment in every area of life – including dramatic improvements in physical health, emotional well-being, and levels of fitness." (267)

A recent article on FoxNews.com had this to say about health potentiation involving a cumulative, exponential and holistic effect: "Nicole Saphier, M.D who is also a radiologist, told 'Fox & Friends' that in modern medical times, cancer is not the 'death sentence' as it was once perceived. (268) It's not necessarily a life sentence anymore, but there is something very powerful about hope and positive thinking and just the support that he has been getting and that is stronger than any sort of treatment we could ever hope to give him (a recent cancer survivor.)" (268).

Notice how Nicole Saphier, MD alludes to the fact that the 'extracurricular' modalities were just as, if not more so, necessary reticent aspects of a medical treatment plan. The self-sufficiency or psychological factors involved with beating cancer are harder to prove and even harder to expound on. Thus matters of faith can be intensively personal and are literally life span, quality of life and eternal prospectus altering.

"So, every healthy tree bears good fruit." (Matthew 7:17; ESV

December 15th:

Like it or not you will have to Move For and Acknowledge Christ There is movement in eternity! Isaiah gives a prophecy that was carried out by Christ, but ultimately will still be fulfilled in the future via a posture in the next life. "By myself (the LORD) I have sworn, 'To me every knee shall bow.'"(Isaiah 45:23; ESV). Movement is part of God's design which reveals his glory in creation. While we confess allegiance with our mouth to Christ, this bringing about salvation is evidenced by the physical act of kneeling. Humanly we are afforded this moral and physical free will, produced by our ability to show or prove via God's design such as when we exhibit humility and a reverent attitude with this pose. Dr. Scott Morris describes our joy in exercising and the physiological changes it incurs while displaying

God's intended endowment: "We are created to move. We have bodies with arms and legs...our body parts bend, stretch, rotate...blood pressure and equilibrium constantly adjust and readjust to the needs and demands of movement. Our bodies are designed to move efficiently. And we can't separate our bodies from our spirt." (276).

God also admonishes his people not to worship false idols in this manner of movement too: "You must not make for yourself a carved image...You shall not bow down to them." (Exodus 20: 4-5; ESV) It is likely that our spirits will be transferrable in nature with regard to motion, whatever form they take after we rise to heaven. And that the given freedom of travel will stimulate growth as Norman Vincent Peale describes: "I hope there will be struggle, for struggle is good. Certainly there will be ongoing development, for life with no upward effort of the spirit would be incredibly dull." (277). One example stated by the Bible that will certainly transpire in its exact specification is that we will assume a lunge position to acknowledge Christ's authority along with a confession of the spoken word. "For the Scriptures say, 'As surely as I live,' says the Lord, 'every knee will bend to me, and every tongue will declare allegiance to God.'" (Romans 14:11).

December 16th:

Is it God's Fault? Take a Deeper Look at the Causation & Solution In the moments immediately preceding his raising of Lazarus from the dead; scripture says, "Jesus...was deeply 'moved' in his spirit and greatly troubled."(John 11:33; ESV) Notice the expression 'moved' to denote a surging of his spiritual healing power portrayed in the situation. Another interpretation of the term 'moved' in the verse is the word 'indignant'. It is likely that Jesus felt mad about, and for the human condition in which Satan had concurred the implanting of evil to bring about suffering and death. The term 'moved' is a parallelism of physical healing that Jesus brought about in a metaphysical manner based on rectifying the injustice of an unfair anomaly that

God did not cause.

Jesus healed people on Earth as proof of his divinity, and it could be said that an extension of his ministry exists in the field of medicine. The healthcare industry is now beginning to acknowledge and further examine the important role that fitness plays in chronic condition stifling. Kenneth H. Cooper, MD says, "The widespread interest in exercise has caused physicians and public health authorities to take an appraising look at aerobics. If properly implemented and supervised, some of them see it as a possible countermeasure to the Nation's Number One health problem: heart disease." (279).

While humans are imperfect, movement (both figuratively toward obeying God and literal bodily segment spatial displacement), can be a sacrosanct method of stimulus that invites God to operate accordingly in your unique situation. "Be open to how God will 'move' in your life as you seek to 'move' closer to God in your pursuit of wellness. Wholeness is not as much about being disease free as it is about experiencing the sacred in your life every day." (280). Both parties involved have an obligation centered on a functional feat. Notice that Jesus did healing miracles for what appears to have been orthopedic problems to remedy and restore anatomical normality plus ambulation in a time-period not even the best contemporary physician and therapist could combine to conclude.

"And they put them at his feet, and he healed them, so that the crowd wondered when they saw the crippled healthy and the lame walking." (Matthew 15:30-31; ESV).

December 17th:

You Can Count Us In For the Full Duration of the Fight In the movie Gladiator, after Maximus is devoid of his family, position and rank of highest general, and even ruler of Rome that Marcus Aurelius wanted to bestow upon him after they are betrayed by the king's very own son, he is sold into slavery. He subsequently gives up on life and refuses to train or take part in the 'bread and circuses' circuit that made its way around the Mediterranean regions in early A.D. I have always loved the dejected and hopeless attitude that Russell Crowe depicted by throwing down his wooden sword and refusing to fight. The Nubian, who admires Maximus for his legionnaire status and the battle experience it entails, asks him: "Spaniard...Why don't you fight? We all have to fight." Maximus grins in a snarky way as if he has experienced more sorrow in his life than anyone previously has ever had in the world, while simultaneously lacerating his arm to cut out the Roman infantry Commander tattoo. Juba, the African, then inquisitively asks, "Is that a sign of your gods? Will that not anger them?" Maximus laughs and continues, embellishing the idea that somehow the stars of fate have set his life in a motion that he cannot turn around and he no longer has any purpose. We can visibly detect the emotion in Maximus' heart by his lack of willingness to take part in physical output needed to defend him in combat.

But this is the beauty of Christian faith, it is not our fate alone, but the story of God and how we weave his will into our substantive fleshly actions that flow out of the state of our heart as we exhibit in exercise. And the state of our heart ultimately convenes from how strong our faith is girding what we do daily. The revelation that the world would not stop for him (Maximus) finally aspersed into action based on the fact that he still had more life to live. For God does not abate the fervor he places in the hearts of men.

"In the few days of our meaningless lives, who knows how our days can best be spent? Our lives are like a shadow. Who can tell what will happen on this earth after we are gone?" (Ecclesiastes 6:12).

December 18ᵗʰ:

   To Pontificate on the Profound Keeps Wickedness at Bay Can God exhibit weakness? And if so, doesn't this contradict what Paul tells us that our weakness is God's chance to strengthen us? Apparently, as laid out in the following Scripture, God can exhibit either extreme end of the spectrum to achieve his desired ends. "And the weakness of God is stronger than men." (1 Corinthians 1:25; ESV).

   Perhaps because he allows us to strive with him and struggle to wallow in our own will before we surrender control, he partially limits his nature so as not to literally consume us with power. But to wrestle with God can be good or even essential for our spiritual growth. Similarly, regular combinations of training with aerobics and weight lifting keep the muscles pliable yet taut. To keep the mind occupied on the theology of Christ is better than sordid, crude thoughts, just as exercise is preferable to screen time, and both holier preferences require effort to be put forth. As William J. Bennett, PhD notes, "So scientists said people must be careful to drink clean water, eat good food, and to keep so vigorous that the body will resist these intruders (bacteria)." (298).

December 19ᵗʰ:

   God's Story For Our Lives: Leaving a Mark Speed is that one great athletic ability that most any athlete desires more of. Is this trait inherited through genetics? Or is speed developed through training variables being properly exploited? The age-old question still exists today, though only partially answered. In life, are the paths we choose a fulfillment of a predetermined destiny, or the result of personal decisions? God has a blueprint laid out for our lives to be impactful in the service of Him and others.

   "'Everything has already been decided. It was known long ago what each person would be. So there's no use arguing with God about your destiny." (Ecclesiastes 6:10).

When we let go and give God control, we are then able to experience the fullness of our destiny. By actively stepping into the story God has woven for us to be a part of, we use the capacity of 'heart' to embrace the hard times and wrestle with the good, creating a spiritual legacy that will last long after we have died.

December 20th:

A Fire Rises through a Taste of the Ephemeral Exercise is a form of stress that when overdone, will actually result in death. However, when applied through the proper prescription, exercise makes us feel more alive. As our heart rates increase, oxygen saturation occurs in the brain tissue and response-induced hormones are released. Because of these hormonal, cardiovascular, and immune system responses, we get the taste of experiences that bring us closer to our eventual expiration. We are made better people by acknowledging the fact that our earthly bodies must face decay and death in this life. Exercise may only occupy 1/24th of our daily expenditures and bustling about, but its effect on the spirit is incalculable.

"After all, everyone dies – so the living should take this to heart." (Ecclesiastes 7:2)

"For our dying bodies must be transformed into bodies that will never die." (1 Corinthians 15:53)

December 21st:

Every Act Matters if you do it For God Fitness can be compared to managing a bank account. Every little bit of exercise you do is a deposit into your overall health and chronic disease prevention. Similarly, for every good thing, we do for others, no matter how small or insignificant it may seem, we will be rewarded by God both in this life and in eternity.

"When you put on a banquet, invite the poor, the crippled, the lame, and the blind. Then at the resurrection of the righteous, God will reward you for inviting those who could not repay you." (Luke 14:14)

December 22ⁿᵈ:

An Artificially Imposed Sense of Fame & Remembrance In the movie Troy, Achilles implores the Greek myrmidon warriors (the elite special forces of the time) he commands just before they single-handedly siege the beach of Troy: "Do you know what's there, waiting beyond that beach? Immortality! Take it! It's yours!"

While this rousing of courage is laudable, trying to achieve fame and eternal glory from purely physical motives, sports championships/accomplishments, or record fitness feats can be futile. This internal inspiration for striving is misguided however, if it is the sole intention and primary source of motivation for valor. Worldly glory does indeed fade. God gives us the true way to have our names remembered: by allowing our good deeds to remain in the world after we die and having our names written in the Book of Life.

"Those who are righteous will be long remembered." (Psalm 112:6)

December 23ʳᵈ:

Leaving Progeny with Generational Heirlooms Through Present Strife The process of aerobic metabolism it utilized by the body for slow endurance activities. This process utilizes oxygen and ATP to cause a cascade effect, so that when an enzyme breaks from a phosphate group, many related functions follow suit.

What we do in life matters and has a cascade effect on our own lives as well as posterity. As Maximus says in Gladiator, "What we do in life echoes in eternity." To be able to bear fruit in life and in eternity, we need endurance physically and spiritually.

"If we endure hardship, we will reign with him." (2 Timothy 2:12)

December 24ᵗʰ:

Indomitable Will & The Quest for Truth Starting and maintaining the rigors of an exercise program offer two very patent and desirable qualities: a continuous striving of the will, and a search for true results. These two characteristics parallel our spiritual walks by creating a desire for heaven, and a constant quest for truth.

Max Lucado states about the desire for perpetual adventure and the character growth it ignites: "The only tragedy, then, is to be satisfied prematurely. To settle for earth. To be content in a strange land." (41) Notice the dividends in eternal qualities that seeking to please God gives, and the restlessness that stirs the heart of humanity that exercise sequentially subverts. Ultimately, the adventurous spirit is diverted to positive manners of expression for God, ourselves, and our neighbors.

Regarding the search for truth, Jesus spoke of this when he said to Pontius Pilate, "I was born and came into this world to testify to the truth." (John 18:37) It makes sense then that because of these two spiritual entities (desire for heaven and seeking truth) that Jesus also said to Pilate, "My kingdom is not an earthly kingdom." (John 18:36)

December 25th:

The Advantages of Alarm Everyone fears death and the vastness that eternity proposes in our hearts and minds to some degree. Seneca says bluntly and accurately, "What hiding place is there, where fear of death does not enter?" (45)

Physiologically speaking, exercise brings us closer to death than we are at rest or optimum homeostasis by applying an alarm to the body inching us toward outright entropy. This temporary, yet significant eustress makes us better human beings by reminding us that our earthly bodies will not taste immortality, but rather will be altered into heavenly bodies. Therefore, since our souls are eternal, life is that much richer with the sweet promises of the Gospel.

"For the wages of sin is death, but the free gift of God is eternal life through Jesus Christ our Lord." (Romans 6:23)

December 26th:

A Renaissance of Reviving the Old, Refining the New We cannot fully comprehend all the possible medicinal benefits of an exercise program. There is simply too much to know regarding the field of kinesiology. This knowledge can and does have an impact on someone physically, mentally, emotionally, socially, environmentally, and most importantly – spiritually. Research is constantly uncovering hidden gems of information and is continuously evolving, proving one exercise method's superiority.

"That's the value of wisdom; it helps you succeed." (Ecclesiastes 10:10)

Similarly, the anagogical nature that God's word uses to describe heaven is too vast for us to understand fully. Max Lucado sums up the dichotomy of earthly life versus the sublime nature of heaven well: "At our most creative moment, at our deepest thought, at our highest level, we still cannot fathom eternity." (57)

"No eye has seen, no ear has heard, and no mind imagined what God has prepared for those who love him." (1 Corinthians 2:9)

December 27th:

The Unseen Work and Battle Strength and conditioning takes place in the off-season, where there is no crowd to cheer you on. Largely, the work is done in private, where no one sees the effort put in until results speak for themselves by enhanced athletic performance. Similarly, the Bible says what we do when no one is looking is largely what determines our level of character. "God will judge us for everything we do, including every secret thing, whether good or bad." (Ecclesiastes 12:14).

In one way, this judgment can be a good phenomenon. The verse gives assurance that God will bless and reward efforts toward bearing spiritual fruit. President Harry Truman elaborated on the private aspect of godliness in a prayer he wrote which says, "Help me to be, to think, to act what is right, because it is right...Make me intellectually honest for the sake of right and honor and without thought of reward to me." (97)

The reason Truman alludes to a lack of reward is because worldly glory is temporal and fleeting in nature. However, we should expect heavenly rewards for good deeds. The promise of eternal rewards further indicates that the battles we face are of an asomatous nature, a truth substantiated in Scripture. "For we are not fighting against flesh and blood enemies, but against evil rulers and authorities of the unseen world." (Ephesians 6:12)

December 28th:

A Society Outside of the Pews, Desks, and Hearth A fitness center fulfills the basic requirements of being what is known in the 21st century as a 'third place.' The idea of this type of congregation stems from the chain Starbucks. The owner of Starbucks came up with the model that each individual needs a social gathering confine outside the realm of home and work. Fitness facilities offer a setting of fellowship in a relaxed atmosphere. Dr. William Bennett says of these recreational outfits and the personal pursuits they contain within them: "You can tell a lot about a man by the way he handles his leisure time." (305).

Does this mean that every gymnasium has to be a 'fitness bubble?' I do not think so, because there are many practical applications that working out has to life experiences. A sense of belonging is had by everyone who populates these settings of kinesiology. Making friends and meeting acquaintances of the opposite sex occurs in a non-vile, mind/ character sharpening environment. God even suggests that man needs a brotherhood of convivial spirit surrounding him, and will be compensated in a mysterious way when they help each other out in similar struggles of life. And what better place to discuss life and spirit than with the pumping of weights?

"Two are better than one, because they have a good reward for their toil. For if they fall, one will lift up his fellow." (Ecclesiastes 4:9-10; ESV).

December 29th:

God Knows your Heart Inevitably, when I read the Bible for teaching and wisdom purposes, an idea pops into my head for multiple verses on how the passage relates faith and fitness together. On the other hand, when I read the Bible (or any book for that matter) for the explicit reason of finding a literary nugget to include in a book I'm writing, my mind goes blank. I believe this series of events ultimately helps me align my motives and intentions with God, and results in me seeking him on a deeper level so that I can be attentive when he speaks.

A pursuit of holiness and supple physique is part of being 'synchronized' with God's plan. In a similar arena, movement needs to take a natural course to be most efficient. Nina Martin, dance professor at TCU who melds movement in performing arts with motor control and teaching purposeful body positioning to persons with cerebral palsy, says of this coordination in her personal experiences: "I have spent a great deal of my professional life reading about cognitive science to try to understand exactly what was happening to me onstage. I knew I wasn't conscious of everything I was doing. I became interested in figuring out ways to access a preconscious state." (306)

Awareness of the body in space allows for real-time spontaneous alterations in arrangement of the trunk and body segments. The premotor cortex plans movements before they occur, similar to how the Holy Spirit guides people in their minds and consciences to act for God.

"Letting the Spirit control your mind leads to life and peace." (Romans 8:6).

"But when you are arrested and stand trial, don't worry in advance about what to say. Just say what God tells you at that time, for it is not you who will be speaking, but the Holy Spirit." (Mark 13:11).

December 30<u>th</u>:

Health Insurance & Eternal Security A client of Kenneth H. Cooper, MD specifically an assembly-line worker, stated an interesting reason that he imbibes on exercise for the good of his work/ finance/ personal life: "For me it's like insurance, I just can't afford to get sick." (307). When you consider this point of view, it's easy to imagine how good fitness levels can be viewed as a safety net of sorts for those who want to avoid chronic diseases that are so prevalent in American society, thereby also aiding in spending less money on healthcare.

Similarly, just as effects of physical activity are lasting, I am a believer in the once saved always saved theory just as results of an exercise program are permanent and cannot be revoked. "The Holy Spirit of God, by whom you were sealed for the day of redemption." (Ephesians 4:30; ESV)

You can always begin anew with fitness, just as we know that no matter what we do, we can never stray so far from God that we are out of range for receiving his grace. It is comforting to know that even Satan is not strong enough to take us out of the will of God. "I give the eternal life, and they will never perish. No one can snatch them away from me." (John 10:28).

December 31<u>st</u>:

The PsychoSocial and Personality Alter Positively with Exercise The term 'social' is found only one time in the NIV translation of the Bible. But make no mistake; Israel was a communal experience during their 40 years in the desert. "Moses assembled the whole Israelite community and said to them, "These are the things the Lord has commanded you to do." (Exodus 35:1; NIV).

So also, there is a psychosocial aspect of exercise which involves meting out the day's hassles in a nonviolent, peaceful canvass. Psychiatrist Bob Conroy says that "Exercise is emotional aerobics." (308). While Duke researcher Dr. James Blumenthal comments that exercise impacts our very personalities linked to by faith: "The decision to exercise could be related to an overall reevaluation in lifestyle behaviors and a change in values. It's difficult to document whether or not the pervasive 'I feel so much better' is a function of exercise, the group setting, or time." (309). Only an epiphany as strong as exercise provokes a very change in our persona.

Author Bio

Patrick Greak grew up in the small town of Liberty in southeast Texas. He became fascinated with all things exercise-related at age 12 while training for football. This interest led him to seek a degree at TCU to study the subject and work in that career field. He graduated with a bachelor's degree in health & fitness and a master's degree in kinesiology, both from TCU. He tries to weave faith and character development for youth into his writings while simultaneously instilling a desire to live a healthy, active lifestyle. He resides in Texas and is happy and blessed to call the Lone Star State his home!

Sources:

1. Plato, The Republic. Baltimore Penguin Brooks, 1955, pg 153.

2. Bennett, William J. Our Sacred Honor. 1997 – Simon and Schuster, pg 240

3. Cooper, Kenneth H. Faith-Based Fitness. Thomas Nelson, 1995, pg 72.

4. Peale, Norman Vincent. Have a Great Day. Wings Books, 1997, pg 34.

5. Bennett, William J. Our Sacred Honor. 1997 – Simon and Schuster, pg 334

6. Shimer, Porter. Fitness Through Pleasure. 1982 – Rodale Press, pg 106

7. Bailey, Covert. Fit or Fat. 1977 – Houghton Mifflin Company, pg 62

8. Bennett, William J. The Book of Man. 2011 – Nelson Books, pg 264

9. Bennett, William J. The Book of Man. 2011 – Nelson Books, pg. 177

10. Bennett, William J. The Book of Man. 2011 – Nelson Books, pg 232-233

11. Bennett, William J. The Book of Man. 2011 – Nelson Books, pg 449

12. Bennett, William J. The Book of Man. 2011 – Nelson Books, pg 180

13. Bennett, William J. The Book of Virtues. 1993 – Simon and Schuster, pg 17

14. Bennett, William J. The Book of Man. 2011 – Nelson Books, pg 239

15. Gilmore, C.P. Exercising for Fitness. 1981 – Time-Life Books, pg. 8

16. Cooper, Kenneth H. The Aerobics Program for Total Well-Being. 1982 – Bantam Books, pg. 18

17. Bennett, William J. The Book of Man. 2011 – Nelson Books, pg. 530

18. Bennett, William J. The Book of Man. 2011 – Nelson Books, pg. 514

19. Aurelius, Marcus. Marcus Aurelius and His Times. 1945 – Walter J. Black, pg. 115

20. Cooper, Kenneth H. The Aerobics Program for Total Well-Being. 1982 – Bantam Books, pg. 211

21. Bennett, William J. (William George Jordan) The Book of Man. 2011 – Nelson Books, pg. 432

22. Bennett, William J. (Thomas Jefferson) Our Sacred Honor. 1997 – Simon and Schuster, pg 322

23. Sheats, Cliff. Lean Bodies. 1992 – The Summit Group, pg. 148

24. Bennett, William J. (Augustine of Hippo) The Book of Man. 2011 – Nelson Books, pg. 505

25. Bennett, William J. (Samuel Taylor Coleridge) The Book of Man. 2011 – Nelson Books, pg. 481

26. Arthur, Michael & Bailey, Bryan. Complete Conditioning for Football. 1998 -

Human Kinetics, pg 251

27. Gilmore, C.P. Exercising for Fitness. 1981 – Time-Life Books, pg. 73

28. Cooper, Kenneth H. The Aerobics Program for Total Well-Being. 1982 – Bantam Books, pg. 210

29. Arnot, Robert. Dr. Bob Arnot's Guide to Turning Back the Clock. 1995 – Rodale Press, pg 164

30. Cooper, Kenneth H. Faith-Based Fitness. Thomas Nelson, 1995, pg 160

31. Superko, Dr. Robert H. and Tucker, Laura. Before the Heart Attacks - Rodale Inc. 2003, pg 205

32. Bennett, William J. The Book of Man. 2011 – Nelson Books, pg. 36

33. Bennett, William J. The Book of Man. 2011 – Nelson Books, pg. 507

34. Arnot, Robert. Dr. Bob Arnot's Guide to Turning Back the Clock. 1995 – Rodale Press, pg 17

35. Bennett, William J. The Book of Man. 2011 – Nelson Books, pg. 379

36. Bennett, William J. The Book of Man. 2011 – Nelson Books, pg. 512

37. Bennett, William J. The Book of Man. 2011 – Nelson Books, pg. 513

38. Bennett, William J. The Book of Man. 2011 – Nelson Books, pg. 117

39. Michener, James A. Sports in America. 1976 – Random House pg 80

40. Bennett, William J. Our Sacred Honor. 1997 – Simon and Schuster, pg 308

41. Lucado, Max. Grace For the Moment, 2007 – Thomas Nelson, page 30

42. Bennett, William J. The Book of Man. 2011 – Nelson Books, pg. 175

43. Lucado, Max. Grace For the Moment, 2007 – Thomas Nelson, page 450

44. Bennett, William J. The Book of Man. 2011 – Nelson Books, pg. 238

45. Bennett, William J. The Book of Man. 2011 – Nelson Books, pg. 238

46. Bennett, William J. The American Patriots Almanac. 2008 – Thomas Nelson, Pg 480

47. Ornish, Dr. Dean. The Spectrum. 2007 – Ballantine Books. Pg 21

48. Peale, Norman Vincent. Have a Great Day. Wings Books, 1997, pg 18

49. Lucado, Max. Grace For the Moment, 2007 – Thomas Nelson, page 428

50. Sherwood, Ben. The Survivors Club, 2009 – Grand Central Publishing, pg 210

51. Lucado, Max. Grace For the Moment, 2007 – Thomas Nelson, page 442

52. Ornish, Dr. Dean. The Spectrum. 2007 – Ballantine Books. Pg 182

53. Ornish, Dr. Dean. The Spectrum. 2007 – Ballantine Books. Pg 87

54. Pelletier, Dr. Kenneth R. Longevity: Fulfilling Our Biological Potential. 1981 – Delacorte Press, pg 240

55. Darden, Dr. Ellington. Living Longer Stronger. Berkley Publishing Group – 1995, pg 116

56. Bennett, William J. The Book of Man. 2011 – Nelson Books, pg. 120-121

57. Lucado, Max. Grace For the Moment, 2007 – Thomas Nelson, page 532

58. Peale, Norman Vincent. Why Some Positive Thinkers Get Powerful Results. 1986 – Oliver Nelson Books; Page 32

59. The Diagram Group. The Complete Encyclopedia of Exercises, 1972, Paddington Press; page 62

60. Bennett, William J. The Book of Man. 2011 – Nelson Books, pg 406

61. Bennett, William J. The Book of Man. 2011 – Nelson Books, pg 278

62. Bennett, William J. The American Patriots Almanac. 2008 – Thomas Nelson, Pg 308

63. Bennett, William J. The Book of Man. 2011 – Nelson Books, pg 469

64. Padus, Emrika. The Complete Guide to Your Emotions and Your Health. 1986 – Rodale Press,

Page 331

65. Bennett, William J. The Book of Man. 2011 – Nelson Books, pg 36

66. Dr. Rosenfeld, Isadore. Dr. Rosenfeld's Guide to Alternative Medicine. 1996 – Random House Inc., pg 47

67. Bush, George W. Decision Points. 2010 – Crown Publishers - Page 3

68. Bush, George W. Decision Points. 2010 – Crown Publishers - Page 2

69. Latash, Mark L. Fundamentals of Motor Control. 2012 – Elsevier Inc. – page 157

70. Peale, Norman Vincent. Have a Great Day. Wings Books, 1997, pg 50

71. O' Neill, Amanda. Historical Facts Ancient Times. Crescent Books, 1992. Page 66.

72. Bailey, Bryan & Arthur, Michael. Complete Conditioning for Football. Human Kinetics, 1998. Page 5

73. Bennett, William J. The Book of Man. 2011 – Nelson Books, pg 177

74. Colberg, Dr. Sheri. The Diabetic Athlete. 2001 – Human Kinetics, page 1

75. Peale, Norman Vincent. Have a Great Day. Wings Books, 1997, pg 14

76. Peale, Norman Vincent. Have a Great Day. Wings Books, 1997, pg 17

77. Bennett, William J. The Book of Man. 2011 – Nelson Books, pg 166-167

78. Cooper, Kenneth H. Faith-Based Fitness. Thomas Nelson, 1995, pg 4

79. Bennett, William J. The American Patriots Almanac. 2008 – Thomas Nelson, Pg 479

80. Bennett, William J. The Book of Man. 2011 – Nelson Books, pg 283

81. Lipschitz, Dr. David A. Breaking the Rules of Aging. LifeLine Press – 2002, pg 142

82. Lipschitz, Dr. David A. Breaking the Rules of Aging. LifeLine Press – 2002, pg 143

83. Lipschitz, Dr. David A. Breaking the Rules of Aging. LifeLine Press – 2002, pg 147

84. Bennett, William J. The Book of Man. 2011 – Nelson Books, pg 485

85. Maxwell, John C. The Winning Attitude. Thomas Nelson – 1993, page 28

86. Lipschitz, Dr. David A. Breaking the Rules of Aging. LifeLine Press – 2002, pg 149-150

87. Peale, Norman Vincent. Have a Great Day. Wings Books, 1997, pg 61

88. Wilder, Thornton. American Characteristics. Harper & Row Publishers – 1979, page 13

89. Carson, Dr. Ben. Think Big. Zondervan – 1992; page 7

90. https://www.ymcatriangle.org/about-y/our-mission

91. Bennett, William J. The Book of Man. 2011 – Nelson Books, pg 502

92. Lipschitz, Dr. David A. Breaking the Rules of Aging. LifeLine Press – 2002, pg 143

93. Carney, Dr. Collen & Manber, Dr. Rachel. Goodnight Mind. New Harbinger Publications – 2013, page 31.

94. Storr, Anthony. Solitude A Return to the Self. The Free Press – 1988, page 3.

95. Bennett, William J. The Book of Man. 2011 – Nelson Books, pg 316

96. Bennett, William J. The American Patriots Almanac. 2008 – Thomas Nelson, Pg 476

97. Bennett, William J. The American Patriots Almanac. 2008 – Thomas Nelson, Pg 477

98. Maria-Remarque,Eriqh. All Quiet on the Western Front, 1987 – Ballantine Books, pgs 60-61

99. Kass, Dr. Leon R. The Ethics of Giving and Receiving, 2000 – SMU Press, pages 42-43

100. Bennett, Dr. William. America the Strong. 2015 – Tyndale House, page 10

101. Bennett, William J. The Book of Man. 2011 – Nelson Books, pg 507

102. Peale, Norman Vincent. Have a Great Day. Wings Books, 1997, page 15

103. Avila, Dr. Patricia G. Fitness for Health and Sports. Bookmark Publishers – 1999, page 29.

104. Bennett, William J. The Book of Man. 2011 – Nelson Books, page 521

105. Bennett, William J. The American Patriots Almanac. 2008 – Thomas Nelson, Pg 481

106. Bennett, William J. The Book of Man. 2011 – Nelson Books, page 360

107. Bennet, William J. Virtues of Courage in Adversity. 2001 – W Publishing Group, page 79-80

108. Darden, Dr. Ellington. Living Longer Stronger. Berkley Publishing Group – 1995, pg 49

109. Challem, Jack; Hunninghake, Dr. Ron. Stop Prediabetes Now. John Wiley & Sons – 2007, page 251

110. Arthur, Michael & Bailey, Bryan. Complete Conditioning for Football. Human Kinetics; 1998; pg 5

111. Foreman, Judy. A Nation In Pain. Oxford University Press – 2014, page 284

112. Foreman, Judy. A Nation In Pain. Oxford University Press – 2014, page 287

113. Bennett, William J. The Book of Man. 2011 – Nelson Books, page 515

114. Peale, Norman Vincent. The Power of Positive Thinking. 1978 – Prentice-Hall Inc. page 107

115. http://www.aol.com/article/2016/05/16/exercise-cuts-cancer-risk-huge-study-finds/21378245/

116. Cooper, Dr. Kenneth. Can Stress Heal? Thomas Nelson – 1997 – Chapter 4

117. Cooper, Kenneth H. Faith-Based Fitness. Thomas Nelson, 1995, pg 208

118. Latash, Mark L. Neurophysiological Basis of Movement. Human Kinetics – 2008, page 52

119. Bennet, William J. Virtues of Courage in Adversity. 2001 – W Publishing Group, page viii

121. Bennett, William J. The Book of Man. 2011 – Nelson Books, page 440

122. Bruce, Dr. Barbara K.; Harrison, Dr. Tracy E. Mayo Clinic Guide to Pain Relief. 2013 – May Clinic page 169

123. Bennett, William J. The Book of Man. 2011 – Nelson Books, page 151

124. Bennett, William J. The Book of Man. 2011 – Nelson Books, page 438

125. Cooper, Kenneth H. Faith-Based Fitness. Thomas Nelson, 1995, pg 128

126. Latash, Mark L. Neurophysiological Basis of Movement. Human Kinetics – 2008, page 50

127. Bennett, William J. The Book of Man. 2011 – Nelson Books, page 469

128. Bruce, Dr. Barbara K.; Harrison, Dr. Tracy E. Mayo Clinic Guide to Pain Relief. 2013 – May Clinic page 158

129. Norville, Debra. Thank You Power. Thomas Nelson – 2007, page 100

130. Russell, Dr. Rex. What the Bible Says About Healthy Living. Regal Books –

1996, page 44

131. Allen, Dr. Charles L. God's Psychiatry. Spire Books – 1953, pages 9-10

132. Peale, Norman Vincent. The Power of Positive Thinking. 1978 – Prentice-Hall Inc. pages 202-203

134. Russell, Dr. Rex. What the Bible Says About Healthy Living. Regal Books – 1996, page 250

135. Morris, Dr. Scott. God, Health, and Happiness. Barbour Publishing 2011, pages 48-49

136. Peale, Norman Vincent. The Power of Positive Thinking. 1978 – Prentice-Hall Inc. pages 202

137. Cooper, Kenneth H. Faith-Based Fitness. Thomas Nelson, 1995, pg 28

138. Kloss, Jethro. Back to Eden. Back to Eden Books, 1939, page 55

139. Lucado, Max. Grace For the Moment. Thomas Nelson - 2007, page 183

140. Kloss, Jethro. Back to Eden. Back to Eden Books, 1939, page 56

141. Peale, Norman Vincent. Treasury of Courage and Confidence. Doubleday & Company, 1970, pg 14

142. Peale, Norman Vincent. Have a Great Day. Wings Books, 1997, page 14

143. Peale, Norman Vincent. Have a Great Day. Wings Books, 1997, page 26

144. Bennett, William J. The Book of Man. 2011 – Nelson Books, page 174-175

145. Bennett, William J. The Book of Man. 2011 – Nelson Books, page 167

146. Bennett, William J. The Book of Man. 2011 – Nelson Books, page 91

147. Warren, Dr. Rick; Amen, Dr. Daniel; Hyman, Dr. Mark. The Daniel Plan. Zondervan – 2013, pg 232

148. Bennet, William J. Virtues of Courage in Adversity. 2001 – W Publishing Group, page vii

149. Bennett, William J. The Book of Man. 2011 – Nelson Books, page 477

150. Beers, Dr. Mark H. (Editor-in-Chief) Merck Manual of Heath and Aging. 2004 – Merck Research Laboratories, page 817

151. Bennet, William J. Virtues of Courage in Adversity. 2001 – W Publishing Group, page vii – ix

152. Gilmore, C.P. Exercising for Fitness. 1981 – Time-Life Books, pg 22

153. Bennett, William J. The Book of Man. 2011 – Nelson Books, page 186

154. Ben Franklin. Poor Richard's Almanac. 2003 – Yankee Publishing, Page 120

155. Yeroulanes, Marines. A Dictionary of Classical Greek Quotations. 2016 – I.B. Tauris & Co.,page 779

156. Latash, Mark L. Neurophysiological Basis of Movement. Human Kinetics –

2008, page 50

157. Peale, Norman Vincent. Treasure of Courage and Confidence. Doubleday & Company, 1970, pg 46

158. Shaver, Larry G. Essentials of Exercise Physiology. Burgess Publishing Company; 1981; page 2

159. Bennett, William J. The Book of Man. 2011 – Nelson Books, page 152-153

160. Bennett, William J. The Book of Man. 2011 – Nelson Books, page 489

161. Bennett, William J. The Book of Man. 2011 – Nelson Books, page 501

162. Cooper, Dr. Kenneth. The New Aerobics. Bantam Books – 1970, page 121

163. Bennett, William J; Our Sacred Honor. Simon and Schuster – 1997, page 371

164. http://www.wellworkforce.com/roi/

165. Warren, Dr. Rick; Amen, Dr. Daniel; Hyman, Dr. Mark. The Daniel Plan. Zondervan – 2013, pg 228

166. Warren, Dr. Rick; Amen, Dr. Daniel; Hyman, Dr. Mark. The Daniel Plan. Zondervan – 2013, pg 231

167. Peale, Norman Vincent. Why Some Positive Thinkers Get Powerful Results. 1986 – Oliver Nelson Books; Nashville, Tennessee. Page 13

168. Peale, Norman Vincent. Treasury of Courage and Confidence. Doubleday & Company, 1970; pages 128-129

169. Martin Luther King Jr., Speech in Detroit, June 23, 1963

170. Gilmore, C.P. Exercising for Fitness. 1981 – Time-Life Books, pg. 11

171. Bennett, William J; Our Sacred Honor. Simon and Schuster – 1997, page 275

172. Austin, Dr. Krista; Diabetes Forecast – American Diabetes Association; September/October 2016; page 58

173. Bennett, William J. The Book of Man. 2011 – Nelson Books, page 421

174. Warren, Dr. Rick; Amen, Dr. Daniel; Hyman, Dr. Mark. The Daniel Plan. Zondervan – 2013, pg 164

175. Sheats, Cliff. Lean Bodies. 1992 – The Summit Group, pg. 166

176. Sheats, Cliff. Lean Bodies. 1992 – The Summit Group, pg. 149

177. Latash, Mark L. Fundamentals of Motor Control. 2012 – Elsevier Inc. – page 213,217

178. MacArthur, Douglas. Reminiscences. McGraw-Hill – 1964; pages 81-82

179. Stanley, Dr. Charles. In Touch – Daily Readings for Devoted Living. In Touch Ministries. November 2015, page 14.

180. Bennett, William J. The Book of Man. 2011 – Nelson Books, page 416

181. Bailey, Dr. Covert. Smart Exercise. Houghton Mifflin; 1994 –page 87

182. Bennett, William J. The Book of Man. 2011 – Nelson Books, pg 176

183. Stanley, Dr. Charles. Handle With Prayer. Victor Books. 1982; pages 11-12

184. Bailey, Dr. Covert. Smart Exercise. Houghton Mifflin; 1994 – page 34

185. Shafer, Sherri. Diabetes Type 2 Complete Food Management Program. Three Rivers Press; 2001 – page 140.

186. Dr. Douglas Brinkley (Editor). Ronald Reagan: The Notes. Harper Collins, 2011, page 155

187. Shaver, Larry G. Essentials of Exercise Physiology. Burgess Publishing Company; 1981; page 187

188. Stork, Dr. Travis. The Lose Your Belly Diet. Ghost Mountain Books; 2016 - page 107

189. Peale, Norman Vincent. Have a Great Day. Wings Books, 1997, page 16

190. Bailey, Dr. Covert. Smart Exercise. Houghton Mifflin, 1994, page 108

191. Morris, Dr. Scott. God, Health, and Happiness. Barbour Publishing, 2011, page 117

192. Bennett, William J. The Book of Man. 2011 – Nelson Books, page 106

193. Bennett, William J. The Book of Man. 2011 – Nelson Books, page 106

194. Arthur, Michael & Bailey, Bryan. Complete Conditioning for Football. Human Kinetics; 1998; page 255

195. American College of Sports Medicine. ACSM's Guidelines for Exercise Testing and Prescription – 6th edition. Lippincott, Williams & Wilkins; 2000; page 138.

196. American College of Sports Medicine. ACSM's Guidelines for Exercise Testing and Prescription – 6th edition. Lippincott, Williams & Wilkins; 2000; page 241

197. American College of Sports Medicine. ACSM's Guidelines for Exercise Testing and Prescription – 6th edition. Lippincott, Williams & Wilkins; 2000; page 244

198. Micheli, Dr. Lyle J. Sportswise: An Essential Guide for Young Athletes, Parents, and Coaches. Houghton Mifflin; 1990, page 28

199. Bennett, William J; Our Sacred Honor. Simon and Schuster – 1997 page 322

200. O' Brien, Tim. The Things they Carried. Houghton Mifflin. 1990, Page 78

201. Arthur, Michael & Bailey, Bryan. Complete Conditioning for Football. Human Kinetics; 1998; pg 6

202. Brophy, James; Epstien, Steven; Nilan, Cat; Robertson, John; Safley, Thomas. Perspectives from the Past: Primary Sources in Western Civilization. W.W. Norton & Company; 1998; page 167.

203. Cooper, Kenneth H. Faith-Based Fitness. Thomas Nelson, 1995, pg 8

204. Gomes, Dr. Peter J. The Good Life. HarperCollins; 2002; page 142

205. Gomes, Dr. Peter J. The Good Life. HarperCollins; 2002; page 171

206. Hole Jr., Dr. John W. Human Anatomy and Physiology. Wm.C. Brown Publishers; 1978; page 474

207. ACSM's Guidelines for Exercise Testing and Prescription. ACSM; Lippincott Williams & Wilkins; 2000; page 4

208. Cooper, Dr. Kenneth. The New Aerobics. Bantam Books – 1970, author's preface page

209. Arthur, Michael & Bailey, Bryan. Complete Conditioning for Football. 1998 - Human Kinetics, pg 5

210. Peale, Norman Vincent. The Power of Positive Thinking. 1978 – Prentice-Hall Inc. page 42

211. Bowers, Elizabeth Shimer. Article in Prevention Magazine; July 2015, page 66. Rodale Inc.

212. Clark DR, Lambert MI, Hunter AM. Muscle activation in the loaded free barbell squat: a brief review. Journal of Strength and Conditioning Research; 2012 April;26(4):1169-78

213. Bennett, William J. The Book of Man. 2011 – Nelson Books, page 152

214. Bennett, William J. The Book of Man. 2011 – Nelson Books, page 124

215. Royal, Penny C. Herbally Yours. Page 104; BiWorld Publishers – 1979

216. Taylor, Dr. Jill Bolte. A Stroke of Insight. Page 39; Viking; 2006

217. Saleka, Siphiwe. Guideposts, page 59, September 2017, Volume 72/issue 7

218. Bailey, Covert. Fit or Fat. 1977 – Houghton Mifflin Company, pg 240

219. Bennett, William J. The Book of Man. 2011 – Nelson Books, page 474

220. Taylor, Dr. Jill Bolte. My Stroke of Insight. Penguin Group; 2006; page 93-94

221. Cooper, Kenneth H. Faith-Based Fitness. Thomas Nelson, 1995, pg 17

222. Cooper, Kenneth H. Faith-Based Fitness. Thomas Nelson, 1995, pg 70

223. Arthur, Michael & Bailey, Bryan. Complete Conditioning for Football. 1998 - Human Kinetics, pages 3-4

224. Peale, Norman Vincent. Treasury of Courage and Confidence. Doubleday & Company, 1970, pg 44

225. Darden, Dr. Ellington. Living Longer Stronger. Berkley Publishing Group – 1995, pg x

226. Bailey, Covert. Fit or Fat. 1977 – Houghton Mifflin Company, pg 241

227. Cooper, Kenneth H. Faith-Based Fitness. Thomas Nelson, 1995, pg 128

228. Arthur, Michael & Bailey, Bryan. Complete Conditioning for Football. Human Kinetics; 1998; pages 3-4

229. Arthur, Michael & Bailey, Bryan. Complete Conditioning for Football. Human Kinetics; 1998; pg 7

230. Yessis, Dr. Michael. Kinesiology of Exercise. Masters Press; 1992, Introduction.

231. Stanley, Dr. Charles. How to Handle Adversity; Inspirational Press; 1989; page 250

232. Bailey, Dr. Covert. Smart Exercise. Houghton Mifflin; 1994 –page 6

233. Cooper, Kenneth H. Faith-Based Fitness. Thomas Nelson, 1995, pg 31

234. Lord of The Rings: Fellowship of the Ring. New Line Cinema; 2001.

235. Bailey, Dr. Covert. Smart Exercise. Houghton Mifflin; 1994 –page 3

236. Bailey, Dr. Covert. Smart Exercise. Houghton Mifflin; 1994 –page 125

237. Latash, Mark L. Fundamentals of Motor Control. 2012 – Elsevier Inc. – page 27

238. Stanley, Dr. Charles. Handle with Prayer. 1982 – Victor Books – page 36

239. Bennett, William J. The Book of Man. 2011 – Nelson Books, page 152

240. Bennett, William J. The Book of Man. 2011 – Nelson Books, page 105

241. Whiston, William. The Works of Josephus. 1987 – Hendrickson Publishers, page 55

242. Bennet, William J. Virtues of Courage in Adversity. 2001 – W Publishing Group, page 107

243. Bennet, William J. Virtues of Courage in Adversity. 2001 – W Publishing Group, page 89.

244.

245. Darden, Dr. Ellington. Living Longer Stronger. Berkley Publishing Group – 1995, pg 50

246. Bennett, William J. The American Patriots Almanac. 2008 – Thomas Nelson, Pg 300

247. Yancey, Philip. The Bible Jesus Read. Zondervan – 1999, page 210.

248. Arthur, Michael & Bailey, Bryan. Complete Conditioning for Football. 1998 - Human Kinetics, page 4

249. Bennett, William J. The Book of Man. 2011 – Nelson Books, page 515-516.

250. Bennett, William J. The Book of Man. 2011 – Nelson Books, page 238.

251. Bennet, William J. Virtues of Courage in Adversity. 2001 – W Publishing Group, page 123.

252. Bennett, William J; Our Sacred Honor. Simon and Schuster – 1997 page 32.

253. Bennett, William J. The Book of Man. 2011 – Nelson Books, page 534.

254. Readers Digest – (Editor: Gayla Visalli). After Jesus the Triumph of Christianity. 1992. Page 21

255. Cooper, Kenneth H. Faith-Based Fitness. Thomas Nelson, 1995, pg 4

256. Arthur, Michael & Bailey, Bryan. Complete Conditioning for Football. 1998 - Human Kinetics, page 253

257. Jay DeMarcus. "Shotgun Angels: My Story of Broken Roads and Unshakeable Hope" Copyright © 2019 by Jay DeMarcus. Used by permission of Zondervan.

258. Cooper, Dr. Kenneth. The New Aerobics. Bantam Books – 1970, page 38.

259. Bennett, William J. The Book of Man. 2011 – Nelson Books, page 282

260. Bennett, William J. The Book of Man. 2011 – Nelson Books, page 161

261. Bennett, William J. The Book of Man. 2011 – Nelson Books, page 475

262. Alcorn, Randy. If God is Good-Faith in the Midst of Suffering and Evil. Multnomah; 2009; page 42

263. Cooper, Dr. Kenneth. The New Aerobics. Bantam Books – 1970, page 39

264. Cooper, Kenneth H. Faith-Based Fitness. Thomas Nelson, 1995, pg 20

265. Darden, Dr. Ellington. Living Longer Stronger. Berkley Publishing Group – 1995, pg 7

266. Bennett, William J. The Book of Man. 2011 – Nelson Books, page 459

267. Cooper, Kenneth H. Faith-Based Fitness. Thomas Nelson, 1995, pg 4

268. https://www.foxnews.com/health/radiologist-on-alex-trebeks-health-update-cancer-is-not-always-a-death-sentence

269. Bennett, William J. The Book of Man. 2011 – Nelson Books, page 368

270. Bailey, Dr. Covert. Smart Exercise. Houghton Mifflin; 1994 –page 160

271. Bennett, William J. The American Patriots Almanac. 2008 – Thomas Nelson, Pg 477

272. Bennet, William J. Virtues of Courage in Adversity. 2001 – W Publishing Group, page 98

273. Bennet, William J. Virtues of Courage in Adversity. 2001 – W Publishing Group, page 53

274. Marshall, Peter. John Doe Disciple. Guideposts Associates Inc.; 1949 – page 133

275. Marshall, Peter. John Doe Disciple. Guideposts Associates Inc.; 1949 – page 139

276. Morris, Dr. Scott. God, Health, and Happiness. Barbour Publishing 2011, page 220

277. Peale, Norman Vincent. Have a Great Day. Wings Books, 1997, pg 78

278. https://www.foxnews.com/opinion/gary-wilkerson-fathers-day-children-hero-in-homeless-god

279. Cooper, Dr. Kenneth. The New Aerobics. Bantam Books – 1970, pages 10-11

280. Morris, Dr. Scott. God, Health, and Happiness. Barbour Publishing 2011, page 251

281.   https://www.foxbusiness.com/industrials/captain-sully-boeing-max-pilots-need-muscle-memory-before-flying

282. Zondervan Handbook to the Bible. Lion Publishing; 1999; page 560.

283.   https://www.foxnews.com/opinion/brit-mchenry-men-embrace-emotion-in-sports-women-should-be-allowed-to-do-the-same

284. Bailey, Dr. Covert. Smart Exercise. Houghton Mifflin; 1994 –page 6

285. Terrazas, Beatriz. Staying in Motion – TCU Magazine, Spring 2019, page 25. Produced by: TCU Marketing & Communications

286. Fields, David. Zondervan Handbook to the Bible. Lion Publishing; 1999; page 564

287. Bennett, William J. The Book of Man. 2011 – Nelson Books, page 476

288. Garrick, Dr. James, Radetsky, Dr. Peter. Be Your Own Personal Trainer. Crown Publishers – 1989. Page 6.

289. Bennett, William J. The Book of Man. 2011 – Nelson Books, page 204

290. Garrick, Dr. James, Radetsky, Dr. Peter. Be Your Own Personal Trainer. Crown Publishers – 1989. Page 5

291. American College of Sports Medicine. ACSM's Guidelines for Exercise Testing and Prescription – 6th edition. Lippincott, Williams & Wilkins; 2000; page 237.

292. American College of Sports Medicine. ACSM's Guidelines for Exercise Testing and Prescription – 6th edition. Lippincott, Williams & Wilkins; 2000; page 241.

293. Bailey, Dr. Covert. Smart Exercise. Houghton Mifflin; 1994 –page 158

294. Crabb, Dr. Larry. Finding God. Zondervan; 1993 – page 17-18.

295. Kidder, David S., Oppenheim, Noah D. The Intellectual Devotional. Rodale Inc.; 2012, page 193

296. Bennett, William J. The Book of Man. 2011 – Nelson Books, page 460

297.   https://www.foxnews.com/opinion/suzanne-hadley-gosselin-i-felt-like-the-worse-mom-ever-then-i-realized-this

298. Bennett, William J. The Book of Man. 2011 – Nelson Books, page 340

299. Bennett, William J. The Book of Man. 2011 – Nelson Books, pages 123-124

300. Bennett, William J. The Book of Man. 2011 – Nelson Books, page 179

301. Bennett, William J. The Book of Man. 2011 – Nelson Books, page 118

302. Lucado, Max. Grace For the Moment, 2007 – Thomas Nelson, page 429

303. Bennett, William J. The Book of Man. 2011 – Nelson Books, pg 226

304. Rosseau, Julie. Guideposts; February 2013; page 72

305. Bennett, William J. The Book of Man. 2011 – Nelson Books, page 169

306. Martin, Lisa. https://endeavors.tcu.edu/rewire-the-brain-control-the-body/

307. Cooper, Dr. Kenneth. The New Aerobics. Bantam Books – 1970, page 13

308. Padus, Emrika. The Complete Guide to Your Emotions and Your Health. 1986 – Rodale Press, Page 87

309. Padus, Emrika. The Complete Guide to Your Emotions and Your Health. 1986 – Rodale Press, Page 91

310. Whiston, William. The Works of Josephus. 1987 – Hendrickson Publishers, page 81-82

CPSIA information can be obtained
at www.ICGtesting.com
Printed in the USA
BVHW080955030820
585324BV00001B/53